A COVENANT FORGED IN BLOOD

A COVENANT FORGED IN BLOOD

JOSEPHINE ROSE PINTO

Paperback ISBN: 979-8-9915518-0-9

eBook ISBN: 979-8-9915518-1-6

For the girls who can never seem to let go of
the ones they loved before.
It is both a blessing and a curse to feel things so deeply.

CHAPTER 1

Veronica Yuller's screams ricocheted through the village square as the necromancers dragged her son's lifeless body forward. A trail of vibrant red blood was left in his wake, leading to the Morta Forest. I pushed my way through the growing crowd that remained deadly silent as Veronica cried. Her wails and screams were piercing, and a part of me wished someone would knock her out to make the intolerable noise stop.

Apparently, the village hunters found her son a short while ago on the outskirts of the forest. Most people knew better than to tread too close to the tree line, but Henry Yuller wasn't very smart. He was a stupid boy who had only seen seventeen years before he died. As I caught a clear glimpse of his corpse, I could tell his death had been nothing short of agonizing, but that didn't come as a surprise.

Many believed the creatures lurking in the forest were left from a time the gods walked the lands. Vicious creatures with teeth like knives and an unforgiving craving for flesh. Regardless of the truth, whatever had sunk its claws and teeth into Henry had shredded his skin in unfathomable directions. And the blood... I'd never seen so much blood in my short life.

Wells, leader of the necromancers, hurried toward the raised slab of stone where the resurrections occurred. It was pure white, completely at odds with the disgraceful dark magic practiced upon it. But that did nothing to stop the necromancers from lifting Henry's limp, broken body onto the stone, staining the white with red. It was beautiful in a way. The sharp contrast of colors.

Veronica ran forward, her eyes swollen and red rimmed from the tears streaming down her cheeks. I fought the urge to roll my eyes. It wasn't like Henry would be dead for long. With half the village performing necromancy as easily as a party trick, nobody truly *stayed* dead here.

Wells nodded toward two of his men who quickly grabbed Veronica, dragging her away so he could begin. I heard several people around me whisper hushed prayers up to Tella, condemning this unnatural act and begging for some sort of divine intervention.

Fools. The lot of them. Didn't they know their prayers would never be answered? There were no more gods. This was it. The evil incarnate in front of us. As black smoke seeped from the palms of Wells' hands, several people gasped like this was something new to see.

He mumbled as he closed his eyes, turning his upright hands down so the smoke seeped over and into Henry's mutilated body. At first, nothing happened. As a group, we fell into a punishing silence, the only sound that of Henry's blood dripping onto the podium beneath the slab.

Then, Henry's chest rose. I watched the exact moment he

gasped his first breath for the second time in his life, and all I could think was how someone, somewhere in the Alosian Kingdom had drawn their final breath at the same moment.

A life for a life.

That was the price of necromancy.

To bring a soul back from death, another must be taken. Be it a child, mother, sister, or brother, it didn't matter. And the necromancers had no regard for consequences or innocent lives lost. They cared for nothing more than the rush that coursed through their veins every time they used their power. And in a place as horrific as Morters' End, their power was required more often than not.

Henry's eyes shot open wide, and as awareness seeped back in, the pain struck. His scream was worse than his mother's as he lifted his head and looked at his body. It didn't last very long as another wave of unconsciousness took him under.

I wondered what part of his soul would be permanently tainted from this. No one that came back to life was ever fully the same. A bit of darkness tended to reside in them, growing and tormenting their already fractured beings. The act itself also heightened the necromancers' powers, helping them become stronger. Although, they remained selective with who they resurrected. The villagers whose souls were already shroud in darkness would cause the necromancers' magic to twist and warp unpredictably. Because of that, wrongdoers were never brought back. Those untouched by evil were the only ones resurrected. As if the necromancers could know such a thing.

A commotion occurred from across the square as two healers rushed forward to take over. The necromancers' magic couldn't repair Henry's injuries but sustained him with enough life that the healers would have a chance to mend his more physical wounds. The more gruesome the injuries and the longer someone remained dead, the more strenuous it was to bring them back. The necromancers would be able to do it within a max of forty-eight hours, but at the cost of magical exhaustion. After that time frame, there was no coming back.

The two necromancers holding Veronica released her, and she instantly flung herself against the slab, gripping Henry's hand in her own as she shook and watched the healers sew her boy back together again.

The necromancers turned, their black cloaks billowing in the breeze as they headed back to the Vacar. Conveniently, their home was the only building in Morters' End not crumbling.

I hated them. Hated everything they stood for. And although I couldn't escape this miserable village, I was aware that the neighboring towns and cities referred to us residents of Morters' End as a 'plague of the land.'

Our necromancers were the reason we were shunned by the rest of the kingdom. They wanted nothing to do with dark magic, and really, I couldn't blame them.

I'd never dabbled in the stuff, and even if I wanted to, I couldn't. I possessed no magic of my own. It was something inherited, and fortunately for me, my family line was as ordinary as they came.

The crowd around me remained tense as the healers continued working. At one point, Henry managed to wake up again only to be rattled with mind shattering screams, causing several people to cover their ears.

I suppressed a laugh as I turned, weaving my way out of the huddled bodies that paid me no mind. Henry's wounds would take a while to mend, and the healing process would be excruciatingly painful.

Good. He deserves it, I thought.

Henry Yuller broke my heart five years ago when I found him with his tongue down Abigail Brester's throat. We'd been together at the time, and he promised me I was the only one. For that reason, I couldn't help but smirk as I ventured away from the square, his painful screams sweet music to my ears.

As I turned down a narrow side road, I hopped over a few puddles and broken cobblestones, dodging the rats that scurried left and right over my boots. The buildings flanking me groaned as the wind brushed against them, causing the rotted wood of their foundations to sway dangerously. A few homes were still crafted from the beige stone of the old ages, but even those were starting to fall apart.

Shadows lingered in the crevices, watching, but I wasn't afraid. I took a guess and assumed it was late morning, but one could never be too sure. With no sunlight, the days and nights blended together in misery.

Aside from the decrepit buildings bound to topple any day now, the foul-smelling air also possessed the permanent stench of death. I was used to it but sometimes still found myself crinkling my nose in disgust.

Now was one of those times as I made my way through the winding roads until I came up to the old greenhouse perched on the edge of a cliff. Even though I wasn't alive at the time when it was flourishing with healthy, beautiful plants, I knew the lack of it now was because of the necromancers. Hundreds of years ago when the sun stopped shining over our home, all the plants and flowers slowly perished, leaving what

I imagined was once a beautiful, bright space with nothing more than decaying fragments.

No one spoke it, but we all knew the sun stopped shining when the necromancers began practicing.

Those who opposed the necromancers prayed to Tella, goddess of justice and righteousness, every fortnight. They believed she bestowed her gift of Purity, a cleansing magic, onto a group of women known as Estelers and that they'd be the ones to free us from this torment. That they'd destroy all dark magic when the time was right.

I believed that was a load of bullshit.

I'd never actually seen an Esteler before, and I no longer believed in the gods. I used to, years ago, but not after everything. Not after my papa died and no one had cared to bring him back.

They'd done nothing. Nothing, as he bled out on the cobblestones six years ago. They let him die.

They let him *stay* dead.

I shrugged off that memory as I stepped through the broken glass door of the greenhouse. No one came here anymore, which was exactly why I did. The silence brought me a sliver of peace. Something rare nowadays.

Another step into the wide room, and I halted. A familiar, yet unnerving sensation slithered up my spine like a snake in the grass. It always did before *he* showed up.

Straightening, I placed my hands on my hips. "Show yourself," I demanded.

Nothing.

Holding my breath, I slowly stepped forward. The sound of a dead leaf crunching beneath my boot filled the unnatural silence. "I know you're here," I continued. "Come out. I promise I won't bite."

At that, a deep, throaty chuckle filled the space around me, echoing off the walls, and prickling the hairs on my arms.

And then he appeared just as he had the night we met, almost four years ago to the day. His bright blue eyes and ebony hair caused a lump to settle in my throat. I watched as he leaned against the crumbling stone pillar, folding his arms over his chest. The black breeches... the white tunic clinging to his defined torso... skin that reminded me of moonlight...

Four years, I thought. *Four years, and he looks exactly the same, all the way down to his clothing. Why did you expect anything different this time?*

Perhaps so I could forget what he really was.

A smirk tugged at the corners of his lips as his eyes pierced mine. "What a shame," he said lazily. "I rather enjoy it when you bite."

I looked away as heat rose into my cheeks. He chuckled again, eating up my clear embarrassment. "What do you want?"

Uncrossing his arms, he shoved his hands into his pockets. "I missed you."

Now it was my turn to laugh. "You missed me? You can see me whenever you like." Narrowing my eyes, I added, "You cursed me with that little trick, in case you forgot."

"You wound me," he said, placing a hand to his chest in mock pain.

One moment he was against the pillar, the next he stood directly in front of me. I didn't so much as bat an eyelash. Four years enabled me to grow rather used to his unnatural movements. And from this close, I saw all the details of his flawless features. Details I dreamt of over the years, engraved into my memory.

Too flawless to be natural, I reminded myself.

I should be able to feel his breath against my forehead. I would have if he were breathing. If he *needed* to breathe. This was another reminder of what he was, and what he *wasn't.*

He lifted a hand and cupped my cheek, brushing his thumb across my skin. I shivered at the contact. Sometimes I could feel him, and other times I couldn't.

"My beautiful Wren," he spoke softly.

There was a time the sound of my name on his lips undid me, but that time had long passed. His eyes trailed down to my mouth. He smelt the same as always, like a midnight breeze.

Swatting his arm away, I took a step back. My hand instinctively went to the dagger sheathed against my thigh. He noted my movement, smirk widening into a full grin. "Come on, Wren, you know a silly little knife won't hurt me."

That might be true, but the thought was still enticing.

"What do you want," I repeated.

He sighed. "You know what I want." And I did, but I needed him to say it. It was the only thing keeping me from falling down the rabbit hole with him again.

In the split second it took me to blink, he moved behind me. "It's been four years," he said into my neck. His hair skimmed my cheek as he dipped his head, kissing my collarbone. I tightened the grip on my dagger. "Four long years that you haven't held up your end of our little deal."

I closed my eyes. I could give this to myself, allow myself to enjoy this moment. Enjoy the brush of his lips against my skin the way I had so many times before. *No,* the voice in my head said firmly. *This is what he wants.*

Forcing my eyes open, I twisted away from him. It felt like waking up from a nightmare only to find I'd entered into the midst of another.

He cast me a bored look. "I don't understand why you put up such a fight against the inevitable."

"Because I can't stand you."

"Lies."

Huffing out a frustrated breath, I swung my arms out wide. "There's no one in this gods awful village I will ever fall in love with, and the last I checked, I can't very well get up and *leave.*"

No one in Morters' End could. Whoever the king was all those years ago when the necromancers began practicing supposedly had the Estelers create a shield around our village. Only those from outside could enter and leave freely while whoever was inside when the shield went up was trapped indefinitely, including their future offspring.

It was our punishment in a way, for the terrible acts committed daily. It didn't matter that a handful of us wanted nothing to do with necromancy. The king didn't care. We were punished as a whole, cast aside and forgotten.

I often wondered why these Estelers hadn't just killed the necromancers when they had the chance if they were blessed with powers from a goddess. If anything, it added to my suspicion that they didn't exist.

As much as I loathed the necromancers, I was thankful they were the only dark magic wielders here. There were other divisions of dark magic... much deadlier divisions, apparently. Creatures born with powers that would send the devil himself scurrying back to Hell. But they all resided in the Kingdom of Enderya across the Aldric Sea.

How the necromancers ended up all the way over here, when their ancestors were from over *there*, was just another mystery to be solved.

Truthfully, I ached to feel the sun on my freckled face just once in my life, but a part of me was glad to be locked in this village. It meant I would never fall in love. And if I never fell in love, I'd never hold up my end of the covenant with Asher.

For a while, whatever *this* was between us had been nothing more than a way to pass the time until I did what I had to do. That was our deal. He saved my dying mother, and as payment, I had to not only fall in love but be loved in return. And then I had to kill that person in order to bring Asher back to life.

I was in no particular rush, and over time our situation turned into something more. Something to quench the desires of our two lonely souls. But that was the tricky thing about giving oneself to another. Feelings were unavoidable. And with Asher's need for me to love a living, *breathing* boy, this thing between us became a tangled mess.

I watched him now as he ran fingers through his messy black locks, memories flashing in my mind from all the times *I'd* been the one with my hands in his hair.

An amused expression took over his face as he realized what I was thinking. Gods, I wished I could stab him.

"You'll grow tired of your excuses, Wren," he drawled. "You can't avoid me or our covenant forever."

As quickly as he appeared, he was gone.

Leaving me surrounded by my memories and the rotting stench of decay.

CHAPTER 2

Time passed strangely in Morters' End. It was often disorienting having day and night morphed into one endless pool of darkness. And yet, every morning I ran to the window in hopes of catching a glimpse of that warm light I'd read and heard stories about. And every morning, I was disappointed.

This morning was no different.

Stripping out of my nightgown, I pulled on a pair of mud-brown breeches and a white shirt. Mama used to complain this was no way for a young lady to dress, but I didn't care much for gowns and fabrics. They were utterly impractical. And even if we could afford any, what use would they have? Living in Morters' End, there was no need to don fancy clothing. It wouldn't fool anybody.

I hurried down the stairs, making sure to hop over the third step from the bottom as it was bound to give out any day now. Like clockwork, Mama was seated beside the hearth, busy knitting a sweater she'd been working on the past several weeks, while Angel was at the small wooden table doing what he did best. Sketching. He was extraordinary with charcoal and parchment, turning any blank space into a masterpiece.

I hovered on the bottom step like a ghost, watching him. Curly brown locks spilling over his forehead, brows furrowed in concentration, hazel eyes darting back and forth over what seemed to be an image of a woman as his hand moved hastily with the charcoal.

I envied his skills. The only thing I was good at was wielding a blade and getting into trouble. As if he sensed my presence, his eyes drifted up to meet mine. "Look who's finally awake."

"Don't act so surprised," I said as I crossed the room to him. Mama didn't so much as glance at me. I should be used to it by now, but the sting was still present. Ignoring it, I sat beside Angel, quickly grabbing the parchment before he could object. "What are you working on?" Even as I asked, I knew what I'd find on the torn scrap.

He ran stained fingertips through his hair and sighed. "It's nothing really. Give it back." I sprang from the seat, taking the sketch with me as I examined the details. The curve of the neck, button nose, full lips, round doe eyes...

"You're drawing her again."

He slumped back in his chair, defeated. "Force of habit."

I fought the urge to tear the image to shreds. Instead, I tossed it back to him. "She doesn't deserve to be portrayed so beautifully, you know," I said as I tugged on my boots. "Not when her soul is so ugly."

Angel's eyes followed my movements. His jaw clenched. "You don't know her."

"And you do?" I hated Zena for what she did to my

brother. I hesitated before adding, "She doesn't deserve *you*, Angel. She never did." Standing on my toes, I reached for my green jacket on the hook beside the door.

"Where are you going?" he asked.

"For a walk."

A second later, he was beside me. "I think I'll join you."

I nodded, then glanced at Mama. Her eyes stayed locked on the yarn in her hands. If Angel didn't have the same eyes as her, I fear I would've forgotten what they looked like. It'd been so long since she looked at me.

I still recalled the countless days and nights I begged and cried for her. I'd go out and stir fights with the local drunkards just to come home with a busted lip or a bruised eye, hoping she'd care. But with every physical wound I welcomed, she inflicted one worse. The type of wound that a bandage couldn't heal.

Pushing down the lump in my throat, I sighed and opened the door, only to be greeted by the usual gray, cloudy sky. "Shall we?"

~

Our rickety house was a few streets away from the village square, isolated behind the skeletons of what were once pine trees, according to the history books in what remained of the old library.

When I wasn't running my body ragged with training, I sought comfort in books. I liked to read about the places outside of the shield. Not that I'd ever see them myself, but it was nice to pretend. I'd devoured all the books still legible about a year ago, so now when I was bored, I'd pick up one I hadn't read in a while and hoped it would feel fresh.

As Angel and I trudged through the mud and dirt, I couldn't help wondering how accurate the books were. They were heavily outdated after all, but I still wondered about the distant villages and cities. Were their roads clean and polished? Did they have plants and flowers growing amid fresh green grass? Were their buildings sturdy enough to stand on their own? Did they have rats scurrying across their food and bodies?

Eventually, the dirt road was replaced with cracked cobblestones leading into the village center. Everything looked the same. Gray, dirty, and broken.

Angel tipped his hat as we passed Miss Pardley's house. The old lady was outside, sweeping dust from her small front step. She smiled and waved as we strolled past. Miss Pardley was a saint as far as I was concerned. She was one of the few who didn't show up that day to watch Papa die. And after that day, she spent a lot of time in our home helping with cooking, cleaning, and making sure our hearts were healing.

Of course, mine did not.

Like us, Miss Pardley hated the necromancers. She was a firm believer in the gods and swore one day the Estelers would rescue us from this evil place. I thought she had a few screws loose, but I kept that to myself.

The smell of freshly baked bread filled the horrid air around me, sending my stomach into a growling frenzy. I grabbed Angel's hand and tugged him in the opposite direction.

"You know," he said. "You can't avoid everything and everyone forever."

My heart flipped in my chest at how similar his words were to what Asher said yesterday. *You can't avoid me, or our covenant forever.*

Shoving those perfect blue eyes to the back of my mind, I continued to drag my brother. "I'm not avoiding," I replied.

"You are, Wren." He stopped, pulling me back to him. I couldn't stand the pity in his eyes as he looked at me. "You have to let go of this anger. Papa is gone, and there isn't anything we can do. You need to move on."

I ripped my hand back. My skin was hot and shaky as I said, "Move on?" I released a humorless laugh. "Just because you hated him doesn't give you the right to tell me how I should feel."

Angel flinched. "I didn't hate him. I loved him, but that wasn't enough." He clenched his jaw, averting his gaze. I fought that overprotective urge to shield my brother from pain. "I know he cared for me, but not the way he did for you. He didn't love anyone the way he loved you."

I felt dizzy. We hadn't spoken of Papa in over two years, and for the life of me, I couldn't understand why Angel was bringing him up now. It was a sore subject, and one I *thought* Angel knew not to tread along. Hearing his words was enough to bring back those horrific emotions. I reached for my brother's hand. "He loved you, Angel. In his own way, he loved you."

He lifted his head with tears in his eyes, and a pang of guilt rushed through me. He wiped them with his free hand, letting out a sigh. "So," he said. "Are you really going to be stubborn forever and deny yourself the sweet bread from the bakery?" He knew I loved the sweet bread. And I couldn't pretend the smell of it now wasn't making my head spin.

So many nights I dreamed of that bakery burning to the ground. Terryn should have given Papa the loaf of bread that day. It was his fault Angel and I were fatherless. Chewing my lower lip, I crossed my arms. "Even if I wanted it, we don't have any money."

"Well," Angel said as he dug his hand into his pocket. I gasped as he pulled out a shiny gold coin. "I'd say we have *some* money."

"Where did you get that?"

He tossed the coin in the air and caught it. "I sold a sketch. It's not much, but I thought I'd treat my little sister to whatever she wanted."

"Angel..." I shook my head. "I don't want you to spend your earnings on me. Save it."

He chuckled. "For what? I know everything made and sold in this village like the back of my hand. There's nothing I want besides seeing you happy again."

I was about to respond, when a figure charging down the cobblestones toward us, arms waving in the air, drew my attention.

I squinted. "Is that—"

"Callin," Angel finished for me.

Callin was out of breath by the time he reached us. Doubled over and panting, blonde hair spilling down his forehead. Angel stepped forward, clapping his back. "Are you alright?"

"Quite so," Callin choked out in between breaths. I fought the urge to roll my eyes.

"Why are you here? We weren't expecting you for another three days." As I said it, I noticed Callin didn't have any of the usual deliveries on him. Nothing besides a scrunched up piece of paper in his hand.

He brushed a sweaty lock of hair from his forehead, green eyes finding mine. "I'm not here to bring deliveries."

Angel raised a brow. "Then why are you here?"

Callin glanced between the both of us. "I thought you two would at least be slightly pleased to see me."

"We are," Angel replied. "It's just unusual for you to show up without deliveries."

Callin was from Telamar, a neighboring village. For the past year and a half, he'd been delivering medicinal herbs, fruits, vegetables, and grain from his family farm to the people of Morters' End. If his family knew of his activities, he didn't say. All I knew was that once a week, Callin's bright blonde head passed through the shield with a wagon pulled by Desi, his mule. He wasn't the only one who'd venture into Morters' End with 'care packages' that, in my opinion, were only given so the deliverers could feel good about themselves, but he *was* the most liked.

While they all brought us things we couldn't obtain ourselves, we were usually able to acquire our own meats. Only the village hunters were trained and allowed to trek into the dead forest where unfortunate animals looking for food would meet their untimely ends. The rest of the goods brought to us were given to the shops and bakers to prepare and then sell. The *kind* deliverers rarely gave their stock out to us upfront since it usually ended in some kind of stampede of people fighting each other to empty the carts.

Callin, however, was a bit more subtle with his deliveries. The elders of the village would kiss his head and bless him, for they really believed he did it out of the goodness of his heart. *I* on the other hand, knew the real reason.

Callin was hopelessly in love with Porticia, daughter of Jarin the blacksmith. She was a scrawny, red-headed girl with a chipped tooth. How the two of them met, I didn't know, nor did I ask. If the only way Callin could dally with Porticia was by bringing us food, then I applauded it and hoped their romance would never end.

"I come with news," Callin said, head whipping around as if searching for a misplaced item. "Is Porticia around?"

This time, I really did roll my eyes. "Give me that." I snatched the paper from his hand, my eyes widening as I read the contents.

"What is it?" Angel asked. "Wren, what does it say?"

Without a word, I handed it to him. As he read it, I watched Callin fidget with a button on his coat. After a moment, Angel said, "Is this true?"

"Do you think I'd run all the way here if it weren't?" Callin was a lovesick fool, so yes, I thought he would.

"What does it matter?" Both heads turned to me. "No offense, but neither of you are in any shape to be considered for the prince's guard."

"Not us," Angel said. "You."

Callin held up a finger. "Well actually—"

"You cannot be serious. I'm a girl, Angel." Was he mad? Perhaps he ingested some of his charcoal this morning.

"Could've fooled me," Callin muttered.

I shot him a poisonous glare before turning back to my brother. "Women aren't permitted in the Royal Guard. And besides, I'd rather run into the Morta Forest naked and let the beasts have their way with me than serve the royals." I'd heard stories of the royal family. No thank you.

Callin choked. Ignoring him, Angel grabbed my shoulders. "Wren, listen to me. You need to at least think about this. I don't know anyone else who can wield a sword or throw a dagger the way you can. You're strong and smart and it's time to put those skills to use. They'd be lucky to have you."

"If you two would listen to me," Callin cut in, drawing my attention. "Women *aren't* allowed, that is correct. I was bringing this here so you could let the others know in advance, not orchestrate some plot to deceive the guards." He looked directly at me. "What if you get caught?"

"She won't," Angel answered. "Or wouldn't, at least. If she actually agrees to it."

I examined him for a moment. Those eyes that focused only on the beauty of this world and capturing it in sketches and paintings. How one could find beauty in a place like this was a mystery, but Angel found a way. He was good, kind, and creative. Everything I was not. And that was why Papa spent years teaching *me* and not Angel how to fight.

"*Wren, my darling,*" Papa would say. "*While your brother resides in a permanent daydream, you see the world for what it is. Hard and cruel. It will break you down until you are nothing more than dust. Do you want that?*" I remember shaking my head. He then turned and pulled a broadsword from the scabbard. He tossed it to me, and I caught it at the hilt, struggling to bear the weight. "*That's my girl. I'll teach you how to turn the rest of the world to dust, Wren. I'll teach you how to fight. How to survive.*"

"How would I even get away with it?" I asked. I wasn't

really considering this. I was merely curious where Angel's mind was going with it.

"We can figure that out later," Angel said. "We can cut your hair off if need be. But please, Wren. You need to do this."

The pleading, desperate look in his eyes set me on edge. "Why?"

"Think about it. What's the one thing you've *always* wanted?"

"A third arm," I said instantly. It would be ideal for managing another sword.

Angel huffed out a frustrated sigh. "I'm serious. You'll get to do what none of us ever could. You'll get to *leave*."

I stepped back. I hadn't thought of that. If I agreed to this madness, I'd get to leave Morters' End. I'd feel the sun for the first time in my life, breathe fresh air, and drink fresh water.

But I'd also have to pretend to be someone I'm not. Not to mention I'd never see Angel or Mama again. "I can't leave you," I said quietly.

Angel grabbed my hand, pressing it to his chest. "You were meant for more than this village."

"And you?" I demanded. "If we're discussing worthiness, you have me beat. There's a whole world out there, Angel. A whole world that would be all the better with someone like you in it."

He shook his head, holding up the paper. "I don't even know how to hold a sword. This is the only ticket out of here, and you're taking it." Before I could argue further, he turned to Callin who appeared to have given up on talking us out of this. "When is this taking place?"

"Tomorrow," Callin said. "The king sent his most trustworthy advisors to collect the most promising young men for potential recruitment."

"What happened to the old guard?" I asked. The issue with being cut off from the rest of civilization was that we were completely uninformed on current events.

Callin frowned. "The official story is they were dismissed." Dropping his voice, he leaned closer. "But word going around is they were ambushed no more than a fortnight ago. Only the captain of Prince Ryder's guard survived."

Ambushed? By who?

"Why not just pull trained soldiers from the military? Why go through every village in the kingdom recruiting men with little to no actual experience?" Angel asked.

Callin shrugged as he rubbed his head. "That's the question, isn't it? Commander Bekencourt of the king's guard was apparently the one who voiced the idea. The king must have liked it since..." he nodded at the paper in Angel's grasp, "... here we are. Anyway, just thought I'd give you the heads up before they ride in tomorrow. They're in Telamar right now."

I snatched the paper from my brother. "Why weren't we given notice about this?" *And why would the commander be so eager to recruit men from Morters' End?*

Callin blinked. "How would I know?"

I took a step forward. "And how are they deciding who gets picked? Is there some sort of physical assessment? A test?"

I felt Angel's warm hand on my shoulder pulling me back as his calm voice filled the air. "I'm sure all your questions will be answered tomorrow when they get here."

"I doubt all of them," I mumbled.

Callin looked between the both of us. "I can't believe

you're actually debating doing this. You're playing with fire, if you get caught—"

"What *is* the worst that would happen?" I asked. I had no idea how things worked in the guard. My books never touched the topic.

Callin shrugged. "I... I don't know. No one's ever broken that cardinal rule. Imprisonment? Death? A smack on the wrist? Who knows?"

"And how long is it?" I asked. "The duration of service?" *Did I ask that right?*

"It varies depending on rank. I know that guards tasked with protecting the royals typically have shorter contracts. They only want the strongest and most capable for that position, so when they age or are no longer cut out for it, they're either honorably discharged or able to pick up lower rankings."

"Interesting," I said as I looked away, the gears in my brain churning.

"But you'd be an idiot to try it. Really, do you think you'll fool the highest ranking guards in the kingdom?" Callin countered.

Angel reached his hand out to Callin. "Thanks for the heads up. You've given us plenty to think about."

Callin hesitated. "It's your funeral." He glanced around the square one more time before sighing in defeat. "If you see Porticia, let her know I stopped by, will you?"

"Of course," I said. Although I had no intention of actually doing so.

Once Callin was gone, we decided to take the long way home past the brook. Fresh water wasn't a luxury we possessed, so the brook was used for both bathing and drinking. As well as the occasional drunkard who decided to relieve himself in it. Disgusting, but our only option.

My nose crinkled as we grew closer, the water a murky brown that was void of my reflection. I was in the process of kicking a stray pebble with my boot when Angel broke the silence. "What are you thinking?"

"Truthfully?" He nodded. "I'm wondering what Papa would think about this. Of me doing something like this. Do you think the risks are worth it?"

Angel chewed his inner cheek. "It's hard to say. Callin doesn't even really know what the risks are. But I do think you're strong enough, and did you hear what he said? It's only a few short years of service and then you'd be free, Wren. Free to continue serving or leave. Whatever you choose, it would be *your* choice."

I continued kicking the tiny pebble until it bounced off another rock and plopped into the dirty water. "I'd find a way to get you out of here when I finished. You and Mama." I would. If I went through with this, I'd free them.

He was silent for a long moment. "That is... a wonderful dream."

I looked at him. "It would be more than a dream. I'd do whatever I needed to get you out of here. Speak to higher ups or do something so honorable they'd feel the need to reward me."

A ghost of a smile flickered on his lips. "I never thought I'd hear you speak so passionately about anything again."

I grabbed his arm. "Because before this, there wasn't anything to be passionate about. But now? Now there's a chance. A chance for us all to get out of here."

His eyes met mine, and he grinned as he wound my braid

around his hand. "You know, we'll have to cut your hair off. If you're going to disguise yourself—"

I swatted his hand away, a laugh escaping my parted lips. "Absolutely not. I will not cut or shave my hair." My long, brown waves were always Papa's favorite feature of mine.

Amusement glistened in his eyes. "You'd be such a handsome guard, Wren."

"You're an ass, you know that, right?"

He draped an arm over my shoulder as we continued walking, passing a few others out for a morning stroll. "I might be an ass, but you, my brilliant little sister, are going to be a Royal Guard."

"I wonder what this recruitment test will entail," I said, waving the crumpled paper in my hand.

"Doesn't matter what it is. You'll pass effortlessly," he said confidently.

"Always the optimist."

"I have a feeling your life is about to change. But regardless, you need to stay alert. Your identity is a secret you'll need to hold safe because while we don't know the full extent of what the repercussions would be if you got caught, I don't think it would be as simple as a slap on the wrist."

"Nothing worthwhile ever came easy, huh?" I said, trying to lighten the mood. I knew I'd need to be careful, more careful than I'd ever been if I was to survive long enough to buy mine and my family's freedom.

I rubbed sweaty palms on my legs. The more I thought about it, the more I wanted this. To be free. To escape the place they claimed inescapable. I could only hope if by some miracle this all worked out, I would be able to escape my most complicated situation yet.

A situation involving blue eyes, a haunting smile, and a promise.

A situation currently leaning on my front door as Angel and I returned home.

Asher was tied to Morters' End as much as the people, so I wondered, if I left, would he be forced to stay? Could I leave him here and live my life out there, avoiding the fulfillment of our covenant? I didn't think he'd hurt Mama in retaliation. After all, there was no time frame set on our deal. If I wanted to take the rest of my life to complete it, I very well could. And there would be nothing he could do about it.

That caused a smile to creep up my lips as I froze several feet away, vaguely hearing Angel ask me what was wrong. I was completely entranced as Asher made his way over to me, each one of his steps mimicking the beat of my heart.

After what felt like an eternity, we stood face to face. His trace scent of midnight breeze wrapped around me like a lover's arm. It was an internal battle to refrain from inhaling it entirely since I knew Asher would be amused by it.

His fingers trailed down my arm, leaving goosebumps in their wake. He smirked as he grabbed my hand, bringing it to his lips. His eyes remained locked on mine as he kissed it. "My beautiful Wren, I've been waiting."

CHAPTER 3

I'm fine, Angel," I called out. "I'll be inside soon."

I sensed his hesitation, but after a moment, the front door opened and closed, leaving me alone with Asher.

I sometimes forgot I was the only one who could see Asher. In the beginning, I thought I had truly gone mad. Seeing and touching a boy no one else could wasn't logical.

Then again, was anything here logical?

The first year I'd known Asher, I contemplated telling someone about him. But every time I approached the conversation, I was unable to voice the truth. It wasn't that I was *physically* unable to tell anyone, but rather a small part of me, the part that cared immensely for him at one point, didn't *want* to tell anyone. He was my secret.

He was mine.

And in a way, I was his.

And in a village where nothing was truly *anybody's*, it was oddly satisfying to have something that belonged completely to me.

I still remembered the night we met.

I'd been in the only graveyard in Morters' End, a dusty old place guarded by rusted gates. This space was meant for those who died of old age and the unworthy. Those who, according to the necromancers, didn't deserve a second chance at life. As if they could decide such a thing.

I was on my knees praying near Papa's unmarked grave when a young man appeared out of thin air. He'd tilted his head and watched me with curious intensity. He was beautiful, and I found myself forgetting why I was in the graveyard in the first place.

"I will help you save her," he'd said. *"I will help save your sick mother if you do something for me."*

I should have declined. I should have wondered how he knew what I was praying for. I should have run as far as my scrawny legs could carry me, but I didn't. I was completely mesmerized by him, and in that moment, I realized I'd do anything he asked.

"What do you want?"

He grabbed my chin, tilting my head until our eyes met. His were like oceans. Unending, dangerous, and thrilling. *"In exchange for her health, I want... you."*

I'd nearly choked. *"Me?"*

"I want you to fall in love with someone. Once your hearts are bound as one, I want you to kill him. His death will free me. As he releases his final breath, I will breathe it in, and it will bring me back from death."

The thing about being close to losing a person was that any option seemed better than facing their quickly approaching death. So I agreed. And before I had a chance to think about what I agreed to, he'd picked up a jagged rock and dragged it across my palm. He raised my hand to his mouth, his eyes never leaving mine. Not even as he let me go, licking my blood from his lips. *"The covenant is forged in blood."*

For a while, I'd forgotten about our covenant. Mama had made a full recovery, a rosy healthy flush to her cheeks, and Asher didn't bring up my end of the deal during the past four years. And with that, my attachment to him became more of an incessant need. He'd held me while I cried, pulled me up when I got knocked down, taught me what it meant to feel things deeply.

I'd been so wrapped up in him that I ignored the truth. He was only around me so I could fulfill the deal we'd made. When he mentioned it again six months ago, something in me cracked. And when I put the pieces back together, I'd built them up stronger.

I was trying my hardest not to let him in again, but the task was easier said than done when he showed up whenever he desired.

Once I was certain Angel wasn't going to come back out, I grabbed Asher's hand and pulled him toward the grove of dead trees. He chuckled. "I love when you get aggressive."

Hidden from view, I let him go. "I don't care what you love. Not anymore." He tilted his head, studying me. I hated how he looked at me. "What do you want, Asher."

He crossed his arms, his tunic tightening. I kept my gaze steady on his face. *Not* his arms. Those arms I touched so many times before...

"I want you to join the guard."

That quickly snapped me out of my thoughts. "*What?* How could you possibly—" A burning rage began pulsing through my blood. "You were following me? You swore to me you wouldn't do that anymore."

He appeared bored as he leaned against a tree. "I said I wouldn't unless I deemed it necessary."

"Oh, so taking a morning stroll with my brother was a necessary reason for you to *spy* on me?"

A muscle in his jaw tensed. "You know how I feel about that word, Wren."

"What, *spying*? That's what you were doing! You had no right—"

"I had every right," he said through his teeth, his stance unnaturally still. I was never scared of Asher, but in moments like this, I was reminded perhaps I should be. "I had every right," he repeated, this time softly. He moved closer, cupping my cheeks.

"Fine." I entertained the idea. "But what makes you so certain you'll be coming with me if I go?" My tone was more mocking than anything, but I sensed the way the words registered with him.

"I'm not certain," he admitted. "But what I do know is that you'll never fully escape me, Wren. We're bound, regardless of the distance between us. In life or death, it doesn't matter. You are mine."

You are mine. You are mine. You are mine.

Years ago, when he first spoke those words, it sounded like a grand declaration of love. But now? A death sentence.

I placed my hands on his chest, pushing him away. "I am not yours. Maybe once, but not anymore." I didn't miss the darkness that seeped into his blue eyes, but I ignored it. "Why do you want me to join the guard?" If I knew anything about

Asher, there was always a catch. More often than not, he calculated things I hadn't even thought of.

He cocked his head. "When are you going to stop punishing me?"

"Punishing you?" I echoed back.

He pushed himself from the tree, shoving his hands in his pockets. He had a way about him that made time itself stand still. "You've pulled away from me. You always knew the requirements of our deal so I don't understand why you were so shocked to hear me repeat them." He pointed a finger. "You owe me a life."

"You want me to fall in love but at the same time are annoyed that I pulled away from you?" I laughed. "Do you hear how contradictory that is?"

He shrugged. "Is it so bad to want both?"

"Yes," I said. "When it's clear all you care for is the fulfillment of our deal." *Not me.* I didn't say it, but I knew he caught my meaning. "Now I'll ask again, why do you want me to join the guard?"

"You claim love will not find you here, and truly, I understand why. So perhaps leaving will give you more options."

I suppressed a grunt as he proved my point. This was all that mattered to him. The constant reminder hurt worse than I cared to admit.

"You think a member of the Royal Guard will have time for romance?"

A devilish grin flashed across his face. "I don't think love cares for positions and rank. I think it sneaks up on you when you least expect it and consumes you. Taking everything you have until you break."

"You speak of love as if it's a thief."

Asher raised a brow, inching closer. "Is that not what it is? Something that creeps up behind you?" I unconsciously backed up as he continued moving forward. "Something that wraps tender arms around your very being like a tightly bound rope, squeezing and demanding every last thing you have to give?"

My back slammed into a tree, causing my movements to halt. Asher, however, did not. He continued moving toward me until our chests were mere inches apart. He pressed both hands against the bark on either side of me, caging me in his grasp. Lowering his head slowly, he brushed his lips over mine. "And when the rope is pulled back, it has stripped you of everything you are. Leaving you utterly and completely alone."

It wasn't until I felt the absence of his body around me that I realized my eyes had closed. When they fluttered open, he stood several feet away, watching me.

Clearing my throat, I stepped forward. I didn't want to speak of love. Especially not with Asher. "Let's be clear. If I do this, it'll be for me. Not *you.*"

He raised a brow. "So you don't want my help?"

"Why would I want anything from you?" I asked.

His eyes narrowed. "How exactly do you plan on disguising yourself tomorrow when everyone in the village knows who you are?" He tugged at my braid, moving his hand before I could hit him. "It's not like you'll have a guard's uniform, so tell me, Wren, what is your plan?"

"Angel has a plan," I said confidently. Although, I wasn't sure he did.

The corners of Asher's lips pulled up in a knowing smirk. "Does he now? Because if you asked for my help, I'd make sure no one here recognizes you. Aside from your family, if that would make you more comfortable."

I sighed. "How?" I hated myself for succumbing to his trap, but if this were to work, I'd need a concrete plan.

His smirk widened to a grin. "Don't you trust me, Wren?"

I snorted. "Trust you? You're joking, right?"

For a moment, I could have sworn hurt flashed in his eyes. "You should trust me. I've kept my word about everything I promised you." I opened my mouth, but he wasn't finished. "If anything," he continued, "I shouldn't trust *you.*"

I ignored his dig. "So no one will recognize me tomorrow. But that doesn't solve the problem of how I'll continue hiding my identity once I leave Morters' End."

His lips twitched. "Look how confident you've become, my Wren. So certain they'll choose you."

I was confident. I might not be good at much, but I was damn sure of how talented I was with any form of weapon. My hand instinctively went to the dagger I kept sheathed at my thigh, only to find it wasn't there. My brows raised as I glanced down at my leg. Nothing. Had I really forgotten it? That wasn't like me.

"No need to demonstrate your skills," Asher said, as if he read my thoughts. "I already know all about what you can do." The way his hooded eyes trailed over my body made it clear he wasn't just talking about my skills with a blade.

The rosy flush to my cheeks quickly diminished as he added, "And besides, the uniforms contain a headpiece so I'm sure you'll be able to tuck away those beautiful brown locks."

"How could you possibly know that?"

He shrugged. "I remember the last time the guards were

here. Granted, it was many years before you were even born, but seeing as they hate to stray from tradition..."

I bit my tongue to refrain from asking exactly *how* long ago this was. Asher wasn't one to talk much about the past, especially *his* past. It infuriated me. He knew me better than anyone, even better than Angel, and I hardly knew him.

However, I did know *some* things. Like how his eyes lit up when the moonlight flickered over the brook, or how his body relaxed when the branches blew in the midnight breeze. I knew he loved the way my body fit perfectly against his, and I knew how much he laughed when I used to create stories of how our lives would be if we hadn't been in Morters' End. If we had been different people.

I knew the way his presence always stirred something in me. I recognized his silence. The stillness of how he moved through the world, like a shadow unattached. My shadow in a way. He was mine, and he wasn't. I knew him and would sense him anywhere and everywhere. Even death. Forever.

But that didn't brush aside the fact there was also plenty I *didn't* know. Would never know because he made it clear he wouldn't tell me.

I chewed my inner cheek as I let my mind sort through the plan he was concocting. He was willing to send me away, potentially *without* him, all in the hopes I'd keep my word. He really didn't get it, did he? I'd never love anyone because he destroyed that part of me. Nonetheless, I'd let him think what he wanted if it meant he'd help disguise me.

"Fine," I said. "I'll do it."

"As I knew you would." He brushed a feather-light kiss to my cheek. "Until tomorrow." And then he was gone.

CHAPTER 4

As I laid awake in bed that night, I couldn't help but contemplate what my life outside the village would be like. I wondered what the sunlight would feel like against my skin. Would it burn? Or be more of a gentle warmth, like the heat that radiates off a dying fire. I hadn't the slightest idea. No one here had ever stepped outside of Morters' End.

I'd be the first.

If this preposterous plan worked.

While I wasn't that concerned about proving my skills, I was as to *why* they were recruiting here. For as long as I could remember, the king had scorned us, and now all of a sudden he was eager to include us? And more surprisingly, in something as important as guarding his son?

I'd like to find out why, but I had more pressing issues to sort through at the moment. Asher claimed I'd be unrecognizable to everyone here, but what about if I left? So many factors came into play. My voice, for instance. Too feminine. Perhaps I should drop it an octave. Or maybe I won't have to speak at all. I could pretend to be mute like old Mr. Walligsby who lived down by the abandoned stables. No one knew how he lost his tongue, but rumor had it that it was bitten off by Sylvia, his pet crow.

My bed creaked as I shifted onto my side, pulling the thin, torn fabric I used as a blanket higher up my shoulder. My bedroom wasn't much bigger than a broom closet. The narrow bed was pressed up against the wall beneath a window, while a broken armoire stood against the other. Those, and a three-legged wooden table was all. I didn't have any keepsakes. Not unless a dozen daggers and three swords were considered personal items.

I shoved my hand under my head, watching the night sky through dirty glass. Sometimes, the only distinctions between day and night were the small bright dots that lit up the sky. When I was younger, I tried to count them all, but eventually, sleep took over. By the time I'd wake, the stars receded to wherever they hid during the day.

Some nights they'd shoot across the sky, a glowing trail of dust in their wake. Papa used to say it was the gods relocating and the most likely time our prayers would be answered. For as the gods drifted through the sky on shooting stars, they heard our prayers the loudest. If they chose to answer, they'd sprinkle stardust which fulfilled any prayer or wish, down to the world below.

I used to believe so strongly. I'd sit by this very window night after night, waiting for the stars to shoot by. And when they did, I'd pray. Pray for a better life for my family, for a way out of Morters' End, for us to be *happy*.

Needless to say, disappointment was a close friend.

Now when I gazed at the moving stars, I saw just that. No gods or prayers or stardust.

I was tracing my finger through the air when one of the floorboards creaked. I froze. Asher hadn't said anything about visiting me tonight. Had something caused him to change his mind? My heart thumped in anticipation as I laid still, waiting.

Showing up in my bedroom in the middle of the night used to be a common occurrence, and one I expected for a time. I remembered the feeling of his arms wrapped around me as we squeezed together on my bed. His right arm draped over my stomach, his left under my head. We fit so completely together, as if our bodies were the missing pieces we both required.

If I closed my eyes, I could almost feel the brush of his lips against my skin, gentle and claiming.

The thought of that now made me shiver. Without turning to face him, I said, "I know you must be feeling sentimental and all, considering tomorrow everything might change, but I thought I made it perfectly clear the last time that I never wanted you in my bed again."

"*What?*"

My eyes widened. That wasn't Asher's voice. Turning slowly, I found a very confused, very *disturbed*, Angel. I forced a smile. "Oh, it's you."

He hesitated, then plopped down at the foot of my bed, causing it to dip slightly. He raised a brow as his eyes rested on me. "I wanted to talk to you, but it seems you were... expecting someone else." Pulling the threads of my blanket, he added, "Do I even want to know who you thought I was?"

For once in my life, I was grateful for the darkness as it hid my flaming cheeks. "I was sleep talking."

His brow inched higher. "Right."

Shifting into a sitting position, I folded my hands in my lap. "So what is it, dear brother, that draws you to my chambers in the dead of night? Do you need ideas for a new sketch? If so, I suggest anything other than Zena. I'm sure whatever else you come up with will be a *serious* improvement."

"Thanks for the helpful tip, but no, I'm not here about sketching. I want to talk about tomorrow."

"Ah, your infamous plan to get rid of me," I teased.

He rolled his eyes and grabbed my hand. "I'm not trying to get rid of you. I'm trying to save you. There's a difference."

"I don't need saving." It came out more harshly than I intended.

He huffed out a laugh. "Yes, I guess you're right about that. You can handle yourself better than half the grown men in this village."

"Correction. I can handle myself better than *all* the grown men in this village."

"I used to watch, you know, when we were younger." He folded his hands behind his head, leaning back against the window. A small smile crept onto his face as he recalled a memory. "I remember Papa training you. I'd look up from whatever sketch I was working on, and I could see you both outside through the window. I remember watching him disarm you over and over again. And sometimes, he'd knock you off your feet so hard I didn't know if you'd get back up."

My throat went dry. I never knew Angel watched me. He never seemed interested in activities that left me bloody and bruised.

"But you always did," he continued. "You always got back up, and I was always so proud of you. Proud to call you my sister."

I felt a sudden urge to lunge across the bed and wrap my arms around him. Bury my head in the crease of his neck the way I used to when we were children and the sounds of thunder scared me half to death. Turning to face me, his eyes glowed in the moonlight. "I hated I was never the strong one. Never able to protect you as an older brother should."

I shook my head. "Angel, that's not—"

"Let me finish," he said softly. I nodded, allowing him to go on. "Especially living in a place like this. I *should* have been able to protect you. But then, when I saw you training with him and watched as you wielded that sword with perfect form, when you threw your daggers with unbelievable accuracy—" he paused, a slight chuckle escaping his lips. "Hell, even the way you managed to disarm and bring Papa, a man double your size, to the ground." I smiled at the memory. Angel reached out and grabbed my hand. "I knew then I'd been wrong. You never needed my protection. You've always been strong, Wren. Strong in ways I cannot even begin to explain. And a place like this?" He waved his free hand through the air. "It destroys the strong and coddles those who follow orders. You were never meant for this."

"And what about you?" I asked. "You think *you* were meant for a life like this?"

He was silent a moment. "I think my purpose is to bring some light to a village corrupted by darkness. Through art." His eyes found mine again, and this time, they filled with promise. "I don't have the skills necessary to be freed from this place, and that's okay. Perhaps I was meant to stay here.

To use my talents to bring color and creativity to this dull, gray life. I've accepted my fate. Now it's time to accept yours."

"I won't leave you here," I said. "Don't accept anything just yet. If this works out, give me a few years and I'll find a way to get you out of here. You have my word."

His returning smile was wistful, as if he didn't quite believe my words. But he nodded, nonetheless.

I picked at a loose piece of skin beside my thumb. "I meant to ask you, don't you think this whole situation is a bit strange? The fact they're recruiting from here? We haven't been acknowledged in years and years, and now all of a sudden, we're being offered an opportunity to become guards?"

Angel's brows scrunched. "It is slightly out of the blue. But maybe they haven't collected enough men in the other locations? Maybe they're desperate?" He shrugged. "Who knows? I'm sure they'll give us more of an explanation tomorrow."

I nodded. Surely they would.

Wrapping his arm around me, he squeezed tight. "So, what do you think the prince is like?"

I snorted. "Well, let me think. Rude, conceited, entitled, arrogant... shall I go on?"

Angel's laughter filled my small room. "Judging the poor guy before you even meet him? Poor form, Wren."

"You asked what I *thought*."

"And what if he turns out to be none of those things? What if he's charming, funny, handsome, and kind?"

I snorted again. "I highly doubt anyone with royal blood will be kind. Or funny, for that matter. But if he is, then good for him. It doesn't affect me. I plan on getting in and out as quickly as I can."

I could basically hear his smile as he replied, "Really? Are you sure it doesn't? Because I seem to remember a little six-year-old Wren running around, claiming she was a princess, just wondering when her dashing prince was going to swoop in and—"

"And on that note," I cut in. "It's time for you to leave." Shoving him off the bed, I couldn't help but smile at the fit of laughter that escaped him.

A somber expression spread across his face as he hovered beside the door. "Don't let the world change you, Wren."

CHAPTER 5

Those first few moments waking up were always my favorite. The moments before my brain began functioning, and the memories of who and where I was came to light.

My gaze drifted across the little room that was mine for the past eighteen years. There was hole in the wall about the size of my fist right beside the armoire from when I first heard about Henry Yuller and Abigail Brester. I'd pretended it was his face.

Another hole was located beside the door in the shape of the knob. When I was ten, I locked myself in my room and refused to come out. Why, I didn't remember. I'd stayed in here about two days before Papa busted the door open. I vaguely remembered him calling me a "*stubborn little gremlin.*"

I swallowed the memories as I stood up. This small space contained millions of them. Some painful, but others so wonderful I hoped I'd never forget them. Like the times Angel would sit with his back against my bed, sketching. Every sketch he made in my room, stayed in my room. That was our rule. I pinned them to every available space on my walls.

I debated taking one with me, folding it up and shoving it in my pocket, but then decided against it. Angel would make me new ones when I freed him. Holding onto that would keep me going these next few years if I succeeded.

I hadn't the slightest clue what to expect today. I tried to prevent my thoughts from straying to a place that would have me changing my mind on this absurd idea as I dressed. I slipped into a pair of gray breeches and a white, long-sleeved tunic. Grabbing my brush from the windowsill, I dragged the bristles through the knots decorating my brown hair.

I was then almost knocked down as my door swung open, and Angel filed in. I sighed. "Do you ever knock?"

Ignoring my comment, his eyes scanned over me. "You can't wear that."

"Why not?"

Angling his head, he shifted his weight. "It's too tight. You can see your..." He waved a hand in the general direction of my chest. Clearing his throat, he tossed a bundled piece of fabric at me. "Here. Wear one of mine. It'll be a bit loose, but better than it being too tight."

I glanced down at my chest. It wasn't like I had much there anyway, but it could still prove to be a complication. Looking back up, I motioned to my hair. "Any idea what to do with this?"

"I was thinking you can have one of my hats for now. It'll have to do until you get cleared and are given a uniform. Just means you'll have to be extra careful today to keep it in place."

A hat? This was his genius plan? "Hurry up and change, they'll be here soon."

I reached for his arm, halting his steps toward the door. "How do you know?"

"A few guards started setting up in the square about an hour ago. The rest should be here shortly." His attention snapped to my table of daggers. "Make sure you have one on you. Wells is *not* happy about this unexpected visit, and I have a feeling it could go very bad, very fast."

I groaned at the mention of that bastard's name. I hated Wells, just as I hated all the necromancers. I used to fantasize about ripping them apart and watching as they begged me to end it. Unfortunately for those fantasies, the necromancers were all but immortal as the dark magic they practiced allowed for a never-ending lifespan.

Although all magic came with a price, I'd yet to see the price of cheating death hundreds of times.

The necromancers could age if they wished or remain at any age of their choosing. Wells was one of the many who preferred to stay young. In all eighteen years of my life, he resided in the form of a thirty-five-year old man, even though he was well over a hundred. Our youngest necromancer was ninety-two, and she kept the body of a twenty-year-old.

After she was born, the necromancers ceased procreating for reasons unbeknownst to me. There was a grand total of sixty-six in Morters' End, and none of them ever died. Ever.

I believed they could be killed, but none of us knew how or were even remotely equipped to try. To strike out against them physically was as good as signing your own death sentence.

They also had rules when it came to reviving the rest of us.

If a person below the age of eighteen died, they'd be brought back as many times as necessary. Once we passed that age frame, we only received one final ticket of resurrection. Because according to the necromancers, only they could live forever.

"Well," I replied to Angel. "I do love to start my day with some drama." I pushed him out the door, swinging it closed. "I'll be down in a second."

I stripped out of my tunic, allowing it to pool around my feet, when something caused me to stop. Using Angel's shirt to cover my bare chest, I spun around to find a very relaxed Asher sprawled out on my bed.

His eyes raked over my half naked body, darkening with lust. When they made their way back to my face, his mouth quirked into a lazy grin.

"Turn around," I demanded.

A brow shot up. "Turn around? You act as if I haven't seen all of you before." Sitting up, he threw his legs over the side of the bed, leaning his forearms on his knees. "Holding up that ridiculous piece of fabric does nothing to stop my mind from remembering every small detail."

I narrowed my eyes, and he matched my glare, testing me. Clenching my jaw, I turned my back to him and finished getting dressed.

"I prefer you without the clothes," Asher said as I faced him once more.

"And I prefer when you're not in my room." I strolled over to the table that held my daggers. I quickly sheathed my favorite, the one Papa gave me, to my thigh. "What do you want, Asher."

He was before me in an instant. After a while, I began

picking up on his silent movements. Standing chest to chest, I inclined my head, eyes locking onto his. They were such a captivating blue.

Lifting a hand, he brushed his fingers through my hair, tucking a strand behind my ear. "I'm here to make you unrecognizable. Or did you forget our conversation yesterday?"

No, I had definitely not forgotten. "Go ahead," I said with a nod.

He twirled my hair around his finger, draping it over my right shoulder. The thrum of his voice tickled the left side of my neck as he whispered, "This might hurt a bit."

Before I could ask *what* might hurt, he lifted his hand which now gripped the dagger I'd just attached to my thigh. He raised it to my neck, and I hissed as a sharp sting filled my senses. I could feel the blood dripping down the side of my throat as a coppery scent wafted up my nose.

He dropped the dagger and cupped the back of my head, his mouth replacing the cold metal. His tongue ran up from my collarbone to the cut. He sucked on the skin, and my eyes fluttered closed. I couldn't help pulling my lower lip between my teeth to prevent any evidence I was enjoying this from escaping my mouth.

I hated that he still evoked such a response from my body. Before I had a chance to do or say something I'd inevitably regret, he pulled back. Opening my eyes, I blinked at the sight of my blood coating the corners of his mouth. I touched my neck, expecting to feel pain, but there was nothing. Not even a drop of blood.

"What did you do?" I asked.

He ran his thumb over the corners of his mouth before sucking the blood off it. "I made you unrecognizable."

I didn't understand how Asher's strange abilities worked. I knew it involved my blood, but that was about the extent of my knowledge. I moved past him to the cracked mirror on the wall, only to find I looked the same. Freckles lining the bridge of my nose, two bright green eyes, and a jagged scar between my eyebrows. "What will they see?"

He shrugged. "Someone else from the village. But the moment they look away, they'll forget they even saw anyone."

Interesting. "What about my family? And the king's advisors and guards?"

"I managed to make it so the illusion won't affect Angel or your mother. But it would take more power than I currently possess to hide your face from those who have never seen you before. The king's men will see you as you are, so make sure to disguise yourself well."

"Angel seems to think shoving my hair in a hat will be enough," I said.

"It'll have to be. No one will expect a girl to attempt something like this, so use that to your advantage." He stepped closer, and this time, I didn't move back. Not even as his mouth hovered beside my ear. "We'll see each other again, Wren. I don't doubt it for a second."

I watched as he vanished, silently hoping he was wrong.

~

The moment my foot hit the bottom step, a handful of berries were shoved into my mouth. "What are you doing?" I forced out in between bites.

Angel opened my hand, dropping more into my palm. It

must have been whatever was left over from Callin's last visit. "You need to eat. It's not much, but you need something."

Once I chewed and swallowed, I headed for the pitcher of water on the table. Ignoring the thought of *where* the water came from, I poured a glass and downed the contents.

Like every morning, I turned to the fireplace where Mama usually sat on the rocking chair Papa built, only to find she wasn't there. Angel quickly brought me one of his fitted black hats, and I stood silently as he twisted my hair into a knot at the back of my head, placing the hat on top.

He stepped away, examining me with the thoughtful look he usually reserved for his art. "As long as they don't stare *too* long, this should be fine," he said.

I held up the glass, vaguely catching my reflection. My hair was completely hidden, and my face was bare. "What if this doesn't work? What if the hat falls off? What if they ask me to remove it?" Granted, the hat fit my head snuggly and I didn't think it would be going anywhere, but there was still a *chance*.

Angel frowned. "It's a risk. I'm sorry if you think I've forced this on you, Wren. If you don't want to go through with it, you don't have to. I've been pushing you because I want you to be free, but if this isn't what you want—"

"I want it," I said, relaxing my shoulders. I'd already committed to this plan in my head, already imagined our life a few years from now on the other side of this shield. I was just... nervous. But nerves were normal, right? Everyone got nerves when doing something out of their ordinary routine. Even if most people didn't do things as extreme as sneaking into the Royal Guard. "What exactly should I be expecting?"

He crossed his arms, charcoal-stained fingers smearing black on his beige tunic. "I assume they'll assess your skills.

Put you through some type of physical test to see if you're good enough. Which, you are."

"You think too highly of me."

He nudged me lightly. "Give yourself some credit."

I was fully prepared to respond with a sarcastic remark when a step creaked behind me. I whipped around just in time to see Mama at the top of the stairs, her eyes glued to me. It had been so long since she looked at me, *acknowledged* me, that I almost forgot to breathe. I barely heard Angel when he said he'd wait outside, my attention wholly on her as she walked down the stairs.

The sound of the door clicking shut snapped me out of it. I willed air into my lungs as she walked to her rocking chair and sat. Her shoulder length auburn hair moved in loose waves as she rocked back and forth. Hazel eyes, the same eyes as Angel's, swept over me as I stood awkwardly.

I didn't know what to say. We hadn't spoken in so long, it almost felt like I was standing in a room with the ghost of the mother I once had. After a moment, she broke the silence. "Interesting look," she said calmly.

"I—" I raised my hand, running it over the material of the hat. "It was Angel's idea."

She clasped her hands in her lap, pushing the chair back and forth with the heel of her foot. "I know all about Angel's idea. I know what you plan to do."

I rubbed sweaty palms against my sides. "What do you think?"

Tilting her head, she blinked. "Does it matter what I think?"

Yes! It has always mattered what you thought! I wanted to scream. *You're my mama. You're supposed to tell me not to do this, not to put myself in danger. You're supposed to tell me you love me, and hold me, and promise everything will be okay.*

"I guess not," I said, the words like poison as I forced them out.

She seemed unfazed. "I thought as much." She paused, then added, "You best be going. Wouldn't want to keep the king's men waiting."

I opened my mouth but was all out of words. Nodding, I turned toward the door, heart thumping in my chest. This might be the last time I saw her for a while. I had to say it. Even if she didn't feel the same for me anymore, I had to say it. I didn't know what I did for her to scorn and abandon me, and right now I didn't care.

With one hand on the doorknob, I turned, taking in every detail of her one last time. "Mama." Her eyes flickered. "I love you."

I could have sworn she flinched at the words. I waited for her to say it back. For her to say *anything*, but she didn't. Instead, she fixed her gaze on the crackling fire.

Wiping away the stray tear that rolled down my cheek, I walked out the door and didn't turn back.

CHAPTER 6

The village square was more crowded than I'd ever seen it. More crowded than the time Finny Tucker fell from his window, shattering every bone in his body. He'd died on impact, but to the surprise of no one, was resurrected shortly after.

Standing here now, I took in many familiar faces as well as a few I didn't recognize. Morters' End was a relatively small village, yet I still hadn't been officially acquainted with everyone here. Of course, they all knew who I was after the spectacle that was Papa's death.

Everything appeared the same, aside from the burgundy tent pitched right in the center of the square. The sound of the flaps smacking in the breeze blended with the quiet murmurs of the people gathered like a tuneless song.

I followed behind Angel as he weaved through the crowd, closer to the tent. Two guards stood flanking either side, attired in military regalia of blue and gold. They were towering, broad-shouldered men, with their hands on the hilts of their finely polished swords. My eyes wandered over every inch of their uniforms, lingering on the headpiece they both sported. Two white cloths connected to an iron cap that came to a point right between the eyebrows. I exhaled slowly.

"Is that what I would wear?" I asked Angel.

He scanned the crowd as if looking for someone. "If not exactly, then definitely similar. But considering the prince's personal guard is a separate division, I assume there will be some form of distinction."

I raised a brow. "Who are you looking—"

"You have absolutely no right showing up here like this!"

I turned just in time to see a fuming Wells round the corner of the tent. His fair skin and black cloak caused his green eyes to pop in a crazy, unhinged manner as he stormed past the guards, directly into the tent. They appeared completely unfazed, and truthfully, I applauded them for not giving Wells the attention he craved with each dramatic meltdown.

Before I could remark on his temper tantrum, the sound of hooves clinking against the cobblestones had me turning to the right where the crowd parted, allowing space for two horses trotting toward the tent. I was familiar with horses. Some of the wild ones would make their way through our shield from time to time looking for fresh grazing space, only to be met with barren, dead land. Some were fortunate enough to escape, while others met a very different end. An end that landed them cooked and pierced on a fork.

The black mare on the left was ridden by a man with a skin color I'd never seen before. It was a rich, dark brown, and his eyes were nearly black. "That's the king's commander, Dimitri Bekencourt," Angel whispered.

I didn't know how he knew these things, but even if he hadn't told me, I would've guessed. Aside from the blue frock coat embroidered with golden detail, Commander Bekencourt carried his head high and his nose higher. He was a man clearly used to being in control and treated with nothing but respect.

As he gracefully dismounted and removed his riding gloves, he grunted in disgust as the stench of Morters' End finally seemed to hit him. A second later, he was in the tent. I grinned as I thought of the surprise he'd find waiting for him inside.

The second horse had a coat as bright as ivory and was ridden by a woman. Truthfully, she was one of the most beautiful people I'd ever seen. Her skin matched that of the commander's, a brown that was almost identical to her hair which was braided tightly and wound into a bun at the top of her head. Her crystal blue eyes scanned the crowd as she effortlessly dropped down, boots crunching the dried dirt below. Smoothing out her midnight blue dress, she halted. A split second later, I realized why.

Wells stormed out of the tent, pausing when he saw her. His eyes widened in recognition and a rage so piercing, I thought he might explode. I instinctively reached for my dagger as he flipped his hand, black smoke seeping from his palm.

"I wouldn't do that if I were you, Wells," the woman said calmly. Her face was coated in amusement. "You do remember what happened the last time you attempted to use your sinful magic on me, don't you?" She unfolded her hand and a bright, golden smoke formed in a swirling motion.

I froze. Sounds of gasps, cries, and prayers emanated all

around me, but I couldn't make out the words. I was too shocked to do anything but stare, wide-eyed, at the magic seeping from her hand like blood pouring from a flesh wound. I'd heard enough stories and read enough books to know what it was. To know what *she* was.

An Esteler in the flesh. Not make believe, but real. Here, in Morters' End.

Wells snorted. "And what do you plan on doing, Drestel? You've been banished from your flock, and you know very well that you won't win against us on your own." He clenched his fists at his side.

I didn't have the ability to process what he'd said as I continued to stare at the Esteler—*Drestel*—in shock. She smiled as she closed her palm, extinguishing her powers. *Purity,* that's what it was called.

"Your time will come, Wells," she replied in the same relaxed tone. "And mark my words, it'll be an Esteler who delivers your final death blow." She cocked her head. "If I have the privilege, I think I'll make you watch as I disintegrate your friends before I do the same to you. I want to see you squirm like the pathetic worm you are as I end your life."

Everyone gathered had gone eerily quiet in anticipation of his response. Not even the rats moved as he stood, shaking with anger. After a moment, Wells opened his disgusting mouth. "*Bitch,*" he spat, before heading back toward the Vacar.

I still couldn't believe what I'd just witnessed. Not as Drestel strolled into the tent with a godly grace, or as Angel gripped my shoulders, turning me to face him. Noticing the vacant look I wore, his features hardened. "What's wrong?"

"They're real," I said, my voice seeming far away.

His brows furrowed in confusion. "Who's real?"

"The Estelers."

The corners of his mouth twitched. "Haven't I always told you to have a little faith?"

"Relax, almighty prophet," I teased. "Just because they're real, doesn't mean the gods are."

"So where do you think their powers came from? Everyone knows the Estelers were gifted with Purity from the goddess Tella when—"

"Stories, Angel," I cut in. "It's just a story for people like *you*, who need an explanation for everything."

He grinned. "You used to believe. Perhaps one day you will again."

Crossing my arms, I sighed. "I'll believe in the gods when I see one with my own two eyes."

My patience was wearing thin as we waited for the flaps of the tent to open. I'd made eye contact with several people, all of whom either waved or smiled in recognition. Who they saw when they looked at me, I didn't know. But it seemed Asher had succeeded in his illusion because as they turned away, a glazed look appeared on their faces. It was as if their most recent memories had been erased and reset.

I let out a deep breath, kicking a loose stone with my boot. A rat scurried across the feet of the man in front of me, but he didn't seem to notice.

After an excruciatingly long few minutes, the flaps were pulled back, and Commander Bekencourt strolled out, followed by Drestel. The crowd went as silent as death.

"I'm sure all of you are wondering why we're here," the commander began, eyes scanning the crowd. "It is by the request of Reid Bryton, King of Alosia, that I, Commander of the Crown, seek out the best possible candidates to reform the guard of Prince Ryder. While initially hesitant to extend this offering to the people of Morters' End, I helped the king see reason that skimming over your... *interesting* home, might prove to be a foolish decision. We could use all the able-bodied men we come across, and seeing as times are changing—"

"What happened to his former guard?" An older man with graying hair interjected.

The commander raised a brow. It was clear he wasn't typically interrupted. "They've been dismissed, and we're searching for eligible replacements."

I wasn't sure I believed him. Callin had said there were rumors spreading that the prince's guard was ambushed and slaughtered. Whatever the truth was, it was clearly valuable enough to be withheld from the public.

Adjusting the lapels of his coat, the commander continued. "We have been—"

"And why would we help you?" This time it was a young woman who cut him off. Sighing, Bekencourt pinched the bridge of his nose. "You trapped us in this village! Innocent people who have no magic and want nothing to do with the evil practiced here! Free us!"

Several others yelled in agreement.

This was quickly becoming a riot. Angry villagers began screaming and throwing whatever they could find. A rock, a shoe. I even saw a pail go flying toward the tent. Unfazed, the commander nodded to Drestel.

Inching forward, she snapped her fingers, and that bright golden smoke reappeared. She motioned her hand at the crowd, and the smoke followed, seeping over the gathered. A moment later, those yelling fell silent. My head whipped around as I examined the people around me. They all seemed... calm.

"What did she do to us?" someone asked.

Commander Bekencourt waved a hand through the air. "Drestel here simply soothed your more *hysteric* companions. Nothing to worry about. Now, may I continue?" When no one responded, he clasped his hands together. "Wonderful. As I was saying, we've made our rounds through every inch of the kingdom, and the king has been gracious enough to extend this opportunity to you, the inhabitants of Morters' End."

He unraveled a scroll from his pocket and cleared his throat. "It has been declared that any man both physically and mentally fit, between the ages of eighteen and thirty-five, may present himself for consideration. He will then be assessed, and it will be determined whether or not his skills deem him qualified to continue training for the Royal Guard." Folding up the scroll, he handed it to Drestel. "Any questions?"

I waited for angry voices to chime in, but there was nothing. Not even a snide remark mumbled throughout the crowd. The commander's obsidian eyes drifted over every one of our faces. As they landed on mine, I couldn't help but feel like they lingered just a bit longer.

Eventually, his voice broke the silence. "Excellent. Anyone interested will be asked to line up outside the tent. Everyone else, clear the square." Without another word, he ducked into the tent, Drestel close behind. Shortly after, the guards followed.

One by one, the crowd dispersed. I watched as some drifted into the crumbling old tavern, while others moved into darkened alleys, undoubtedly up to no good. My heart sped up as I spotted Henry Yuller. The color had not yet fully returned to his face, but he was looking... healed. Pity. He was seated in a chair with wheels along the bottom, his mother holding onto the handles behind him. As his eyes locked on mine, he smiled. For a moment I forgot it wasn't me he saw. Slowly, I raised my hand and waved. He looked like he was about to say something, but his mother quickly spun the chair, pushing him away from the tent.

Eventually, I was left standing alone with Angel. I wasn't surprised to find no one lined up. If he hadn't shown me this was my only chance at freedom, I wouldn't be here either.

But this *was* my chance. My one shot at escaping. Before I knew what I was doing, my feet moved in the direction of the flaps. I glanced back at Angel once. He nodded and smiled, placing his hand to his chest. He didn't have to say it. I knew what he meant.

Using that as my final piece of encouragement, I strode the last few steps and pushed into the tent.

CHAPTER 7

As soon as I was inside, my attention locked on the group of four huddled around a small table, speaking in hushed tones. The white tarp that covered the ground now contained a trail of dirt as I moved farther inside. A few candles sat along various wooden ledges that jutted out from the rods holding the tent, as well as one large, half melted candle in the center of the table. Before I observed anything more, four sets of eyes met mine, glaring at me as if I strolled into the tent naked. I instantly regretted this.

I felt the heat rushing to my cheeks. Commander Bekencourt's gaze held me in place, the intensity in his dark eyes sending a chill down my spine as he braced his hands on the table. "Yes?"

I opened my mouth, then shut it abruptly. My voice. Angel hadn't helped me with my voice. And now all I could do was hope for the best. Clearing my throat, I tried to deepen it. "I'm here to present myself." It came out strained and guttural. When no one responded, I added, "As a potential candidate for the Royal Guard... sir."

I forced myself to stand tall. Drestel was studying me, as were the two guards. Gods, why was I so good at embarrassing myself? The room had fallen silent. I could hear each strained breath that entered and left my lips. The commander moved around the table, crossing his arms. The way he was staring at me... the way they were *all* staring at me...

I began to panic. They knew. Of course they knew I was lying. Did I really think I would get away with this ridiculous plan? That I could put on a silly hat, talk like a man, and it would work? I braced for the tongue lashing I was no doubt about to receive when—

"Not a very good listener, are we?"

"I..."

Folding his hands behind his back, the commander cocked his head. "I believe I made myself quite clear when I stated all potential candidates were to wait *outside* the tent."

Oh. *Oh.*

I was definitely not off to a good start.

"I'm so sorry. I'll just—" Taking a step backward, I pointed to the opening between the flaps. "Should I go back outside and wait?"

Drestel stifled a laugh as Bekencourt sighed in annoyance. "That seems quite unnecessary considering you're already here. What's your name?"

"Wren," I said quietly.

He took a slow step forward. "Wren what?"

"Wren Hibreaker, sir."

"Wren Hibreaker." He spoke my name as if it were a prayer being answered, and for some reason, the sound of it on his lips made my skin crawl. "And how old are you, Mr. Hibreaker?"

I stood up tall. "Eighteen as of last month."

He proceeded to circle me, heavy boots dragging along the tarp. He was examining my figure, probably wondering what business a scrawny little thing like myself had attempting to join the guard. But then again, what did they expect to find in Morters' End? No one here was exactly the epitome of healthy. We learned to survive on minimal nutrients and whatever Callin and the others managed to smuggle in.

When he completed three full turns, he looked me hard in the eye. "And why is it, Wren Hibreaker, you desire to join the Royal Guard?"

I couldn't stop the words as they fell from my mouth. "You've seen this place, can you blame me for wanting to leave?"

Bekencourt's eyes narrowed as he rubbed his chin. "I see. Hopefully your reasons will expand to align with our own." Taking a few steps toward the table, he leaned against the dark wood. "Well, Wren Hibreaker, show us what you can do." There was challenge in his eyes, and I was happy to meet it.

He nodded toward the guards, and they raised their practice swords. The taller of the two tossed one to me. I caught it easily with my left hand, adjusting my grip and getting a feel for the weight.

"Disarm both of my guards, and you'll be taken back for basic training." From his carefree manner, I could tell the commander didn't expect this to end in my favor. It caused me to smirk as the guards inched closer, shifting into position. I couldn't help it, I loved a good challenge.

One blink later and the guard to the left lunged. I had just enough time to dodge out of the way, coming up on his side where I drove the pommel of my sword into his abdomen. He angled himself, giving me the opening I needed to duck under his arm as he swung the sword at my chest.

Both guards might have been large and muscular, but I was small and agile, and I'd use that to my advantage. I blocked his next swing with my own blade, the sound of metal scraping metal echoing through the space. Twisting to the side, I brought the sword down hard on his forearm. He cursed as his grip slipped, sword falling to the ground.

I laughed, wiping my sleeve across my sweaty forehead. "One down, one to go."

The second guard moved so quickly and swung with such unexpected force, I didn't have time to move out of the way. The air escaped my lungs as the sword dug into my stomach. I hunched over as he swiftly raised it again, preparing to bring it down in a sweeping motion.

I dropped and rolled to the side. By the time he realized, I had my leg hooked around his ankle. I pulled back, and he stumbled. This was my chance. I swiped the sword across the back of his legs, and his knees buckled from the sudden blow. Another jab later, and his sword had fallen beside his comrade's.

I stood between both disarmed guards, smiling like a fool, chest rising and falling rapidly as I attempted to catch my breath. I almost forgot how much I loved this. The thrill of the unknown that came with swordplay.

It'd been so long since I trained with anyone. It was always Papa and I, but once he died, I had nobody. Angel wasn't at all interested in swinging a blade at me, and I didn't have friends in Morters' End. Most of the girls stayed away from me, claiming I didn't *act* like a girl should. That was the same reason the boys stayed away too.

Until Asher. He trained with me.

I swallowed those memories because the look of utter shock on the commander's face was too good to miss. "Very well, Wren Hibreaker," he said. "You'll come with us." He snapped his fingers, and the guards opened the flaps.

"Wait, that's it? It's that easy?"

Drestel laughed. "Not even close. You've only passed the recruitment stage. Once we get back to Caelestis, the real work will begin." Her smile made me shift uncomfortably.

I moved for the parted flaps when Commander Bekencourt blocked my path. "Where do you think you're going?"

"Am I not allowed a moment to say goodbye to my brother?"

He eyed me. "Once you walked into this tent and declared your interest, you gave up access to your outside life. As of now, you are a trainee for the Royal Guard. You should have said your goodbyes beforehand."

No. *No.* I had to see Angel. I didn't care about anything else.

I moved around him, only to find the guards now blocking the exit. I whirled, anger and panic coursing through me. I could tell from his expression he wasn't going to budge, so instead, I hurled myself at the guards. My sudden movement sent them stumbling back. Unfortunately, even the element of surprise was no match for the four hundred pounds blocking me in.

I could take them out if I wanted, even without a sword. I still had my dagger, and I happened to know sixty-five different ways to kill a man with it. But *that* wouldn't end in my favor.

I steadied my shaking hands. "Please, I'm begging you."

The commander's mouth straightened. "Guards do not beg." He looked to Drestel who seemed to understand the unspoken words. "Take this as a lesson, and be grateful because the next time you fall out of line, it will not be as painless."

I didn't know what was happening until Drestel moved closer, golden smoke seeping from her palms. I knew what she was doing. I shook my head, tripping over my feet as I moved away. As if I could avoid the inevitable.

My head turned as another guard entered the tent, halting in front of the commander. "Take Mr. Hibreaker to the horses. We'll give it another hour or so to see if anyone else lines up before we leave."

The guard nodded, a step behind the golden smoke as he moved for me. I wanted to scream but knew it would be useless. My Angel. I wasn't going to get to say goodbye.

The smoke reached me, wrapping around my body like a blanket of warmth and light. The last thing I saw was the satisfied smile on the commander's face before I passed out.

CHAPTER 8

The sound of hooves trotting on uneven ground echoed in my head for the last hour. I fidgeted in the uncomfortable seat of the wagon, the beam of wood digging painfully into my lower back. My legs were numb, but I didn't dare move. One of the guards sat across from me while the others rode ahead alongside the commander and Drestel.

I was the only person from Morters' End seeing as no one else had lined up outside of the tent. Not that I'd expected them to. A lump sat at the base of my throat as I thought of Angel. How I didn't get to say goodbye.

I distracted myself by staring at the sleeping guard before me. He was a wide framed man with scarred fingers that twitched every so often, making me wonder if he was having a nightmare. His head was tilted back, arms crossed over his chest as he snored. The white flaps attached to his headpiece moved with each exhale, occasionally smacking his mouth which caused him to gargle and choke before readjusting his position, not once bothering to open his eyes.

I rolled mine, averting my gaze to the greenery around us. Nothing about where we were was familiar. The dirt path was flanked by wild bushes and shrubs as well as a blanket of trees, moonlight flickering through the branches to illuminate the ground. I wished I could see them more clearly, but there wasn't enough light.

I tried fighting the oncoming wave of exhaustion. Whatever Drestel did to me hadn't worn off yet. By the time I'd woken up, we were already out of Morters' End, and it was dark. But even in my unconscious state, I felt the exact moment we passed through the shield. As if chains I didn't know I wore broke free, releasing me. A weight lifted off my shoulders. I was out.

One of the wagon wheels dipped into a hole, the movement and sound causing the guard to jolt upright, blinking himself awake. I watched as he got his bearings before settling down. I tried to swallow, but my mouth was unnaturally dry. I opened and closed it several times before asking, "Water?"

He glanced at me, then rummaged through the rucksack beside him. A moment later, he shoved a cannister into my grasp.

I twisted the lid and tipped my head back as fresh water poured down my throat. I couldn't get enough of it. I didn't know if it was because of the Purity leaving my system or the fact that this was the first water I'd ever had that wasn't from the disgusting brook, but I couldn't stop drinking it.

Eventually, I handed it back empty. "Thank you." He nodded, looking like he was about to sleep again so I quickly asked, "Where are we?"

"Almost there," he drawled, his voice low and raspy.

"Almost where?"

"Camp."

I sighed, knowing I wasn't going to get much more out of him. He closed his eyes but flicked one open to stare at me as he added, "You should sleep. We won't be there for another hour at least, and you'll need all the rest you can get."

I didn't want to sleep. I wanted to know exactly where we were. But the heaviness that soon set over my eyelids wasn't something I could fight for long. So inevitably, I gave in.

I heard voices as I opened my eyes. Many of them. And I felt something too. Something *hot* piercing my skin. It took me several moments to adjust to the light around me, a light so bright, I wondered if perhaps I died in my sleep.

I didn't get a chance to catch my bearings as I was ushered out of the wagon, landing on surprisingly steady feet. We were stopped at some sort of clearing surrounded by dense woods. Tents almost identical to the one in my village were pitched around the open expanse of land as men in different uniforms drifted about. Some were sprawled out on what I realized now was *grass*, while others were busy carrying logs of wood to and from various firepits.

Bekencourt and Drestel were nowhere to be seen. Angling my head to the guard beside me, I asked, "Where did the commander go?"

"Back to Caelestis," he replied, moving out of the way as a young boy in torn breeches unhooked the horses from the wagon, clicking his teeth as he directed them toward a makeshift stable. "The king required his presence. He continued on with Drestel as soon as we arrived here this morning."

"And where exactly is *here*?"

"Drapolin Forest," he said absentmindedly. I rummaged through my memory of all the places I'd read about. After a moment, I recollected enough to know we were just outside of Skantra, a small fishing village on the coast of the Aldric Sea. I knew that Caelestis, the capitol city, was about a two day journey from Morters' End so we probably had a few more rest stops along the way.

Before I could ask anything else, he took off down the hill to join the other guards around a long table. The sound of someone clearing their throat had me turning to find another guard with spectacles resting low on his nose, staring at me. He was sat at a smaller table, a stack of parchment before him. Ink from the end of his quill dripped onto the table as he asked, "Name?"

I squared my shoulders. "Wren Hibreaker."

He looked me up and down, disbelief flashing over his features as he took in my narrow frame. Shaking his head, he directed his attention back to the sheet. "Age?"

"Eighteen," I said.

"Origin?"

"Morters' End."

His quill froze before he scribbled it down. "Right, Hibreaker. Head for the tents and get yourself associated with the men you'll be training with for the next few weeks."

He didn't glance at me again, so I quickly thanked him and turned on my heels. I was about to walk down the hill when I stopped. I'd been so distracted since I got off the wagon that I hadn't even taken a moment to appreciate how everything was glowing vividly in a way things never did in Morters' End. Slowly, I tipped my head back, and my breath halted as the warmth of the sun kissed my face.

I closed my eyes as they began to sting. A sound escaped my lips, something between a laugh and a cry because right now, I didn't know what I was feeling. Tears fell freely down my cheeks as I soaked in the warmth I'd craved my entire life.

"Crying before training even starts? Guess they're really bringing the weak ones out to play."

A chorus of laughter followed the remark. Lowering my head, I opened my eyes to a group of young men. The one in front stood with his feet shoulder's width apart, arms crossed, and a snide expression I would be glad to rearrange with my fist.

He snorted. "Don't tell me you can't speak either. Gods, what hole did you crawl out of, Pipsqueak?" The four boys behind him laughed again as if on cue. Each one had a bow slung across their backs and quivers filled with arrows.

I stepped closer. "The kind of hole that taught me how to break every single bone in your spine in under thirty seconds." I smiled as he shifted back. "Shall we give it a try?"

They all fell silent, considering me cautiously. *Good*. After a moment, the one in front shook his head and pushed forward, heading for the line of trees, his companions trailing close behind.

That went well.

I knew we would all be fighting for our right to be here, but I really hoped that wasn't how all my encounters were going to go because if so, I was in trouble. I was already at a disadvantage with the secret I possessed. I'd need to do better at keeping my anger in check. I didn't need any enemies.

Gods, why couldn't Asher have found a way to make me unrecognizable to everyone? My throat hurt from straining to deepen it to an unnatural tone. Exhaling, I dropped down to tie the laces of my boot that came undone. As I stood back up, my attention landed on a dark-skinned boy crouched over a firepit. He was watching me intently. Not in the mood for another altercation, I turned around and headed to the far end of camp.

It didn't seem like anyone was keeping that close of an eye on us at the moment, so I'd enjoy my taste of freedom while it lasted. This was the first time in my life I was able to bask in the sun, and I wasn't going to let anyone else ruin it.

I'd concluded that grass looked softer than it felt. After finding an open area behind an empty tent, I plopped down onto my back and tried to enjoy the warmth. It didn't last long as I was unable to stop scratching the exposed parts of skin the grass rubbed against. I tried ignoring it as I raised a hand to the sky, parting my fingers slightly so the sunlight could flitter through the gaps onto my face.

I wondered how Angel would sketch it. If I closed my eyes, I could almost picture him here. Lips slightly parted, curly brown locks spilling over his forehead as he decided which yellow to use. He'd try several different shades, but none of them would be right. He'd grow frustrated and then stop. A moment later, he'd pick up the white and *yes*, that would be it. Mixing the yellows, whites, and oranges, he'd do it. He'd find a way to capture the unattainable beauty in the sky above.

While that caused me to smile, it also sent a pang of guilt through my chest. Did he think I left without saying goodbye on purpose? Did he see them take me out and put me into that wagon unconscious? Did he try and stop them?

Sighing, I leaned onto my forearms, surveying the vast expanse of forest before me. Wildflowers of all colors and shapes grew down the hill. I wondered where they led to. Perhaps somewhere wonderful. *One day,* I reminded myself. *Get through recruitment and the next few years, then you'll have your freedom.*

"Did someone give you orders to lounge around?"

I nearly jumped out of my skin at the husky voice. One of the guards was standing beside the tent, arms folded across his chest. He looked like he could snap me in two with his fingers alone.

I pulled myself to my feet instantly, brushing the grass from my breeches. "No, sir," I said, keeping my head angled down.

He moved closer, his boots crushing the ground beneath him. "Look at me."

I did as he asked, raising a hand to shield the sun from my eyes. He wasn't exactly young, but not old enough that wrinkles were gracing his face either.

"What task were you given?"

My brows scrunched. "I wasn't given a task."

He cursed under his breath, mumbling something about a man named Regs never doing anything right. "Firewood then," he said. I must have looked confused as he added harshly, "Take your scrawny little legs, collect an axe, and chop some wood. Everyone earns their meals here."

I nodded. "Of course, sir."

He stepped to the side, extending a hand for me to pass. Just as I was about to hurry away, he added, "What's with the hat, recruit?"

I stilled. I could hear my heart thumping in my ears as I grasped for the first excuse I could come up with. "An accident, sir. Healer stitched me up and said to keep it covered until it heals."

He made a *humph* sound, and I waited for him to make me remove it. It wasn't too late to escape into the woods. He might have been larger than me, but these scrawny legs of mine were fast.

"Make sure you get it looked at when we get to Caelestis," he said, surprising me.

I nodded, taking that as my official dismissal and moved as fast as I could to find an axe.

CHAPTER 9

By the time I'd collected enough firewood, the sun had set, and the familiarity of the dark sky cloaked me like the embrace of an old friend. I had a few cuts and scrapes from carrying the chipped pieces of wood which stung as I brushed my hands against my thighs.

Several fires had been erected, framed by long, thick logs to sit. All the recruits were scattered, sloshing back the liquid in their mugs, and eating whatever animal the hunters managed to catch. The guards sat around their own fires, paying no mind to the rowdy groups.

My eyes scanned for an empty seat. I didn't realize how starved I was until the smell of food found its way to me, teasing my grumbling stomach. I caught sight of the boy who'd been watching me earlier. He sat with four others, but he seemed distracted. His eyes darted back and forth around the camp as if he was searching for someone. Whoever it was, I hoped they wouldn't mind if I took the open seat beside him.

Silence washed over the group as I approached. I cleared my throat. "Is this spot taken?"

Tension released from his shoulders as he looked at me through amber eyes. "Nope, all yours," he said eagerly.

I nodded, taking a seat at the edge of the log. I felt his stare like a cold gust of wind but tried to ignore it. The three on the log beside me had fallen back into conversation, and the one across the fire was busy ripping into his food.

I grabbed a spare plate and began pulling apart chunks of meat that were left on the side of the pit. As I dug in, my stomach flipped in delight. After that, I couldn't stop myself. I was shoveling it in faster than I could chew.

A chuckle sounded beside me. "Usually when people say, 'eat like your life depends on it,' your life doesn't *literally* depend on it."

I turned to him and blinked. His cropped black hair glistened in the firelight. I was about to respond when a voice broke in. "Who says that? I've never heard anyone say that in my life."

My gaze shifted to the person seated across the fire. From his face, he couldn't be much older than me, but his body? I'd never seen muscles that big on someone my age. He was so ginormous, he took up two spots on the log. With slightly angled eyes and olive skin, I gathered he came from a different region.

The man next to me shrugged while taking a swig from his mug. "Someone's said it." He then stretched out his hand. "Name's Alicai."

I gave it a firm shake. "Wren."

"I'm Zavier," the other chimed in with a finger in the air.

Dropping my hand, Alicai snorted. "Did anyone ask?"

Zavier frowned. "Rude." His pin-straight dark hair fell over his forehead, concealing part of his left eye. "So, Wren," he continued as he bit into the mystery meat. "Where'd you come from? I'm from the Raptyrs."

I remembered reading about the Raptyrs before. They were a vast range of mountains composed of sharp peaks hidden in the clouds, and low valleys great for agriculture and farming.

"My folks were so proud when I passed the recruitment test," he went on. "How about yours? Did you—"

"If you don't stop blabbering on, I'm going to cut your tongue out," Alicai said, pinching the bridge of his nose. "Do you ever shut up?"

Zavier shot me an apologetic smile.

"I'm from—"

"He's from Telamar," Alicai said calmly. "Like me." He noted the bewildered look on my face, but his eyes told me not to question him. Strange. Why was he lying for me?

Zavier pointed between us. "You're both from Telamar? How are you just meeting now?"

Alicai rolled his eyes. "Because you big chunk of muscle, not every place in the kingdom is as close knit a community as where you come from. We don't all huddle around a campfire singing songs every night."

"First of all, we don't sing. Ever," Zavier replied. "Second, if you've never met, how do you know where he's from?"

At some point, the others began listening intently. "We've seen each other around before," I said, saving Alicai who couldn't even come up with an explanation for his ridiculous lie. "Haven't we?"

"Yes," he responded, leaning forward onto his knees. I cast

him a wary look. Whatever this was about, I intended to find out.

"So," I cleared my throat. The guttural, scratchy tone was the only *manly* voice I could do, and by some miracle, it was working as no one seemed suspicious. "What's the plan here? There must be at least fifty recruits, right? The prince doesn't need that many guards."

"They're going to weed us out," the red-headed man on the other log said. I watched as he dragged a stick through the dirt. "By the end of the training and tests we're going to be put through in Caelestis, they'll narrow it down to twenty-five of us."

"And what about the other twenty-five?" I asked.

The blonde man next to him shrugged. "Get sent home I imagine. Real disappointment to wherever they came from."

The third one elbowed him. "That's not true." Turning his gaze to me, I was greeted by gray eyes threaded with hints of green. "One of the guards said they'd probably send whoever wasn't chosen to the Haldro Mountains to train for the military."

Okay, so regardless of what happened in the capitol, I wouldn't be sent back to Morters' End. *Hopefully.* But still, I didn't want to join the military. The further I got from Angel, the harder it would be to get him and Mama out. Besides, I felt like I had a clear plan here aside from one question. "How long is the service?"

The redhead raised a brow. "Eager to be done already?"

I shook my head. "No, I just... no one's told me anything really."

He laughed. "Relax, don't crap your pants, I'm only messing with you." He continued dragging his stick around.

"Five years? Right?" He turned to the others for confirmation.

"I think it's seven," Zavier said. "But I guess we'll find out when we get there."

Five or seven years. I fought to keep my breath steady. That was a long time to keep a secret. I also needed to find out exactly what would happen if I got caught, not just assume the repercussions like Angel and Callin had.

The blonde man glanced over both shoulders before leaning closer, dropping his voice to a whisper. "Have you guys heard what's been said about Ryder's former guard? Apparently what really happened is that they were ambushed. No one knows why, but it seems the king isn't too bothered about looking into it further. Strange, right?"

Now *that* sparked my interest. Callin had said something about an attack. If this was true, it was definitely odd that the king wasn't pushing to find the men who almost killed his son. Even more strange how the truth was hidden from the people with a story of the former guard being released from duty.

"Oh, please," Alicai snorted. "Who knows what really happened?" He finished the contents in his mug and tossed it to the ground. I spotted an extra and quickly reached for it, filling it from the pitcher. I was glad to find it was water.

"I'm more intrigued about the prince," Zavier added.

"Why's that?" I asked.

"Don't tell me you haven't heard the stories about him." I hadn't but decided to keep that to myself. Stretching his massive arms behind his head, Zavier said, "I heard he set a tavern on fire then stole the owner's horse."

The red-headed man chuckled. "I once heard he ran

around the castle grounds stark naked at dawn. Gave all the servants such a fright, I think one of them ended up in the healers' sanctuary from a heart attack."

Alicai huffed out a breath. "I highly doubt they were frightened. Have you *seen* portraits of the prince? He's very easy on the eyes. That servant probably had a heart attack from a strong desire to jump his bones." Everyone hooted, and I found myself smiling as well.

"Besides, I've got a better one," Alicai added. "I heard he took the virginity of his older brother's betrothed. Lucio never forgave him, and that's why he fled to the Haldros' to take position as a general."

I was rendered speechless. While these rumors were all good fun, I hoped they weren't true. How were we meant to guard someone so reckless? I hoped he was a well behaved, quiet prince so I could complete my duty as easily as possible.

Then again, I was jumping ahead. I knew I was talented with a blade, but these men around me... they were bigger and definitely stronger. What if I wasn't as good as them? Papa would be angry at me for even doubting myself, but I couldn't help it.

Before anyone else could share tales and stories they'd heard, a heavy silence fell over the camp, the only sound being the crackling of the flames. The guards stood up, making their way toward the center. One of them cleared his throat, drawing everyone's attention. "Time to put the fires out. Two men per tent. Get some rest, we leave at sunrise."

Crap.

I'd have to share a tent. Dread washed over me as the fires were extinguished, and everyone headed for the rows of tents.

Zavier and the other three were gone by the time I turned around, leaving me alone with Alicai.

He smiled widely. "Guess it's you and me."

I forced a smile in return. "Guess so."

He spun on his heels and headed into the chaos. I had to jog to keep up with his fast pace. "I'll try not to be too offended by how much you clearly don't want to share a tent with me," he said.

"I never said that." I followed him through the flaps of a tent near the edge of the clearing. It wasn't much, just two cots, a small table with a pitcher of water, a bar of soap, and a half melted candle.

"You didn't need to." He dropped onto one of the cots, crossing his feet at the ankles. "I could hear it clear as day in your voice. But trust me, I'd be nervous too if I was pretending to be someone I wasn't."

I froze, but quickly relaxed, not wanting to make it seem like his words affected me. I pushed down on my cot, causing the wooden legs to groan. Alicai had cut me off before I could say I was from Morters' End earlier, could that be what he was talking about? But *he* was the one who lied first, telling them I was from Telamar.

Stop panicking, I told myself. *He doesn't know you're a girl.*

I decided my best course of action now would be getting him to admit he lied. I'd change the angle, make it so *he* was the one being questioned. "Do you actually remember seeing me?" I asked casually. "You know, back home?"

He angled his head. "I think so. You visit the Ashriven Tavern often, right?" I opened my mouth to say yes, then clamped it shut, realizing what he was doing a little too late.

He grinned. "Hesitation will always give you away, make sure to remember that."

I grinded my teeth. "There is no Ashriven Tavern, is there?"

He leaned back. "Oh, there is. Well, there *was*. It burned down two years ago."

Right. No more tiptoeing. "Why did you tell them I was from Telamar?"

"Because no one here would be too pleased to know where you really came from."

"And how would you know where I came from?" I narrowed my eyes. "I don't know you."

"Ah." He grinned again. "But I know all about you. Tell me, how's the water in Morters' End?" I stilled, and he chuckled, folding his hands behind his head. "How long do you plan on doing this little dance? Because I've got all night."

Nope. I wouldn't fall for this. Denial was my greatest friend in this situation. "I wouldn't know," I said calmly. "Never been there."

He rolled his amber eyes. "Callin said you were stubborn, but he didn't say you were delusional."

Callin? What did Callin have to—oh. I was an idiot. A complete idiot. Alicai was from Telamar, the same village as Callin. How did I not realize that? Somehow, hearing his name settled the nerves wrapped around my insides a bit.

I must have taken too long to answer because Alicai continued. "He told me a friend of his from Morters' End, a very *stupi*d girl named Wren, would be trying to sneak her way into the guard. He told me to find you. Said if I couldn't tell which one you were, that you had a ghastly scar between your eyebrows and puffy green eyes."

"My eyes aren't puffy," I seethed. I was furious. Why would Callin tell anyone? He hadn't even known if I was actually going to go through with it.

"They are a bit, especially right now when you look inclined to kill me."

I slowly lowered my hand, reaching for my dagger. I'd do anything to keep my secret, too much was riding on it. I couldn't fail. Especially not this early on. "Give me one good reason why I shouldn't." I dropped the false voice, easing back into my natural tone.

He trailed my movement. "Because you're going to need allies. *Friends* who can help you with this absurd plan if you don't want to get caught."

"Why would you help me? You don't owe me anything."

"True," he said. "But I owe Callin, and this was his request. To help his lunatic friend if she tried to do the dumbest thing possible." He rubbed his jaw. "Do you realize what you've gotten yourself into? If you get caught they'll throw you in the dungeons. And typically, they'd let you rot there, but now? Things are different. If these rumors about an assassination attempt are true and they find you *sneaking* around the guard, they'll assume the worst. They'll torture you and everyone you love to get answers, and when they don't get any, what do you think will happen? You think they'll just believe you? They'll kill you."

I swallowed. I figured I'd be imprisoned, and that was enough for me to be careful, but I didn't think about how the current tension in the guard would affect me as well. If Angel knew this, I doubted he'd have encouraged me. But it was too late. I was here and accounted for. I couldn't very well go running away. Alicai was right, I'd need someone in my corner I could trust. But could I trust *him*?

I studied him for a moment. He had several opportunities to tell the guards about me already, but he didn't. That had to count for something, right? "I have a question," I said.

"Shoot."

"How did you know it was me?"

"Not many people are stupid enough to stare directly at the sun," he said. "I tried to get your attention, but you had this murderous glare in your eyes after that group of hunters walked away. I decided I didn't want that dagger of yours embedded in my throat."

I smiled. "Wise choice."

He sat up, long legs sprawled out in front of him. "You're going to need me for this to work. Which means you better not mess up, because I don't feel like getting dragged down with you as an accomplice."

"You do know I'm not actually planning on hurting anyone, right? I just wanted to get out, and this was my only chance."

"Knowing that alone would be enough to have me thrown in a cell with you," he said. "Which is why we need to do everything we can to keep your secret a secret." He reached over the cot, pulling up a gray rucksack. Digging a hand in, he pulled out a pair of scissors. Making a *snip, snip,* motion, he grinned. "What do you say, care for a haircut?"

CHAPTER 10

Within a matter of seconds, I snatched my dagger from the table, flipped it in my grip, and directed it straight at Alicai. "Take another step with those scissors, and I'll drive this blade straight through your palm so hard it comes out the other side."

Alicai slowly raised his hands in surrender. "Well that's a bit excessive, don't you think?" He shoved the scissors into his pocket and ran a hand through his hair. "Callin failed to mention just how psychotic you are."

I kept my dagger raised. "What makes you think I even need a haircut?" Truthfully, it was only hair, and I knew I was making a fuss over something that would grow back, but it was a reminder of Papa. He loved my hair.

Alicai leaned against the pole in the center of the tent. "Because it looks like your head is swollen under that hat. So unless you just have a big head, I'm guessing you've tucked all your hair away. And besides, I'd hardly say we're strangers now."

Fighting the bubbling surge of annoyance, I slammed the dagger down. "I don't care who you are or what you know. You're not cutting my hair."

He rolled his eyes. "You sound like such a brat. Just take the damn hat off."

As annoying as he was, I found myself doing what he asked. Clinging to the soft material of Angel's hat, I pulled it off and dropped it on the cot. I watched Alicai as my hair cascaded down, ending at my mid back. "Happy?"

He stepped closer, twirling a lock around his finger. "You have *a lot* of hair."

I swatted him away. "And I intend to keep it that way."

"What's the big deal? It's just hair," he stated, leaning against the table. "You're going to have a ridiculous amount of trouble trying to wind it all up into the headpiece we have to wear." Slowly, he dragged the scissors from his pocket. "Let me cut some off. I'm trying to help you."

Help me? I wasn't used to people wanting to help me nor did I usually need it. No one ever did anything without something in return. He might owe Callin a debt, but how far would he go? "What's the catch?"

He blinked. "Catch?"

"What do you really want?"

He shook his head. "I don't want anything except for you to sit your stubborn ass down and let me help you. Why does there have to be some ulterior motive?"

I examined him momentarily. The curve of his nose, the slight stubble lining his jaw, the openness in his amber eyes that led me to believe he was telling the truth.

"Fine," I forced out. I extended a hand, halting him in his

tracks as he grew closer. "But you only cut off as much as I tell you. Alright?"

"Okay, okay." He sat on my cot, ushering me to sit in front of him. Grabbing a section of hair, he held the length between two fingers. "Is this good?"

I tilted my head, getting a glimpse of where he secured it about two inches past my shoulders. I swallowed but nodded. Facing forward, I closed my eyes. "Have you done this before?"

He gathered all my hair and tugged on the ends, keeping it tight. "Nope."

Before I could change my mind, I heard the snip of the scissors. Once the pressure released, I looked down where long strands of hair covered the ground. Immediately, I reached for my head, sucking in a sharp breath. This was *not* what we agreed on.

I spun around. "This is so much shorter than what you said!"

If he noticed the rage in my voice, he didn't seem fazed. Ignoring me, he bent down and collected the hair from the floor. He strolled out the tent, returning a moment later empty handed. Silently, he dropped the scissors back into the sack and began digging around for something else.

"I can't believe how much you just cut. Did you even—"

"Stop talking." He turned to me, this time with a small mirror in his grip. "I think it suits you better. Here." He handed me the mirror. "Take a look for yourself."

I held it up to my face, taking in my new appearance. My hair now fell in loose waves against my collarbones. The ends curved inward, framing my face, and somehow making my green eyes appear larger. I ran a finger over the scar between my brows before slamming the mirror into his chest. "Where did you even get this stuff from? I thought we weren't allowed to bring anything."

"Do you like it?" he asked, ignoring my question as he touched my hair.

I pushed his hand away. "Do you want me to stab you?"

He opened his mouth, then wisely shut it as he put the mirror down. "Of course we were allowed to bring stuff from home," he replied after a moment. "As long as it was packed and ready to go before the recruitment test. These are just a few things I couldn't leave behind. Sentimental value and what not."

"Sentimental over a mirror and scissors?"

Alicai laid back on his cot. "My father's a tailor back in Telamar. The scissors were his, and the mirror was my mother's. She died when I was six." He studied the space around me. "Where's your stuff?"

I nodded to the dagger. "You're looking at it."

"That's all you brought?"

I brushed a finger through my hair. "It's all I need." We sat in silence for a moment before I added, "Thank you. For your help."

He didn't answer, and I thought he'd fallen asleep until he asked, "What are they like? The necromancers?"

It took me some time to pull out the correct string of words. "Wicked," I said firmly. "They're corrupt, power hungry animals who consider themselves gods." Papa's bloody, broken face flashed in my memory. I fisted the blanket. "I hope they all burn in Hell." Fortunately, Alicai didn't push the discussion further. "How did you know I wasn't..."

"Evil?"

I nodded. I knew the rest of the kingdom looked down on us like we were no better than the necromancers themselves. Who knew what other rumors and lies had spread throughout the years.

"That's all Callin," he said. "He'd tell me all about you and your people after he'd return home from his weekly deliveries. How not all of you had the evil touch. I didn't believe him at first. Hell, I still didn't fully believe him until I saw you earlier. I can't explain it, but when I watched you tip your head back at the sky smiling, I knew he'd told the truth."

I glanced at my dagger on the table. As if reading my thoughts, he added, "You might not be *evil*, but I still think you're a lunatic."

"And don't you forget it."

He let out a short laugh. "Night, Wren."

I laid down and pulled the blanket up to my shoulders, stashing my dagger under my pillow just in case. Itchy as the cot might have been, it was an upgrade from my bed back home. I closed my eyes, releasing a deep breath. "Goodnight."

"Wren?"

"Yes?"

"Please don't stab me in my sleep."

The following morning, our camp was swiftly packed, and we headed out on our journey. Alicai left the tent when we woke up so I could change into the uniform I failed to notice beneath the cot the night before. Ours were considered 'trainee uniforms' which contained a set of navy blue pants and tunic with black trimmings around the wrists and ankles.

They didn't seem to fit anyone right, and I wondered how many people had worn them before us.

Alicai offered to store my clothes in his rucksack which I gladly agreed to. We weren't given headpieces yet, so Angel's hat would have to do for now. As we joined the others, I noticed I wasn't the only one wearing a hat today, so hopefully that kept me from being singled out and questioned.

We ate a rushed breakfast of leftover meat before being ordered to take down our tents. Several wagons had arrived, each large enough to hold fifteen people. We were shoved inside, squished beside each other on the two long wooden benches that took up the interior. The roof was covered with a white tarp, and a wooden door locked us in, preventing any glimpse of the scenery we passed.

Less than a minute after the doors were bolted, we were moving. I sat between Alicai and Zavier, and aside from them, I recognized no one. The incessant chatter and laughter that erupted when we first departed lasted about an hour. Two hours in, we stopped and were allowed out to relieve ourselves.

Alicai guarded the small, secluded area I found so I could drop my pants away from the wandering eyes of the other men. Shortly after, we were off again.

The concept of time evaded me as we sat side by side in the stuffy wagon. Sometimes we'd hit a bump or go over a rock, and whoever sat on the edge would go flying into the door. I wasn't sure how long we traveled, but by the time the horses stopped and we were allowed out, it was nightfall.

"We'll camp here tonight," a guard named Kurtis announced. We'd made it all the way to the outskirts of Driscal, which meant only another five hours to Caelestis. We instantly got to work re-pitching our tents in the clearing.

Several recruits chopped and gathered wood for the fires, while another group took off into the woods, crossbows strapped to their backs, on the hunt for our dinner. About forty minutes later, we dispersed around the fires, eating rabbit and wild boar.

I watched Zavier frown at his plate. I'd already inhaled my first serving and was on my second, yet he still hadn't touched his food. "Don't like rabbit?" I asked.

He glanced at me, and my gods, he really was a giant. The muscles in his arms alone were larger than my head. I wondered where they found a uniform big enough for him. "I can't eat this," he mumbled.

"And why not?" Alicai asked. It was just the three of us around the pit tonight. The others from the night before were scattered amongst other groups, but I wasn't complaining. The fewer people I had to speak to, the easier it was to maintain this illusion.

"I had a pet rabbit once." Zavier lifted a piece off his plate, dangling it with disgust. "So I can't eat this."

Alicai blinked. "You... had a pet rabbit?"

Zavier nodded. "His name was Twitch. White as snow with two black circles around his eyes. Every time I'd hold him, he'd make this jumping motion. Hence the name."

"*Twitch*," Alicai repeated, dragging out the word. I looked down, stifling a laugh. There was something oddly amusing about the thought of Zavier holding a small rabbit named Twitch in his massive hands.

Alicai snatched the plate from him a moment later. "Give me that," he said, taking a bite. "Rabbits were meant to be eaten, not cuddled up and given strange names."

I had to agree. Coming from a place where the next meal

wasn't guaranteed, it didn't matter how cute or fluffy an animal was. Food was food.

Zavier moved as if he were about to vomit. "Why not eat the boar instead?" I offered. "I'm sure the other groups have some left."

He shook his head vigorously. "I think I lost my appetite."

Alicai shrugged. "More for me."

Not long after, we were putting out the fires. We would be leaving for Caelestis at first light. "They're really eager to get us there, aren't they?" Alicai said, stomping his boot over the remaining embers.

Zavier yawned as he stood, stretching his arms out to the side. "Do you blame them? They probably just want to get all of this done as quick as possible. After that failed assassination attempt on the prince, it makes sense."

"So you do believe his former guards died in an ambush," I stated. "You don't think they were released from duty?"

Zavier shot me a knowing smile. "Royal guards aren't just released before the end of their service without cause such as insubordination or failure to meet their duties. Stuff like that. And even then, it *rarely* ever happens. So, do I think an entire division of guards were dishonorably discharged? No. Not a chance. There was foul play involved."

I chewed my inner cheek as my mind raced through everything I'd read and learned about this kingdom. If there were people who had motive to murder the prince, I didn't know of them.

"Do you think I can stay in your tent tonight?" Zavier begged. "Samuel snores louder than a potato being yanked from the dirt."

I looked at Alicai who only shrugged, shaking his head.

"Don't look at me. I have no clue what the hell he's on about. But anyway," He clasped Zavier's shoulder. Alicai actually had to *reach up,* Zavier was so tall. "The answer's no, buddy. You know the rules, two to a tent..." His voice drifted as he strolled away, whistling to himself.

I smiled apologetically at Zavier, said goodnight, and followed after Alicai. Once in our tent, I waited until the remaining voices quieted before asking, "Do you have soap?"

He tilted his head as he sprawled out on his cot. "Come again?"

"Yesterday I saw a bar of soap on the table. Did you bring it?"

"Why?"

I tossed my hat onto the small table, running my fingers through my hair. "Because I'd like to go clean myself. Do you want any more details?"

He reached over and yanked his rucksack from the floor. After digging for a moment, he tossed the white bar of soap at me. "And where exactly are you going to do that?"

"I found a place." After I'd finished pitching the tent while the others were still chopping wood and securing our dinner, I snuck off for a bit. Not long enough to draw attention, but enough that I ended up stumbling across a small lake behind some bushes and shrubs. It was isolated, so I wouldn't have to worry about being seen. And besides, I waited until now, when everyone had gone to bed.

He watched me for a moment, then bent over to untie the laces of his boots. "Enjoy."

"I'll be back soon." I hastily grabbed the blanket from my cot and headed through the flaps.

CHAPTER 11

The lake water was a bit on the chilly side, but I didn't mind as I dunked my head under. I rubbed the soap between my hands, placed it on one of the rocks lining the water's edge, and ran soapy fingers from my scalp all the way down.

The moonlight glistened over the clear water, allowing me to see the small fish and sand colored rocks along the bottom. After my hair was rinsed out, I cleaned my body. Twice. Back in Morters' End, we didn't bathe often. It was a long, drawn-out process to fetch the contaminated brook water, boil it clean, and then fill up a soaking tub. Safe to say I didn't miss *that.*

I was in the process of scrubbing my back when a noise between a gasp and a shriek escaped my parted lips. My heart was pounding in my chest as my gaze shifted to the hanging rock at the far end of the lake. On that rock, one knee bent and a smirk plastered on his face, was Asher.

"I must say, the short hair suits you."

I lowered myself so the water rested against my collarbones. How had I forgotten about him? I'd been so consumed with my own thoughts and the chaos of everything around me that I hadn't stopped to wonder if he'd been able to follow me through the shield. Seeing him perched on the rock, the image of unearthly beauty, it was clear he had.

He leaned back, the corners of his lips twitching as if he could hear my heart racing from across the lake. Wrapping a hand around his knee, he asked, "Mind if I join you?"

"I'd rather you didn't."

He flashed from the rock to the water's edge, less than five feet from where I was submerged. Crouching down, he tossed a stone. I watched as it bounced five times before sinking to the bottom.

"Why?" he asked. I felt the water heating around me as he trailed a finger over the surface. "Do you not trust yourself around me?"

I waded backward toward the center of the lake, trying to put as much distance between us as possible. But there would never be enough. He was a part of me as much as my own soul. "How did you get here?"

"You know how it works, Wren. I thought of you, and—"

"No, not *here*, as in the lake. But out of Morters' End."

His brow lifted. He was so achingly beautiful, the tempter of my darkest desires. Every curve, sweep, and cut of his features appeared as if the gods themselves chiseled him to creation. Although after everything, he hardly deserved my admiration.

And yet, when he was near, I was drawn to him like the moon is drawn to the sun. Rising each night in hopes of catching her, only to be disappointed by their eternal opposing orbits.

"Did you really think I wouldn't be free to leave as you were?" When I said nothing, he laughed. "Oh, Wren, it's going to take more than some magical shield to keep us apart. You and I are bound by blood. Where you go, I will go. Did you forget?"

I didn't forget, but I was hoping. Hoping that when Drestel's Purity released the shackles that bound me to that vile place, it had released *only* me. Sadly, I was mistaken. "Seeing as you're free, why don't you go somewhere else then? Find another person to make a deal with."

He appeared bored. "That's not how this little arrangement works. I cannot engage in another covenant when ours is yet to be completed. And I'm too intrigued to see who it is that takes your heart to leave now."

His smile was anything but warm. These last few days were the most we'd spoken of our covenant in years. And after all this time, I still didn't know for certain what it truly entailed.

"You've given me no time frame," I stated. "But I am curious, in the slim chance that I *did* fall in love, how would you even know? How long would I have before I had to take their life? And how would I have to do it?" I'd never asked these questions before because I'd really believed I was enough for him. That our simple life was enough. I only had myself to blame.

"Careful, Wren," he drawled. "Or I might start to think you were worried. Any of the guards caught your eye? Hm?"

I dug my nails into my palms. "I'm glad this is amusing to one of us."

He chuckled. "All jokes aside, there is a matter I wanted to speak with you about. I know you can take care of yourself," he stated. "But... be careful."

Was that concern in his voice? "Be careful of what?"

He ran a hand through inky hair that curled along the ends. "These attacks on the prince aren't over. You know I've always been able to sense these things."

He had. Whenever something bad was about to happen, he'd often known it in advance. The way he described it to me was like an old injury aching just before a storm hits.

"So it's true then," I said. "He was attacked."

Asher nodded. "Before you start asking, I don't know the details or who was responsible. All I know is his entire unit of guards was slaughtered, save for his captain who managed to get them both to safety."

A million questions raced through my mind, but I knew Asher didn't have any further information for me to pry from him. If he knew anything else, he'd tell me. He'd never withhold things that could potentially keep me safe. Afterall, I was his one ticket to resurrection. If something happened to me, he'd... well, I didn't know what would happen to him if I died. But I knew he wasn't willing to take the chance, so as much as I currently despised him, I trusted him to warn me of any risks he was aware of.

I gazed at my reflection in the still water. What exactly was I getting myself into? "So no leads, no known cause, and no one's doing anything about it."

"As of now, that's how it seems. But, Wren."

His strained voice had me looking up to see his eyes glazed over as if he was suddenly carrying the weight of the world. "Yes?"

The look quickly vanished. "You need to be alert. If there's another attack and you're there, I can't—"

"I know," I said. "You can't help me." Through our bond, I was the only one Asher could make physical contact with. Even if he wanted to protect me, he couldn't do much. Not that I needed his help anyway. I was perfectly capable of looking out for myself.

I held my breath as I dipped down, letting the cool water wash over me entirely. When I resurfaced, Asher was gone. I made my way out of the lake and wrapped the blanket around my shivering body.

Once dried, I donned my uniform and sent up a silent prayer to the gods I no longer believed in.

~

We arrived in Caelestis at ten the following morning. Everyone in the wagon fell into nervous silence as the sounds of hooves clicking along the cobblestones came to a stop. Muffled voices from outside filled the quiet, but before I could decipher what I was hearing, the wooden door unbolted and swung open. I squinted as my eyes adjusted to the morning light.

In single file, we hopped off the ledge onto the crunching gravel of the courtyard. I angled my head upward, embracing the warmth as I exhaled a deep breath. A strong hand gripped my arm, yanking me forward. "Would you stop doing that?" Alicai hissed.

"Stop doing what?" I asked, pulling my arm free.

"Smiling up at the sun like a drunk eyeing his next drink."

"First of all, I wasn't smiling. Secondly, if you ever pull me like that again, I'll tear your arm from its socket. Okay?"

Alicai scoffed, mumbling something incoherent under his breath. I watched Zavier hop out of the wagon, the entire contraption shifting under his weight. "No one should have that much muscle on their body," Alicai said, crossing his arms.

I smiled. "You're just jealous because you have the body shape of a string bean." That comment earned me a wave of curses.

Zavier was scanning the growing crowd, and once his eyes landed on us, he smiled and headed over. The courtyard was swarmed with armed guards of varying ranks, servants, gardeners, and recruits as they continued unloading the wagons.

"Have you guys ever seen anything so massive?" Zavier asked.

Alicai snorted. "Do you *own* a mirror?"

The two of them began bickering, but the sounds were washed out as I turned to see what had Zavier so amazed.

The castle rose up behind me like a tower of shimmering silver, the highest peaks covered in a blanket of clouds. Every square inch was composed of ashy-gray stone, and four identical towers lined the corners, connected by open walkways where guards were stationed, bows nocked and at the ready for any threat below. It was the most magnificent structure I'd ever seen. Not that I had much to compare it with.

Heavy footsteps to my right had me whirling around where a guard made his way up the steps. His uniform was similar to the others, the only difference being the golden patch embroidered over the right breast. He carried himself in such an undisturbed manner, I got the feeling he wasn't one to care about the opinions of anyone. He was strongly built, his uniform clinging snugly to his arms as he clapped his hands, ordering attention and silence. His tanned skin accentuated the golden specks of his eyes, and a slight stubble lined his jaw. He was incredibly handsome, even with the headpiece shielding the sides of his face.

His eyes scanned the crowd, assessing the quality of men brought in for such an important position. After several moments of silence, he finally spoke. "I'm Captain Blanning, head of Prince Ryder's guard." His voice was deep and raspy, like stone rubbing against stone.

A symphony of hushed whispers fell over the group. By now, mostly everyone had heard the stories of what happened to the former guard.

"Well, isn't he a sight for sore eyes," Alicai whispered, nudging my arm.

I nudged him back. "Would you shut up?"

Captain Blanning clasped his hands behind him, lips pulled taut. "I am well aware of the rumors regarding the fate of the previous guards, so I will say this once and only once. My men were ambushed, attacked, and slaughtered a little over a fortnight ago. You will all handle this information with the utmost discretion, seeing as you are now—in one way or another—in service to the crown. No further information is being released at this time, so it would be in your best interest not to ask." A new type of silence washed over us.

"Those men laid down their lives in protection of the prince, as will you if you are deemed fit for the role." He paused, considering his next words. "I want you all to take a look around. At the men beside you, across from you, behind you." I scanned the crowd, locking eyes with several other recruits.

"You are all here because throughout the entire kingdom, you have been considered the best of the best," he continued. "This is not a weight to carry lightly. These next two weeks of training and tests will be daunting and push you both physically and mentally past any point you can imagine. Some of you will break. But the rest of you... the *best* of you, will rise. Twenty-five of you in two weeks' time will be sworn into the personal guard of Prince Ryder where you will remain for the next seven years, gods willing. After your service has ended, you will have the option for discharge or reinstatement into different areas of the guard upon a physical assessment. Those of you still able bodied will also have the chance to re-enlist for service with the prince. If any of you are having second thoughts, speak up now."

The captain waited a moment, eyeing us down, but no one said a word. "This might seem hasty," he added. "But we don't have the luxury of time. The prince needs a formal guard sworn in now more than ever. Men sworn to protect and lay down their lives for him, and him alone, should the need surface."

Seven years. I'd have to maintain this illusion for seven years if I succeeded. *It will be worth it,* I told myself. I had a feeling I'd need the constant reminder.

The sound of sniffling had me sneaking a peek at Zavier. Was he *crying?* Shaking my head, I turned back to the captain. "You will be split into two groups," he said. "The first round of training will commence in exactly two hours' time. You will be assessed on your skill, strength, integrity, and thought process. There will be a ranking board displayed after every session so you can see where you stand. Those with the most points will have their names at the top, while those failing to meet the criteria will find their names toward the bottom. After the two weeks are up, the twenty-five at the top of the ranking will move forward."

He snapped his fingers, gaining the attention of two castle guards who moved toward a stone archway. "You will also find that you will be earning a wage for your training period," he added. "The first half will await you in your rooms upfront, while the rest will be given out at the end of the two weeks, regardless if you pass or fail. Afterwards, if you remain, you will be put on a salary. In the meantime, you will be shown to your living quarters where it will be three to a room. There is a common room where you may converse and socialize when you are *off duty*." I don't think anyone missed the emphasis on those words.

Without so much as a nod of dismissal, Captain Blanning retreated through the door behind him.

The castle guards then began shuffling us down the narrow pathway under the stone arch that led to the back of the castle. I stumbled as a heavy arm draped over my shoulder. Zavier tossed his other one over Alicai, huddling the three of us close together. "Guess we're going to be roommates," he said cheerily.

I only had a second to catch Alicai's eye before we were waved through the arch, the weight of my secret crushing down on me like a stack of bricks.

CHAPTER 12

"That is the ugliest thing I've ever seen," Alicai remarked. I couldn't help but agree as my eyes raked over the sloppy brush strokes of the massive painting on the wall in our sleeping chamber.

It was a painting depicting a half-naked woman gazing at her reflection in the clear waters of a lake. However, the reflection staring back at her was distorted. The face cracked, eyes drooping, the skin a gray pallor. It was disturbing. If Angel were here, he would have commented on the lack of texture, vibrancy, or some other fancy term artists used.

Pushing the thought of Angel to the back of my mind, I examined my new room. Three beds took up three walls, and two hefty armoires stood flanking the door that led to the common room. The gray paint was chipping off the walls, and the ceiling had a slight yellow tint from water damage. Along the wall to my left was another door that led into a small bathing room.

Zavier quickly jumped on one of the beds, causing me to

claim the one opposite. That left Alicai the middle bed directly underneath the hideous painting.

He sighed as he slung his rucksack onto the mattress. "Guess I'll be having nightmares for the foreseeable future."

I cleared my throat, earning his attention. *What do we do?* I mouthed silently.

Before Alicai could respond, Zavier got up and headed into the bathing room to freshen up before training. Once the door closed, Alicai began pacing. "This isn't good. This is really not good."

I swallowed down the panic. "We can't tell him," I said firmly. "No one else can know."

"Don't you think I'm aware of that?" Alicai hissed. "But what the hell are we supposed to do? Do you really think you won't slip up in the next two weeks? And how are you going to get dressed? Are you just going to wear your hat to sleep? He's going to know something's up." He ran his hands down his face and groaned. "I shouldn't have agreed to this. Damn you, Callin."

My eyes stayed locked on the door, waiting for the knob to turn. "I can change in the bathing room," I said. "And the hat... I told one of the guards I had stitches and was meant to keep my head covered. I can say that."

Alicai looked at me like I had ten heads. "Stitches come out, Wren. How long do you think that excuse will last?"

I crossed my arms over my chest. "We don't have many options right now. It's not like we can just kill him."

Alicai paused, raising a brow. "Now *that* is an idea."

I rolled my eyes. "They already have him accounted for. They'll know if he goes missing. And what are we going to do with the body? Drag him through the hallway with forty-seven recruits watching?"

"You're right," Alicai said on an exhale.

"And would you stop that damn pacing!" I yelled quietly. I sighed as I dropped my head into my lap, tapping my foot against the floor as I continued to think.

Realistically, I could try and get away with it. But in the confines of our room, what if I got complacent? I'd need to be on my guard all hours of the day and truthfully, a slip up would be inevitable. And what would be worse? Getting caught now or later? It *would* pay to have both Alicai and Zavier in my corner...

Although I didn't know Zavier well, he seemed like a nice guy. Then again, that could all be for show. Would he be more likely to tell on me if I hid the truth from him and he found out by accident? He gave off the impression he was a strict rule follower, someone who took immense honor in this position. Would he see my deception as a sign of disrespect?

"Time's up," Alicai whispered as Zavier strolled out.

Zavier paused, both hands mid-adjusting his breeches when he saw us looking at him. "Oh, crap, did I piss on myself again?" He bent at the waist, checking the material.

Alicai blinked. "*Again?*"

Zavier straightened up, an embarrassed smile on his face. "It happens sometimes. Don't tell anyone, alright? It'll be our little secret."

Alicai leaned against the wall, crossing his legs at the ankles as he narrowed his eyes. "Are you good at that? Keeping secrets?"

I shot him a warning glare, but he wasn't looking at me.

"Of course I am," Zavier said, a tad on the defensive side. "Why?"

Alicai shrugged. "Just wondering. Never know when the information might prove useful." He turned, catching my eye before he walked into the bathing room.

This was going to be a long two weeks.

~

The three of us had been split amongst the two training groups. Alicai was with the first, while Zavier and I were with the second. When Alicai returned to our room three hours later, sweating and breathless, Zavier and I barely had a moment to prepare ourselves before we hurried out the door.

Thankfully, Zavier didn't question me when I changed in the bathing room, and I was even more thankful to know we were required to wear the headpieces stored in the armoires. Captain Blanning was clear that from here on out, when training and on duty, it was essential we wore them so we'd get used to the weight.

"This thing is making my head itch," Zavier groaned as we proceeded down the hallway toward the sparring room. The guards' corridors and training rooms were kept in an extension off the back of the castle, connected through an open walkway. Gray slabs of stone lined the walls, the only light seeming to flow from torches in the iron sconces attached to the stone every few feet, casting a dim glow over the section below it.

I tugged at the white cloth that shielded the sides of my face. "Mine feels perfectly comfortable." Truthfully, it was a bit itchy, but I was in no position to complain. The iron cap came to a rugged point between my eyebrows, concealing my scar.

We crossed the threshold into the room, a spacious area with high walls and an arched ceiling made of glass. Sunlight penetrated through, illuminating the wooden floors and weapons secured against the walls. I recognized broad and short swords, rapiers, iron staffs, axes, crossbows, and daggers. The few others I wasn't familiar with, I was eager to get my hands on and learn how to use.

Captain Blanning strode to the front of the room a moment later where he stood on a raised platform in front of the wall of weapons. Two guards flanked him, their expressions void of emotion.

The irrefutable aura of confidence he exerted was enough to make me still. His eyes scanned us, his mouth drawn in a tight line. "Today's lesson will be simple," he said, voice toneless as he cut right to the chase. "You will partner up and be given a broad sword each. We will work on disarming, form, and technique."

Blanning pulled a sword from its holder on the wall. Flipping it in his grip, he tossed it to the nearest recruit who fumbled and dropped it, his face turning bright red. Someone snickered, and as I turned my head, I realized it was the recruit I'd threatened back in Drapolin Forest. He must have felt me looking as he met my gaze, a sinister grin forming. I quickly looked away.

Don't make enemies. Don't make enemies. Don't make enemies.

Blanning clenched his jaw and picked up the sword. He moved through the room like water running downstream, weaving in and out of where we stood. Not a single person moved a muscle. I kept my gaze straight ahead, even as he stopped in front of me. Even as his golden eyes hardened on mine, and he shoved the sword into my grasp.

Everyone was staring at me, and I did my best to seem unfazed, but a voice in the back of my mind kept screaming that they knew I was lying. That they knew I was a girl. As I adjusted my grip on the sword, I realized they were only looking because the captain hovered over me. It was a natural thing to stare. It had nothing to do with me.

I released a steady breath and rolled my shoulders back. "Perfect form," Blanning said as he circled me. "Firm grip, but not too firm that you'll struggle with movement. Ideal starting stance..." He nodded as he finished his lap around me before moving back to the platform. "Everyone else! Grab a training sword and partner up!"

I waited while they hurried over to the large chest beneath the weaponry wall, the sound of scraping metal echoing through the space as swords were dug out. Zavier came back a moment later, tossing his and catching it effortlessly in his right hand.

"Really? You're pairing up with that pipsqueak?" the recruit who'd snickered earlier said as he walked by.

"My offer still stands, you know," I said with a smile. "To break all the bones in your spine if you'd like to be my partner instead." *Really, Wren? That's how you avoid making enemies?*

He eyed me up and down once before scoffing. When he walked away, I turned back to Zavier who was giving me a questionable look. "What?" I asked.

He shook his head. "Nothing."

Blanning gave a few more instructions and then we began. I raised my sword steadily as Zavier and I circled each other. I loved this dance, the energy that thrummed through me from anticipation. Zavier lunged first, driving his sword straight. I blocked it with my own effortlessly. "Come on," I teased. "You can do better than that."

Zavier grinned. "We're just getting started."

We circled each other some more, and I noticed the way he kept rolling his right shoulder. It was an unconscious movement, but I noted it. I cut to the left as quickly as I could, uppercutting his sword with my own. His grip slipped, and the sword wobbled. Before he could adjust, I spun around him, raising my sword and bringing it down swiftly across the center of his. I grinned as the hilt slipped from his hand and clinked against the floor.

Blanning was making his rounds through the room, adjusting forms and correcting technique. He passed Zavier and I just as I disarmed him, earning me a hint of a smile and a nod of approval. Pride swelled in my chest. There was a fine line between drawing too much attention and ranking high for this session. I'd need to excel if I wanted to earn my spot.

"Good move," Zavier said as he picked up his sword.

"You'll need to do better at hiding that." I nodded to his right shoulder. "It's your weaker side, isn't it? But also your dominant side. Your shoulder roll is your tell." Normally, I wouldn't want to help my opponent, but I'd prefer to be in his good books.

"That obvious, huh?" Zavier asked as we started up once more. "It's an old injury but keeps flaring up."

He lunged a second later, but I was faster. I hooked my right foot around his ankle, pulling him off balance. He stumbled a few feet and as he turned, I was already on him, driving my sword against his with force. He managed to adjust his grip, using his left hand for support so my blow didn't land the impact I was hoping for. I pulled back, getting ready to strike again, when he ducked, coming up on my other side. He drove the blunt end of the blade into my forearm which caused my arm to vibrate in pain. My hand spazzed, and the sword fell to the ground. One of the guards marked it on his clipboard.

I picked up the sword, rubbing my muscle. "Sorry about that," Zavier said. "You alright?"

"I'll be fine," I replied. "That was a nice move, I'll give you that."

A cheesy grin spread over his face. "Can't let you get all the praise, now can I?"

I was surprised to find myself laughing. "Let's not get too cocky yet." Before he could respond, I ran forward with my sword raised. Zavier lifted his in a defensive maneuver, expecting me to come straight down. But Papa taught me the art of deceiving one's opponent. I smiled as I spun the sword around my head while pivoting to the right, bringing it down behind Zavier's left knee.

His leg gave out and he dropped to the ground, disarmed. Fortunately, these were only practice swords so he wasn't *really* hurt. We'd both have bruises tomorrow, but nothing worse than that.

Blanning stopped before us, hands clasped behind him. "Excellent," he said. "Again."

CHAPTER 13

I collapsed onto my bed in a fit of heavy breaths and sore muscles. The training went...well. It was demanding and draining, but it went well.

By the time we completed the three hour session, it was safe to say we were thoroughly exhausted. I could still hear the sounds of metal on metal, panting, and the occasional curse like the melody of my favorite song.

This was where I felt the most alive. With my hand gripping the hilt of a blade, faced with a challenge. This was where I excelled, where all my pent up anger and rage and regrets could seep through my pores, directly into the blade as I swung, dodged, and thrust.

After washing up and changing into fresh uniforms stocked in the armoires, the three of us walked to the dining hall for dinner. Until the initiation ceremony, we weren't permitted to enter the main section of the castle.

"At least it'll only be two weeks," I said as we turned a corner.

Alicai cursed under his breath. "I feel like a prisoner. This is how they treat the men they expect to guard the prince with their lives?"

"It makes sense," Zavier added. "Why would they allow fifty strangers to wander the halls after everything that happened?"

I had to agree. And as someone who knew what it truly meant to be a prisoner, this really wasn't so bad.

A few recruits stood outside the dining hall, examining a wooden board attached to the wall. Two of them shook their heads as they walked into the room, and as we approached, I realized it was our rankings for the day. All fifty names were written in ink and beside them, were a series of stars. Five being the max, seeing as no one passed that number.

"Bullshit," Alicai mumbled. I followed his gaze to find his name at the twentieth spot with two stars beside it.

"At least you're in the top half," I replied, although it didn't do much to correct the bitter look on his face. I continued skimming the board, grinning when I found my name.

Zavier whistled. "Number eight. Nice, Wren."

Top ten. Not too far at the top to put the focus on me, but high enough that I was noticeably *good.* I had four stars beside my name. Whatever that meant, I'd take it. Zavier's name was ranked eleventh with four stars as well.

"Who's Davin Hardcastle?" Zavier asked, tracing his finger over the name at the number one spot with five stars.

Alicai grunted. "Some jerk-off in my group. His father's a soldier so he grew up near the training fields in the Haldro Mountains. Unfair advantage if you ask me."

We entered the dining hall a moment later which

consisted of three long oak tables extending the length of the room, each side containing equally long bench seats. Many of the spots were already filled, the sounds of laughter and conversation flowing through the air. The four wrought iron chandeliers hanging from the ceiling held hundreds of flickering candles, setting the room in a warm glow.

We decided to claim the seats at the end of the third table, and as soon as I sat, I began shoveling roast chicken, mashed potatoes, and spinach onto my plate.

We sat in silence as we stuffed the food down our throats. It might have been plain, cold, and dry, but compared to what I was used to, it was delectable. Once satiated, I pushed the plate away. "What do you think they'll have us do tomorrow?"

Alicai downed the contents of his glass, a watered down beer I thought tasted like liquid garbage, then wiped his sleeve along his mouth. "Hopefully something other than swordplay."

I raised a brow. "Why? You do realize swords are the most used weapons in the guard, right?"

"You're wrong," he replied, tapping a finger against his head. "The main weapon is your mind. To be able to anticipate threats and strategize the best courses of action to take when faced with them."

Zavier slapped a hand on the table, a short chuckle escaping his lips. "Do you mean to tell me you can't wield a sword?"

"I *can* wield a sword," Alicai snapped.

"Would explain why you ranked twentieth today." Alicai growled as Zavier patted his back. "Ah, don't beat yourself up over it. Wren kicked my ass today."

That caused Alicai to smirk, amber eyes finding mine. "*That* doesn't surprise me."

The doors pushed open as Captain Blanning filed into the dining hall. My body went rigid as I viewed the man behind him. I hadn't seen Commander Bekencourt since the day I left Morters' End. There was something about him, something that set me on edge, like an unwanted hand raking up my spine.

They headed to the front of the room where Blanning waited slightly behind the commander. Dimitri Bekencourt appeared the very image of authority as he looked down at us, obsidian eyes drifting over every face while he cleared his throat.

"Captain Blanning has informed me that your first session went promisingly well," he stated. "Just know it will only become more intense and challenging from here on out, so it would do you well to stay humble. However, I am not here to speak of your training session today."

I watched his finger run over his inner wrist. A small, insignificant gesture to most, but I knew better. It was the type of movement one did unconsciously, usually over an old wound. I knew it well, as I constantly did the same over my scar.

A heartbeat later, he dropped his hands to his sides. "Prince Lucio is returning tomorrow from the Haldro Mountains, and a ball is being held to celebrate his return to court." He glanced at Blanning, something passing between their gazes I couldn't decipher before he turned to face us once more. "After some discussion with the captain and king, we decided tomorrow's training would be a bit... different. You will be split into four teams, and the task will be revealed to you upon arrival. It will be a matter of working together and coming up with a valuable plan on the spot because as guards, we do not always have the luxury of planning. Whichever team wins the task tomorrow will be rewarded with the opportunity of attending the ball."

Murmurs and whispers spread throughout the room until Bekencourt cleared his throat, demanding silence. "You will not be obligated to attend should you be on the winning team, but the offer is there. The ball is set to commence at promptly six in the evening tomorrow. Training will begin in the morning at seven on the hilltop beside the Tyro Forest."

"Why?" one of the recruits at the front of our table asked.

Bekencourt angled his head, repeating the question. "Why?"

"Why would we be allowed to attend the ball? No offense, Commander, but isn't that a bit of a safety concern?"

"Oh, crap," Alicai whispered. "Bekencourt's going to rip him a new one."

I watched as the commander smiled, the motion void of any warmth. "Matters of security have already been handled, recruit. Mind your rank."

"What do we wear if we win and choose to attend?" someone else asked.

Bekencourt inhaled a frustrated breath. "If you have any more questions that lack importance, please direct them to your captain." Without another word, he walked down the aisle and out the doors.

"You aren't prisoners," Blanning said, taking the commander's place.

"Could have fooled me," Alicai mumbled.

"You're free to leave the castle grounds and venture into the city as you please when you're not training. If you wish to wear something other than your uniform, there are plenty of tailors and shops dispersed throughout Caelestis. Anything else?"

When no one responded, he nodded. "Now, for matters of the teams..." He pulled out a scroll and began reading off names. I was glad to find Alicai, Zavier, and I were all on the second team. After the names were read, Blanning left.

Once the doors closed again, conversation sparked back up, a new sense of motivation flowing through the room. Most people here were from towns and villages that had never seen anything as extravagant as a ball before. I wondered what Angel would say if he knew I had the possibility of attending one.

He would probably begin sketching up the most elegant and extraordinary gown for you to wear, the voice in my head replied. I smiled at the thought, ignoring the ache in my chest.

We returned to our rooms shortly after, everyone wanting to get a good rest before tomorrow. Once Zavier closed the door to the bathing room, Alicai grabbed me.

"Do you think he suspects anything?"

My brows scrunched. "Who? Zavier?"

Alicai nodded.

"No," I replied. "I don't think so."

"I've been thinking about it," Alicai said. "And I'm wondering if you should just tell him. I know it's a risk," he continued, cutting me off before I could speak. "But wouldn't it pay to have someone else looking out for you? Trust me, this is a risk for me as much as it is for you now. I'm guilty by association. I just don't know if he would be more annoyed if he found out later on that we were lying to him."

I chewed my inner cheek. "I thought the same thing." Crossing my arms over my chest, I leaned against the wall. "We can always threaten him, right?"

"Threaten who?"

Our heads darted to where Zavier stood, drying his hands.

"Eavesdrop much?" Alicai said, keeping his voice casual.

Zavier shook his head. "No, don't do that. Don't make me feel crazy. I've dealt with exclusion most of my life, and I really don't feel like going through it again here." His eyes drifted between us. "I know you guys are talking about something you don't want me to know. You did it earlier too, didn't you? Is it me? Did I do something?"

Alicai groaned. "Don't be so dramatic."

"You know, I wanted to room with you because I thought there was potential here for friendship. Brotherhood, even."

"This is training for the guard," Alicai said. "Not some sort of bonding experience."

Genuine hurt flashed in Zavier's eyes. Gods, I hoped I wasn't going to regret this. "It's not you," I said. "Alicai and I have been speaking about something, that's true. But it's a personal matter, and I'm not sure I can trust you."

"What do I have to do to earn your trust then?" Zavier asked. "You two didn't even know each other before this, yet you trust each other without consequence. How is that fair?"

"You're acting like a child," Alicai murmured.

"Swear it," I said. "Swear on your life that whatever it is I tell you, you'll take to the grave. Because so help me, if you breathe even a word of this to another living soul, I'll make you regret your entire existence."

Zavier's eyes widened in shock. "I swear," he said, swallowing. "What could be this important?"

I sighed. "I'm not who you think I am."

Zavier blinked. "Am I supposed to know what that means?"

I glanced at Alicai. If Zavier tried to run and tell someone, there would be a dead body in our room in a matter of seconds. Which would be a real shame because I was starting to like him. But I felt like I had to do this, I needed to learn to trust. It's what Angel would want me to do if it meant earning extra protection. Between Alicai and Zavier, it would be easier to conceal my secret. Without another word, I tore the headpiece off. My hair quickly unwound from the bun, brushing against my collarbones.

Zavier stumbled back, falling onto his bed as if he'd been struck. "Wow, okay." He scratched his head. "So you're a girl. You—" He looked to Alicai. "You knew this?"

"Yes," Alicai said.

I had my hand on the hilt of Papa's dagger sheathed at my side as Zavier shook his head a few more times, sorting everything out. "I'm so embarrassed."

Now it was my turn to look confused. "What?"

"I admitted that I accidentally pee on myself sometimes in front of you." His cheeks heated. "I *examined* myself in front of you to check."

"*That's* what you're worried about?" Alicai asked, dumbfounded. "That doesn't even compare—"

"It's fine, Zavier," I cut in.

He ran his hands down his face. "You disarmed me. *Three* times."

My lips quirked up in the corner. "Yes."

"Why?" he asked.

"Because I'm talented with a sword," I began, but he raised a hand, silencing me.

"Why are you doing this?"

"Because it was my one chance at freedom," I said on an exhale. "I'm not from Telamar. I'm from Morters' End."

I waited for him to freak out, but all he did was tilt his head to the side and say, "And?"

And? Hadn't Alicai told me everyone in the kingdom hated the people from Morters' End? Alicai seemed just as surprised by Zavier's reaction. "You do know about Morters' End, don't you?" Alicai asked.

Zavier moved, the springs of his bed whining under his weight. "Obviously I know. Necromancers and shields and what not," he replied, swatting a hand through the air.

My brows scrunched in confusion. "You're not... you're not afraid of me? You don't hate me?"

"Is there a reason I should be afraid of you?"

"Well, no." Not at the moment at least.

He tapped a foot against the floor. "I never judge a person by where they come from. We don't get to choose the places we're born or the families we're born into. I only care if you're a good person."

"Alright then," I said somewhat awkwardly. "Good to know."

"I'm more interested in knowing exactly *how* you managed to end up in this situation." He leaned forward, mischief glimmering in his dark eyes. "I bet there's quite a story."

A smirk tugged at my lips as I sat on the floor. Leaning against my bed, I told him everything.

The next two hours flew by as the three of us shared stories of our homes and families, treading carefully down the line of getting to know one another. Once Alicai finished telling us about the time he was chased through Telamar by a herd of sheep, we decided to call it a night. And for the first time in a long time, I slept in peace.

CHAPTER 14

My teeth were chattering as the brisk morning air brushed against me the following day. All fifty of us were standing on top of the hill, the entrance to the Tyro Forest several feet ahead. The towering trees grew closely together, casting the forest floor in darkness and shadows. It reminded me of home.

Blanning arrived five minutes after seven with ten other guards donned in castle patrol uniforms. We'd already split into our teams and were spaced out evenly. Blanning noted it, a glimmer of approval flickering in his eyes before it faded out to the stern, hard-pressed expression of our captain.

"Good morning, recruits," he bellowed. "I hope you're well rested as you'll need all the mental and physical energy you can muster for this session. The task is simple. One of the guards is tied up and hidden in the forest. In this situation, he's the prince and has been kidnapped. Working together with your team, you must find and rescue him by bringing him out of the woods. These ten guards behind me are going to be working against you, trying to prevent you from your mission. You will be given two hours to complete the task. Whichever team rescues the guard wins the prize of attending the ball. The rest of you will be required to attend mandatory training tonight in wake of your failure. If none of you manage to succeed in the time frame, you will all be training tonight, and I will be greatly questioning your abilities. Understood?"

"How is this realistic?" one of the recruits asked. He was tall, but that was all I could make out from his features with the uniform on.

"That's Davin Hardcastle," Alicai whispered. "Shame he's not on our team."

"We don't need him," I said confidently. And I was confident. I worked extremely well in the dark so as long as my teammates didn't do anything stupid, I didn't see why we wouldn't win.

"Anything can happen," Blanning said with narrowed eyes. "Look at what happened to the guards before you. Do you think they ever believed they'd be murdered in an ambush?" Davin angled his head down. "No. They did not. Preparation is necessary for any situation. Do I think the prince will be kidnapped and held in a forest? No, but you need to learn to work together as a unit. You'll need to stop viewing yourselves as individuals and begin to see that you are all parts of one whole. A functioning team of protection for the prince. Now, I'll ask again. Do you understand?"

"Yes, captain," we all said in unison.

He nodded. "Wonderful." Turning toward the ten guards, he whispered something before they all took off into the woods, gearing up to torment us. "We'll begin in ten minutes. Your mock prince has left you a trail of sorts to follow. Whether or not you can decipher it is up to your skills."

"That's not part of the trail!" Kai yelled. "It's just a fallen leaf."

"It's the *only* fallen leaf, genius," Alicai spat. "Do you think that's just a coincidence?"

"Do I think it's a coincidence that leaves fall off a tree? No, it's nature!" Kai raised his arms to the side in frustration.

We were huddled as a group beside a tree stump. The captain had given each team ribbons of different colors, ours being red. I adjusted mine around my bicep before glaring at the two of them. They'd been arguing for the last five minutes about the odds of the leaf being the beginning of a trail.

"Do you see the way these roots and twigs are broken?" someone named Easton asked. He was hunched over a few feet away, examining the ground. "This only happens from a serious impact. As in the weight of a fully grown man stepping on it. I think this can be a trail."

"It could just be where one of the guards ran. Doesn't mean it'll lead us to the prince," Zavier replied, then scratched his head. "Or do we just say guard? Mock-prince guard?"

"We're wasting time fighting like this," I said as I flexed my hand against the practice sword we were all given. "Our best bet is splitting up."

"Are you crazy?" I looked at the stocky man sitting on the stump. I wasn't sure of his name, but he had a bright red beard braided toward his collarbone. He'd definitely be forced to cut that. "Splitting up leaves us all prone to getting attacked. Then who's going to rescue the guard? Plus, Blanning said we needed to work together."

"I agree with Wren," Kai stated. "There's twelve of us. What if we split up into pairs? That way we're not alone and can cover more ground. We'd still be working as a team if we came up with a plan."

"Perfect," a recruit named Davie said. "Alicai and Easton can both follow the paths they think are right, and the rest of us should start venturing further into the woods. Start around the edge of the tree line, then when we're spaced apart enough, head inward. It'll give us a better chance of spotting the guards trying to take us down too."

We all nodded in agreement. I paired up with Alicai while Zavier went with the bearded man. "There are three other teams out there who all want to win," I said. "Try to avoid conflict if you can."

Easton pulled the sword from his sheath. "Don't think we'll be able to avoid all conflict, especially if we get near the guards. But do your best."

Everyone began to disperse when I whipped my head around. "Wait! Remember, we *all* need to leave the woods with the guard. If only two of us make it out with him it's still a failure. This is about us working together, so we need some sort of code if one of us finds him."

Easton tilted his head back, making a cawing sound that echoed through the wide expanse of land. We all looked at him as he shrugged. "That'll work, right? Make that sound if you find him. And if we hear it, we'll retrace our steps back to this spot, and we'll leave together."

Once we all agreed and finally had some sort of plan, we split up. Alicai left the leaf on the ground, and we walked in the direction *he* thought we should go. I was about to tell him he was wrong when about a hundred feet from the first, we found a second identical leaf. He bent down, twirling it between his fingers. "What were you about to say?" he asked with a grin.

I rolled my eyes. "Keep moving."

He left the leaf so we could find our way back to the meeting spot in case we got lost. We moved in silence for a while longer, the occasional sound of a distant voice or footsteps echoing around us. There was something eerie about this place. It wasn't as bad as the Morta Forest, especially since I doubted we'd run into anything like the beasts that had their way with Henry Yuller, but knowing we were being *watched* was just as haunting.

The sound of a branch snapping behind us had me spinning around. Nothing. "You need to relax," Alicai said, eying the ground like a hunting dog.

"There are trained guards monitoring us to make sure we don't succeed. Sorry I'm keeping my eyes out for them."

"Good. You do that, and I'll lead the way to victory."

"Your little leaf theory is a stretch and—" The words died on my lips as he turned, holding up another leaf. I grinded my teeth. "Just hurry up."

We made it several more steps before two leaves laid flat on the dirt like a fork in the road. "Looks like we're splitting up," I said.

He didn't argue. "Stay alert," he called over his shoulder as he went left.

"Always," I replied as I ventured to the right.

I had the shaky feeling I was going the wrong way. I hadn't seen another leaf since we split up roughly twenty minutes ago, and I was beginning to think I should turn back and try to catch up with him, when someone dropped down in front of me.

I stumbled back, wondering *why* one of the recruits was hiding in a tree. That was until I realized *who* it was.

"Hello, Pipsqueak."

I wasn't afraid of him, I just didn't want any unnecessary problems. But it seemed he'd had it out for me since we crossed paths in Drapolin Forest. Sighing, I gripped the hilt of my sword.

"Your obsession with me is flattering but also kind of creepy," I said. "Considering I don't even know your name."

He bared his teeth like an unhinged animal. Really, *what* was his problem? "Brior," he answered. "And you'll do well to remember it seeing as I'll be Captain of the Guard one day."

That caused me to laugh. "Right, that's why your name wasn't even in the top ten." He stepped toward me then paused, eyeing me up and down. "Is there a reason you're hiding in trees when we're meant to be recovering the guard?" I asked. "Don't tell me you're scared of the dark."

"Doesn't surprise me you wouldn't think to get some height for a better vantage point. After watching you eyeball the sun, it was pretty clear you weren't the brightest."

I resisted the urge to draw my sword, deciding this once to take the high road instead. We were wasting time, and I wanted to win. Not because I wanted to attend the ball, because really, I had no desire to do that, but I needed to be on the winning team. I needed the captain to know my name and respect me.

"Well, enjoy," I said, moving to pass him when he sidestepped me, blocking the path. He crossed his arms over his chest as if that made him more of a man. "Get out of my way." My patience was dwindling.

"And why would I let you get any closer?"

So I *was* going in the right direction. This idiot didn't even realize what he'd just admitted. With a sigh, I drew my sword. So much for the high road. "You sure you want to do this? Going to be pretty embarrassing when you get knocked down by the pipsqueak."

He growled as he pulled his sword and charged at me. He swung aggressively, giving me just enough time to raise my own in defense. This was different than fighting with Zavier who *wasn't* actively trying to hurt me.

My arms were shaking, my teeth clenched as I held my ground, mustering enough strength to shove him back. I didn't give myself a chance to catch my breath or wait for him to readjust as I spun under his arm, coming up behind him. Before he could turn, I swung the sword into his lower back, causing him to groan in pain.

"Dirty fighter," he said as he spat on the ground.

"There's no such thing," I replied with a grin. "You do what it takes to win." Papa taught me that.

Brior was too angry to fight with intention. He ran at me, arms swinging wildly, and I barely had to move as he tripped over my foot, landing on the hard dirt. The white flaps of his headpiece were covered in brown and red as a deep gash now covered the skin beside his nose. He must have landed on a rock or a broken branch.

He was about to stand when something caught his eye behind me, making him stay put. I spun just in time to see one of the guards, sword already swinging. I ducked, but the blade smacked into the top of my headpiece, pushing it to the side.

That was the last thing I needed. I quickly adjusted it, backing up a few steps to give myself enough room to lift my sword. This guard was massive with a jutting belly that was barely contained beneath his uniform. Judging by his size, I doubted he could run fast. All I needed was to get around him, and I'd be fine.

I brought my sword up to meet his, the clash of metal reverberating down my arm in a familiar manner. I spun it to the side, but he parried the blow. *He's a trained guard, what did you expect?*

I managed to catch Brior out of the corner of my eye tripping over himself as he ran toward one of the trees and quickly began climbing. I crouched low, rolling out of the guard's way, and as I moved, I drove the sword into the back of his left foot, right against his Achilles. He cursed as he fell to his knees, and I took that as my opening. I shoved the sword into the sheath and ran.

I ran until I came to an open field and right in the center, bound to the trunk of a hefty oak tree, was the mock prince. I paused, examining the perimeter. I had no doubt the other nine guards were here, watching. The second I stepped into the field, they'd attacked.

Damn it, where was the rest of my team?

My breath caught as one of the recruits sprinted out from the tree line on the opposite side, a bright blue ribbon tied around his arm. He was fast, I'd give him that, but not fast enough as a hoard of arrows rained down on him. They were only practice arrows, but they still hurt. The recruit fell as one smacked into his back. He tried to pull himself up as two guards drifted from the woods and dragged him away as he screamed and kicked.

Right. I'd need a plan. The grass in the field was tall. Tall enough that if I crawled, I might be able to avoid being seen. And from the way the arrows came down, it seemed they were mostly being fired from the other side. I glanced around once more, looking for any sign of another red ribbon, but my team was nowhere to be found. Time was ticking, and I needed to move now.

Taking a deep breath, I laid on my stomach and dragged myself through the grass, pulling my body with my arms. I chewed my lower lip to hide my wince as I occasionally crawled over a rock that dug into my groin. I stopped every few paces, making sure I didn't hear anything, then kept moving. I didn't chance looking up. I just hoped I was going in the right direction.

My arms were burning by the time I spotted his dark boots. His eyes were trained on me, and although his mouth wasn't gagged, he didn't say a word. I slithered up beside him and pulled out Papa's dagger, silently tearing through the binds.

"Okay," I whispered as I came back around. His eyes were as brown as the bark of the tree. "We're going to crawl out of here, alright?"

He nodded, remaining silent. I made him go first so I could keep my eye on him. I sucked in a sharp breath as my forearm came down hard on a rock. I could feel the dampness soaking my uniform a moment later. Hopefully the cut wasn't too deep.

We made it about fifty feet before the sound of muffled screams echoed behind us. They knew he was gone. A second later, arrows whizzed past my head, landing in the grass. "Cover your head!" I silently yelled.

The guard in front of me did as he was told, folding his arms over his head as we waited for the arrow shower to halt. While they were re-nocking their next round, I pushed his boot to keep moving. Another fifty feet, and we were at the tree line.

He pulled himself through, and just as I was about to stand, one of the arrows hit my calf. I bit my lip so hard I tasted blood but forced myself up, even as it throbbed and tingled. It didn't pierce the skin, but the speed was enough that I'd have an awful bruise.

"Don't be such a baby, let's go," an irritable voice called out.

I stilled as Alicai came into view. "About time you showed up," I said.

"I'm sorry," he sarcastically drawled as we began running, our guard between us. "I was taking care of some other pressing issues. You know, like keeping your ass from getting taken out by the other teams."

It was then that I noticed Davie off to the right, cleaning blood from his knuckles as he stood over the unconscious body of a recruit from the green team. He locked eyes with me and began heading in our direction. "What? We had to keep them out of your way."

Footsteps and heavy breathing sounded from behind and to the left, causing me to spin and withdraw my sword. Rilee held his hands up in surrender, his red ribbon torn and stained with dirt. "Woah," he panted. "Just me."

"How did you guys know where I was?"

"We were on the other side of the clearing," Davie said, nodding toward Rilee. "Saw you right after that other recruit got bombarded with arrows."

"We also saw four green team guys sneaking up behind you, probably planning on taking you out of the equation before you could make a move for the guard," Rilee added.

"And let's just say we got them first," Alicai said with a devilish grin.

Davie hooted. "Did you see—"

I didn't let him finish that sentence as I cut in, "How about we focus on getting out of the woods and actually winning before we start talking, hm?"

"Don't take it personally," I heard Alicai say as he slowed down to take up the rear. "That's Wren's way of saying thank you." Without another word, he tilted his head back and made the signal sound as we grew closer to the meeting spot.

I exhaled a relieved sigh when I noticed everyone else showing up at roughly the same time. Making sure all twelve of us were there, we hurried out of the Tyro Forest, our mock prince guarded between us.

We were panting as we crossed the last line of trees. I squinted as my eyes adjusted to the morning light, noting Blanning watching us with a raised brow. "And with six minutes to spare," he said. "Looks like we have our winners."

CHAPTER 15

We had breakfast after the session, and while my team was all planning on attending the ball, I was the only one who decided not to. No matter how much they tried to convince me, my answer was no. I would join the other recruits tonight for more training.

"Come on, Wren," Zavier begged. "It's because of you that we won in the first place."

I stabbed my fork into the cold eggs. "You're welcome. But I still don't want to go."

"Why not? Why are you so against it?" he asked.

"I can't wait to see the prince in person finally," Alicai said, ignoring our conversation. "Time to put a face to all those scandalous rumors."

Zavier shook his head. "Why are you so fascinated with the prince?"

"I can't help it," Alicai grinned devilishly. "I love a man of mystery."

"Well, I can't wait to see the dessert table." Zavier stabbed his fork into a piece of fruit. "I've heard they import the chocolate from Saratala. I've always wanted to go and see the cacao trees there." His voice dripped with longing.

"Of course you have," Alicai snorted. "Are you sure all that sugar agrees with muscle?"

I stood up from the bench. "I'll catch up with you guys later." I could tell Zavier wanted to say something else, but Alicai smacked his arm, neither of them stopping me. Seeing as we had some free time, I decided to take a stroll through the gardens.

The sun was beaming over the gravel pathways that wove in and out of the hedges and shrubs. Some were overflowing with flowers that reminded me of a color wheel itself, the petals so rich and vibrant, I stopped several times to bury my nose between them, inhaling the sweet scents.

The grounds were fairly empty aside from a few noblemen and women out for a morning walk. Seeing my uniform, they nodded and smiled as I walked past. I did my best to fake a smile in return, but it was difficult. I despised these people. Living in luxury, eating the finest foods, wearing the most expensive clothes. The only worries they had were whether or not they'd find a suitable match at court, and if their names would be the center of this week's gossip.

Remember why you're here, I told myself. *In the long run, it'll be worth it.* Right. I'd need to suck it up and get used to it because if I succeeded, this would be my life for the next seven years. Seven years, and then I could hopefully see Angel and Mama again.

I strolled past one group of young women dressed in ridiculously large gowns that made them look like colorful blueberries. They were comforting a blonde girl crying her eyes out on a bench in one of the alcoves. Apparently, Lord Pennyroth, a rich nobleman who'd been courting her for several months, just announced his engagement to another.

I stifled my laugh as I changed direction, walking down a narrow path. As I came to the end, the gravel was replaced with white stones leading to a rounded area cocooned by white rose bushes. In the center was a fountain made of slick white marble, the same marble as the benches erected around the exterior, each one finely polished.

I leaned over the fountain, gazing at my reflection before running my fingers across the surface. Straightening, I prepared to continue my stroll when I saw him. He was standing on the other side of the fountain, watching me with a tilted head and bright hazel eyes. "Angel?" I croaked.

No, it couldn't be. I rubbed my palms over my eyes in aggressive circles, clearing my vision and gripping onto my last thread of sanity.

When I tore my hands away, no one was there. Shaking my head, I splashed a handful of water on my face. Perhaps I really was going mad.

~

There weren't many recruits in the common room later that evening. The ball would be starting soon, and mostly everyone was either getting dressed to attend or resting up before training. I couldn't rest if I tried, so I was sat around one of the tables with a few others. A broad-shouldered man named Sanyulin, and two smaller recruits named Avril and Rays.

"I can't imagine this going over well," Avril said, crossing his booted feet on the table. His skin was a shade darker than the commander's, his eyes as gray as the Morters' End sky. "Lucio and Ryder seeing each other again. I heard they haven't spoken since the incident."

"What incident?" Rays asked, running a hand through his cropped blonde hair.

Sanyulin snorted. "Do you live under a rock? Ryder slept with the princess Lucio was set to marry. What was her name..." He snapped his fingers, trying to remember.

"Lorianna," Avril replied. "Princess Lorianna of Tryfel."

Tryfel was a kingdom past the Haldro Mountains rich in spices, silks, and allegedly the finest jewels known to man.

"Yeah, that's it," Sanyulin said, leaning back in his chair. "They say that's why Lucio left. I don't know, if that was me, I think I'd kill my brother."

"Because one prince murdering the other would go over really well," Rays added, taking a swig from his glass. "Besides, you know what they say about the second born child in a royal family."

"What do they say?" I asked.

Rays smirked. "The firstborn carries all the duties and responsibilities. They have to appear professional if they're to be king or queen one day. But the second born... well, the second born can do as he or she pleases. They have more freedom for mistakes, especially with their abilities to cover up scandals."

"Clearly their abilities aren't very good if everyone knows about Ryder's activities," Sanyulin smugly replied.

I was about to ask a question when the door to my room swung open. Alicai half ran, half speed-walked, down the hall. "Sorry to interrupt whatever's going on here," he said to the three others as he gripped my arm. "But I need to borrow

Wren." Without another word, he yanked me out of the seat and into the room.

Once the door closed, I tore my arm back. "What is wrong with you?" I demanded. "I told you, if you ever pulled me like that again I'd—"

"Yeah, yeah, yeah." He waved a dismissive hand through the air. "Tear my arm from its socket, I remember. Honestly, I could write a book full of your threats."

I had half a mind to punch him in the face but stopped as I looked between him and Zavier. They'd both changed out of their uniforms into formal wear. Alicai in black trousers and a white button down, Zavier in similar trousers and a crimson waist coat. "You look nice," I said to them both, my anger quickly diminishing.

"We know," Alicai replied as he walked to my bed.

"What are you—"

With a self-satisfied smirk, he held up a gown made from ivory silks with golden beadwork woven into the bodice. A lilac ribbon was secured around the waist, separating the top half from the full, flowing skirts that contained the same golden beadwork along the hem. It *was* beautiful, but they were crazy if they thought I was putting it on.

I ran my fingers along the stitching. Whoever made this put a lot of time and effort into it. I dropped my hand. "No."

Alicai blinked. "No?"

"I know what you're doing, but I'm still not going."

Alicai's jaw clenched. "Do you always have to be so stubborn?"

"Do you always have to insert yourself into things that don't concern you?" I snapped back.

Zavier stepped between us, raising his hands like a mediator about to break up a brawl. "Come on, Wren," he said gently. "This kind of opportunity never happens. The next time we attend a ball will most likely be as guards lining the wall. The only reason we're even going is because of *you*." He nodded to the dress. "Can you at least try it on?"

I tore my narrowed eyes from Alicai's rageful face. "How do you know it'll fit me?"

Zavier smiled. "We took one of your uniforms and found a seamstress on some hidden back street. She didn't ask questions and luckily already had this made in a similar size."

"You both do realize how insane this is, right?" I asked. "This is just setting myself up to get caught."

"Don't you think we've thought of everything already?" Alicai huffed out. "It's not like you could just wear your brother's hat. They wouldn't even let you through the door dressed so informally, so that eliminates being disguised. And besides, hats aren't allowed. Apparently it's disrespectful." He shrugged his shoulders. "Anyway, we've got you covered."

"It's one night, Wren," Zavier pleaded. "You've given us this opportunity, so let us do this for you."

I looked at the gown once more. "Fine," I huffed out. "I'll try it on. But that doesn't mean I'm agreeing to this." Zavier grinned from ear to ear as Alicai shoved it into my hands.

I headed for the bathing room to change when something occurred to me. Turning, I added, "For the record, even if I did decide to go, you geniuses forgot one thing."

"Oh?" Alicai said, adjusting the cuff of his shirt. "And what's that?"

"How exactly am I meant to walk out of here in a dress?" They shared a quick glance. "What is it?"

Mischief glimmered in Alicai's eyes. "Do you trust me?"

"Do I have a choice?"

He held up a finger. "Nope. And to answer your question, we've already planned it all out. Most of the recruits would have left for training by now, and those attending the ball should be leaving any second. If anyone else is lingering around, they won't even notice you because this tomb of a man" — he motioned to Zavier — "is going to cause a distraction."

I decided it was best not to ask questions. My fate was tied to both of them now, so if I got caught, they'd be in trouble as well. Probably not as much as me, but enough that they'd most likely get sent home. Regardless... I trusted them.

In the privacy of the bathing room, I stripped out of my uniform and stepped into the gown which, to my surprise, fit perfectly. The sleeves hung off my shoulders, exposing my chest and neck, the lacy bodice giving my breasts a slight boost. The lilac ribbon fitted right above my naval while the skirts pooled around me like liquid moonlight.

I looked in the mirror, and for a moment, I allowed myself a glimpse at the life I never had. A life where a girl's mind was filled with thoughts of fabrics and colors and securing a new dress for every minuscule occasion. A life where I'd have sat beside the window in a flowing gown, my hair curled and styled to perfection while I read a book on poetry. A life where suitors would line up outside my incredibly wealthy parents' door, each one offering more than the last at the chance for my hand.

I looked beautiful. I *felt* beautiful.

It was disgusting.

I quickly threw away thoughts of that other life just as the door opened, and the two fools stumbled inside. That life was for someone else, not me.

"What if I was naked?" I asked as they cleared their throats and adjusted their shirts.

Neither of them answered as they openly gawked at me. I snapped my fingers. "Hello? Hi, yes, eyes up here please."

"You look incredible," Zavier said as Alicai pushed further into the room.

"Flattery isn't going to make me agree to this, just so you're aware."

I ran my hands down my sides, pausing when I realized I didn't have my dagger. I began moving things around in search of it when Alicai grabbed my chin and shoved me onto the small stool.

"Sit, and don't move." He dabbed a thin metal object into what looked like pressed charcoal, then dragged it along my upper lash line before I could object. After both eyes were finished, he dipped a finger into something red, smearing it over my lips. He stepped back, examining me from head to toe. "Perfect."

He handed me his mother's mirror, and I couldn't hide my surprise at how the black lines made my eyes appear larger, fuller, the red stain on my lips also making them more plump than usual.

"It's one night, Wren," Zavier said. "Can't you just have fun with us for one night? Who even knows if we'll all make it to actually being in the guard."

He had a point. Angel would encourage me to go if he were here. That thought alone had me pushing the mirror back to Alicai gently. "Alright. I'll go."

He grinned over his shoulder at Zavier. "Told you it'd work."

I rolled my eyes. "Hurry up before I change my mind." I hoped no one would notice my absence at training tonight. Seeing as everyone was worried about themselves, I doubted they'd concern themselves with my whereabouts. If anything, I could say I decided to go into the city. After all, I *was* on the winning team, and that meant training wasn't mandatory for me.

I found my dagger on the floor beside my bed and quickly lifted the skirts, sheathing it to my left thigh. I didn't have any fancy shoes, so my old, brown boots would have to do.

I smoothed out the bodice as I stood by the door. "So when is this distraction of yours taking place?"

Alicai glanced at the ticking clock above one of the armoires. "Right about—" A mixture of screams and curses sounded from the common room, followed by hurried footsteps and slamming doors. "Now," he finished.

"What did you do?" I hissed.

"I may have let loose an angry hive of bees," Zavier said nonchalantly.

My eyes widened. "What is wrong with the two of you? You know what, don't even answer that, it would take too long. Where did you get bees from?"

"The how and why aren't important," Alicai said. I was going to kill him later. "What matters is that you get out of here. *Now.* While whoever's still here hides in their rooms." He pushed me to the door.

"I'm not walking into a room full of angry bees!"

Zavier slouched against the armoire. "Just make a quick run for the main door, turn left, and head across the walkway.

Listen for the sounds of music and voices and follow it. We'll meet you at the ball."

Before I could protest further, Alicai opened the door, and Zavier shoved me out. Oh, I was going to kill them *both* later.

The sound of buzzing filled my ears as I tried to turn the knob to no avail. Those bastards locked me out. I had two options. I could either stand here and pray the bees darting around didn't sting me, *or* I could make a run for it.

I went with the latter. How those two idiots were going to clean this up, I didn't know or care. This was their mess.

I took off into a full sprint, hiking up the skirts of the gown so I didn't trip. *This*, I reminded myself. *This is why I don't wear these things. Completely impractical.*

I continued running, and I didn't stop until the sound of music and voices filled my ears.

CHAPTER 16

I never cared about fitting in, but right now I had to if I didn't want to draw attention. Keeping that in mind, I confidently strolled through the large, golden doors of the ballroom.

The marble floors were freshly polished, portraying the inverted reflections of those who wandered across while large white pillars rose up from the ground wrapped in green vines. The cream-colored walls were covered in gilded mirrors of all shapes and sizes, and from the ceiling hung elegantly crafted chandeliers, illuminating the room in a golden glow.

The left wall was taken by a long white table containing trays and dishes of various assortments of meat, cheese, bread, and dessert. Smaller ornately decorated tables were dispersed throughout the room, framing the large open space where men and women twirled and spun in a synchronous dance to the music.

The dais was positioned in front of two glass doors which led out to the garden. The platform was covered in a red silk rug and two golden thrones. One for the king, and one for the queen. But the royal family was nowhere to be seen.

I carried myself as gracefully as I could manage down the remaining steps, doing my best not to bump into anyone. There had to be at least two hundred people here, and by the looks of the clothing and jewelry, they were all courtiers, lords, nobles, and their families. The highest and wealthiest of society. And mixed into that crowd were the recruits as well as numerous guards stationed around the room, clinging to the walls, observing.

I thanked one of the servants who offered me a flute of glimmering golden liquid. I brought it to my lips and almost moaned at the delightful taste and bubbly sensation as it ran down my throat. I stilled as Easton and Kai strolled past me, half afraid they would recognize my face. But as they moved, recognition was the *last* thing I saw spark in their eyes.

Gross, I thought as they walked away. I was worried over nothing. No one would recognize me here. If anything, I looked more like the daughter of some mighty lord.

I wondered where Alicai and Zavier were and if they managed to get the bees out. A fit of laughter escaped me as I envisioned them walking in, covered in red bumps from being stung. Honestly, they'd deserve it.

I moved past the buffet table, my stomach growling as the smells of roasted duck, rosemary crusted chicken, sweet peach pie, and many other foods blended together. I reached for a plate but stopped myself, my hand hovering above the surface.

As quickly as it arrived, my hunger vanished, transforming into something much more deadly. I gazed around the growing crowd once more. People were dancing, laughing, and spinning to the lovely music while others ate from plates of food piled so high, my family would've been full for a week. The laughter, the gowns, the music, the food, the people...

It was too much.

While my family and the few others I cared for were starving back in Morters' End, these people were living a life of luxury. They didn't give a second thought to those less fortunate, those so wrongly treated and betrayed by the very man whose castle they now occupied. I clenched my teeth and fists.

I had to get out of here. I had to get out of here *now*, before I did something that would jeopardize everything I was working toward.

I didn't care where I was going as I pushed past the crowd and out the doors I'd come through just moments before. I didn't go back the way I came. Instead, I walked in the opposite direction, striding through the wide halls covered in portraits of royals long since buried.

I walked and walked and walked until the sound of music became a distant memory. I cut left down a dimly lit hall, this one a bit narrower. The sound of voices coming from the other end had me opening the first door I could get my hands on. Once inside, I quietly shut it as the voices grew louder then died out as they moved further away. When I was certain they were gone, I relaxed.

Was I crazy? What exactly would I have done if it was a guard, or a lord, or the king himself? I shuddered at what *that* encounter would've been like. I wasn't sure what excuse I could've created to justify straying so far from the party.

But the people were gone, and I was okay. I dropped my hand from the doorknob as curiosity took the best of me. Turning to see what room I stumbled into, my eyes widened. I'd made my way into the royal library.

As I took it in, I began wondering if there was anything in this castle that wouldn't leave me speechless. Rows and rows of towering shelves filled to the brink with books covered the walls, and that was just the bottom level.

As I gazed up, I saw three more levels, the open mezzanines revealing even more shelves. I took a step further into the room, my booted feet silent against the carpeted floors. Long, mahogany tables were distributed in the rounded area, each one containing candelabras spaciously positioned every few inches for optimal reading light. In the far-right corner stood a massive stone fireplace between two shelves with red-velvet plush couches positioned in front. The crackling flames and warm light created a comforting, magical feeling. I always associated books with magic. The purest, most thrilling form.

Aside from the sounds of the fire, the library was eerily silent as I stood alone, like a drop of water in an endless sea. A smile bloomed on my lips as an idea sprung to mind. If everyone was at the ball, that meant I had the library to myself.

I hiked up the skirts of my gown as I wandered to the nearest bookcase. I pulled the first book my eyes landed on from the shelf and plopped down onto one of the couches. It was so soft, it felt like sinking into a cloud. I blew dust off the cover, opened the first page, and read.

My eyes darted from page to page like the words would soon vanish and it would be gone forever before I could finish. I wasn't sure how long I sat there, but as I heard the door open and close behind me, I knew it'd been too long.

I watched from my spot on the couch as a young man who couldn't be much older than myself strolled into the room, hands stuffed into his pockets, golden shirt cuffs glimmering in the candlelight. He moved to the center of the room, directly across from where I was now hiding, and stopped.

My heart began racing as his eyes darted around, dark brown hair brushing against his forehead. "Who's there?" His voice echoed through the room, bouncing off the walls, sending my heart flipping in a nervous frenzy.

I sank further into the couch, praying he didn't see me. I closed my eyes and pressed the book to my chest as I waited.

And waited.

And waited.

I waited for the sound of footsteps, for him to speak again, for anything. When I was certain I waited long enough, I lifted my head just enough to peer over the back of the couch.

I shrieked as I was greeted by a pair of dark blue eyes. The surprise sent me shifting backward, and the next thing I knew, I was on the ground, my book halfway across the floor. I cursed under my breath. I was about to pull myself up when a hand came into my line of sight.

My gaze locked onto those blue eyes staring down at me with playful amusement, dark brows raised as if he were holding in a laugh. I glanced back at his extended hand as he wiggled his fingers.

"You know," he said, "when someone offers a hand, you're meant to take it."

Shoving my pride down my throat, I grabbed it, allowing him to pull me up. He then walked to where my book landed and retrieved it, his eyes scanning the cover.

I took this moment to observe him further. His hair was the darkest of browns and yet, in the firelight, I noticed lighter streaks running through the waves. The edges rounded into soft curls falling against his ears and forehead. His skin was fair, only a shade darker than my own, and he was tall. Tall enough that I had to angle my head to see his face as he came back over. Defined muscles flexed through the sheer material of his white shirt, and I felt my cheeks heating traitorously at the sight.

The sound of his laughter snapped me from my clear ogling. I raised a brow as he handed the book to me, his full lips pulled into a smirk. *Was he laughing at me?* I snatched the book out of his hands.

"And what's so funny?" I demanded.

He shook his head, smirk spreading into a full grin of pearly white teeth and dimples. Gods, of course he had dimples. "I'm just trying to figure out what's wrong with you."

My eyes widened. "*Excuse me*?"

"Well surely there must be something wrong, no? I mean, what other explanation is there for someone so beautiful to be hiding in a library, reading a book on the construction of ancient roads during a ball?" He nodded to the book I clutched so tightly my fingers might break. "And ancient roads? Really? Even a romance novel would be more interesting than that."

Who *was* this guy? And what nerve! Fighting the urge to slap him, I released a calming breath. "First of all, if you'd like to know what's wrong with me, I'd be happy to show you. Although it'll probably end with you in an infirmary." His eyes danced with delight and surprise at my words. "Secondly, there's nothing wrong with preferring the company of a good book over fake, egotistical people. And lastly, I *hate* romance novels."

I shoved the book into his chest, causing him to step back.

"Clearly *you* should stop judging books—and *people*—by their covers."

If I hoped that would scare him off, I was mistaken. If anything, he seemed even more intrigued as he put the book down on the table. "Fair enough. But who's to say you're not also one of those fake, egotistical people?"

"Clearly, I'm not. And what's your excuse for being in here and not at the ball? I'm sure there's plenty of women waiting for some handsome young man to ruin their lives."

He leaned against the fireplace, smirk returning. "You think I'm handsome?"

"I—" I shook my head. "I didn't say that."

He shrugged. "It was implied."

I smiled, eyes narrowing. "Whatever makes you feel better. Now if you'd be so kind as to *leave*, you're aggravating me, and I was here first."

His brows shot up as he laughed, running his fingers through the tangle of curls. "Do you not know who—" He paused, studying me as Angel often studied his art. Whatever he was about to say, he decided not to.

He gripped the mantle of the fireplace, causing the muscles in his back to tense. "I've never had much interest in large parties. Being around people you barely know tends to spoil all the fun." His eyes focused on the flames. "Besides, there's nothing interesting about half the people in there, and I'm not one to waste my time on dull conversations or assignations that lead to nothing."

A hint of a smile played at my lips as I stood beside him, watching the flames dance. "I always found the most interesting people were the least expected."

Blue-gray eyes like a raging storm locked onto mine. There

was a slight intensity in them and in the sudden roughness of his voice as he said, "It would seem so." I noticed deep shadows under his eyes that I hadn't seen at first. Shadows gifted only to those who barely slept.

Clearing my throat, I moved, leaning my back against the neighboring bookshelf. "So, you like to read?"

"I do. The library is only ever empty like this when a ball or event is happening, so I take advantage of it when I can. But it seems someone interrupted my plans tonight."

My mouth opened. "*You* interrupted *me*."

"It's okay, I forgive you," he replied. Was he delusional? I was about to argue further when he asked, "Where are you from? I've been to enough of these balls to recognize faces, and I've *never* seen yours before."

I interlocked my hands together, resting them against my skirts. "Are you sure? Maybe you just don't remember."

He moved closer. "Trust me, I would remember you." He stood a bit too close for a casual acquaintance.

I shifted to the side, putting a healthy distance between us. "I thought this ball was being held for Prince Lucio's homecoming."

"It is," he said as he took up my previous spot against the bookshelf, crossing his feet.

"Well that's quite rude then for him to skip his own party." I perched on the arm of the couch. "None of the royal family was present when I stopped in earlier."

His lips twitched as his gaze drifted to my leg swinging back and forth. It was then that I realized he was looking at my boots. Dirty brown boots under a beautiful gown. I quickly stood, fixing the skirts over them, but he'd already seen. His eyes held that same curious amusement they had when he helped me off the floor.

"Maybe they're at the ball now," he said. "I know Prince Ryder enjoys being fashionably late."

I snorted. "I hear that's not the only thing he enjoys."

He stilled. "And what is it that you've heard?"

"Well, let me see." I tapped my chin. "There's quite a few scandalous stories going around about him."

He chuckled. "Give me an example."

"I heard he ran through the castle grounds naked."

"Is that so?"

I nodded. "I also heard he bedded his brother's fiancé, and that's why Prince Lucio fled for the Haldro Mountains." I placed my hands over my chest. "Poor guy couldn't handle the heartbreak."

He laughed again, the warm hues from the fire highlighting his sculpted jaw and cheekbones. He *was* handsome, but I would never tell him that. "I must say, that's a new one. What else have you heard?"

I rubbed the back of my neck, trying to remember what Zavier said that night. "Oh!" I exclaimed once it came to me. "Apparently, he set some tavern on fire and stole the owners horse."

"Do you think he stole the horse first and *then* ran around the castle grounds naked? Or was he naked when he stole the horse."

I couldn't help the burst of laughter that escaped my lips. It had been so long since I truly laughed that the sound was foreign to my own ears.

He pushed off the bookshelf, closing the distance between us. My laughter died as he raised a hand, tucking a strand of hair behind my ear. "You have the most soul-stirring laugh..." His eyes scanned me, trailing over my scar, darting across my freckles, my lips...

We were so close I felt his breath brush against my face. He smelt like burnt sugar. "Do you believe them?" he asked softly, although there was a hint of something heavier present. "The stories?"

I was finding it difficult to focus on anything besides the nearness of his lips to mine. "I—"

The door swung open, and two guards burst inside. I sprang away as the stranger I was close to kissing cleared his throat.

I mentally slapped myself. What had gotten into me? I went from wanting to wring his neck to wanting to jump his bones in a matter of minutes. I needed to lay down. Or have a drink.

The guards seemed just as uncomfortable as I was. One of them stepped forward, bowing at the waist.

Why was he—

"I apologize for the intrusion, Your Highness," the guard said, causing me to blink in confusion. "But your mother has requested your attendance. Prince Lucio has arrived, and they're waiting for you."

No. *No.* I turned my head, eyes wide as the man beside me sighed and strolled over to the door.

The other guard held it open and said, "Your father is also very displeased at you wandering around alone, considering..." He glanced at me, halting his next words. He was clearly unaware that I knew exactly why the king wouldn't want his son wandering around alone.

Holy gods. The *king* was his father. And if Lucio had just arrived, that meant he was—

He looked at me from the doorway, that devilish smirk glimmering. "In case you were wondering about the stories, I did run around the grounds naked." A wink later, Prince Ryder and the guards were gone.

I stared at the closed door, raising a finger to my lips as I recounted the events of the last several minutes.

Prince Ryder.

Before I could throw myself into the flames from pure embarrassment, I hurried to the door where the lingering scent of burnt sugar filled the air.

CHAPTER 17

"Okay, I take back what I said about the captain," Alicai muttered while chewing. "Ryder is by far the most handsome man I've ever seen."

I snatched another flute of golden liquid off the tray of a passing servant, downing the contents of my fourth one this evening. I couldn't tell if Alicai was amazed or concerned, but as he grabbed the now empty flute from my hand, I opted with the latter.

"Woah there, I'm all for having a good time, but we have training in the morning. In case you forgot."

I didn't answer as I scanned the room for another tray of that glorious liquid that made my vision blurry and thoughts cloudy. I wasn't sure why I came back to the ball, but standing here now with the prince only a few feet away, I was regretting my decision. "Where's Zavier?" I asked, eager to change the conversation.

"Where do you think?"

I turned toward the buffet table, and sure enough, there

he was, attempting to cram as much food as possible onto a small porcelain plate. I was trying my hardest not to look over at the dais where the royal family now sat, but my self-control vanished as quickly as the contents of my flute.

For what it was worth, Alicai was right. Ryder had a way about him that made everyone in the room swoon and whisper. Married or single, male or female, it didn't matter. This ball might be in honor of Prince Lucio's return, but it was clear who the center of attention really was. And gods, I could kick myself for letting him get close to me the way he did in the library.

It was stuffy, and the ash from the fire was fogging my judgement, I told myself. Yes, that was it.

Prince Lucio on the other hand looked nothing like his brother. From his lavishly embellished blue trousers to his white and gold frock coat embroidered with the royal coat of arms. His hair was as bright as the sun, falling in loose waves around his face, enchanting his dark brown eyes. And from the way he threw his arm over Ryder's shoulder, the both of them laughing with a group of young men, it was clear that whatever had broken Lucio's engagement to Lorianna wasn't because of his brother.

They both stood at the base of the dais as the two seats were now occupied by the king and queen. Lucio had his father's hair, while Ryder's features were more closely tied to their mother, Queen Rosamund. Her chocolate brown locks and rosy cheeks accented her kind, gray eyes as she spoke hushed words to her lady's maid beside her.

Looking at King Reid felt... wrong. Perhaps it was because I knew behind the mask was a man capable of terrible things. A man capable of condemning an entire village to a life of suffering for the crimes of some. I knew *he* wasn't the one responsible for the shield, as that was his ancestor's doing, but he did have the authority to remove it.

As if sensing my anger, Alicai rested a hand on my forearm, pulling my mind from thoughts of regicide. "Are you alright?" There was genuine concern in his voice.

"I'm fine," I said as I rubbed the sensitive skin where I'd cut myself earlier in the field. And just in time as another servant crossed my path with a tray. I quickly snatched a flute and brought it to my lips, but Alicai was faster. He grabbed it from me before I could get a taste.

"Where were you?"

"What?" I reached for the flute, but he pulled it back.

"I said, *where were you*?" He placed it on the table behind him. "Zavier and I got here, and you were nowhere to be found."

My blood raced to my cheeks as I unconsciously glanced at Ryder. His head was tipped back as he laughed at something Lucio was whispering in his ear. I looked away before Alicai noticed. "I needed some air. What did you two do about the bees?"

"Yeah, Alicai, what did *we* end up doing?" Zavier carefully placed two towering plates of food on the table. He crossed his arms as he nudged Alicai. "Go on, tell her."

Alicai released an exasperated sigh. "He did most of the work."

"Most of the—" Zavier snorted. "I did *all* of the work." Looking at me, he shook his head. "It's a long story that involved nectar, a jar, and a very large shoe." I opened my mouth, but he raised a hand. "And *don't* ask about the shoe. I'm not ready to talk about it."

Clearly I wouldn't be getting any answers tonight. Zavier dropped into a chair and dug into his hefty plates. I was reaching for the flute when Alicai bumped my arm. "Seems like you've caught someone's attention."

He motioned to the dais, and I knew what I'd see before I turned. Ryder's eyes were locked on me. He smiled knowingly, and I suddenly wanted to crawl under the table. The corners of his lips curved into the same smirk he wore in the library, making my insides heat. If I was going to be a member of his guard, this was an issue.

I angled myself so I couldn't see him. "Not my problem."

Alicai's eyes widened to the size of the plate. "Not your *problem?* The prince is staring at you like you're the only damn person in the room, and it's not your problem?" He shook his head. "If he was looking at me like that..."

A flicker of blue flashed in the corner of my eye, drawing my attention as Drestel and another woman in a matching blue dress strolled toward the dais and stood beside Commander Bekencourt. Captain Blanning was also there, his attention focused wholly on Ryder. If he was here, I wondered who was orchestrating the training tonight for the recruits.

"Who is that?" I asked, pointing to the woman with Drestel. Her hair was just as icy as the look in her brown eyes. Her red lips were pulled into a thin line as she gazed bitterly at the crowd. Drestel on the other hand was smiling, her eyes glowing as she watched the dancing couples.

"The king's lapdogs," Alicai said. "Drestel and Pryler, his personal Estelers."

I turned, a puzzled look on my face. "What do you mean *personal* Estelers?"

Alicai shrugged. "It's just common knowledge that those two have been at the sides of every king in the Alosian Kingdom for as long as anyone can remember."

"Really?" I glanced over my shoulder at the two women who didn't appear a day over twenty-five. Clearly the necromancers weren't the *only* ones who could live forever. "Where are the rest of them? There can't only be two."

He pulled out a chair and straddled it. "No one really knows if there's any others left. Hell, I've only ever seen and heard of Drestel and Pryler. But from the stories that've been told, at least in Telamar, the Estelers resided in the Forgotten Mountains. Not that anyone would ever be able to find them anyway." His amber eyes darkened. "No one who goes into the mountains is able to find a way back out."

I'd read plenty about the Forgotten Mountains back in Morters' End. They stretched on for hundreds of miles at the north-western edge of the kingdom. Nothing but sharp, steep peaks and dark, dangerous valleys. Even the books held warnings about entering the region, stating most people would find themselves disoriented and lost after just several steps. There had to be some sort of magic involved. Something ancient.

"The terrain is unforgiving," I replied. Drestel was now beside the king, whispering something in his ear. "So they work for him?" I asked. "Why?" It seemed shocking that beings who possessed godly gifts of justice and righteousness would aid someone so horrific.

Alicai let out an irritated huff. "Do I look like some sort of Esteler expert to you? Go read a book."

Zavier shook his head at Alicai as he munched on his food. Turning, he ushered me with his fork to take a seat. I obliged, feeling like we were miles away from the ball going on around us.

"You have to understand, Wren, no one really knows anything about them for certain," Zavier said with a full mouth, causing Alicai to grunt in disgust. "But legend has it that Drestel fell in love with the king hundreds of years ago, and he manipulated her into using her Purity to do whatever he wanted. She roped Pryler into joining her with all the promises of riches and status the king gave them. I think that's why Pryler has a permanent scowl on her face. She never forgave Drestel or herself. They sold their souls and were cast out from their *holier-than-thou* sisters." He took a swig from his glass, then wiped his mouth with the back of his arm. "It seems the king treats them well, and they must be comfortable here."

I shifted, glancing back at the dais only to find it was short one person. Scanning the crowd, my blood froze in my veins as I spotted Ryder strolling across the marble floor. Beautiful girls stepped in his path, begging for a dance, and throwing themselves in his direction. While I was sure he'd had his fair share of women, he didn't seem interested in any of them.

How could he be when his eyes were glued to me?

For what, I didn't know, and I didn't plan on staying to find out. I quickly sprang to my feet. "I'm not feeling very well," I said to Alicai. Zavier went over to the buffet table again, his massive back to us. "I'll see you in the room."

Without a second glance at the prince, I walked hastily to the door. "I told you to stop drinking!" Alicai called, but I didn't turn around. I didn't want to know if Ryder stopped, or if he was watching me, or even *following* me. No, he wasn't that stupid.

I hurried out of the stuffy ballroom and down the empty halls. A short while later, I rounded the corner and crossed the open walkway that led to the guards' corridors. Moonlight illuminated the stone path as I lifted my skirts and broke into a run, the night breeze kissing the exposed skin on my neck. I tried to ignore who it reminded me of.

Out of breath and panting, I pushed open the door to the common room. Training was still going on, so no one was here thankfully. I hurried to my room and closed the door, leaning my back against the wood. I closed my eyes, breathing slowly.

Once calm, I opened them, only to be greeted by another nightmare lying on my bed. Asher's arms were folded behind his head, eyes raking over me in a way that sent a shiver down to my bones. "My beautiful Wren." His voice was thick with desire. "That dress on you is doing unfathomable things to me."

I didn't know what I was doing or why I did it, but in that moment, I didn't care for logic. I needed to flush out my thoughts, and as much as I'd hate myself in the morning, Asher was the perfect escape. I didn't have the mental strength right now to remind myself of the covenant or the fact he was only here because of it. No, I didn't care. Not now.

I kicked off my boots and stripped out of the dress, letting it pool around my feet. His eyes darkened as his gaze drifted over my body. As he took in everything I once gave him. Everything I swore I wouldn't give him again. Yet here we were.

I locked the door and moved toward him. His hands gripped my hips, and he pulled me down, flipping us so I was pinned below him. A growl escaped from somewhere deep in his throat as I kissed him. As I begged him with my lips and hands to help me forget.

Forget my run-down home in Morters' End. Forget the look in Papa's eyes as the life left his body. Forget Angel and his charcoal. Forget the absence of Mama's affection these past few years. Forget the countless nights I cried myself to sleep, all bloody and bruised. And forget the prince. Forget his stupid blue eyes and stupid smile and everything else in this stupid kingdom.

And that's exactly what Asher did.

CHAPTER 18

I lost track of time as the next several days blended into one. Wake up, train, and then train some more. Unlike the other recruits, I wasn't interested in doing anything else during my free time. It was the insatiable need to keep my mind occupied that drove me to the training room after hours.

With every dagger thrown and every sword swung, I felt a bit more at ease. I trained until I collapsed, sweat covered and bruised. I needed this. I needed the release it gave me from the ever-churning gears in my mind.

The night of the ball was the first and last time I'd seen Ryder. And while I couldn't seem to get it out of my head, I wouldn't let our little encounter steer me away from my goal. And besides, it wasn't like he'd expect to find the elegantly dressed young lady from that night in his guard. I was hiding in plain sight, as one might say.

Unfortunately, the drama of that night didn't end there. To say Alicai was suspicious would've been an understatement. When he returned to our room that night, it was almost as if he sensed I was keeping something from him. He strolled in, his usual light demeanor gone. He'd stood over me like death himself coming to collect a lost soul. After several long moments of his hard gaze fixated on me, I cracked. "What?"

"What happened tonight." There was no hint of playfulness in his voice.

"We're back to this question?" I asked.

"Something happened with the prince, didn't it?"

I studied him for a moment. His tall, lanky frame, dark skin, and bright amber eyes. Those eyes that watched me so closely it was like he saw right through my lies. The only other person who could do that was Angel. I chewed my lower lip. "I ran into him in the library."

His eyes widened slightly, shoulders stiffening. "You ran into him?"

I nodded, pulling my knees up to my chest. "That's what I said, isn't it? We talked, he left, no big deal. He doesn't know who I am, and he'll forget about it by tomorrow."

"When were you in the library? And—"

I groaned. "I'm tired, can we not do this right now?"

His eyes narrowed once more before he backed down. "Fine," he said bitterly. "But we're not done with this conversation."

That conversation was days ago, and Alicai was *still* pestering me about it. He even roped Zavier into his nosy little schemes, having him ask me what Ryder and I talked about, how it happened, and several other pointless questions during our training sessions. As aggravating as it was, it gave me the extra push I needed. Enough of a push to have Captain Blanning approach me several times to praise my skills.

"What's your name?" Blanning had asked.

Wiping smeared blood off my cheek, I said, "Wren Hibreaker."

"Wren Hibreaker," he repeated, tasting the sound of my name on his tongue before nodding in approval. "A warrior's name at that."

I'd managed to contain my grin until he walked away, but once he was gone, I was smiling from ear to ear, grateful to have him recognize my talents. Talents Papa drilled into me from a young age so I'd always have means to defend myself.

My satisfaction faded as I noticed Brior shooting me a dirty look. "He's just jealous," Zavier said in a hushed tone, spinning the staff around in his grip. His right eye was swollen and bruised from the day before when I'd hit him with the pommel of my sword. I'd apologized, even offered to run down to the kitchen and get him ice, but he laughed, claiming he deserved it for doing Alicai's dirty work.

Although Zavier made light of the tension between Brior and I, I couldn't help but feel slightly on edge. If Brior found out my secret, he might kill me himself instead of ratting me out. Really, I was hoping he wouldn't make it into the guard, and by the way he constantly ranked low, it was a very real possibility.

While Zavier and I continued training that day, I felt my thoughts slipping to Asher. I hadn't seen him since the night of the ball either, and thank the gods for that. It was a mistake. My emotions were running wild, and seeing him in my bed like shadows and mystery given physical form, I gave into those darkest desires of mine. The desires I kept sheltered and hidden in the deepest parts of my soul.

Days later, I still felt the lingering trace of his fingertips on my body. The invisible kisses still burning in all the places he left them. He didn't mention a word of our covenant that night, and maybe that's why I gave myself to him. He knew which buttons to push and which ones to leave untouched.

Today at archery training, I didn't think of those things. I thought of nothing but the crisp morning air stinging my cheeks as I drew the bow string taut. My breath wrapped around the arrow like a silent prayer, coaxing it to land true. I focused my gaze on the target, a circular mound of straw containing three colored rings. Black along the edge, blue near the middle, and red for bullseye.

Blanning had lectured us for an hour last night about how a sword and dagger were not always efficient means of defense. Sometimes the targets would be too far, and by the time we reached them with our swords drawn, it could be too late.

Archery was never my strong suit, but as I released my hold on the string, the vibration reverberating through my hands, I almost shrieked in surprised delight as the arrow landed just outside the red marker. "Did you see that?"

Zavier clapped his hands in encouragement. Taking the bow from me, he nocked his own arrow. "That was good, but I could do better." He pulled the string back, aiming for the target.

"Are you sure you should be doing this?" I glanced guiltily at his swollen eye.

He chuckled, his massive form shaking. "I could do this blindfolded." I was glad I stood behind him as he released the arrow because I didn't want to give him the satisfaction of seeing how shocked I was when it landed directly in the center target.

In the short time I'd known Zavier, he told me bits and

pieces about his home. Because the Raptyrs were such a secluded and demanding mountain region, there wasn't much they could do there. In the valleys, the elders planted and harvested vegetables and plants with medicinal and healing qualities, while the younger generations trained vigorously along the sharp peaks so high up, Zavier claimed the air was thin enough to cause unconsciousness.

They trained their bodies and minds on those peaks and in the ice cold caves from sunup to sundown. It explained why he looked the way he did. But aside from his looks, Zavier had a kind and rare soul. I think Angel would have liked him.

Besides their training and daily midnight meditation services, the small amount of downtime they had was dedicated to archery. When he told me, I laughed in his face at the thought of him carrying a dainty bow and arrow. But watching him now, I wished I could swallow my laughter back up.

Last night I asked him if everyone in the Raptyrs was built like him, to which he admitted that most but not all of them were. The women weren't nearly as large, he'd said, but they made up for it with agility and fiery ambition.

I thought life in the Raptyrs sounded like a dream, so it puzzled me why he wanted to leave so badly. That's when he told me that due to their natural and earned strength, at the ripe age of nineteen, all healthy men were sent off to the Haldro Mountains to join the military.

Zavier, having just turned eighteen, didn't want that. So when word came around about recruitment for the guard, his family encouraged his decision. He left behind both parents, a six-year-old sister named Korai, and a grandmother.

I whistled as he jogged over to retrieve his arrow. "Lucky shot!"

He raised a brow in silent challenge. "Okay, Hibreaker, let's see you do better."

I peered at the other end of the field where Blanning was swinging his arms in anger, his mouth forming words I couldn't hear as three healers lugged an injured recruit back toward the castle, blood leaking from his side.

"Fine." I snatched the bow, a mischievous look crossing my face. I was never one to shy away from a challenge.

Mama used to mumble prayers to the gods, shaking her head as I'd stumble through our front door bloody and bruised from a fight. "*I can handle myself,*" I'd say as Angel did his best to clean my wounds.

"*One of these days, Wren, you're going to try your luck for the last time,*" Mama would reply. Six days later she fell ill, and I was in the graveyard making a deal with a ghost.

I grabbed an arrow from the quiver. "What do you want me to do?"

Zavier rubbed his smooth chin for a moment, thinking, and then said, "I managed with one eye, let's see you do with both eyes closed."

I looked around. The castle was behind us, the Tyro Forest ahead of us. We were spaced out several feet from each pair of recruits, so even if I missed, the odds I'd impale someone were slim.

I released the tension from my shoulders and pulled back the string. Closing my eyes, I exhaled a slow breath. I'd done this at least a hundred times today, so I let my body fall into position from memory alone.

"Get ready to eat your words," I said as I released. My eyes remained closed for the duration of time it took the string to stop vibrating. I waited for a laugh from Zavier, admittance that I was better than him, for a slap on the back, for *anything*.

But the only noise was a collection of sharp breaths, and then nothing. Complete silence.

"*Wren*." Zavier's voice was as tight as the bowstring. "*Open your eyes*."

Had I overshot? Did my arrow land on another target? Did I *shoot* someone? Slowly, one at a time, I peeled my eyes open to find my arrow lodged directly in the center red target. Less than an inch away from Prince Ryder's head.

CHAPTER 19

I stopped breathing as Ryder pulled my arrow from the target. *Where the hell did he even come from?* I was half aware of Blanning yelling while the two guards flanking the prince drew their swords, attention on me. Everyone was watching me.

Blanning finally caught up, checking if Ryder was harmed, but the prince merely brushed him off. The captain then turned to *me*, his face so red he might've popped every blood vessel in his head. He moved to step forward but was stopped by Ryder's hand. Ryder whispered something to his captain that made him relax. And while the guards also stood down, re-sheathing their swords, I knew if I made any sudden movements they would strike me down instantly.

Oh gods, this was *exactly* the wrong kind of attention. Would they kick me out? Imprison me? They'd definitely learn my identity then. And with an almost fatal — yet accidental — attempt on the prince's life, they would think I really was trying to kill him. They'd kill *me.*

I grounded myself, refusing to shake as I waited for my punishment. There was no running from this. I didn't even bother looking at Zavier, I knew he was just as panicked as me. I really thought I had this. Thought I would've at least made it past the training stages. How embarrassing.

Tossing my arrow back and forth in his hands, Ryder walked toward me, his black riding cape blowing in the wind. With each step he took, even the birds in the trees held their breath. There was something oddly appealing about the way he carried himself. A sort of certainty... a *confidence,* that made it impossible to look away.

A million thoughts ran rampant in my mind, but I ended up focusing on the slim chance that he'd recognize me. That sent an entire new wave of panic through me.

Don't be ridiculous, I told myself. Nothing about me looked familiar. My scar was hidden under the sharp point of the headpiece, and my freckles... lots of people had freckles, right? And green eyes, they were common enough.

I held my breath as he finally approached, his brown curls woven with hints of gold. I averted my gaze so he couldn't examine me too closely.

"You have quite the aim," he said in a light tone. I blinked, refusing to look up. Sighing, he crouched down. "You know," he whispered, "Blanning's not as tough as he seems. Really, he's a big, cuddly bear underneath all those stern looks and harsh words. You have nothing to fear from him, or me, for that matter. I should've been more conscious of where I was going." He chuckled, standing up straight. "Hell, I must look like an idiot walking in front of targets during an archery session, huh?"

I bit my tongue at the remark I wanted to make. "Those

guards are the idiots," I said instead, my voice deep and firm, just as Alicai and Zavier instructed me. "Aren't they supposed to be paying attention?"

"Stand up straight," he said after a moment.

Swallowing hard, I lifted my head to find him scanning my face curiously. From this close, his dark circles appeared like smudged charcoal, and I couldn't help wondering what kept him awake at night. It seemed ridiculous they could *add* to his already handsome features, but somehow they did.

"You're right," he added. "They're gods awful at their job, so I guess it's a good thing they're only temporary." He handed the arrow that almost ended his life back to me. "I think this belongs to you. And with an aim like that, I'm looking forward to having you as one of my guards." He flashed me a smile that probably sent girls throwing themselves at his feet.

A second later, he shoved his hands into his pockets and headed down the hill toward the castle, whistling a light tune, as if he didn't just have a near death experience.

A hint of a smile brushed my lips. Perhaps there were worse men to guard than Ryder.

~

Whatever Ryder had said to the captain must've been enough to keep him from scolding me the way I sensed he wanted to.

Training wrapped up after that incident, and Blanning cast me a look that seemed to say, *Get your ass in line, Hibreaker.* Aside from that, I was also knocked down three spots on the board and lost a star. I was now ranked tenth.

Better than getting kicked out, I reminded myself.

When we returned to the guards' corridors, I made it very clear that if Zavier mentioned any of this to Alicai, I'd find that hive of bees again and let them loose while he bathed. And on that note, we parted ways.

Zavier went to the healers' sanctuary to pick up salve for the deep gash on his arm while I headed to the sparring room. My palms were slick with sweat as I pushed open the heavy doors, entering my little slice of isolation.

The other recruits frequented the city during our time off, getting their fill of ale and women at the local pubs and brothels or playing cards at the gambling halls, as Alicai preferred.

Zavier however, did his best to leave every session with a new injury so he could see Tavrina, one of the castle healers. She was young, beautiful, and had taken a warm liking to the future guardsman. I, on the other hand, wanted to keep training.

"*You don't become the best by resting when you're tired,*" Papa told me years ago. "*The best push themselves past the point of exhaustion. Past the point of pain. They only rest when they're about to break. And then they do it all over again.*"

Pulling the broadsword from its holder on the wall, I began the motions that were as familiar to me as breathing. A drive there, a twist here, a duck and parry... it was a dance.

I continued thinking about Papa's words as the hours ticked by, my uniform soaked with sweat. I wanted to be the best. But aside from that, the burn and pain of pushing my body was the only thing that kept me in check. The only thing that kept me from forgetting who I was. The only thing—

"Wren Hibreaker." I spun around to find Commander Bekencourt leaning against the doorframe. My sudden surprise appeared to thrill him as he cocked his head. "You look as if you've just seen a ghost."

I cleared my throat, standing up a bit straighter. "No, Commander. I just didn't expect you to remember my name, that's all."

"And why would I not remember the name of the star recruit who rescued the mock prince? Hm? Or the same recruit who fired an arrow that almost killed the *real* prince?"

I opened my mouth, but he raised a hand. "Relax, I'm not here to reprimand you. I was just passing by and couldn't help but notice your dedicated training." He glanced at the sweat I felt dripping into my eye. "Do you ever rest?"

I slid the sword back into its holder. "I'll rest when my thoughts do."

His following laugh gave me chills. "And what is it that's troubling your thoughts? I hope all of this isn't proving to be too much for you. I can only imagine how difficult it must be integrating into proper society after coming from... well, you know." He waved a hand through the air, his expression one of fake sympathy.

"I'm more than capable of handling everything being thrown at me," I said with a clipped tone. I couldn't stand him. And not just because he wouldn't let me say goodbye to Angel. There was something about the way he watched me, as if he knew something I didn't.

He smiled, but it didn't reach his cold, vacant eyes. "I'm glad to hear it. Keep it up and you'll prove to be a very valuable member of this team. And remember, those with value are often rewarded."

My brows scrunched in confusion.

He clicked his tongue, casting me a sidelong glance.

"Come now, Wren, do you think me a fool? After all, I was there when we took you from that place you call home. I saw how you reacted to being denied a moment to say goodbye. You'd love to see your brother again, wouldn't you?"

I swallowed, unsure of what else to do except nod. Of course the commander of the king's guard didn't forget a single detail.

His smile widened, teeth flashing. Leave it to him to make a typically warm gesture feel threatening. "I thought as much. Keep doing your part, and perhaps down the line, we can... negotiate. How does that sound?"

It sounded fantastic. It was everything I'd been hoping for. But I didn't trust him. "Why?" I asked.

He blinked. "Why?"

"Why are you doing this? Are you offering rewards to the other recruits as well if they succeed in their duties?"

He chuckled. "As of now, just you. Let's keep this between us, hm?"

I didn't think I had a choice so I nodded again. Besides, it wasn't like anyone would believe me. Still, I couldn't shake the uneasy feeling...

"I think I'll be going now," I said. I tried to pass him, but he stayed in front of me, blocking the doorway. My fingers itched for my dagger.

A heartbeat later, he stepped to the side, extending his arm. A power move. I didn't give him another look as I darted out of the room, suddenly desperate to wash myself clean of the feeling of his stare.

The following morning, a bundle of nerves settled into my stomach as I watched several guards drag a black, padded mat into the sparring room. We were coming up to the end of the two weeks of training, and today's session would be hand to hand combat. Both groups were here, all forty-nine of us lining the exterior of the room.

We were short one man, Padlyn Drugsmot, who was still in the healers' sanctuary with a shattered arm after falling off one of the climbing walls. I didn't know how this would affect his ranking, but seeing as he missed several days of training, I didn't think a position in Ryder's guard would be waiting for him.

My body was aching today which wasn't a good sign. I'd barely rested last night as Bekencourt's face haunted my dreams. I also wasn't the best at hand to hand fighting. Give me a dagger or a sword and I would excel. But hand to hand? Most of the men here were double my size. They'd flatten me instantly.

I'd need to focus more on identifying my opponent's weaknesses and then using them to my advantage. It was my only chance at winning. I didn't know how many ranks I'd be knocked down if I lost, and I wouldn't be ignorant enough to think it wouldn't affect my overall scoring.

I stood between Alicai and Zavier as Blanning headed to the front of the room. "Right," he said, eyes darting across his scroll. "Ravenswood and Dornic! To the mat!"

Okay, so we were getting right into it then.

I watched as both men pushed their way forward, standing on opposite sides of the mat. They bent their knees and raised their arms in starting stance. "First one pinned down for three seconds loses. Same goes if your feet leave the mat. Understood?" Both men nodded without taking their eyes off each other. "Begin!"

Their fight lasted all of two minutes. Ravenswood was a foot taller than Dornic, but Dornic was a stocky build and didn't budge easily. He had Ravenswood pinned below him, forearm blocking his airway when Blanning called time.

The next several pairs went as quickly as the first, and each time, the heavier recruit won. I was *definitely* at an unfair advantage. I was tightening my belt buckle when Blanning called, "Hibreaker and Lewis!"

Lewis? I didn't know a—

Shit. I internally groaned as Brior stepped up to the mat, eyeing me down hungrily. It seemed he was still bitter about our little rustle in the woods. I moved for the mat when Zavier grabbed my arm. "He has it out for you, remember that. Don't let him get his hands on your headpiece."

Brior didn't know my secret, he just didn't like me for some reason. If anything, he might try to take my headpiece off to bash my face in with it just for fun. That was a likely possibility. I nodded as I stepped to the mat.

I bent my legs and raised my arms as Blanning called for us to begin. Brior and I circled around the perimeter of the mat in a clockwise direction, neither wanting to make the first move.

"Come on, Hibreaker," he spat. "Let's finish what we started."

Definitely still bitter. "Pretty sure the last time ended with you eating a mouthful of dirt. You still feeling confident?"

That did it. Brior lunged, reaching for my legs. I didn't have a chance to react as he slammed me into the mat. The air escaped my lungs, and my vision went blurry. He kept his knees on either side of me, pinning my shoulders down with his forearm.

"One... two..." Blanning's voice echoed in my ears.

I kicked my foot up as hard as I could, grinning when it connected with his back. He tipped forward, his arm releasing me. I rolled out of the way as his body crashed down.

He was up a moment later, and we resumed our circling.

"Kick his ass, Wren!" Alicai yelled.

"The only thing you'll be kicking is the wall when you fail to make it into the guard," Brior said as he moved for me again.

Fortunately, I remembered from the day in the woods that Brior moved with anger rather than strategy. When he came close enough, leaving himself completely exposed, I cut to the left at the last second, kicking my leg out. He tripped, falling face first onto the mat.

I jumped on him, pinning him down with my hips. "Just like the woods, huh?" I whispered.

He growled and bucked up, moving me enough to give himself a chance to turn. He grabbed me by the throat and drove me down onto the mat. I struggled for breath as my arms moved wildly in response. He used his free arm to pin my shoulders to the mat.

I could distantly hear Blanning calling time, and then yelling louder for Brior to get off me. But he didn't budge. His face was red with anger as his grip tightened around my throat, blocking off all available air supply.

"Such a little pipsqueak," he spat. "I don't even need two hands to choke you out."

"That is enough!" Blanning's voice echoed as he grabbed Brior by the back of his uniform and yanked him up.

I gasped as my hands went to my neck, coaxing the oxygen to flow into my lungs. Alicai and Zavier were there in an instant, propping me into a sitting position.

"I told you to let go, and you blatantly ignored me." Blanning fisted Brior's shirt, keeping him in place. "And because of that, you forfeit your win." Brior's eyes widened, and he was about to protest when Blanning added, "And you'll be knocked down in ranking for this." He let Brior go and headed to the front of the room.

"That's ridiculous!" Brior yelled. "I won fair and square!"

Blanning spun, his face red with rage. "You tried to *kill* one of your fellow recruits. If I hadn't pulled you off, Hibreaker wouldn't be breathing anymore. A disregard for orders and rageful behavior has no place in the guard. It's that kind of recklessness that could put your entire unit and your prince in harm's way."

Brior opened his mouth but Blanning raised a hand, silencing him before he could start. "Say another word, Lewis, and you'll be removed from the premises entirely. Any chance of you making it into any rank will be completely revoked." Brior clamped his mouth shut. "Now get out of my sight."

He stormed out of the room, not even casting me a wayward glance. It was then that Blanning looked at me. "You alright?" I nodded as Alicai and Zavier pulled me to my feet. "Good. Franklin and Rivers! You're up next!"

CHAPTER 20

The final round of training was today. After the initiation ceremony tomorrow, everything would be different. For the past two weeks, it had been fifty of us. It was strange to think some of these familiar faces would be sent home or shipped off to other locations around the kingdom where their skills might be needed. By this point, most of us knew who would remain.

After Brior's outburst, Blanning had him removed from the ranking board entirely. Apparently, he tracked down the captain after we'd all cleared out of the sparring room and gave him a piece of his mind. I didn't know what he said or where he was sent off to, but a part of me felt like I could relax now that he was out of the equation. One less threat.

As of now, I was ranked sixth. I didn't want to jinx myself, but I was confident I was safe. Same for Alicai and Zavier. Zavier ranked in number eight while Alicai was now eleventh. Although Alicai trained with the other group when we weren't all together, I heard he impressed the captain immensely, especially during the mental examinations a few days ago. It was one of the few I struggled with.

Having been placed in a mock hostage situation, we had to withstand questioning and torture for six hours without breaking or giving away any pretend information we were given. I would have done fine if my wrists hadn't been bound with rope.

I'd panicked as memories came back in hot flashes. Memories of standing in the village square with my hands tied behind my back as I was forced to watch my neighbors beat Papa to death.

Apparently, I blacked out at one point, and when I came to, one glance at Blanning told me I didn't pass that test. But I'd made up for it everywhere else, and that had to count for something.

Today's final session included both groups again. All forty-eight of us trudged out at the crack of dawn to the hill behind the castle. Blanning and several other guards led the way through the damp grass, the fog so heavy I lost sight of them. From the looks being shared, it was clear no one had any inclination about what this final assessment would entail.

The captain stood beside a metal table containing strips of black cloth. I raised a brow, turning toward Alicai who appeared equally confused.

"By the end of today, twenty-three of you will leave this castle and be sent elsewhere," Blanning began. "Some of you will be asked to join the ranks in the Haldro Mountains, while others will be recruited to guard duty in villages throughout the kingdom."

His eyes trailed over us like a mother bird watching her young prepare to take flight. "Some of you will be sent home.

Your remaining wages for your time here will be waiting for you upon departure." Clearing his voice, he stepped closer. "The twenty-five of you who have been awarded the honor of joining the Royal Guard will be initiated in tomorrow morning at half past nine. There will be no celebration, no parties, and *no* drinking. This isn't some achievement won, celebrated, then carelessly tossed aside. You will swear your *life* to defend the prince. Do you understand?"

"Yes, Captain," we said as a group.

"All of you who remain must report to me. While off duty, you're free to do as you please. But know this, I have eyes and ears all over this city. I won't keep you on a tight leash unless you give me reason to." His gaze scanned over us again, and I swore they hovered on me a bit longer. "Everything else will be explained after the initiation."

He grabbed a strip of cloth off the table. "A guard's duties are never fulfilled. We're on high alert, day and night, for any and all possible threats. At night, it can be especially difficult to assess a situation when you can't see. That's why when our eyes fail us, we must rely on our other senses to guide and defend."

He summoned over the first recruit, Sanyulin. I knew how gifted he was with a sword. It wasn't so much in the way he struck, but in the swiftness of his feet that made him excellent at dodging blows and maneuvering away from every strike of his opponent. His kind, hazel eyes reminded me so much of Angel's, I couldn't help but stare.

"You'll each be blindfolded and given a sword," Blanning bellowed loud enough for everyone to hear. "One of the senior guards behind me will be your opponent. Your task is to disarm him by relying on your other senses. Most importantly, you must trust yourself. Trust your body, your skills, and your mind. Swinging the sword for the purpose of swinging will do nothing. As guards, we must always think strategically. Always plan our next move and the one after that."

He handed Sanyulin a practice sword. "If you can't disarm your opponent after five minutes or they disarm you, you fail this session. Regardless of the outcome, when you finish, you're to go back to your rooms and wait. Final rankings will be posted on the board tonight. The top twenty-five names will be sworn in to the prince's guard."

The captain motioned for one of the four guards behind him to come forward. He stepped into the circle of white powder spread along the grass. The guard was tall and muscular, his uniform worn and weathered from countless years of servitude to his king. A king whose head I wouldn't mind seeing on a pike.

He unsheathed his sword and positioned his feet equally apart, his right slightly ahead of his left. A tell-tale sign he'd surely lunge forward from the left.

Sanyulin lowered the blindfold over his eyes as Blanning's voice echoed through the clearing. "Begin!"

~

It was an absolute disaster.

I watched each recruit make it to the front of the line, put on his blindfold, and get knocked down in under a minute. I chewed on my nail, cringing as one after the other fell.

They weren't listening to what Blanning said. Rather than moving with a purpose and using their other senses, they swung their swords as clumsily as a newborn foal taking its first steps. It was pathetic. And from the disgruntled expression coating the captain's face, it was clear he thought the same.

There were fifteen of us left on that hilltop, and as Zavier stepped forward, reaching for the blindfold, I held my breath. Even if he failed this, I was certain he passed enough of the other tests to still be qualified. But regardless, I was... nervous.

As I glanced between Zavier and Alicai, the latter with his hands folded behind his head as he watched in anticipation, I realized how much I cared for them both. Through all the lies, deception, and twisted logic emerged the beginning foundations of a bond that wouldn't be easily broken.

As Blanning screamed for them to begin, I mumbled hushed words under my breath, imagining I could somehow direct Zavier on which way to move, when to duck, and when to strike.

I whispered as the guard spun to the side, angling the pommel of his sword directly at Zavier's right cheek, "Duck under his arm and hook your foot around his ankle."

He couldn't hear me, but by some gods given miracle, he did exactly what I said. Just as the guard prepared to strike, Zavier crouched low enough to slip under his arm.

With the split second of surprise, Zavier hooked his foot between the guard's legs, pulling him off balance. As the guard stumbled, Zavier swung the sword with perfect accuracy into his side. I exhaled as the remaining recruits cheered, glancing at Blanning who raised a brow, his interest piqued.

Although this was far from over, Zavier was the first to strike a guard. His victory, however, was short lived as a moment later, the guard drove the blunt end of his sword into

Zavier's, sending it outside the circle where it fell silently to the grass.

Even though he'd been disarmed, Zavier pulled the blindfold off with a smile. He gave Blanning a curt nod, holding his head high as he walked back to the castle. The captain was clearly impressed. Not only by the way Zavier put up a fight, but by how professional he was when he lost. *That* had to earn him points.

Next up was Alicai. His session lasted all of thirty seconds as he made the same mistakes as everyone else. He swung blindly with no purpose and when easily disarmed, spat out a string of curses that had even Blanning's eyes widen in shock. He stormed down the hill, foul words spilling from his mouth the whole way. For everyone's sake, I hoped they stayed out of his way.

"Hibreaker," Blanning called. "You're next."

I stepped up to the metal table and grabbed a cloth. Lifting it over my headpiece, I rested it against my eyes. The warm hilt of the sword was in my hand a moment later. Warm from the countless tight grips and sweaty hands that held it before me.

I rolled my shoulders and stepped into position. Feet shoulder with apart, knees slightly bent. I raised the sword with my left hand, keeping my grip firm, but light. My heart was thumping in my ears, but not from nerves.

As the sound of Blanning's voice echoed through the clearing, instructing us to begin, I smiled. The good thing about being from Morters' End, a place without sunlight and constant dark skies, was that it prepared me for this.

I *always* relied on my other senses in a fight. When I trained with Papa, I used the slight tang of metal in the air to direct me as he swung. The sound of his body moving through the wind, telling me where to strategically land a blow. I used my *sixth sense*, as I liked to call it. The gut feeling I trusted more than any type of vision to guide me toward victory.

So as the guard brought his sword down, I raised mine. With the first clang of metal on metal, I felt right at home.

Everyone around me went silent a moment later. I kept my eyes closed beneath the blindfold which allowed me to focus more. I stood still, waiting, *listening*. I knew the guard was behind me, could feel the phantom brush of his body as he passed me, the light sound of his feet on the grass.

He raised his sword, causing a slight thrum to echo through the air. Those untrained to hear it wouldn't notice, but I did. I waited until it was an inch away from my shoulder before I spun rapidly, raising my sword to meet it.

I wasn't surprised to find I was correct. A few cheers sounded around me before it went silent again. The guard pulled his sword away, and I stepped back. A rush of wind kissed my right cheek and *there*. I met his blow once more. While I had him in my vicinity, I rounded out my sword, arching it like a rainbow, and just as his own slipped free, I thrusted mine forward.

Based on the disappointed sounds around me, I knew I'd been close but must have just missed my target.

Come on. You've trained in the dark your entire life. Finish this.

I stilled for another moment, honing in on my hearing. A slight crunch of grass to my left, a whiff of metal, and I was arching backward, bending my back at a painful angle as I felt the sword whizz past my face. *I've got you now.*

Without hesitation, I rotated, bringing my sword around at an angle as quickly as I could. I felt it come in contact with something firm. A chorus of gasps sounded, and I had flashbacks to when I almost killed the prince with my arrow.

I tore the blindfold from my eyes as Blanning called time. The guard was standing in front of me, my sword still wedged between his left arm and his side. I hadn't disarmed him, but I did manage to strike him. I glanced at Blanning as a hint of a smile appeared. "Well done."

"We're not being marked based on how we speak," Alicai stated. "He's not going to deduct points for what I said."

Zavier shook his head as if he couldn't fathom how Alicai could be so stupid. "Presentation matters. How we present ourselves *matters*. Blanning's not going to want someone in the guard that breaks out swearing in front of highly decorated officials if he bangs his toe on the corner of a cabinet. You react too quickly."

I stifled my laugh as memories from earlier resurfaced. Not only did Alicai have a curse filled meltdown after he failed the last training test, but to make it worse, he then banged his foot so hard when we got back to our room, the words that flew out of his mouth were so horrific I felt dirty just recalling them.

Truthfully, I knew how painful stubbing ones toe on the armoires in our room could be. They stuck out just enough that in the dark, it was near impossible to navigate around. Alicai was currently losing the battle between himself and the piece of furniture.

He snorted. "Decorated officials, would you shut up? Maybe your problem is you talk like you have a stick shoved up your—"

"Look, I know we're all feeling tense right now, but let's just try and relax, okay?" I didn't know why I was suddenly so nervous myself. It wasn't like all three of us could get bumped down that many spots from one training test. At least I hoped not.

"Wren's right," Zavier said as we walked down the hall to where the board—and our inevitable fate—were waiting. "What's meant to be will be. Let's just hope for the best."

Three recruits shuffled past us, two of them consoling the one in the middle who looked like he was between crying and screaming.

Alicai whistled. "Looks like someone got bad news."

I ignored him as we continued moving, my heart thumping in my chest so aggressively I was shocked I couldn't see the outline of it through my uniform. As we grew closer to the board, the chaos increased. We had to shove our way through the crowd that was filled with mixed emotions to get a glimpse at the ranking.

I couldn't get to the front, but I was able to make out the top three names. Davin Hardcastle had retained his number one position, number two was gifted to Easton, and the third slot was—

A hand slapped my back. "Well done, Hibreaker. Nice climb to the top."

I vaguely recalled saying thank you to whoever it was. I was too shocked to see my name in the third spot with four and a half stars to do anything else. A sense of pride filled me.

"I did it, Papa," I whispered as a tear fell down my cheek. I felt a warmth as I said it. A warmth that could only be his presence.

I basked in that feeling for a moment longer before continuing to scan for the only other two names I really cared about. A nervous heat began crawling up my neck as my gaze passed the seventh spot, and I still didn't see Alicai or Zavier's name. I stood on my toes to get a better view and—

There it was. Next to number ten was Zavier. Relief washed over me, but it wasn't complete. It wouldn't be until I saw Alicai's name. A pain in my ass he might have been, but I would be lost here without him. While we bickered like small children, I knew now with full trust that he would have my back through anything. Zavier, too. And I would do the same for them.

I never had friends growing up, but I imagined this was what it felt like. Loyalty and love and a desire for them to succeed too. Never one above the other, but all of us together.

My eyes kept skimming as my heart kept racing.

Number eleven...

Number twelve...

Number fourteen...

Just when I thought I might throw up from panic, I found his name at the eighteenth spot. I didn't need to see anything else. I didn't care who else made it as long as I had them.

I turned and pushed back through the crowd, eager to find my boys that I'd gotten separated from. It took me a minute, but then I spotted Zavier's towering form. I couldn't hide my excitement as I ran toward them, almost knocking them both down in an embrace.

"Woah." Alicai's voice was muffled against my arm. "I think she might like us, Zavier."

Zavier's deep chuckle reverberated through me. "I think you might be right about that." I pulled back, unable to hide my smile as I looked between them both. My friends.

"Top three? Not too bad, Wren," Zavier added with a clap. "Look at you showing us all up."

"Eh, she could've done better," Alicai said.

I rolled my eyes. "Well it seems Zavier was right about one thing."

Alicai raised a brow. "And what's that?"

"That mouth of yours did get you knocked down."

Alicai's returning wave of curse words had Zavier and I laughing all the way back to our room.

CHAPTER 21

The sunlight illuminated the black marble floor of the throne room the following morning. The twenty-five of us who made it to initiation lined up in two rows, facing the dais where the king and Ryder sat.

The twenty-five best in the kingdom.

The captain made his way down the front row with the High Priest of Caelestis at his side, blessing each recruit turned guard with holy water as they recited the oath.

It was probably a bowl of water from the kitchen.

I watched through the sheer white material of the headpiece as Zavier and Alicai took their oaths, bowed their heads, and allowed the High Priest to bless them.

We were given our official uniforms this morning. They were such a deep blue they appeared black with bronze stitching around the seams, knee-high brown boots, and a leather belt with enough slits to hold various weapons. Our official swords would be given at the end of the ceremony.

I straightened as Blanning and the priest approached me

next. A flicker of pride shone in Blanning's eyes before his usual authoritative, stern mask fell into place.

I mimicked his motion, holding up my right hand, palm facing the prince. It was a symbol of submission. A way of saying without words that everything I was and would become was in service of Ryder.

"Wren Hibreaker, repeat after me." Blanning's voice was firm and unwavering. Having watched him carefully these weeks, it was clear why he'd been given the role of captain. "Through foreign and domestic threats, I swear my allegiance and loyalty."

"Through foreign and domestic threats, I swear my allegiance and loyalty," I repeated. I felt Ryder's eyes on me, and although I was taking an oath to *him*, I couldn't bring myself to meet his gaze. Especially not as Bekencourt took up residence behind the king, staring at me.

I repeated the next several lines, partially unaware of the words as they came out. It wasn't until the final half of the oath that my attention snapped into place.

"From this day forth, I will put Prince Ryder's life, safety, and well-being before my own," Blanning continued. "Where my fellow men falter, I will rise. I will cease to walk blindly, comfortably, heedlessly..." *That* was a mouthful. Taking a deep breath, I repeated.

He motioned for the priest to step forward. "...I will do everything in my power to keep him safe. Even when my service ends, until the day I die, I am his."

My gaze remained on the ground as I recited the final phrase. "I will do everything in my power to keep him safe..."

The priest mumbled hushed blessings, and as the holy

water dripped down my head, I spoke the final words. "Until the day I die, I am his."

As the water hit the black floor, I could've sworn it hissed.

~

Once the ceremony ended, the first rotation of guards was sent out. Alicai was stationed at Ryder's bedroom with Kai, while Zavier accompanied the prince with three others.

I wasn't on duty, and since it was midday and I had nothing else to do, I went back to the gardens. I felt less burdened in nature. The branches swaying in the wind, the diverse collection of flowers, the birds chirping... it was soothing.

Most courtiers had already taken their daily strolls so only the gardeners were out now, efficiently trimming the hedges and planting new blooming flowers along the path.

I kept to myself as instructed. "*Be seen and not heard,*" Blanning said. "*The best way to gather information is to seem invisible.*"

If that wasn't the gods damn truth.

Earlier, I passed several members of the king's council, the highest nobles in the city who made decisions on matters of the kingdom during weekly meetings with the king. I saw them as I left the throne room, and they made no effort to conceal their voices.

Their conversation wasn't important to me as matters of a dairy farm didn't spark my interest. However, it was fascinating to know that as a guard, people would say anything around me.

I stopped where the gravel was replaced by white stone.

Aside from the trickling water cascading down the fountain, it was silent. No birds chirping, no insects buzzing, nothing.

It wasn't my intention to come back here, but my legs carried a mind of their own. I took slow steps, lifting my boots heel to toe as I walked to a marble bench and sat.

While every other section of the garden was bursting with vibrancy, everything here was white. And for a color meant to represent light and goodness, there was an unsettling feeling of *wrongness* that radiated through the space.

Last time I was here I hallucinated seeing Angel. Resting my head against the back of the bench now, I wondered what he'd say if he knew. I would've remained in that position, allowing the sunlight to kiss my freckled face, had a sudden burst of laughter not pulled me from my thoughts.

My head snapped up, eyes opening. Standing on the other side of the fountain, watching me, was a young man. My hand instantly went to the hilt of my sword as I stood abruptly.

The laughter continued. A sinister laugh that would've sent most people running in the opposite direction. Everything in me screamed to *go*, to pretend I saw nothing, but the curious part of me...

"Who's there," I called.

No answer, just more laughter. A laugh, that although expended no warmth, seemed eerily familiar. I stepped to the side so I could see the figure more clearly, and as I did, the air was sucked from my lungs.

No, I thought. *It couldn't be. Not again.*

My hand fell from the hilt as I looked directly into the eyes of my brother. "Angel?" I breathed.

The laughter stopped, his head tilting as he watched me. How could this be? How did he get free? Was this Bekencourt's doing? I took a few more steps around the fountain. "Angel, say something." I approached slowly, as if he were a wild animal. I hadn't been crazy the other day, I *had* seen him.

He continued watching me, a distant look in his eyes. I was about to reach for him when I stopped myself. Angel's eyes had specks of blue around the irises. The eyes in front of me were green and gold rimmed. As I examined the rest of his features, I noticed that although similar, they were not my brother's. The nose was too curved, cheekbones too high, eyebrows too thin...

My hand went back to the hilt, and this time, I unsheathed the sword. "What are you?"

The person who looked like Angel but was definitely *not*, began laughing again. A laugh that now felt like a thousand tiny cuts spreading over my body at once.

He opened his mouth, and the voice that followed was neither feminine nor masculine. It was more of an unnatural combination of the two, like a rogue breeze flowing in the wrong direction. "Guard your prince, and guard him well," he sang in a melodic tune. "His enemies stretch far and wide, and even some reside at home."

What in Hell—

I blinked, and in the split second it took, he vanished. I spent the next several minutes searching every path, maze, and alcove, but he was gone. As if he simply vanished into thin air.

As simple as magic.

I ran straight for the library. I made sure Ryder wasn't anywhere near here as a part of me worried that seeing each other in the same setting we met would spark recognition. I also didn't know if guards were allowed in the library, but desperate times called for desperate measures.

I tried to move quickly in case someone came over and yelled at me to get out, but because of the countless volumes of books, it was taking longer than I intended to find the section on magic. Book after book, all on Purity. *A holy magic*, one of the books said. *A means of cleansing and purifying the dark and disastrous complexes of the world.* Whatever the hell *that* meant.

I kept looking, but for some reason, there was nothing on the topic I was searching for. Dark magic. I knew whatever I saw in the gardens was not of the good kind, and that left me unnerved. The sound of that sinister laugh still reverberated in my ears like nails scraping down a smooth surface.

The clock struck six just as I reached for another book. Cursing under my breath, I quickly shoved it back and hurried to my room. I had roughly a half hour until the rotations switched.

Honestly, I should've rested all afternoon like Flint, the guard I'd be stationed with tonight, but with everything going on, sleep was the furthest thing from my mind.

I made it all of two steps into my room before coming to a halt. "What are you doing here?" I asked flatly.

Asher dropped the book he'd taken off Alicai's bed, leaning against the wall beneath the horrific painting. His white tunic was unbuttoned at the top, revealing his chest. With his sleeves rolled up, the smooth muscles of his forearms flexed as he crossed them.

I forced my gaze to meet his, focusing on his eyes. *So blue*, I thought. *So achingly, annoyingly, perfectly blue.* A lazy grin spread over his face. "Would you believe me if I said I missed you?"

CHAPTER 22

"You should take that painting down," Asher said with a grimace. "It's so—"

"Are there people that can change their faces?" I blurted out. "People who can appear as someone else?" All the blood rushed to my head as I leaned over my bed.

Asher turned with a raised brow. He sat on the floor beside me, long legs thrown out in front of him. "That's an extremely random question."

I grunted as I rolled onto my stomach, resting on my forearms. "I'm serious. Is there some kind of magic that would allow such a thing? I checked the library but—"

"First of all," he cut in, "the chances you'd find something of that matter *here*, are slim to none. Secondly, where is this coming from?"

I chewed my lower lip before finally admitting, "I saw Angel today."

"*What*?"

"Well, it wasn't *really* Angel, but someone wearing his

face. If that makes sense. It wasn't the first time it's happened either."

He shifted. "When did you see it?"

I noted how he said *it* and not *him*. "Today in the gardens. The first time was a few days ago in the same spot. I thought I was going crazy."

"You're not crazy," he said firmly, jaw clenching. He ran a hand through his hair before continuing. "They're called Facelings. Although I'm pretty sure in some places, they call them exactly what they are. Face Changers."

"Care to elaborate?"

"They're not exactly people, but a type of creature that has no identity of its own. It's a segment of dark magic, the power they have. They shift themselves into what their prey wants to see most. It makes sense that you saw Angel. But, Wren." He grabbed my face between his hands, eyes filled with something I couldn't distinguish. "They're dangerous. They'll lure you in using the face you trust most, and when they get you alone, they'll tear you apart until you're nothing but mangled body parts."

That sounded delightful. The Faceling I saw didn't seem like it wanted to tear me apart limb from limb. It seemed... curious. Like I was. And then there was that strange song it sang that I hadn't even dissected yet.

"Can they speak?" I asked.

"Why? Did it say something to you?"

"No," I lied.

Another moment passed, and I shifted onto my back again, dangling my head over the side of the bed. If Alicai hadn't cut my hair, it'd be sweeping along the floor.

Asher stood up, adjusting his sleeves. His eyes found mine,

and four years' worth of emotions flowed down our bond. Love and lust, hate and pain, agony and betrayal.

It was a bond we forged in blood. *My blood.* All for a covenant I still hadn't fulfilled.

"Wren, did you hear me?"

I blinked. "What?"

He smirked, doing up his top few buttons in a sensual manner. "You're going to be late for your first rotation. Wouldn't want to keep the prince waiting." Something dark flashed across his eyes, and then he was gone.

Hopping off the bed, I twisted my hair and put on the headpiece. After a final sweep through the room, making sure I had everything, I hurried out the door.

Three days passed since the initiation, and if I learned anything so far, it was that Ryder liked to smile. A lot.

Sometimes I wanted to smack it off his face while other times I wanted to run my thumb across his lips and taste them with my own. I was losing my mind and *not* in a good way.

In only three short days, we all fell into a synchronous step. As we'd stroll through the castle, Ryder made jokes. And while the captain instructed us to keep a straight face when on duty, the prince went out of his way to make us laugh or pull a smile. Whoever we passed, be it a servant, lord, or beautiful courtier, he made a habit of stopping to say hello. He was sunshine in human form, and it was intoxicating.

The times I was on rotation, I walked behind him. I picked up on the little quirks he had, like the way he cracked his fingers when awaiting news, how he ruffled his hair when nervous, and how his body went completely rigid in the presence of his father.

With every day that passed, the circles under his eyes grew darker. Heavier. Stationed outside his door at night, I wondered if he'd fallen asleep or if he was lying there, tossing and turning as some wicked thought kept him awake. I wondered if he had nightmares like me.

Speaking of nightmares, the song the Faceling sang continued to plague me while I slept. It was a puzzle I couldn't piece together. *Guard your prince, and guard him well. His enemies stretch far and wide, and even some reside at home.*

I didn't know enough about Facelings to conclude if it was lying. But I also wasn't a fool. I heeded its warning everywhere I went, constantly searching for something out of place or someone out to spill royal blood. But it was difficult. Especially when I knew nothing about the former attack against Ryder. Nothing except that his men were slaughtered and disemboweled.

A clacking sound shook the thought from my mind. I was in the games room with Alicai, our backs against the wall, as Ryder and Ambrose started their third billiards game of the evening.

Ambrose was one of Ryder's closest friends. He was the son of Lord Davincourt, an awfully corrupt man in high favor of the king. I didn't know why Ryder entertained Ambrose's company. He was an arrogant snob, and the two of them couldn't be more different.

Where Ambrose had the face of a saint, he was nothing short of the devil. He tricked young women into sleeping with him with the promise of marriage, only to reject them the next day, ruining them. He gambled, drank, and started brawls everywhere he went but was never reprimanded. Courtesy of his father blackmailing everyone in the city.

Ryder was chalking his cue stick, brown curls swept messily to the side.

"You know who I ran into last night at the Iron Oak?" Ambrose asked, leaning against the cherry wood billiards table, sipping on brandy. His blonde hair hung low on his forehead, one lock falling over his left eye, highlighting the scar from his hairline to ear. If I found out who did that to him, I'd kiss the ground they walked on.

Ryder braced his hands against the table. "No, but I have a feeling you're about to tell me."

"Gisella," Ambrose said, a wicked grin spreading over his awful face. I didn't know who Gisella was, but as Ryder huffed out a breath and rolled his eyes, I could tell he did.

"I've said it once, and I'll say it again. I'm not interested."

Ambrose lifted his glass. "So you'd have no issue if I bedded her?"

Ryder laughed. "Good luck with that." He positioned his cue at the white ball, pulled back, and struck. It shot across the table, knocking a striped ball into the corner holder.

Ambrose lowered the glass, shaking his head. "I don't know what happened to you. The old Ryder was constantly entertaining beautiful women in his bed. I used to admire that. Now I have a feeling it doesn't matter *who* I introduce you to. You'd refuse every last one."

"And you'd be right," Ryder answered instantly.

Ambrose struck the white ball, sending two solid colored balls into the holder. He angled his head at the prince. "Tell me you're not still pining over that girl you met in the library."

I sucked in a sharp breath just as Alicai choked, exploding into a fit of coughs.

Ambrose turned, noticing our presence for the first time this evening. His eyes narrowed over Alicai. "Get a hold of yourself."

Ryder, to my surprise, filled up a glass of water and handed it to Alicai, patting him on the back. Even Ambrose seemed stunned. Most people didn't even acknowledge their guards, let alone offer them a drink. Then again, most people weren't Ryder.

Alicai mumbled his thanks as he downed the contents. Ryder asked him again if he was okay, and when Alicai nodded, the prince took his empty glass and placed it on the table. My heart swelled with something I didn't understand.

"Why exactly do we need guards in here?" Ambrose asked, annoyance heavy in his voice. I wished I could take that cue and shove it up his—

"Because, Ambrose, someone tried to kill me last month. In case you've forgotten." Ryder's demeanor shifted. He stood taller, more regal. "My guards are doing their job." He turned and winked at us.

"Did they ever end up figuring out who was behind that?"

Ryder shook his head no, but something in my gut told me that wasn't the full truth.

Ambrose grunted as he peered at the clock. "Well, I'm so glad you have your guards to keep you company seeing as I have to go, or I'm going to be late for a very important meeting with a *very* beautiful redhead." He smirked before hurrying out the door.

The prince racked his cue and leaned against the table, running his hands over his face. We left the room a few minutes later, and I couldn't help wondering what Ryder would say if he knew how close that girl from the library really was.

"Tell me again the point of this?" I groaned, sitting cross legged on the floor, eyes closed.

"It's meant to relax your mind and clear your thoughts. Have you really never meditated before?" Zavier asked. I opened one eye and glanced at the giant man sitting across from me. He was the picture of ease, gently breathing in through his nose and out through his mouth.

We'd been doing this every morning and afternoon when not on rotation. He tried getting Alicai to join us initially, but he laughed in our faces, claiming we were wasting our time.

It had been two weeks since the night in the games room, and everything seemed relatively normal. Well, as normal as this kind of life could be. There weren't any more assassination attempts on Ryder, and I managed to carry on with my secret intact.

I was cut off from the library a few days ago when the librarian scolded me, claiming the books were off limits to those in our *rank*. I had half a mind to tell the wrinkly old man exactly where I'd love to shove one of those books, but I didn't think Blanning would approve of being called in over something so trivial.

The books I managed to read before my banishment had absolutely nothing on dark magic. Not even a single mention of those two words, and the ones on the Estelers were mostly written in a language I wasn't familiar with, so that option was quickly ruled out.

I began thinking about Asher. I hadn't seen him since the day of the initiation. Wherever he was, he made no effort to see me. I should've been relieved, but all I felt was a gaping hole of emptiness in my chest. He was one of my guiltiest pleasures. Although I chased him off with harsh looks and vicious words, a part of me, my most loathsome part, wanted him near.

Going to the sparring room would've cleared my mind, but I stopped visiting a week ago after the commander showed up again, indirectly casting threats. I still didn't understand his fascination with me. Every time we were in the same room, I felt his focus drift to me like a beacon of death.

I shuddered at the thought of those cold obsidian eyes as I attempted to meditate. "This is doing nothing," I whined. "I'm just as anxious and my thoughts are just as active as they were before."

I opened my eyes and rested my chin in my hands, elbows digging into my inner thighs. Zavier's lips curled into a small smile, his eyes closed. "That's because you're fighting it. You don't want it to work because you're afraid of what you'll feel when your mind stops racing."

I had enough of this today. Pushing myself up, I tugged on my headpiece. "I'm not afraid," I said. But even as the words left my lips, I knew they were a lie.

CHAPTER 23

Today was the Bringing. A festivity held every six months where people from all over the kingdom came with gifts, words of praise, and even disputes that needed settling on a more official level.

The throne room was decorated with countless vases overflowing with beautiful, blooming flowers and detailed carpets lining the freshly polished marble floor. If I looked close enough, I could've sworn there was *real* gold woven into the material. What a waste.

Castle guards were stationed against the walls, each with a hand on their hilt, prepared for any threat against the crown as hundreds of people from all over the kingdom waited for their turn.

I was situated on the dais, slightly behind Ryder. As much as I hated to admit it, he was becoming a prominent reason for me staying in the guard. Aside from my other goals, I felt *eager* to protect him. The rumors made him out to be a rash, entitled, arrogant snob, but they couldn't have been further from the truth. Regardless of the fact I swore an oath, I realized I wanted to be here. It shocked me.

The king was seated beside Ryder on an immaculate throne of jewels and crystals that I couldn't name if I tried. Prince Lucio wasn't in attendance as he had to hurry back to the Haldro Mountains to deal with an altercation between the different legions. And since Queen Rosamund was on holiday at their second palace on the island of Cresta, only the prince and king were present for the Bringing.

I watched as two of the guards by the door assessed and cleared the next couple of people into the room. I grew rigid at the way the middle-aged man pulled the young boy forward from his shirt collar. The boy couldn't have been older than ten, his forehead lined with sweat and soot stains.

The man bent at the waist before addressing the king. "Your Majesty," he said, then turned his gaze to Ryder. "Your Highness." Ryder nodded in greeting.

"Well," the king said, his eyes lingering on the state of the young boy. "Seeing as your hands are bare of gifts, what is it that's troubling you..."

"Linus," the man said. "My name is Linus Havinwerd, Your Majesty."

The king raised a brow. "And the boy?"

Linus, seemingly just remembering the young boy he was nearly choking, glanced down at him with disgust, shoving him forward. "Well, go on, tell your king your name."

The boy stumbled over his feet, his arms shaking as he interlocked his hands together. As I got a better look at his face, I noticed his left eye was swollen shut, purple skin framing it like a beacon. I grinded my teeth just as Ryder sat upright, all calmness gone from his posture.

"M-my name i-is Ty, Your Majesty."

Linus took a deep breath. "For the last several weeks, I've noticed things going missing from my home. It started off small, a silver spoon here, a gold-rimmed plate there. My wife and I questioned all the maids and ended up firing more than half of our household staff." He pushed a stray lock of hair away from his heavily wrinkled face.

"I thought we'd taken care of the problem, but to my surprise, we hadn't yet caught the culprit. For two weeks nothing else went missing. It wasn't until the night before last when my wife and I were attending the opera that her entire jewelry box vanished."

He grabbed Ty again, shaking the boy like one would aggressively empty a money sack. "I found *this* weasel last night sneaking in through my chimney. He's stolen enough from me to start a small fortune for himself, and I want justice."

My heart hurt for Ty as his right eye widened in fear. He was visibly shaking now. From the state of his clothing and the scabs lining his exposed skin, he hadn't had an easy life.

"Very well, then," the king said, no sign of compassion on his face. "Ten lashes for the boy."

Linus began clapping and voicing his thanks as Ryder slammed his hands on the arms of his chair, fury in his eyes as he glared at his father. "He's a *child*. You cannot possibly plan on whipping the boy." He turned to Linus. "Surely you'd much rather prefer compensation for the missing items."

Linus didn't look like the type of man who was financially affected by this loss. I had a feeling it had more to do with his pride than anything else.

"The boy needs to be taught a lesson," Linus said. "I will agree to the ten lashes."

Ryder flew out of his seat. "Where are his parents?" When Linus didn't answer, Ryder jogged down the dais steps, holding up a hand to halt the guards before they started moving. He crouched down in front of Ty who now had wet trousers and a puddle under his feet. "Where are your parents?" Ryder asked him gently.

Ty's bottom lip quivered. "T-they're dead, Y-Your Highness." He didn't have to say anything else.

Ryder stood upright and motioned for the closest guard. "I want you to take Ty here and get him cleaned up and fed. Then I want you to send a message over to Miss Evangeline's Orphanage in Westcroax to have someone come and pick him up."

My chest ached at his goodness. Ryder was proof that the apple *does* sometimes fall far from the tree.

The guard glanced at the king who was staring at his son. Seeing no objection, the guard nodded, grabbed Ty by the hand, and hurried him out of the room.

Two servants rushed over and began cleaning up the mess on the floor as Linus opened his mouth to object, but Ryder beat him to it. "I am sorry about the situation, but can you really blame a young boy who was undoubtedly starving and living on the streets? I am not condoning his actions, but surely you have a heart and can appreciate the position he was in."

I didn't think Linus did at all, but he nodded anyway.

Ryder clapped him on the shoulder. "You will be compensated with three pouches of silver to make up for the missing items. My guards will see to it on your way out."

Not waiting for a reply, Ryder turned and walked back up the dais steps. He stopped in front of the king. "I'm not going to apologize for refusing to allow you to hurt a young boy."

There was an iciness in the king's expression. "What's done is done."

And that was the end of it.

Hours continued ticking by as the captain and commander accompanied each individual to the foot of the dais. Mostly every man, woman, and child that stepped forward brought a gift of their own. Soon enough, the room was overflowing with baskets of fresh vegetables, pails of fruit, grains, baked goods, and even livestock that a stable hand brought around to the barns.

Some came to offer words of praise to their king, while others demanded retribution for an altercation with a neighbor, family member, or stranger. Two men had to be escorted out when they began brawling due to some lack of payment.

Really, I wasn't paying much attention to what they were saying. I was wholly focused on protecting Ryder.

Although his attack was now something of the past, I wouldn't grow complacent. It was becoming more and more pressing on my agenda to find out what actually happened. It just didn't make sense to me. In a castle so well guarded, how was it possible that the assailants could strike, let alone get away? How did they manage to kill an entire unit of the best trained guards? And why did the king seem so unbothered by it? Looking at him now, lounging on his throne in his royal garments and crown, I wanted to be sick.

He didn't speak often, and while some might view it as a sign of weakness, I saw it for what it really was. He was observing. Observing every interaction, unspoken word, gesture, and expression. In a way, he knew these people better than they thought. And because of that, he was dangerous. Like a hawk perched on a branch waiting for the perfect moment to strike. The thought of him finding out my secret terrified me more than I would ever admit.

The next man to come forward stumbled, his feet bare and caked in mud. His trousers were torn in several places, patched over with different colored fabrics. It was a strange way to present oneself to the king, and by the looks on the other guards faces, this wasn't a common occurrence.

They all gazed at him with disgust, like he was no better than the pigs outside. It caused a muscle in my jaw to tick. The way they judged those less fortunate was despicable. Especially when there were things the king could implement to improve their quality of life.

The man tripped once more near the foot of the dais and fell. One of the guards trudged over and yanked him up by his arm. He wobbled for a moment before regaining his balance. He was skinny, his tunic hanging off him like it was two sizes too big. His arms were shaking as he bowed, gray hair falling over his forehead. "Your Majesty."

My eyes drifted to the king who leaned forward, resting his chin in his hand. "And what have you brought for this Bringing?" he asked.

The man continued to shake, but I didn't think it was from fear. Malnourishment was as close a friend to me as a dark sky, and I recognized it when I saw it. He glanced at Ryder out of the corner of his eye. Such a small movement, but as he did it, I noticed the flex of his jaw. Slowly, my hand drifted to the hilt of my sword.

The man straightened, clasping his hands together in

front of him, his necklace swinging freely above his tunic. It looked like an elongated dart made entirely of glimmering steel. "I do not have any fancy goods or expensive wines. I come with nothing more than a question."

Alicai and I glanced at each other. What was going on? Something about this entire situation felt... off. The king angled his head as he extended a hand. "Please, go on."

"Do they know the truth?" the man asked, each word clipped with malice. That was all he said, a small smile forming on his lips as the color drained from the king's face. *What was he talking about?*

Before anyone could get another word out, the man clicked his tongue, and his smile transformed into something sinister. "I'll take that as a no. And with that, I bid you all farewell with one parting message."

Bekencourt stepped in front of the king. "A message from whom?"

The man's eyes flicked to Ryder. "The Kindrahs of Enderya."

The next several moments happened quickly as the man yanked his necklace free, throwing the dart with unhuman-like speed and accuracy at Ryder's throat. Without hesitation, I tackled the prince, shielding his body with my own. I heard metal scraping as swords were drawn and... laughter?

I twisted my head just in time to see Blanning pin the attacker to the floor. "There will be more!" the man screamed in between laughs, his yellow, cracked teeth showing. The guards began lockdown protocol, securing all exits. "We won't stand down! Where I failed, two more will step forward! And if they fail, three more after that!" His words became mangled as he was dragged from the room. "Your precious prince's blood will spill, I swear it! I..."

The room erupted into a state of chaos, and there I was, pinned to the prince. I was about to get up when a lock of hair fell down my forehead. *Oh gods.* My headpiece must have shifted when I threw myself at Ryder. I looked up, my eyes meeting Alicai's. His widened immediately before he started moving closer to cover me. But he was too far away and wouldn't get to me before someone noticed.

I had to take the entire piece off to fix it, and I couldn't do that in the middle of the room. Panicking, I looked around. There were guards everywhere, but they were focused on clearing out the remaining guests. The king was already evacuated which meant Ryder was next.

I didn't have much time, seconds at best. I had to get out of here *now.* Ryder would be fine if I left him. I did my part. My eyes landed on the large tapestry that concealed an entrance to the tunnels. Without thinking, I pulled myself up and made a run for it, not chancing a look back.

I pushed through the fabric, entering one of the dark passages that ran beside and beneath the castle. The sound of footsteps trailing me caused me to move faster. Maybe it was Alicai? No, he would have called my name by now. What if someone saw?

Turning around wasn't an option. Inhaling a deep breath, I willed my shaking legs to move faster. The sound of dripping water blended with the hurried footsteps, and I prayed to the gods I didn't believe in to keep me from slipping and face-planting on the damp stone.

My chaser was relentless. Every time I tried to lose him, the sound of his steps behind me echoed a moment later. My lungs were burning by the time I came through another tapestry, leaving me on the other side of the castle. I turned to the right and spotted the music room. I didn't pause to catch my breath as the footsteps and labored breathing were growing closer.

I ran harder. If I continued this way, I'd end up near one of the towers where I could descend the winding stairs to the levels below. To the maze of abandoned passageways that haven't been used in over a hundred years. *According to my book.* I would lose my follower there.

The footsteps were gaining, but I was so close. Almost at the tower. I could see the gray stone alcove and the small windows. I'd make it, I would—

"Wait!"

I skidded to a halt at the sound of that voice. I knew that voice. I'd know it anywhere. I panted as I glanced around, only to realize the mistake I made. I ran to the eastern tower, not the western. This tower didn't have a staircase. It had nothing besides a wooden door, which, as I tried the knob, was locked.

I was trapped.

Trapped, with Ryder standing behind me.

His footsteps slowed, and he finally came to a stop. *Why did he follow me?*

"Please," he begged. "Please stop running. I just want to... I want to thank you. You saved my life."

I bit my tongue, gazing out the small window overlooking the Tyro Forest.

"Please," Ryder repeated. "What's your name?" When I didn't answer, he sighed heavily. "Very well. You leave me no choice."

What was he about to do? Order my execution?

"I'm your prince, and I command you to tell me your name."

I couldn't help it. I burst out laughing.

He sucked in a sharp breath, and I knew I made a big mistake. A firm hand gripped my shoulder, spinning me around.

His wide eyes scanned my face, and eventually, he said the two words I hoped I'd never hear. "It's you."

"You must have me mistaken for someone else," I said, angling my head down and maintaining that deep voice I worked so hard on.

"No, I don't." He gripped my chin firmly, forcing my head up. Those storm cloud eyes focused so intently on me, I wanted to shrink away to nothing. "I'd recognize your laugh anywhere."

Before I could object, he pulled the headpiece off, my brown waves falling against my shoulders. He dropped it, the sound of metal on stone ringing in my ears. He didn't notice, or maybe he just didn't care as he moved closer. As close as we stood that night in the library.

Delicate fingers ran down my cheek as his dark brows knitted closely together. He seemed so intent on memorizing every detail of me. Like he was afraid that if he broke his concentration, I'd slip through his fingers. Again.

He opened his mouth, but the sound of footsteps made him snap it closed. He peered over his shoulder, back to me, and then to the jammed door. Before I could ask what was going on, he shouldered the door, popping the lock. Grabbing my headpiece, he shoved it in my hands and pushed me inside.

Worried eyes met mine as he whispered, "Don't make a

sound." The door clicked closed before I could catch my breath.

I stood in the storage closet as my heart thumped unsteadily in my chest. I vaguely heard Ryder claiming he was fine and only ran off to get some air. It must have been the guards who approached.

I waited several moments after they walked away before pushing the door open a crack. No one was there.

Tucking my hair back into my headpiece, I walked. I walked as swiftly as I could back to the common room, ignoring my shaking hands the entire way.

~

I didn't know how long I'd spent pacing back and forth. I had one hand braced against my forehead, the other at my side. We'd all been sent out to guard during the Bringing, and no one was back yet. I felt myself slipping into a panic attack.

Ryder knew.

So much for seven years of service and then freedom. I'd need to leave... *now.* Forget about my plans. Maybe I'd work my way back to Morters' End. I hated it, but Angel was there. And what was I going to do out on my own without him?

You can't, the voice in my head demanded. *If you leave, Morters' End will be the first place Bekencourt looks for you.*

Shit. I didn't think of that. With his creepy fascination with me, I doubted he'd just forget about it if I abandoned station. And if I ran elsewhere, he'd probably threaten Angel and Mama until I made myself known.

So leaving wasn't an option. But I wouldn't be able to stay much longer. Maybe Ryder already told Blanning. Would they be coming to escort me to the dungeons? Oh gods. This was really it. I was so scre—

The door swung open to the common room, halting my thoughts. I stilled as a chorus of voices seeped in. Some of the guards went to their rooms while others dropped onto chairs and sofas. No one paid me any attention. That was a good thing, right? It meant they weren't aware of anything. *Yet.*

Sanyulin paused when he saw me. "We were wondering where you ran off to. Great work saving the prince, by the way. Definitely put yourself at the top of Blanning's list." Good. Maybe my noble act would keep them from punishing me too harshly. Sanyulin raised a brow. "Where *did* you go?"

"I wasn't feeling very well." Not exactly a lie.

"Yeah, you don't look great," he said as he sprawled out on the green sofa. Alicai walked in next, watching me cautiously. "But your rotation starts in ten minutes, so I'd get a move on if I were you."

Crap. I forgot tonight was a double shift. Cursing under my breath, I pushed past the guards still piling into the room. I didn't have to look to know Alicai was on my heels. "What happened when I left?" I asked.

"They locked him up. It's going to be a long, painful night if he doesn't start talking."

In the madness of this afternoon, I didn't have time to stop and think about the attack. I hadn't heard the word Kindrah in years. It was what the dark magic wielders in Enderya, the kingdom across the Aldric Sea, were referred to as. It was said that some of the magic practiced there was so twisted and evil, it drove countless men and women to their deaths.

Just the thought of it gave me chills. While the necromancers were wicked, their acts unnatural and wrong, they didn't scare me. But I knew if I met a different type of Kindrah, I might feel different.

Although, I did come across another type. The Faceling. But like the necromancers, the Faceling I met didn't scare me. It just intrigued me. Perhaps that was just as dangerous.

I kept quiet as we continued walking. I still couldn't piece together why they were going to such lengths to assassinate the prince. It wasn't as if Ryder was in line for the throne, that was Lucio's right as firstborn. It didn't make any sense.

I decided to lock those questions and thoughts away for later as we approached the ivory door of Ryder's bedroom, relieving the two guards. Really, I'd rather be anywhere else right now, but abandoning post would be suspicious.

I didn't know what Ryder had done with the information, and I wouldn't incriminate myself just because I was worried. Besides, he shoved me in the closet. Would he have done that if he wanted me caught?

"He's a bit shaken up after everything, but he's in there. The room was checked over twice," Easton said before hurrying off with another guard named Tril.

We resumed their positions on either side of the door, hands draped over our hilts. We stood that way for several minutes in complete silence until Alicai asked, "Do you want to tell me what happened when he ran after you?"

"Nope," I replied.

I could hear his teeth grind. "You forget that if you get caught, Zavier and I are going to go down with you."

"I would never rat you two out," I said earnestly.

"Doesn't matter. We share a room with you. Do you really

think Blanning won't believe that we knew? Now I'll ask you again, what happened?"

I shrugged, feigning nonchalance. "Nothing. He never caught up to me."

I didn't enjoy lying to Alicai, and I knew I could trust him, I just... I needed to sort this out myself before I dragged him further down with me.

For two hours we stood there, the tension so thick I could feel it tightening around my throat. Eventually the door creaked open, and we both turned in surprise as Ryder stood in the doorframe. He was shirtless, wearing only a pair of black sleep pants that hung low on his hips.

He glanced at Alicai, then me, where his gaze froze. He looked me over quickly before resuming that charming, tilted smile I was certain could start wars. "It seems I'm in need of assistance." His voice was thick, causing the hairs on the back of my neck to perk up in twisted delight.

I cleared my throat, angling my head to Alicai. "Go assist the prince, I'll stand—"

"No," Ryder said abruptly, causing my gaze to flicker back to him. "Your assistance will do just fine."

It wasn't as if I was in a position to say *no*. As Ryder stepped aside, holding the door open, I looked at Alicai. His eyes seemed to say, *You're not getting out of telling me about this later.*

Then as I entered the room, the door slammed shut, leaving me alone with the prince.

CHAPTER 24

I hovered beside the door as Ryder crossed the room, taking a seat at the edge of his bed. It was massive, covered in black silk sheets and countless pillows. He braced his hands behind him, exposing the entirety of his torso.

His body was sinfully flawless. The portrait of rugged, defined perfection. The flames from the torches secured against the walls highlighted the lines of each muscle, dip, and curve as he inhaled and exhaled steadily.

I clasped my hands behind me, nails digging into my skin as I forced the words out. "How can I be of assistance?"

He tilted his head, tousled curls falling to the side. "Drop the act."

While a part of me was terrified he would expose me and ruin everything, the other part felt oddly comfortable around him. *Too* comfortable, seeing as I scoffed and crossed my arms over my chest. "Excuse me?"

"Take off the headpiece."

I hesitated before removing it. He knew who I was, there

was no point looking any more foolish than I certainly already did. He now held my life in his hands. And from the dark glimmer in his eyes as they raked over me, I had a feeling he knew it too.

Without a word, he stood, strolling to the table near the fireplace. For someone so bubbly and full of life, his room was awfully dark. His walls were a deep gray, and the midnight curtains were pulled tight across the windows, denying any flicker of moonlight from entering.

His toned back muscles flexed as he filled up a glass with amber liquid. Turning, he leaned against the table, eyes on me as he slowly brought the glass to his lips. I couldn't look away. It was like invisible hands held my head in place, forcing me to watch him. I hated it.

When finished, he put the glass down and gripped the edges of the table. "I have two questions."

"Only two?"

A hint of a smile played on his lips. "For now. How did you end up in my guard?"

"That's none of your business." I slapped a hand over my mouth, eyes widening. I was making this worse, but I couldn't control myself.

Amusement lit up his face. "Fair enough, it's your secret to keep." He tapped his finger against the wood. "Okay, second question. Why did you run from me during the ball?"

That was a question I wasn't expecting, and one I didn't particularly know the answer to. I released a deep breath. "If you're just playing with me before alerting the other guards of my deception, then please just get it over with." The not knowing was torturous.

He frowned. "What makes you think I have any intention of telling someone?"

My brows raised. "Why wouldn't you?"

"Perhaps I have more interest in keeping you as my own little secret." The corners of his lips curved up. "Can you tell me your name?"

I chewed my inner cheek. I wasn't sure I believed him fully, but he'd find out my name regardless of if I told him or not. "Wren Hibreaker," I said.

"Wren," he repeated. The sound of my name on his lips had my insides twisting in a heated manner. "What a uniquely beautiful name." He ran his fingers through messy hair. "I haven't been able to stop thinking about you, Wren."

"Yes, I'm sure watching as I threw myself from the sofa was quite memorable."

He smiled. "It was. It's not every day that I cause a girl to fall so ungracefully onto the floor. Or to run from me during the middle of a ball." I laughed, and his eyes brightened at the sound. "I've dreamt about you nearly every night since."

I arched a brow. "Well that's kind of creepy considering we only met once."

"Is it?" he asked, pushing off the desk. Everything about the way he moved was mesmerizing, like the rippling effect of water after a pebble disrupts the tranquility. "Here I was thinking you'd find it romantic."

"I told you in the library, romance isn't really my thing."

His throat bobbed at my words, the pulse in his neck speeding up. "I have another question. Well, more of an observation."

"Yes?"

"It was you that fired the arrow during archery practice, wasn't it?"

"I fired lots of arrows during practice," I said innocently. "You'll need to be more specific."

His eyes narrowed. "The one that nearly took my head off."

"Ah," I said. "Yes, I do remember that one. And if I remember correctly, you were foolishly standing in front of the target."

"Careful," he warned, although his voice was light with humor. "Or I might start to think you have it out for me."

"My eyes were closed. I didn't see you."

"Oh? Do you often fire arrows blindly?"

I flexed my fingers. "Not particularly, but it seems I'm just as talented without having to *see*. I doubt you can say the same."

He stepped closer. "Believe me, my talents in the dark are unmatched. Care to find out?"

I felt the heat rush to my cheeks as I moved back. *Damn him*. "Not at all."

He must have noticed the change in my demeanor as his smile faded. He sighed heavily. "You have my word, Wren. I'm not going to tell a soul about you."

"You could just be saying that. How do I—"

The words died on my lips as he lowered in front of me, sitting back on his heels. The prince was *kneeling* before me.

"You have me on my knees. I swear to you, I will not tell anyone about your secret. Is this enough?"

Why was he doing this? My voice was nothing more than a whisper as I asked, "Why?"

He pulled himself to his feet, towering over me now.

"Because you intrigue me." He said it as casually as stating the weather.

I blinked. "What? Why?" I knew I sounded like a fool repeating myself, but I was still too stunned from the sight of him on his knees moments before to form a coherent sentence.

"You're just... you're a breath of fresh air in this stuffy castle."

"You don't know me." *And if you knew the truth about me, I doubt you'd feel that way.*

"But I'd like to," he said. "You have piqued my interest in every way, Wren Hibreaker. I'd like to know more about you."

I backed up, putting several feet between us. "Even princes can't always get what they want," I said as I smoothed out my uniform.

He smirked, coming closer again. I was beginning to think he took every word I said as a challenge. He raised a hand to touch me, then lowered it. "Do this one thing for me. Please."

"I vowed my life to you. Is that not enough?"

"Not even close. I want to know you, and I want you to know me. I want you to look at me the way you did in the library before you knew I was the prince."

I wasn't sure why I agreed. Perhaps it was to end this conversation so I could leave, or maybe it was so he didn't go back on his word about keeping my secret. Or *maybe*, it was because a part of me wanted the same things he did. "Fine," I said after a moment.

His smile made the flames burn brighter, as if even they were delighted by this new agreement.

I put my headpiece on, and as I moved to the door, a

warning voice screamed in my mind that I was crossing a line. A dangerous line that couldn't be uncrossed.

"Wren?" Ryder's voice sliced through my thoughts.

Hand on the doorknob, I turned. "Yes?"

He smiled, and this time, with genuine gratitude. "Thanks for saving my life."

~

I watched from the large window in the main hall as Ryder took a morning ride the following day. His horse, Atri, was a beautiful, black thoroughbred. Ambrose rode beside him while three guards took up the rear. Their horses were slightly smaller than Atri but just as fast.

I returned to my room shortly after where Alicai and Zavier were waiting. Alicai hadn't said a word to me since last night, but I had a feeling the silent treatment was going to end now.

I clicked the door closed behind me and leaned against the cold wood. Exhaling a deep breath, I said, "He knows." There was nothing but tense silence for several moments, and I could all but *hear* the rage bubbling inside Alicai.

"Well that's just wonderful," he said calmly. *Too* calmly.

"Nothing happened. I think he just wants a friend," I replied. It wasn't a lie, just not fully the truth.

Alicai laughed bitterly. "Trust me, he doesn't want a *friend.* This is a game to him, and you're the new shiny prize. Once he beds you, he'll fix the sheets for the next girl that catches his eye." He pointed a finger at me. "I thought you were smarter."

I moved, fists clenched, when Zavier stopped me with a

gentle hand on my shoulder. "Leave her alone," he sternly said, gaze hardening on Alicai.

I didn't need Zavier to defend me, but I didn't push him away either. I tried to not let Alicai's words affect me, but I felt my chest tightening by the second. I thought about Ryder sitting on his bed like it was an open invitation. No. *No.* It seemed to be more than that. He wouldn't go through all this trouble for something so fleeting. Once I was certain I wouldn't wrap my hands around Alicai's throat, I stepped away from Zavier.

"Don't question what I'm doing in order to survive," I spat. "I'll do what I have to do to keep any of this from getting out. Think what you want, Alicai, but you're wrong. And don't you *dare* question my intelligence."

His amber eyes flicked between us both before he huffed out a humorless laugh, throwing his arms out wide. "When this ends badly, you'll see. I refuse to be dragged down with a sinking ship because you've got some crush on the prince. Anyone else, Wren. Literally *anyone* else. But no, you choose the one person that could have us all hanging with the snap of his fingers."

"Alicai," Zavier warned.

"Don't." I put a hand on Zavier's arm, but my eyes were trained on Alicai. "There is *nothing* happening between Ryder and me, and he's not going to tell anyone. I trusted you both, now it's your turn to trust me."

"I trust you, Wren," Zavier said.

But it wasn't his admittance I was waiting on. Alicai stared at me for a long while before shaking his head. "I won't go down with a sinking ship," he repeated before leaving the room.

I stepped forward, but Zavier stopped me. "Let him cool off," he said. "He'll be fine. He's a hothead, you know."

Oh, did I know.

Zavier left shortly after to go to the healers' sanctuary, most likely to see Tavrina. With my free time, I headed back to the gardens. Specifically, to the spot where I saw the Faceling. While most of the flowers here had the sweetest fragrance, the white roses reeked of death and decay. It reminded me of Morters' End. Of *home.* Strange that a place I hated so strongly could still carry that title.

A part of me hoped to see the Faceling again so it could explain its riddle and maybe offer up some information on *why* Ryder was being hunted. Or maybe, the selfish part of me wanted to see Angel's face again. Even if it wasn't really him.

As the sun drifted, morning shifting into afternoon, the Faceling didn't show. Dark, gray clouds crept across the sky, and with the first crackle of thunder, I headed back into the castle.

CHAPTER 25

"Someone better start speaking, or heads are going to roll."

I tensed at the king's harsh words and unforgiving tone. Apparently, during the middle of the night, the would-be assassin took his own life. And given the blood vessels bulging from the king's head, he clearly wasn't pleased.

Ryder was seated at a mahogany table that was brought into the throne room, and although I stood against the wall behind him, I could see the ghostly look on his face through the gilded mirror across the room.

Captain Blanning fidgeted in his seat at the other side of the table. "The guards who were stationed outside his cell can confirm no one entered or left. Not once." He grimaced. "The prisoner had stitches on his inner right thigh. From the amount of blood in the cell, it was clear he tore them open to get this." He paused, lifting a pine green needle so thin, I squinted to see it. "He poisoned himself," Blanning added, dropping it onto the table.

The king rested his chin on his fist. His expression was unreadable, but if I had to guess, I'd say he was picturing Blanning's head on a pike.

"What in *Hell* is that?" Duke Halorast asked. The middle-aged man in charge of foreign affairs leaned forward in his seat beside Ryder.

Blanning began to respond when the commander rose from his chair, cutting him off. "Never heard of the prindleberry bush before, Halorast?"

The duke shook his head, shoulder length white hair moving slightly. "It's native to the Feros Mountains of Enderya," Bekencourt said, holding up the needle. "While the fruit that grows on the bush is harmless, you have to watch out for the needles. One simple prick causes a full body paralysis that stops the heart."

Lord Winward, the king's advisor, gasped as Bekencourt drove the needle into his own hand. I wished he'd drop dead on the spot, but unfortunately, he remained unharmed.

Bekencourt laughed as he flicked the needle back to the captain. "Funny thing is, the needle only ejects one dose of poison. After the initial prick, it's as harmless as the fruit it grows beside."

"And how exactly do you know so much about a plant that grows in enemy territory, Commander?" Halorast asked.

Bekencourt smiled. "I make a habit of knowing everything I can about our enemies. Perhaps it's something you'd consider adopting, given your title."

Halorast clamped his mouth shut.

"What a terrible way to die," Ryder said as he examined the needle, surprisingly chipper for someone who was almost killed twice.

Something coated the king's face as he glared at his son, but it was gone as he turned back to Blanning. "I want the body burned and not a word of this getting out. Rumors and fear spread like wildfire, and I don't need the people of this kingdom panicking over who's behind these attacks."

"But, Your Majesty," Winward blurted. "This is now their second attempt. I've said it before, and I'll say it again. This is all but declaring war. Lucio *must* be informed so he can prepare units. An act of such magnitude cannot go unpunished. If they've managed to breach the castle, we should be evacuating immediately, and the people need to be warned that the Kindrahs have attacked. Who's to say they won't start infiltrating the city? The people should be given the chance to protect themselves in advance."

I stiffened. I'd had a feeling after yesterday that it was the Kindrahs who were responsible for the slaughter of Ryder's old guards, but this confirmed it.

"They seem to be interested in only one person," Bekencourt said, eyes trained on Ryder. "And until we figure out why our prince is the target of this twisted game, the information should remain classified."

I didn't miss the look Blanning shot at the king, as if there was something he was urging him to say, but the king grunted in agreement. "There is no reason to stir up mass hysteria. Evacuating sends a message of fear, so we will be staying put. We must demonstrate a united front, therefore this stays between the members of this room and the guards."

Winward's head darted back and forth as if he couldn't quite believe what he was hearing. I also couldn't believe the laid-back attitude of not only the king, but the commander as well.

"What about the commoners who were in the room when the prince was attacked? They heard what was said," Halorast added. "We *all* did."

"How many had gotten through the doors at the time?" the king asked.

"Four, Your Majesty," Bekencourt replied.

The king nodded. "Have the guards track them down. Bring them in and lock them up. Charge them with whatever crimes you deem necessary to prevent their neighbors and friends from asking questions."

Blanning raised a brow. "Life threatening charges?"

"We must do what is necessary," the king answered.

He would do anything to conceal these attacks... but why? And why was no one questioning the motivations behind them? I didn't understand. I also didn't know enough about the Kindrahs as a whole to piece together my own theories.

I looked through the mirror at Ryder. He was still, a distant look in his eyes as if he were somewhere else entirely. I wanted to be where he was.

"And what are we supposed to do now?" Blanning asked, frustrated as he glanced at the prince. There was a fatherly love in the way he looked at Ryder. Love, and deep-rooted, unyielding loyalty. I guess after everything they'd seen and gone through together, it made sense. Just from one quick glance, I knew he cared for Ryder more than the king ever had. It made my chest tighten.

"The Kindrahs will keep coming," Blanning went on. "Are we supposed to do nothing?" His eyes were pleading with the king, and I couldn't shake the feeling there was a deeper meaning.

The king was stern, testing. "No, Captain. What we're

going to do is wait. When they inevitably try again, I want them captured." He gave no explanation on *how* they would capture them, but I had a feeling it would involve Drestel and Pryler.

That answer didn't seem good enough for the captain, but with one look at the king, he stood down.

"And you," the king said sharply, eyes drifting to his son. Unspoken words flowed between them, and I sensed Ryder go rigid. "You go absolutely nowhere without guards from here on out. *Nowhere*. Am I clear?"

Ryder lifted his head, ocean eyes meeting mine through the mirror. "Crystal."

"What do I get out of this?" I asked from the chaise in Ryder's room that night. "I'm not answering your questions and getting nothing in return."

He looked up from his spot on the floor, back pressed to the wall beside the fireplace. "You can ask me whatever you like."

"What makes you think I care to know anything about you?"

He grinned. "Oh come on, you're not fooling anyone. Look me in the eyes and tell me you haven't thought about kissing me since that night in the library." My cheeks flushed traitorously, causing his grin to widen. "We can give it another go if you'd like."

I tried to ignore what the thought of kissing him did to me. I'd never admit it, but I did wonder what it would be like. I wondered if he'd taste like the burnt sugar I smelt every time he was near. I wondered if he'd be gentle or claiming and rough. From the looks of him, I assumed it'd be the latter.

I needed to stop. These thoughts were dangerous. I was already way over the line by associating with him on a friendly level but fantasizing about him? I had to keep my focus on my long-term goals. I couldn't afford distractions like this. Especially when he was being targeted for unknown reasons that I was now determined to figure out. Because if he died, what would happen to his guards? There'd be no chance to free Angel and Mama. I *needed* Ryder to live for my own benefit.

There may have also been a part of me that wanted him to live because I was starting to care for him. I refused to fully admit that to myself though. Instead, I pulled my hair over my shoulder in attempts to cool off my heated neck. I heard Alicai pacing outside the door, simmering with anger.

Ryder thought he was the only one who knew my secret. And as we sat there, his eyes glued to me as if I was the perfect challenge, I knew he wouldn't rest until he pried *all* my secrets. Or died trying.

"I think I'll pass on that offer," I said with a smile. "But since you've agreed to answer my questions, why are the Kindrahs trying to kill you?"

He coughed. "Starting with the easy ones I see."

"That's not an answer."

"Do you think if I knew why, we'd still be dealing with this?"

I shifted, crossing one leg over the other. "Well why is no one trying to figure it out or asking questions? Am I the only one who doesn't understand their motivations?"

Ryder sighed. "You're not the only one. And that was more than one question. It's my turn now."

I noted how quickly he dismissed the topic, stashing it in my thoughts for later. "Go ahead," I insisted.

He extended a leg, resting an arm on his bent knee. "What are you running from?"

His question caught me by surprise. "I'm not sure I know what you mean."

"You went through all this trouble tricking everyone into believing you're someone who you're not. *And* you joined the guard." He cocked his head to the side. "You're running from something. I want to know what."

Just like that, my insides turned to ice as my defense mode kicked in. "I'm not running from *anything*. Maybe I wasn't interested in living a boring life. Maybe I didn't want to get married and have children just to stay home all day cleaning up after them and my fat husband with an alcohol problem."

His lips curved into a smirk, left dimple showing. "Are you telling me you have a fat, alcoholic husband and children?" He whistled, leaning his head back. "And here I was thinking I was pursuing a single woman."

I rolled my eyes. "No, I'm not married, and I don't have children. It was an example. And you aren't pursuing me, you're just a hopeless flirt who can't help himself."

He frowned slightly, as if my words stung. "It's your turn, ask away."

I contemplated pushing him further about the attacks, but I didn't think strolling down memory lane, reminiscing on his dead guards was something he'd be eager to do.

Instead, I asked, "Do you actually like Ambrose? Or are you forced to spend time with him because of his father's relationship with the king."

"Ambrose?" He seemed genuinely puzzled. "That's a random question."

I shrugged. "You two are nothing alike. He's a self-centered *ass*, and you're—"

"I'm what?" he teased, tapping his boot against the carpeted floor. "Because I can finish that line with a few thoughts of my own."

"I changed my mind," I replied. "You're also an ass."

He leaned forward, challenging me. "Would you rather speak about body parts? Or do you want me to answer your question. Honestly, I'm okay with either."

My cheeks heated instantly. "Answer the question."

"Shame, I was hoping you'd pick the other option." He dragged his gaze over me slowly, a cocky grin on his face. "Ambrose wasn't always this way. Granted, he's always been full of himself, but he wasn't always so—"

"Obnoxious?" I cut in.

Ryder laughed. "We were born two months apart, so I guess we've been friends since birth." He looked down at his clasped hands. "Our mothers were also close friends. Lydia died about six years ago during childbirth. Losing his mother and baby brother in the same hour took something from him. His father has never been... *warm,* and with the absence of Lydia, Ambrose became a miniature version of him."

Ryder looked... regretful. As if for some reason, he blamed himself for how his friend turned out.

"He started doing horrible things," he continued. "Lying to girls and robbing them of their virtues. He makes sure every suitor knows it too, so the girls are undesirable and ruined. He starts fights almost every night at the taverns and brothels, claiming no one can do anything about it because of who his father is. I've tried to talk to him. Tried to bring him back to the Ambrose I learned to ride horses and climb trees with. The Ambrose who was too shy to kiss a girl for the first time, I had to kiss her first to give him the courage."

He brought both knees up to his chest, resting his forearms across them. "But it wasn't just that. Ambrose pretty much grew up in the castle with me. And growing up in a place where everything is given, you start taking what you have for granted. I'd like to think I never lost sight of that, but he did."

"You feel responsible for him." It was more of a statement than a question.

"In a way, yes," he replied.

None of this changed my opinion on Ambrose. If anything, it made me despise him more, seeing how Ryder hurt over him. We all lost people. We all had trials and hardships. I watched Papa get brutally murdered. Ryder watched his entire unit of guards die. Loss was loss, and while I did feel bad about Ambrose's mother and brother, it wasn't a reason for him to be an awful human being.

Ryder cleared his throat. "What's your favorite memory?"

"I don't have any," I said instantly.

"Everyone has memories."

"I don't have any favorite ones," I clarified.

He stood up and sat on the other side of the chaise which suddenly felt too small. He draped an arm over the back, studying me. "I don't believe you."

I picked at a loose string on my uniform. I didn't know how far I wanted to go with the truth, but without realizing it, a memory surfaced. Guilt coated my chest as I recalled sitting at the cliff edge near the old greenhouse with Asher a few years ago. We'd been looking up at the stars as the waves crashed against the jagged rocks below. It was one of those nights where I so desperately craved *more.* I wanted to touch the stars, to feel the light from them against my face. I didn't know how Asher did it, but he managed to pull one of them from the sky. He'd held it in the palms of his hands as it blinked and flickered, the light so bright I had to shield my face.

He couldn't hold it for long, the power of the star too strong for him to contain. Eventually, it flew from his hands and retook its place in the night sky as if it had never left. When I looked beside me, Asher was gone.

It was a month and six days before I saw him again after that. The energy it took for him to obtain the star completely drained him, sending him off somewhere I couldn't find. I never let him do anything like that again for the fear of losing him forever. But even then, I didn't forget what he did for me. The lengths he'd gone to make me happy. Thinking of those times fractured a part of my heart as I knew it would never be that way again. We might be bound, but we couldn't be further apart.

"Wren?"

I jumped at the sound of Ryder's voice. I must have zoned out as he was now sitting closer to me, his thumb rubbing away the stray tear that was falling down my cheek. "I'm sorry, I didn't mean to make you upset," he said.

I shook my head. "It's not you, I just—" I couldn't tell him about Asher, so I went for the only other person that would warrant such emotion from me. "I was thinking of my brother, that's all."

Ryder watched me intently, his hand still resting against

my cheek. I wanted to lean into it. Lean into the feeling of him. "Do you miss him?"

"Every day," I said.

He stretched out a leg. "You know, I never did ask you where you came from."

I could feel my pulse jump at his words. It was only a matter of time before he asked. "A place much less luxurious than this," I said. "I really don't want to talk about it."

He nodded, always so understanding. I then made the mistake of looking at his lips.

"*Wren*." He said my name again, but this time it was more of a warning growl. My eyes darted up to meet his which were now a shade darker. "You need to stop looking at me like that." He gripped my chin, and I could tell he was fighting something within himself.

I swallowed. "Like what?"

Three knocks sounded at the door. Alicai's signal our rotation was switching. Was I really in here that long? I sprang up from the chaise, putting as much space between us as possible while I tugged on my headpiece.

He was breathing heavily, as if he'd been holding his breath the last few moments. I felt hot, my pulse pounding throughout my entire body. Too close. That was way too close.

I was pulling open the door when Ryder said, "Thanks for the company." I glanced back, noticing now how the shadows of the dark room intensified the circles under his eyes. The stain of sleepless nights. I hoped tonight sleep would find him.

CHAPTER 26

I rolled my shoulders as I stepped out of Captain Blanning's office. We were all required to give weekly reports regarding any concerns we had for the prince, our own rotation schedule, and our performance. It was one of my most dreaded parts of the week. I respected our captain immensely. Would even go so far as to say I liked him, but being alone with him made me ten times more paranoid he would discover my secret. It wasn't the same as being in a room with the other guards where he could easily focus on someone else. No, during our reports, it was me and the captain. That was it. So far I'd done well at keeping up my ruse, considering I was still here.

I was definitely growing into this role, but I still had to remind myself that one small misstep and everything would be over.

Fortunately, it seemed Blanning was distracted lately. Sometimes I forgot that he was just as affected by the previous assassination attempt as Ryder. The captain lost all his men. Men he'd trained and stood by for years, all gone in the same day.

Blanning had a distant look in his eyes, and when he replied to my statements and questions, his answers were slow and scrambled, as if someone shook him upside down, jumbling his thoughts together.

Once I finished my report, I was dismissed and was now trying to find Ryder. My rotation started ten minutes ago, but my meeting had gone overtime.

I found him a few minutes later in the hall of windows, which was exactly what it sounded like. The ceiling, floor, and walls were all constructed of thick glass. He loved it here. He loved the blood pumping feeling that something could go wrong at any given moment. I realized that three days ago when he showed me the secret tunnel from his bedroom to the west wing of the castle. The passageway opened up behind a patch of cerulean forget-me-nots.

Initially, I tensed at the thought of him sneaking out. I wondered if anyone else knew about it and if I should tell someone. Then my mind spun in a different direction that had a twinge of unwarranted jealousy rushing through me. What if this was a tunnel he used to sneak in late night companions? I wasn't with him *every* night so who knew what he did?

I wouldn't put it past him, seeing as Ryder was a free spirit. He liked to tread along the edge, pushing the boundaries and bending the rules. It made me wonder if that was why he'd taken a liking to *me*.

It was a similar thrill to walking on glass, I assumed. I probably would've liked it here too, if I didn't know about the section that shattered last year, sending one of the servants plummeting to his death. His body was found cracked open, bleeding on the stones below. It was safe to say I had a newfound fear of heights.

I pushed down that fear as I caught up to Ryder and Kai. Ryder must have sensed me approach as he glanced over his shoulder, a smirk spreading across his sinful lips. I wished he'd stop looking at me like that.

We passed a group of young courtiers, each one more ridiculously glamoured up than the last. The bodices of their gowns were so tight, it was shocking their breasts hadn't fully slipped out. I rolled my eyes as they batted their lashes when Ryder greeted them.

They giggled like idiots, fanning themselves as their gazes raked over him slowly. They were probably picturing what he looked like under those clothes. It took all the restraint I had not to shove them through the glass.

Thankfully, he left it at that. As their giggles and whispers faded out behind me, I wondered *why* I was so bothered by the way they looked at him. Everyone looked at him. Servants, eligible courtiers, even those who were married. It didn't matter who it was, they all looked at Ryder in a way that said, *I'd face any punishment for a moment alone with you.*

And why wouldn't they feel that way? Ryder was absolutely beautiful. Looking at him felt like being drunk on sunshine, and while I had no claim to him, I couldn't push down the undiluted rage that surfaced whenever a beautiful girl looked at him. I hated myself for it.

I was so lost in thought, I didn't realize he stopped until I almost walked into him. We stood in front of the games room, and when I saw *why* we stopped, my rage began bubbling again.

Ambrose was leaning against the wall, and he wasn't alone. Lorzo, the son of Duke Halorast, and Garrick, one of Ryder's distant cousins, stood beside him. Who I didn't recognize, was the blonde girl standing between them. She looked like she stepped out of a painting with porcelain smooth skin and brown doe eyes. Even her nose was curved in the most perfect of ways, leading down to red full lips. Her lavender and gold tea gown exposed just enough cleavage to have Ambrose drooling.

"Where the hell have you been?" A wide grin took over Ambrose's face as he threw an arm over Ryder.

"I've been *here*," Ryder emphasized. "Where have *you* been?"

Ambrose waved a lazy hand through the air. "Accompanying my father on one of his business endeavors. Wouldn't want to bore you with the details."

Garrick eyed Ryder warily. "Are you doing alright? I haven't seen you since before the... well, you know."

A muscle in Ryder's jaw twitched. "I'm fine. Just trying to stay alive," he teased. I knew some people needed to find humor in their trauma so they didn't lose it completely, but seeing it come from Ryder was strange.

Garrick also seemed to notice it and was about to reply when Ambrose interrupted. "Gisella was just asking about you. I told her you've been fairly busy, isn't that right?" His words were rigid as he raised a brow to Ryder, a silent question passing between them.

I looked at the girl again. So *this* was Gisella. She curtsied, bending low. "I've missed your company, Your Highness. I hope you've been well."

"The best I've ever been," Ryder replied.

She frowned. "Are you sure?" She reached out a gloved hand, running her fingers over the bare skin of his wrist in slow, flirtatious circles. "You know, I'm always available if you want to talk about it."

"There's nothing to talk about," Ryder said. "I was almost killed, and my guards were slaughtered. There's really nothing else to say."

Gisella's eyes widened to the size of the moon, and I almost choked at his bluntness. It was then that I realized none of his friends knew about the second attack during the Bringing. I wondered how difficult it was to keep that information to himself.

"Ryder, I'm so sorry," Gisella said. Her voice was so polished and elegant, it had to be rehearsed. "How have they not caught those horrible men yet? I hope they're each hanged for their awful crimes." She wiped at her eyes. "You poor, poor thing."

She had no idea what she was talking about. But then again, most people throughout the kingdom didn't even know about the attack, still believing his former guards were dismissed.

Ryder had clearly told his friends the truth, but by the way he appeared wholly done with this conversation, I could tell he was regretting it. "I'm fine, really. Still in one piece."

"You know Ryder," Ambrose said dryly. "Always the center of attention." Was he kidding me? I wished I had one of those prindleberry needles right now.

Ryder only shrugged. "You know me."

Lorzo raised a brow as he looked between Ambrose and Ryder. It seemed a silent game was being played here. Although, from the uninterested gleam in the prince's eye, he didn't seem eager to play.

"You shouldn't say such horrible things!" Gisella said, swatting Ambrose with her hand. "What a terrible thing you must have gone through, Your Highness. It's both a blessing and a curse to be as handsome as you, since it clearly drives lesser men to do unforgiveable things."

Oh, that was it. I couldn't help the fit of laughter that slipped out. Kai shot me a look that said, *What the hell are you doing?* Garrick appeared surprised but amused, Lorzo looked like he would rather be anywhere else, Ambrose was still gazing down Gisella's dress, and Gisella... she was red with anger as she took me in.

"Is something about this funny to you?" She pushed past Ryder who was on the verge of laughter himself. "After everything that happened, you should have a little more respect and understand how important your position is." Her gaze drifted to Ryder. "The prince is truly something to be protected."

"Oh, I understand my position," I stated, unable to keep my mouth shut. "But I'm struggling to understand yours. If you're trying to come off as obsessive and desperate, you're doing a fantastic job."

Kai gaped at me as Gisella gasped. Before another word could be uttered, she turned on her heels and stormed off down the hall. Ambrose quickly followed, and as much as I didn't like the girl, the thought of him taking advantage of her vulnerability made me want to kill him even more.

Garrick and Lorzo left a few moments later with Kai, who Ryder asked to accompany them. Kai hesitated as he weighed the risks of disobeying the prince or Blanning, ultimately deciding on the latter.

When the two of us were alone, Ryder turned to me. "That wasn't very nice."

"Sincerest apologies, Your Highness," I said as I bowed obnoxiously low.

He hooked his finger through the front of my weapons belt, drawing me closer. I inhaled sharply at the sudden movement and how his gaze lowered to my lips.

Realizing *where* we were, I shoved out of his grasp, adjusting my uniform. "Do you think this is all a big joke?"

His brows scrunched. "What?"

"Whatever you're doing." I gestured between us. "You're putting me at risk of getting caught. It might be all fun and games for you, but this is life or death for me. What do you think will happen if they find out?"

Ryder stilled. "No one is going to find out. I swore to you. I went to my *knees* for you."

"Just because you don't verbally tell anyone doesn't mean these little actions of yours won't get me caught. You need to stop touching me."

The corners of his lips twitched. "I quite like when you order me around. Of course, I'd like it more in a different setting, but this will do." He smiled wickedly. "For now."

I ignored his words and what they did to me as I began scanning the hall.

"What are you doing?" he asked.

"Waiting for Kai to return so I can get away from you."

"You'd abandon your station so easily?"

My eyes narrowed. "Don't test me."

"And where exactly do you plan on going once you leave me?"

"Outside." There was a door to the right that opened to a set of cascading white steps leading to the garden.

"Well it just so happens I'm now in the mood for some fresh air too," he said as he pushed the door open, stuffing his hands in his pockets. "Join me?"

As if I had a choice.

CHAPTER 27

The gardens were more crowded than usual for this time, and each person we passed looked at Ryder as if they were gazing upon a god. A wealthy merchant from Reysitte, the city at the base of the Haldro Mountains, dropped to his hands and knees, kissing the ground in front of us like an imbecile.

"You must find this all absolutely ridiculous," Ryder said as we made our way into the less congested hedge maze.

"No, not at all."

He angled his head as if to say, *Oh, please*.

"Alright," I sighed. "It's the most ridiculous thing I've ever seen. That man actually *kissed* the ground. Do you think he swallowed some gravel?"

Ryder laughed, and I felt the tension from our previous conversation evaporate. "It's strange, most people don't even react that way when they see my brother. And he's the one who's going to be king someday."

We moved to the side as several priests shuffled by, brown

robes skimming the dirt. "You and Lucio seem pretty close," I pointed out as we continued our stroll. "I'm assuming the rumors of why his engagement fell through weren't accurate."

He rubbed the back of his neck. "When you told me in the library that people thought *I* was the reason…" He shook his head. "I told Lucio about it, and he couldn't stop laughing."

I remembered Ryder whispering to his brother the night of the ball, both of them laughing to the point of tears in their eyes. "You told him after we met."

"I don't think he's ever laughed so hard." He glanced at me with a lazy grin. "So thanks for the entertainment."

I tapped a finger against the hilt of my sword. "Why did they end their engagement then?"

Ryder looked ahead as we rounded a corner of magnolia bushes. His curls were wind tossed, and I wondered if they were as soft as they looked.

Stop it, I scolded myself.

"Let's just say Lorianna prefers a more feminine touch in her bed."

Oh. *Oh.* "Does her father know that?" Surely as the King of Tryfel, he'd want his daughter to make an advantageous marriage. I couldn't imagine ending their engagement went over well.

"I'm not sure," Ryder replied. "Lorianna and Lucio have been friends since they were wetting the bed. I think it would've been strange if they married. Like marrying a sibling. All I know is that a few months ago, he went to Tryfel without telling our father, and they officially ended the engagement. Lucio never told me what reasons they gave, but whatever it was didn't cause any division between our kingdoms."

I wondered how the king reacted to his heir going against him like that. I looked down as I kicked a loose stone. "And the people..."

Ryder faced me again, and I noticed for the first time tiny specks of silver floating around his deep blue irises. I'd never seen a color like them. "You know what they think." He winked, an arrogant smirk plastered on his face.

I rolled my eyes. "Right. The troublesome brother couldn't keep it in his pants and ruined everything." I cut him a sidelong glance. "Sound accurate?"

"I love that mouth of yours."

"I don't see the point in sugar coating things."

"Trust me, I've noticed." He extended his hand, ushering me ahead as we exited the maze. "I have a feeling you'd love the Iron Oak."

"What's that?" I asked.

His eyebrow arched upward. "You've been here over a month, and you haven't been to the Iron Oak?" He seemed genuinely baffled. "What do you do when you're not on rotation?"

"Clearly I don't go to the Iron Oak," I said. "What is it?"

"One of the more discredited taverns in the city. You've probably passed it, it's right beside—"

"Ah, and there lies the problem. I haven't been to Caelestis yet." I stopped, narrowing my eyes at him. "And should I be insulted you think I'd *love* a place like that?"

He ignored the question. "You haven't been to the city? We'll have to fix that right away."

I laughed as we resumed walking. "Let me guess, you're going to be the one to take me?"

"If you'd like."

I snorted. "I think it would spark more rumors if you strolled into the city hand in hand with your guard."

His eyes locked onto mine. "Who said anything about holding hands?" I felt my cheeks burning up. He grinned, stepping closer. "But I'm really enjoying how flustered the idea of it's making you."

"I'm not flustered."

"You're getting redder by the second."

I was about to say how red *his* face would be when I slapped him, prince or not, when I got the feeling we were being watched. It wasn't until now that I realized where we were. The water was pouring down the fountain like falling shards of glass when I spotted it.

"Wren?" Ryder nudged me, but I couldn't look away as the Faceling watched me through my brother's eyes. A slow, sinister smile crept across its lips.

"Wren, what is it?" A firm hand gripped mine. I couldn't even move to tell him *this* was exactly what I was talking about. Actions like this would get me caught.

I was frozen as the Faceling walked around the fountain, stopping close enough for me to see it clearly. The hairs on the back of my neck stood up as it raised a finger to its lips.

Ryder dropped my hand and grabbed my shoulders, turning me to face him. "Are you alright? What just happened?"

The Faceling didn't move, arms slack at its side. "You don't see that?" I asked.

Tender fingers gripped my chin, turning my head. "See what?"

When I didn't respond, Ryder moved his hand to my cheek, rubbing his thumb up and down the little bit of skin available beneath the headpiece. "Hey," he said softly, eyes glazed over with concern. "Talk to me."

I tilted my head toward the fountain, only to find the Faceling was gone. My confusion was followed by panic as a piercing scream echoed through the gardens.

Ryder dropped his hand, and we ran.

I ran so quickly I thought my heart was going to explode. Gods, *why* were these gardens so massive? I'd always been a fast runner, but Ryder was faster. He shot past me only to slow down as we came upon a hidden alcove under a canopy of draping vines.

I was going to kill him for this if Blanning didn't kill me first. Ryder ran toward the screaming without hesitation. What if it was a trap? Or another attempt on his life? Sometimes he was so careless, I questioned his sanity.

All my anger quickly vanished at the sight of a body sprawled out on the gravel. The lifeless form of a young girl. A child, too young to be dead. There was a woman beside her, weeping as she clawed at the girl's dress. As if she was reaching for any trace of remaining life.

But there wasn't any left. I watched numbly as the woman was hauled back by guards. She kicked, screamed, and begged while she was dragged from the gardens into the confines of the castle. The door closed on her screams, and I felt like I was suffocating. The entire concept of breathing seemed foreign to me as Tavrina and two other healers carried the girl's limp body away.

At some point during the chaos, Ryder was escorted inside by Kai, Sanyulin, and another guard named Brax, who all happened to be close enough to hear the screams. I couldn't move. Not as the gardens cleared out or as the sun began setting. The first droplets of rain were what finally had me dragging my feet back into the castle.

I couldn't get the image of the girl out of my head. Of her fiery red hair sprawled around her like a crown of flames. Or the stillness of her body. Of her chest that would never rise and fall again.

There weren't any wounds or blood, and aside from her weeping mother, no one else seemed remotely surprised. As if the sight of a dead child was a common occurrence. I couldn't wrap my brain around it as I walked into the common room. I found the off-duty guards gathered around the fire, tipping back mugs of ale, laughing and singing. None of them knew what happened, and none of them noticed me. Alicai and Zavier were on night rotation, so with nothing keeping me, I hurried to our room.

I knew he was there before the door clicked shut. I paused, waiting for him to make himself known as the light from the candle in the sconce flickered, the wax nearly melted down to the end of the wick.

I sucked in a sharp breath as a hand snuck around my waist, pulling my back roughly into something firm and cold. His chest. *No heartbeat*, I reminded myself. He nudged my head, exposing the left side of my neck and pressed his lips to my skin. He left a trail of kisses from my ear to my collarbone, marking me as his.

No, my mind screamed. *Enough.*

I twisted from his grip, reaching for Papa's dagger tucked under my shirt. I saw the surprise in Asher's eyes as I slammed him against the door, blade to his throat.

"If getting on your bad side means ending up in this position, remind me to do it more often," he said, grinning like he took some kind of sadistic pleasure from this. I knew I couldn't hurt him, but my dagger glimmering against his flawless skin did something to me.

Asher was beautiful in the way things often were when they were dead, like lovely pressed flowers. He was a boy frozen in time. A kiss of death, and when I was with him it felt like plunging into the depths of an uncharted sea. Dangerous, exhilarating, and wild.

He moved faster than I could anticipate, knocking the blade from my hand and pinning the front of my body against the wall. I struggled, but his grip was firm and unyielding as he pressed himself into me from behind. His lips brushed my ear. "This position's not so bad either."

"Let go of me," I spat.

A moment later, I was free, rubbing at my wrists as I shot him daggers with my eyes. Satisfied, he dropped down onto my bed, watching as I took off my weapon belt and hung it over the hook on the wall. "I saw the Faceling again."

Asher sat up straight. "What happened?" he asked flatly.

"Nothing. One second it was there, the next it was gone. Then there was a scream, and a girl was dead." I picked at the skin beside my fingernail. "Do you know anything about it?"

"Why would I?"

I sighed, sitting down beside him. "I don't know, it's just... there was nothing wrong with her. She looked like she was in a deep sleep."

"Necromancy."

My head spun. "What?"

He ran a chilled finger down my leg, his hair hanging like a cascading waterfall of liquid midnight. "You've only seen the side of necromancy that brings someone back to life. That girl you saw? That was the price."

A life for a life.

He didn't stop there. "Someone in Morters' End must've died, and the necromancers brought them back." He brushed the back of his hand down my cheek. It felt like the remaining traces of a fever dream. "You know how it works, Wren."

"But she was a *child*," I stated.

He shook his head. "It doesn't matter. They can't choose who pays the price. It could've been anyone. It could've been you."

I swatted him away, and he stood up, leaning against the wall. "You have to admit, there's something wonderfully dreadful about death. Don't you think?"

His words were nothing more than background noise to my thoughts. My mind was reeling as I recalled every dead body the necromancers brought back over the years. It was one thing to know what would happen but another entirely to see the aftermath of necromancy firsthand. I groaned as I thought of Henry Yuller's stupid face. Why did he deserve to be brought back? No one *made* him go near the Morta Forest. What happened to him was his own doing. Why did he get to live again when someone else had to die?

"Why does the king even let the necromancers live?" I asked. "I understand containing them, but if their actions are the cause of death for so many outside the shield, why not just take them out?"

Asher scoffed. "You can't just 'take them out'. The necromancers are far too powerful, and the only ones who could match them would be the Estelers. Even then, I can't see their golden little magic tricks doing much damage."

"Well, the Estelers did manage to trap them. I wouldn't underestimate their *golden little magic tricks* if I were you."

His returning smile held something I couldn't place. "Perhaps *you* underestimate the necromancers," he said. "You've only seen a fraction of their abilities. And they have the power of numbers. It would take more than just Drestel and Pryler to bring them down."

I swung my leg. "So the necromancers win. They can keep doing whatever they want while innocent people die."

Asher didn't reply, so I let my thoughts stir for another minute. If there were other Estelers somewhere, how could they just sit back while all of these evil acts were committed? How far would things have to fall before they intervened?

"What were you doing in the gardens?" Asher asked, interrupting me.

"What?" I was standing now, pacing back and forth. "I was with Ryder. We were—"

I slammed into Asher's chest. He steadied me, and as I looked into his eyes, I found something resembling... anger? "Why were you out for a stroll with the prince alone?"

I stepped back. "I'm his guard. He's not meant to be by himself."

"Guards don't engage or have flirtatious conversations." Asher inched closer, and I had the strangest sense of déjà vu as I moved back. "Guards don't hold hands or blush or—"

"Asher." My voice was surprisingly steady. "Are you *jealous*?" Just the thought of it was absurd, but from the tight lips and sour expression, I didn't know what else it could be. Then again, to be jealous required feelings, and Asher felt nothing for me besides a desperate need to complete our deal.

He cocked his head. "Answer the question."

"Do you hear how ridiculous you sound? Why do you care what I was doing?"

"I will *always* care what you're doing." He said it with as much certainty as if he were pointing out the sky was blue. "And because in case you've forgotten, you still have your end of the covenant to fulfill."

"As if you'd let me forget," I spat.

He grabbed my wrist as I tried to turn. "The prince is quite an interesting choice for you. I must say, I didn't think you had it in you." He sounded so bitter, so full of resentment.

I tore my arm free. "I didn't *choose* him for anything. Especially not your ridiculous covenant."

"It wasn't so ridiculous when I saved your mother, was it?" He clenched a fist, resembling what I imagined the center of a storm to be. "You think I don't know of your secret meetings with him? Of the nights you spend huddled around the fire, pretending you don't want *more*?"

I swallowed, backing up until my legs hit the edge of my bed. I tripped, falling onto my back. Asher moved as gracefully as dancing shadows, slowly lowering his body over mine. I knew he'd never force himself on me, never take anything I didn't offer, and that steadied some part of my racing heart.

"Do you think I don't see the way he looks at you when you're unaware?" He brushed the hair off my forehead. "He looks at you like he wants to *devour you whole*."

"Is that any better than how you look at me?" I shot back. "You would eat my heart out then convince me I made you do it."

His lips skimmed over my ear as he whispered, "And you'd enjoy every second of it." He pulled away, bright eyes glowing like stars in a dark sky. We stayed that way, staring at each other. Two lovers, friends, enemies.

"Whatever you think is happening with the prince, you're wrong." Even as I said it, I tasted the lie. But I wouldn't admit it. Never. Not to myself and certainly not to Asher. "But you do *need* me to fall in love." I clicked my tongue and smiled, only aggravating him more. "Seems someone doesn't like sharing."

He bent down, wrapping his hand around my throat. "You're mine, even if I lose you for a while to another. Because when all is said and done, that'll be the one fact that remains. You'll always be mine."

"What if I choose not to hold up my end?"

"We've been over this, Wren," he said. "One doesn't have a choice where love is concerned. But you'd be wise not to test me. I've been patient, but patience only lasts so long when you're dead."

CHAPTER 28

A commotion in the common room pulled me from bed the following morning. With eyes still full of sleep, I tried to focus my blurry vision on Zavier who jolted upright at the noise. Alicai's bed was empty.

"What the heck is going on?" Zavier groaned as he began dressing himself.

"Guess we're about to find out." I headed into the bathing room to change into uniform. After I secured the headpiece down and clicked on my weapons belt, I stepped aside as Zavier closed the main door behind us.

We were hurrying down the hall, Zavier on my heels, when I stopped short, causing him to ram into my back. The guards were filtering in and out of the room from the main hallway, a combination of fear, panic, and annoyance flashing across their faces.

Zavier grabbed ahold of Easton, tugging him toward us. "What's going on?"

Easton looked as if he hadn't slept a wink in the last twenty-four hours. "We can't find Ryder." I tensed as Zavier and I shared a quick glance. "Tril and Micah said some blonde noblewoman was trying to get in his room this morning, claiming she wanted to see him. When they opened the door his bed was empty."

I had no doubt that noblewoman was Gisella. What did she want with Ryder? And in his bedroom this early? *You have no right to be jealous,* I scolded myself. He could do whatever he wanted. It wasn't as if there was anything between us. He wasn't mine.

I shook my head. None of that mattered right now. "That makes no sense," I said. "His bedroom is four stories up. It's not like he could just jump out the window."

Easton rubbed his face, a mixture between exhaustion and frustration. "The thing is, he had about a twenty-minute timeframe to leave when Tril and Micah went to use the latrines earlier on this morning."

My eyes widened. "They *both* abandoned post? Why the hell would they go at the same time?"

"Where's Blanning?" Zavier asked.

Easton's head was darting back and forth, and I could tell he was growing antsy standing here. "He doesn't know yet. We were hoping to find Ryder without bothering the capt—"

Zavier started saying something, but I wasn't paying attention as I remembered the hidden passageway in Ryder's room. Underneath one of the rugs was a latch that led down to the tunnels. It was an old castle, so it made sense that not many people would know about it or think to check it.

I knew where I needed to go. I darted out the room before

anyone could ask where I was going. Most of the guards were scouring the halls looking for him, none of them realizing he wasn't *inside*. Or at least I didn't think so.

I all but flew down the corridors, narrowly avoiding the servants with arms full of fresh laundry and bedding. It was still early, the sun just rising over the horizon as I bolted out a side door. The grass was covered in fresh dew, the morning haze wrapping around my ankles as I ran.

It took longer than I thought to get around the side of the castle, stopping as I came up to those now familiar blue forget-me-nots. I was panting, my heart thumping in my chest as I tried to catch my breath.

I brushed past the bushes, crouching down near the tunnel entrance. It was a five-foot hole cut into the gray stone, shielded by a mossy iron grate overtaken with plant life.

And that grate was slightly moved to the side. He'd been here.

"I knew it," I said as I stood up, trying to figure out *where* he would've gone. I didn't want to assume the worst, but it was hard not to fear the Kindrahs had gotten to him. Ryder wouldn't just leave on his own accord, especially after that very clear warning from his father. No, he was taken.

I backed up just as a hand flattened over my mouth, another wrapping around my chest. My eyes widened in shock as my body instantly went into defense mode. I drove my head back as I simultaneously dug the heel of my boot into the assailant's foot.

It was a masculine voice that groaned out in pain, his grip on me loosening enough that I was able to break free and draw my dagger. I spun, blade at the ready to drive it home, when I stopped.

"*Ryder?*" I quickly re-sheathed my dagger, reaching for him as he tilted his head back to stop the blood from dripping down his nose. *I gave the prince a bloody nose.*

"I'm experiencing so many firsts with you," he said with a laugh that turned into a cough.

I covered my mouth with my hands, unsure of what to do. Unsure of how to make this better. "I'm so sorry. I didn't mean—"

"Don't ever apologize for defending yourself." He lowered his head as the trickle of blood began to slow, using the hem of his riding cape to wipe it away. "And for future reference, I'm all for a bit of pain as long as there's more pleasure involved."

There it was. I rolled my eyes. "What in the gods names are you doing out here? Do you have any idea how insane the guards are going looking for you?"

He leaned against the pine tree to his left. "Yet you knew exactly where to find me."

"You snuck out to what—lure me outside?"

He appeared so unbothered and entertained at the same time. "Yes," he said as he reached behind the tree, tossing a bundle of fabric at me. "Get changed."

I fumbled with it, separating a long-sleeved white tunic from a brown riding cape. I held them up in both hands. "Get changed for *what*?"

"I'm taking you to Caelestis."

I laughed. "That's funny, it sounded like you said you were taking me into Caelestis." I waited for him to laugh with me, to admit he was only joking, but he didn't. "We're not going into the city. The rest of the guards are all but flipping the castle upside down looking for you, and it's only a matter of time before your father—"

"He's away for the day, so what's the harm? Come on, Wren, live a little." His smile was playful and tempting and that's what made it dangerous. It was so difficult to say no to him, especially when the idea of spending time alone with him thrilled me.

I opened my mouth then shut it. "Is there something you need to get? Surely if you just go back inside and tell Blanning you want to go—" I didn't finish the sentence as I looked again at the clothes in my hand. He'd brought these for *me*. He snuck out for *me*. I glanced at him. "This is because I told you I've never been to Caelestis, isn't it?"

The look on his face told me I was correct. I shook my head. "Ryder Bryton, you have lost your mind."

He grinned. "Well, Hibreaker, here's to hoping you help me find it."

I held up the tunic he gave me, raising a brow. "This is huge."

"It's mine. I didn't have time to go rummaging for anything nice, but with the cape over it, I figured it'd be fine."

I couldn't believe I was agreeing to this, but if there was one thing I'd learned about Ryder, it was that once he set his mind to something, it was hard to steer him away from it. "Turn around," I said on an exhale.

The corners of his mouth twitched as he slowly faced the other way, his brown curls kissing the base of his neck. I quickly removed my uniform, my legs and arms glazed over with goosebumps as the brisk morning air caressed my bare skin.

I took my headpiece off and tugged the tunic over my head, immediately warming from the feel of it. The feel of *him*. It rested against my mid-thigh, leaving only a small part of my legs visible beneath the knee-high boots. I pulled on my weapons belt next, tightening it around my waist, and finished it off with the wool riding cape.

"I'm dressed."

Ryder didn't hesitate to spin around, his eyes raking over me several times before he cleared his throat and shook his head, stepping closer. He reached for the strings of my cape, tying them in a knot against my chest. I had to angle my head back to see his face. To study the slight stubble coating his jaw and the few random freckles scattered around his cheeks.

I was so lost in the sight of him I almost missed it as he said, "I think seeing you in my clothes might be my new favorite sight."

"Well, I wouldn't get used to it."

"I think it's too late for that."

We didn't waste any more time as I hid my uniform behind the bush, and we hurried to the stables where he graciously tipped the stable hand to keep his mouth shut. He looked like a prince of night on Atri, while I was given a smaller, beige horse named Fern.

I mimicked Ryder's motion as I climbed into the saddle. I couldn't tell him I'd never ridden a horse before. Most people knew how, and if he realized I didn't, he'd begin asking questions.

I gripped the reins tightly as I adjusted my weight, fighting the urge to wrap my arms around Fern's neck and stay that way until we got to Caelestis. Luckily, she seemed more... *reserved* than Atri, and within ten minutes or so, I had the hang of it.

Well, enough that I could fake knowing what I was doing without raising suspicion.

It was a short journey into Caelestis, only a little over two miles. Ryder pulled the hood of his cape over his head, concealing his curls. We tied the horses to a tree near a small stream behind the shimmering bronze gates at the entrance of the city. The off-white cobblestone streets glimmered like moonstones against the cream buildings, while the terracotta roofs were texturized from countless years of exposure to the elements.

Wooden shutters were thrown open at the windows, the curtains blowing in the breeze, while narrow lines of wire stretched across the street from window to window, containing hundreds of white triangular flags. People of all colors and ethnicities hurried left and right, winding down the narrow roads that branched off the main one.

Bells chimed from vendor carts as men in aprons waved down potential customers, each claiming *their* goods were the best in the city. Competing smells of caramelized peanuts, molten chocolate, bread, roasted meats, and forged metal wafted through the air, mixing with the delicate scent of blooming flowers that lined the walkways.

The buildings lower levels were framed with colorful signs marking the wide array of shops the city had to offer. The sounds of hooves clicking against the cobblestones echoed in the distance as black carriages were pulled through the streets. I stepped back as a group of children ran by, giddy and laughing as their red-faced mother chased them with a fist in the air.

I felt Ryder watching me as I made no effort to hide my smile. This was everything I never had and everything I always wanted. But as my gaze drifted to a man perched on a wooden stool, easel and blank canvas before him, my smile quickly faltered.

His right hand balanced a slip of wood covered in a variety of colored paints, while his left gripped a brush. Something in me twisted as I thought of Angel. Of how his talents would've flourished in a place like this. He should've been here. Not me.

I looked at the towering marble statue to the right. I knew who it depicted without reading the bronze plaque at the base. The broad, muscular shoulders, the garments draping down the length of his body, the bare feet, and the crown of stardust that sat atop his perfectly sculpted head. Alteria, the god of night.

A group of young boys hurried past the statue, arms overflowing with ornately decorated wreaths full of white flowers. They hung them on every door, while vendors handed out the same flowers to every person that passed, free of charge. Soon enough, the entire city was flooded with them, like a sheet of freshly fallen snow.

"What are they doing?" I asked.

"Preparing for the Scorching."

My head turned. "The what?"

A small smile played on his lips. "The week-long celebration to honor the Estelers and how their powers came to be."

A young boy with deep blue eyes and cropped blonde hair ran to me. Without a word, he dropped a white flower in my hand, then ran off in a fit of giggles. I held it to my nose, breathing in the sweet scent.

"Lilies," Ryder said. I turned to him with a raised brow. He laughed, pointing to my hand. "The flowers, they're lilies."

"I knew that," I lied. After a moments consideration, I asked, "Can you tell me about the Scorching?"

Ryder folded his hands behind his back. "Centuries ago, the gods walked the land. While some retreated to the stars for their eternal rest, a few remained a while longer. One of them was Tella, goddess of justice and righteousness. Alteria chained her to the land, claiming her gifts were needed to balance out evil and keep the humans honest and good. She was bound to walk amongst the mortals until the end of time, never to return to the sky with her fellow gods. She yearned for her lover, Durling, god of the holy flame, but because of Alteria's need for her here, she could never see him again."

I listened intently as he continued. "To keep the story short, Tella eventually figured out a way to maintain her duty *and* return to the stars. She gave her powers to a group of women who then became known as Estelers. Their magic, which they later called Purity, was born from the goddess herself. Once Tella gave it up, her chains were broken, and she was free. Free to return to her lover and tour the night skies with him for all eternity."

"Do you really think there's other Estelers still out there?" I asked.

Ryder nodded instantly, as if he had not a single ounce of doubt. "I do. Most people think that because the Estelers won't intervene with mere human issues, it means they're not there. But they have the blood, wisdom, and powers of a goddess. Obviously they're not going to concern themselves with minor things. I think it would take something extreme for them to come forward again."

Interesting. I wanted to ask what his thoughts were on Drestel and Pryler constantly intervening on his father's behalf, but something else popped into my mind. "Why is it called the Scorching?"

A dimple flashed as he looked at the city before us. "For seven days during sunset, fire rains from the sky. It's said to be the tears of Durling as he wept for Tella when she didn't return. Many believe it resembles the seven decades it took for her to finally go to him after she'd been freed."

"But why?" I asked, now fully emersed in the story. "If she loved him so much, why didn't she go to him as soon as she was free?"

Ryder's eyes danced between gray and blue as he turned, watching me like I was the only person on the busy road. "If you were trapped your entire existence and finally freed, would you be so quick to return home? Or would you live for yourself first?" His words weighed down in my stomach like a sinking stone.

"And do you believe it?" I asked.

He tilted his head, studying me. "Everyone has to believe in something. If not, then what's the point?"

Yes, I thought. *What is the point?* I glanced at the children pulling long strings of flowers through the streets. "Why the lilies?"

"When Tella's chains broke, all that remained was a pile of white lilies. So after that, they became a symbol of the holy week. It doesn't start for another two months, but it's never too early to celebrate."

When I didn't respond, he grabbed my hand, causing heat to flood my cheeks. His amused smirk returned. "As much as I love admiring your reactions to me touching you, I want to show you something."

I had every intention of putting an end to this and telling him I wanted to be treated just like his other guards, but all thoughts of doing so evaded me as I was swept up in the moment.

This felt a bit like freedom.

He pulled me toward one of the side roads when I noticed a figure standing behind a vendor cart. My eyes narrowed as I tried to get a better look.

Shaking it off, I turned from the city center and followed the prince.

CHAPTER 29

Standing on the balcony of the town house, I tipped my head back with closed eyes, the warmth of the sun brushing my face. The breeze was crisp, the air carrying the rich fragrance of the Tyro Forest from the east.

"I've never seen anyone do that," Ryder said.

"Do what?"

He huffed out a laugh. "Admire the sun and sky the way you do. Like every time you see it is the first."

I blinked, turning to where he leaned against the iron rail. "When you've spent so long in the dark, you learn to appreciate the light."

He said nothing as he studied me, as if I was a puzzle whose pieces never quite fit. I could sense the storm of questions brewing in his mind, but he kept his mouth shut.

"What is this place anyway?" I asked. Potted plants filled the outdoor space, concealing us in our own private forest. "Do you live a secret life as a botanist?"

"Unfortunately, I can't add that to my long list of talents," he teased. "This is just a little haven Lucio purchased four years ago to escape our delightful father. I come here when I need space to think."

I rested my forearms on the railing. Down below, the winding roads of the city branched off of the main one like spider legs. "For someone meant to wear the crown one day, your brother seems like he prefers being away from all this."

"He's a free spirit," Ryder replied. "The shackles of being king never appealed to him. My father thought making him a general would scare him into coming home, but it did the opposite. Lucio was meant to rule, just not a kingdom."

"So what will happen when your father dies if Lucio doesn't want to be king?"

Ryder sighed. "I think he's just hoping Lucio will get his head on straight and accept his birthright."

"Have you ever thought about it?" I questioned. "Being king?"

He laughed, eyes scrunching in the corners. "Gods, no. I hate being at court." He cast me a sidelong glance. "But I don't have to worry about any of that. My father's also completely in denial and believes his reign will never end. As if death is avoidable."

Didn't he know it was? The king could easily have a necromancer brought in to make sure he never stayed dead. The thought of it made my skin crawl. I stiffened as the memory of the girl in the alcove crossed my mind. Dead because someone was given a second chance at life.

"What's wrong?" Ryder asked. His eyes focused on my white knuckled hands gripping the rail.

"That girl who died. You just... you just left. All of you did. You went back into the castle and carried on with your lives while a *child* laid dead in your gardens." His jaw clenched. "Do none of you care? Is life so insignificant to those of you with rank that you brush it off like dust from your shoulder?"

"Ask me where I went," he said softly.

"What?"

"Ask me where I went when I left the gardens." I stared at him. "Go on, Wren. Ask me."

"Where did you go?"

"I went to her mother. The girl's name by the way was Salma. I went to her mother and sat with her, holding her hand while she cried for hours. The tunic I wore is still stained with her tears."

I didn't dare breathe as he continued. "I sat with her, not because I had to, but because no one should bear the weight of grief alone. And you know what? In that moment, she didn't care if I was the prince or a beggar off the street because when people are so completely broken, they take comfort where they can." His eyes found mine again. "That's what I was doing when I left the gardens."

I didn't know what to say. I swallowed, suddenly feeling terrible as I looked at his hardened features. "I... I'm sorry," I said at last. "I didn't know."

He said nothing for a moment, and I thought this outing of ours had come to an end when he added, "I had a sister."

I stilled as he ran a hand through his tangled curls, exhaling a shaky breath. "Her name was Adelina. I was eight when my mother had her. I still remember how nervous I was to hold her small body for the first time. I was so afraid if I moved the wrong way, I'd crush or drop her. She was beautiful. One eye blue, the other brown, and the softest coating of blonde hair on her head."

He had a distant look in his eyes, like he was back in that room holding his baby sister. I noticed how all his muscles seemed to tense at the memory. "She lived for four days and six hours before she died. For the longest time, no one knew what happened. We had the best healers in the kingdom brought in, and with each examination, they all said the same thing. She was perfectly healthy."

I had a feeling I knew where this was headed. "There was only one explanation." His voice turned icy. "A necromancer brought someone back to life, and my baby sister paid the price." Tears rimmed the edges of his eyes. "My father had every intention of forcing Drestel and Pryler to go to Morters' End to destroy the necromancer responsible, but they wouldn't. *Couldn't*, was more like it. They're strong, but not strong enough on their own."

I thought about Asher's words as I looked back at Ryder. At his pained expression. "I didn't know you had another sibling," I said quietly.

"Not many do. My mother kept the pregnancy a secret. Those who knew were told Adelina died from a lung condition. That she passed peacefully in the middle of the night."

I sensed from his rigid composure he didn't want to speak about this more. "Why did you bring me here?" I asked.

His eyes softened, that haunted look retreating back to the restless, broken section of his heart. "You said you've never been to the city, and I wanted to be the one to show you. This was the only way we could be just Ryder and Wren."

"Oh." I didn't know what else to say. *Perhaps tell him*

there is no Ryder and Wren. There never will be. I pushed the intrusive thoughts away. I didn't want to fight right now.

"How did you get that?" he asked.

"Get what?"

He motioned to the line between my eyebrows. "Your scar."

My hand unconsciously went to the long strip of scarred skin. Images and memories of Cazimir, one of the necromancers, danced through my mind. Of the night after Papa was buried that I scaled the side of the Vacar.

I remembered the smell of rotting flesh as I tiptoed through Cazimir's chambers, the dim flicker of candlelight atop his nightstand outlining his sleeping frame. I was going to kill him. Kill him for landing the final death blow to Papa. I stood above him, watching as he breathed. As his eyes fluttered behind his eyelids. I hoped he was having the worst form of nightmare. The kind that would leave him sweat-soaked and screaming.

As I raised my dagger, preparing to drive it through his chest, his eyes opened. Before I knew what was happening, we were tumbling on the ground. The surprise caught me off guard long enough for him to pin me down. One hand gripped my wrists, the other held *my* dagger above my face. The dagger Papa gave me.

Cazimir marked me that night with my own blade. He left a rugged line across my forehead that let every necromancer know I was *never* to be resurrected if I died. I never told anyone about that night. About the twisted smile exposing his yellow teeth as he finally released me.

The next morning, I told Mama and Angel I sleepwalked

into my armoire. Its jagged ends were sharp enough to make the story believable.

I couldn't tell Ryder the truth, so I opted for the closest I could get to it. "I was wronged and seeking retribution."

"Is that all you're going to give me?"

"That's all you need to know." I could tell he was debating whether or not to push me further, but as usual, he respected my boundaries. Before I could stop myself, I asked, "What keeps you up at night?"

His eyes locked on mine. "What do you mean?"

"You don't sleep very well." An observation, not a question.

"That obvious?" I nodded, and he exhaled a deep breath. "I still remember the names of all my guards who died the night of the attack. They fought so bravely to protect me. To make sure I got out of there alive. Some of them had families. Letters from their children and wives were tucked into their uniforms while they bled out on the dirt." I felt the pain of the memory radiating off his voice.

"I repeat their names every night. I see their faces, the bloody, torn remains of their bodies every time I close my eyes. So, I repeat their names. Over and over, and by the time I finish, the sun is rising, welcoming a new day. A day they'll never see." He ran his hand over his face. "I *can't* have anyone else die for me. I won't allow it."

I wanted to ask what exactly happened that night. *How* it happened, but I could never bring myself to ask him to repeat such traumatizing memories. "Your guards..." I said slowly, "... they did what they were sworn to do. To protect you at all costs. To give their lives for you entirely."

His eyes were glossed over with something I didn't recognize. Something that made my stomach flip and hands shake as he stepped closer. "And what about you?" he asked.

"What about me?" I barely heard my voice as he lowered his head.

"Have you given yourself to me? Are you entirely mine?" He ran his thumb over my lips as he moved to take that final step. To cross the line there would be no returning from. I pulled back, stumbling over one of the potted plants.

I shook my head. "I can't."

He frowned. "But you could in the library? We almost did, before we were interrupted."

"That was different."

"How?" He took a step closer.

"I didn't know who you were."

He stopped as realization and hurt set in. "Ah, I see. Because of my title, because I'm a *prince*, that changes things."

I swallowed the bitter taste in my mouth and nodded. "Yes." There were a million and one other reasons why, but I couldn't tell him.

He watched me for another moment, his eyes searching for any sign that I didn't mean it, but I was good at concealing how I felt. I'd been doing it for years.

He cleared his throat and smiled. It wasn't a real smile, but he was a gentleman and wouldn't force me into giving him what he wanted. What I could never give him, regardless of how badly I was starting to yearn for it myself. "We'd better head back," he said at last.

I followed him down the narrow pathway into the house. Even though Asher wasn't here, his words still rang in my ears. In my heart.

I didn't know what I'd truly done when I agreed to that covenant.

CHAPTER 30

Ryder and I had to return to the castle separately as the guards—and now Blanning—were searching for him. I'd quickly gone to the tunnel entrance and changed back into uniform before meeting Ryder near the tree line of the Tyro Forest.

Blanning and several other guards found us there. Ryder crafted a story about needing some time to himself after everything that happened, claiming he'd only wanted to go for a walk along one of the woodland trails. He said he forced me not to tell anyone and to accompany him, just for safe measure.

The way Blanning looked at him was more with pity and worry than anything else. He made it clear that this couldn't happen again, at least not until the Kindrah situation was resolved. Other than that, he seemed to believe the story.

However, the other guards looked at *me* with a bit more skepticism. Several of them had seen me in the common room earlier today, and I wasn't sure they bought what Ryder said.

But he was their prince, and if Blanning let it go, so would they. That didn't mean I hadn't received several dirty looks and curious glances since we'd returned.

I was in the process of shoving a forkful of venison in my mouth when a tray dropped down across from me. My gaze rose to meet Alicai hovering beside the wooden bench, glaring.

Placing my fork down gently, I folded my hands together and smiled sweetly. "Are you waiting for a formal invitation?"

He snorted and sat down. I waited. One minute... two minutes... by the third minute, I asked, "Where's Zavier?" Trying my best to spark any sort of conversation.

He shrugged, spooning garlic mashed potatoes into his mouth. "Off doing gods know what with Tavrina. You would think they'd find somewhere else to rendezvous after the head healer caught them in a storage closet half naked."

I choked on my water. "*What?*"

"Honestly, I'm just impressed he knows what to do with his—"

I held up a hand, stopping *that* sentence. "Alright, I'm eating. Thank you for the images that will now give me nightmares eternally."

He smiled. "My pleasure."

Pushing that thought as far back in my mind as possible, I asked, "What about you? Some of the guards here are very handsome. And that nobleman's son... what's his name? Brannon?"

His hand stilled on his spoon. We never spoke about it, but I knew Alicai preferred men. I saw it in the way his eyes wandered when some of the guards took their shirts off, their muscular chests slick with sweat. That, and the fact he always voiced his opinions loud and clear. But when I tried having a serious conversation, Alicai shut down completely, his defense mode in full swing.

When he didn't respond and looked inclined to bend the spoon in half, I added, "It's not something to feel ashamed of, you know."

"*I know that,*" he snapped. A few moments later, he sighed. "How was your day?"

I stabbed my fork through a brussels sprout. "Fine."

"Oh, please."

I looked up. "Oh please what?"

"Something's going on."

"Nothing's going on," I insisted, chasing a rolling sprout around with my fork.

"You can lie to everyone else, but I see right through it. I know you, whether you want me to or not. And your little tryst with the prince? It's made the other guards suspicious."

"It wasn't a *tryst,*" I seethed. "And what do you mean they're suspicious?"

Alicai shrugged. "I overheard Flint, Easton, and Micah speaking about how strange it was that you happened to find Ryder and instead of alerting anyone, basically ran off with him." He shook his head. "You need to stop this, Wren. What do you really expect to happen here? That you two will live happily ever after? Be realistic. The moment someone higher up finds out, you'll be arrested. And with the assassination attempts..."

I knew where he was going. We'd spoken about it that first night in our tent. I'd instantly become suspect number one, and they'd question and threaten not only me, but my loved ones. Especially since I was from Morters' End. They'd think I had ties to dark magic. I *knew* all of this, yet I'd allowed Ryder to distract me.

I was starting to see his intentions for what they were. He wanted more. More than I could ever give him. Avoiding him wasn't an option or even a possibility, so I'd need to just hope our last conversation on the balcony would be enough for him to abandon the chase. I was still determined to find out the Kindrahs motives, and for that, I'd need to stay close. I just needed to be strong enough to maintain the sliver of a boundary we still had.

"We are just friends," I said for what felt like the hundredth time. I didn't know who I was trying to convince more. Alicai, or myself. "I can't very well shut him out completely. What if he gets angry and tells my secret?" I didn't think he would, but I was just trying to back up my reasoning.

Alicai sighed. "Lies, lies, lies. Everyone knows how to do it except when it comes to matters of the heart." I tried keeping my expression neutral as he twirled his spoon at me. "And your heart is written all over your face."

I knocked the spoon away. "Yours isn't as bad as Ryder's though," he added. "His face is an open book, spread wide for anyone smart enough to see."

"What's that supposed to mean?" I asked.

"The way he watches you. It's only stolen glances, but if I can see it, who's to say someone else won't?"

"I thought this was just a game to him? What was it you said again? Oh, right. Once he beds me, he'll fix the sheets for the next girl that catches his eye."

Alicai shrugged, unbothered by my tone. It was so frustrating how he always pulled a reaction from me. "That's probably still the case. You're just putting up more of a fight than he's used to. I imagine he's enjoying the challenge."

I clenched my fist. The sound of the giant clock on the wall ticked away, and when I looked up, I almost sighed in relief to be finished with this conversation. "I have to go."

A formal dinner was being held in the king's dining chamber for his council, and Ryder would be there in place of his brother who was still in the Haldro Mountains. And from what he told me earlier, Lucio was in no hurry to return.

I didn't bother saying goodbye as I discarded my tray, but as I glanced behind me to where Alicai still sat, he didn't even seem to notice I left.

Twelve guards including myself lined the wall of the dimly lit room. The scarlet wallpaper combined with the black glass table made the king's personal dining room feel more like an execution chamber.

From where I stood, I had a clear view of Ryder. And while I kept my eyes on him, as it was my *job*, he didn't look at me at all. His attention was focused completely on the men and conversations flowing around the table. There were sixteen of them, but the only two I recognized were Duke Halorast and Lord Winward.

Although, the man sitting at the right side of the king looked oddly familiar. It took me a minute to register who his tossed blonde curls and hazel eyes reminded me of. I realized it when he smiled, his shoulders rolled back in an arrogant manner.

It had to be Lord Davincourt, Ambrose's father. I hid my

disgust as his eyes raked over a servant's chest when she bent down to fill his glass. *Like father, like son.*

I glanced back at Ryder to find his head tilted back in laughter, his eyes crinkling in the corners. He was so lovely to look at. In a room full of old men and ugly souls, Ryder glowed with all the beautiful wonders of life. He must have felt my stare as his eyes found mine. Pain and longing replaced the humorous vibrancy that was there a moment earlier.

"Eye contact can be a dangerous thing," the commander whispered beside me. I instantly went rigid as his breath seeped down my uniform.

"I'm afraid I don't know what you mean," I said flatly.

"No?" His shoulder dug into mine. "Illicit declarations of love or even promises of death can be spoken through the eyes. There's a specific type of intimacy that comes with eye contact. Not to mention the danger it can lead to when a third set of eyes picks up on it."

I shifted on my feet. "Quite an imagination you have."

He chuckled. "Perhaps. But you know what I didn't imagine? The prince out for a stroll with a mysterious young lady in the city today. Piercing green eyes and silky brown hair. And you know what I didn't see? His guards." He clicked his tongue. "Blanning might buy whatever it is that comes out of that boy's mouth, but I'd hope the rest of you would be a bit smarter."

It *was* him this morning beside the vendor cart! "You must be mistaken," I said firmly. "The prince wanted to go on a walk today in the woods, and I joined him. Whoever you saw in the city must have just been a look-alike."

"Let's cut the pretense, shall we? You and I both know there are indiscretions occurring here that would be of the utmost interest and importance to the king if he should find out, hm? To have such blatant disregard for rules in a unit as high up as the prince's is punishable in ways you cannot even fathom."

I stiffened. "Again, I'm afraid I don't know what you mean."

Bekencourt sighed. "Here I thought you and I were having an honest conversation. No matter, you may act oblivious all you want. But I do wonder, how do you think your brother would enjoy life outside of Morters' End?"

Every muscle in my body tightened. I didn't dare move or breathe as Bekencourt bent closer. "Do you know what happens if someone tries to escape the shield without the Purity from an Esteler?" he asked.

I didn't. Apparently someone tried to leave once, but the results were so horrific it was never spoken about.

"Let me paint a picture for you," he said. "I'm sure you're familiar with that, seeing as your brother is an artist, correct?" My body was trembling as I fought the urge to strangle the man beside me.

"Yes, I know all about him," he went on. "But no matter, back to the point. If someone tries to leave the shield without Purity, whether by their own free will or shall we say *force*, their body will decay from the inside out in a matter of excruciatingly painful minutes. Think of it as fire singeing the vines of a plant, causing them to shrivel to nothingness. That is exactly what would happen to all the organs, veins, and muscles in the human body. It's terrifying, really."

"What do you want," I said through clenched teeth.

Bekencourt chuckled softly. "What I want isn't important, but what you want is. Remember what's at stake here,

Hibreaker. Succeed, and you will see your family again. Unharmed."

Succeed at what? Keeping Ryder safe?

He was gone a moment later, the sound of his receding footsteps echoing in my mind. I turned to the direction he'd gone, the swinging door the only sign he had been in the room at all.

CHAPTER 31

Bekencourt's threats plagued me as I walked down the hallway later on. I couldn't understand his angle. Surely if he knew my real identity he would have told the king by now. Maybe he was just targeting me because I was from Morters' End. Regardless, I had enough going on at the moment, and watching my back for the commander wasn't something I was particularly eager to do. It seemed he'd made it his personal goal to torment me into... behaving?

My steps slowed and my thoughts faltered as I turned a corner into the Great Hall of Tapestries. Each one depicted tales and history of the kingdom ranging from the coronation of the first king, to an image of Reeza, the first Esteler, kneeling on a pile of white lilies. But neither of those were what caught my attention.

At the far end stood Micah and Flint. They were in conversation, but the moment they spotted me, the words died on their lips, and I fought the urge to turn on my heels.

"Hibreaker!" Flint called. "Where are you going?"

So much for an escape. I strolled toward them, remembering what Alicai told me earlier. "What are you two doing?" I asked, trying to keep my voice casual and light.

"Funnily enough, we were just talking about you," Micah replied.

"Oh? And what about me?" My heart was thumping in my chest a mile a minute.

Flint kicked his boot up against the pillar behind him, crossing his arms over his chest. "Just how crazy it is that someone like you beat out so many of the others during recruitment."

I blinked. *Really*? "Recruitment was a while ago, not sure why you're still harping on that. And what exactly do you mean, *someone like me*?" My eyes narrowed. I was trying so hard to keep my composure, but I didn't do well with insults.

Flint shrugged. "Come on, Hibreaker. Men thrice your size were booted out while you stayed. Even after you almost killed the prince. And no offense, but from the way you went down on the mat with Brior, how exactly do you think you'd defend the prince against someone larger than you?"

Before I could snap at him, Micah chimed in. "By any chance, did you know Blanning before this? Family friend or something? Come to think of it, I don't even know where you're from."

I was almost too stunned to speak but also somewhat relieved their thoughts weren't somewhere else. "You think I've been given special treatment?" I asked. "What, that I *bribed* my way into the guard?"

They glanced at each other. "Your words, not ours," Flint mumbled.

I snorted. "I'm not even going to entertain this. That's

bullshit honestly. And do you really think size is all that matters in this position? I'll remind you that it was *me* who rescued the prince during the attack at the Bringing. And how fast are the two of you? I'd wager I'm quicker. More agile and better equipped with a sword, too. Next time you have a problem, how about you speak to *me* instead of gossiping like a couple of young girls."

Micah's smug expression snapped away, replaced by tight lips and narrowed eyes. "You want to take this to the sparring mat?"

I stepped closer. Even though my mind screamed for me to abort this, my body was thrumming for a fight. "Why waste time going all the way there? If you were good at your job, you wouldn't need the safety of a mat. Do you think if someone tried to assassinate the prince again, they'd pause to go to the sparring room?"

Micah opened his mouth before clamping it shut as his eyes trailed to something behind me. I turned just in time to see the queen and her ladies in waiting walking down the hall. They were far enough away and too deep in conversation to notice us, but Flint and Micah bolted off before I had the chance to turn around.

Not wanting to get reprimanded for doing *nothing*, even though I technically wasn't on rotation, I quickly walked in the opposite direction, pausing when I noticed something out of place. I'd ventured down this hall enough times to know each tapestry inside and out, but there was one that made me stop. It was the way the right corner was tucked under, like someone moved it recently. Being the nosy person I am, I lifted it slightly off the wall and peered behind it, surprised to find the entrance to a dark tunnel.

I thought I knew where all the tunnels were, but clearly I missed this one. I quickly grabbed a torch from the wall and climbed in, smoothing out the tapestry to cover my tracks.

I was greeted by darkness, the distant sound of dripping water, and scurrying feet. It was cold, the stone walls damp. My boots splashed through puddles as I stepped over the remains of dead mice. The stench was horrid, but I'd smelled worse.

Fortunately, the tunnel contained only a single path of winding turns. No options for getting lost. *Only trapped.*

I held the torch above me, examining the stone ceiling that matched the walls and floors. It was hard to picture it as anything but a tomb. Perhaps my tomb should one of the stones fall.

The sound of voices caused me to stop. The space was too narrow to draw a sword, so my dagger would suffice. I gripped the hilt tightly, waiting.

But as I waited, footsteps never followed, and the voices didn't draw closer. It wasn't until I noticed two circular slits in the wall behind me, a dim light filtering through, that I found the source of the sound.

I stood on my tiptoes to line up my eyes with the holes. Clearly someone was up to no good. As my eyes adjusted, I realized the peepholes led into King Reid's private office. *Oh, someone was definitely up to no good.*

I watched the king pace back and forth, his golden surcoat abandoned for a basic tunic. He ran a hand through cropped hair as the second voice continued, "There's been whispers about a group of Kindrahs assembling in Evamort." Captain Blanning stepped into view, leaning against the wooden desk. His face displayed the remnants of many sleepless nights. His usual handsome features were sunken in, golden eyes now a diluted, washed-out yellow.

The king continued to pace. "I told you to leave it be."

Blanning appeared unfazed. "The villager I spoke with overheard one of the Kindrahs in a brothel talking about their plans to push further east."

The king stopped. "East?"

Blanning nodded. "They're heading for Morters' End." I hissed as the torch slipped, the flames burning my fingers. I tried to hold still as the captain ran a hand down his exhausted face. "This goes against everything in the agreement. They're making a mockery out of—"

"Watch your tongue," the king said through his teeth. "Do not lecture me, Blanning. You seem to forget you are not the boy's father." Blanning looked like he wanted to strangle him.

My brows scrunched together. *What agreement*? My legs were burning as I pressed harder into my toes.

The captain sighed, more in pent up annoyance than defeat. "Apologies, Your Majesty. Why is it you think they're heading for Morters' End? To retrieve the necromancers?"

The king scoffed. "No one in that village can leave without Drestel or Pryler." He stilled for a moment then added, "Let them go." Blanning cocked his head, but the king held up a hand. "Let them enter the village. The shield will keep them trapped, as it does for anyone practicing dark magic. Once they're enclosed, you may act, Blanning. You may act as you see fit."

The captain pushed off the table, taking a wary step forward. "What exactly are your orders here?"

The king chuckled. "Like you said, what they're doing

goes against the agreement, so I'm giving you a gift, Blanning. The gift of vengeance for your fallen comrades. Take Bekencourt, Drestel, Pryler, and as many guards as you find necessary. Once the Kindrahs are in Morters' End, burn it to the ground. It won't kill them, but I'd love to see what they do when they have nothing. No food, shelter, or even humans to torment. It would be rather interesting to see how long it takes for them to turn on each other, no?"

"You're speaking of mass murdering an entire village." Blanning's voice was nothing but a whisper. "There are *sympathizers* to the ordinary people of Morters' End. They'll riot."

The king pinched the bridge of his nose. "The sacrifice of a few for the greater good. Quite frankly, it's something I should've done long ago."

Blanning shook his head. "This is *genocide*."

"Are you arguing with me, Blanning?"

There was silence for a moment. "No, Your Majesty. I will make sure it gets done."

The torch slipped from my hand, the flames hissing as they hit the damp stone and quickly extinguished.

Their conversation went on for another minute or so, but I didn't hear anything else. My ears were ringing, and my breathing grew ragged as I paced back and forth. I barely heard the office door open and close, the room now empty. I had to do something. I had to *tell* someone.

I didn't care for most of the people in Morters' End, and I definitely didn't care for the necromancers. But I couldn't let Angel, Mama, and the few others who were innocent burn to death. I had to figure out how to stop this. Perhaps I could tell Ryder. I could—

A sudden breeze kissed the back of my neck, sending a shiver down my spine. "Wasn't life much easier under the stars while we laid by the brook? Where the only sounds were the steady stream of water and the pounding of your heart?"

The outline of Asher leaning against the stone wall was all I could see. Since my torch fell, the only light was from the dying fire in the king's office shining through the peephole.

I wasn't in the mood for this. *Or* him. Not now.

I continued pacing, clenching and unclenching my fists as I moved. Even in the dark I felt his blue eyes on me, marking every movement I made as if he were engraving it to memory.

"Do you remember, Wren?" he asked when I didn't respond. "Do you remember those nights? When I named the stars after you?"

Of course I remembered. But right now, I didn't care.

"Not the small, delicate stars though," he continued. "But the ones that burned so fiercely. So brightly and strong, we wondered if they'd ever go out. If somehow they would drain every spark until they were nothing more than stardust and memories."

He pushed off the wall and blocked my path. "But they never did, did they? They never burned out. They continued to glimmer and shine as brightly as the midmorning sun. *Those* were the stars I named after you." He raised a finger, running it down the side of my face.

Even with the iciness of his touch, I felt my body warming. My heartbeat slowing to a relaxed, steady rhythm. A rhythm that belonged to him.

But it wasn't real. Nothing was real when it came to Asher. Our entire relationship, whatever it had been, was built on our covenant. Nothing he did was because he cared for me.

"Do you ever grow bored?" I asked. His finger stilled. "Of having no one else to speak to and torment but me?"

He dropped his finger gently, pressing his forehead against mine. Such an innocent gesture, but from him, something else entirely. His lips brushed mine like the shadow of a kiss. "How could I ever grow bored of you?"

He pulled away, and the absence of him felt like a missing limb. I never understood it. How I could feel so much and so little for him all at once. *We're bonded through blood,* I told myself. That was the only logical explanation.

"I have to go back to Morters' End," I managed to say.

He turned, eyebrows slightly raised. "And why's that?"

"Don't act like you haven't been here the entire time. I know you heard the king."

"You can't save them, Wren."

My fists clenched at my sides. "Like hell I can't."

"And how," he asked, "do you plan on doing that? You're a two days' journey away, and even if you managed to return in time, once you crossed that shield, you'd be stuck again without the Estelers to bring you out." He paused, leaning his right shoulder against the wall. "I know you, and I know this isn't just about playing hero on a rescue mission. You want revenge."

I moved away, but he grabbed my chin, forcing me to face him. "Tell me, Wren, how exactly are you going to fight not only the necromancers, but the other Kindrahs you know nothing about? Do you know how far their magic reaches? Do you know what they can do? No, you don't." He dropped his hand, holding my gaze. "You're not going."

"I'd rather burn fighting to save my family there then continue living here indebted to *you*," I spat as he turned, his white tunic a fair contrast to the black curls along the nape of his neck.

He stiffened, his muscles contracting through the light material. "No."

I laughed. "No? As if you have a say in the matter. As if you care if I—"

He whirled on me, his eyes glowing shards of ice. "I will *always* care. And if I have to tie you down to keep you from entertaining this stupid idea further, I will."

"All you care about is our deal," I said through my teeth. "Don't act like you give a damn about *me*."

He watched me carefully, jaw clenching. He opened his mouth then shut it. A moment later, he repeated, "You're not going."

"Go to Hell," I snarled.

He shoved his hands into his pockets. As he walked away, he called over his shoulder, "If you insist. But just know, wherever I go, I'm taking you with me."

CHAPTER 32

After pacing for several more minutes, I picked up the torch and decided it was time to leave. I took a few steps, touching the wall for guidance, when I heard what sounded like a rock bounce across the ground. I waited, and when I didn't hear it again, continued moving.

Three steps later, another noise echoed through the narrow space. *Stupid rats.* I couldn't tell if the sound was behind, in front, or beside me. Everything blended together in the dark, making it impossible to discern the location of sounds.

I picked up my pace as the walls curved, leading back toward the tapestry. It wasn't until it happened a third time, significantly louder, that I grunted in frustration. "Seriously, Asher? You want to play games with me right now?"

No response.

I huffed out a breath, rolled my eyes, and kept walking.

I was nearing the tapestry. A sliver of light was shining through the holes in the fabric. Just a few more steps...

A sudden burst of laughter sent the torch flying from my hands, landing somewhere ahead of me. I knew that laugh. When I'd heard it the first time, it felt like a thousand cuts opening and closing all over my body at once.

A dark figure appeared in front of me, and although I couldn't see anything besides the outline of its long body, I knew who it was. *What* it was.

I kept myself steady, voice firm. "What do you want?" Its head tilted like a trained animal learning a new command. "Well?" I pressed. "Why are you following me? What did your riddle mean?" I stepped closer to the Faceling. "Why me?"

It laughed again. I remained still, my patience simmering on the border of murderous intentions as I waited for it to stop. "So many questions, and so many answers," it sang in a melodic tune. "Are you sure you ask the right ones?"

"Is there a specific question I *should* be asking?"

It chuckled again. "I will tell you what you do not realize you need to know."

Everything out of the Faceling's mouth was a damn riddle. "What does that even mean?" I tried to keep the annoyance from my voice, but it was a challenge.

"Guard your prince, and guard him well. His enemies—"

"Yeah, yeah. His enemies stretch far and wide, I know."

There was a stillness to the creature that was so unnatural. So foreign, I didn't know how I'd missed it the first time in the gardens. After a moment, it sang, "Morters' End is not at its end. Not yet, and then..." Its voice faded out.

I smirked, crossing my arms. "What's the matter? Run out of rhymes?"

"Someone is coming," it said in a hushed, brittle tone. "Your prince is not all they want, but he is truly worth a lot."

It paused again, its hands moving like it was physically pulling the words from its mouth. "A shedding serpent, red like blood." It choked, then vanished.

If someone was coming, I had to move. *Now.* I picked up my pace and ran for the tapestry. I'd sort out this new collection of riddles later.

~

My mind was reeling between the Faceling's words and the fact that my home would soon be burnt to a crisp.

Oddly enough, what Asher said in the tunnel left me with *some* comfort. It would take the captain a few days to get to Morters' End, so I had time to come up with a plan before he marched.

My pressing issue was remembering the riddle. Before I could forget, I pulled a piece of parchment and charcoal from under my bed and wrote down everything the Faceling said.

A shedding serpent, red like blood.

Was it literal? I saw plenty of snakes around the gardens. But what would its shedding skin have to do with anything?

No, it had to be symbolic. But of what? I'd read countless books but never came across anything about a serpent. I sighed as I wrote the words for the hundredth time. As if writing them would somehow give them meaning.

"What is it?" Zavier asked.

I put the paper on my lap and glanced at him. He sat on his bed, back to the wall, arms folded behind his head. I hadn't seen him much lately. Any free time he had, he spent with Tavrina. And after my conversation with Alicai, I now had a visual of exactly *what* they did.

His silky hair was pinned to his forehead, still wet from his bath. "What do you know about the Kindrahs from Enderya?" I asked.

"You're still thinking about that?" I turned to where Alicai sat on the floor, twirling his dagger around.

"What do you want to know?" Zavier asked, ignoring him.

Alicai rolled his eyes. "She wants to know about the attacks. Don't you, Wren? As if we have any more knowledge on it than you do."

"Do you not find it strange the king wants to wait for them to strike again? He's putting not only Ryder but all the guards at risk by keeping us like sitting ducks. Don't you want to know why?"

I didn't mention what I'd overheard in the tunnel, or the fact that there was definitely more going on here than we thought. The king and Blanning were talking about an agreement. *But agreement of what?*

"Obviously. But there haven't been any attacks since the Bringing. Maybe they went back to whatever hole they crawled out of," Alicai said.

Zavier shifted. "I've heard stories of some of the Kindrahs being able to vanish into thin air, transporting themselves wherever they wanted. That would make it nearly impossible to go out and hunt them. Maybe the king has a point."

I shook my head. "I just don't get it. Why Ryder? He's not in line for the throne, and he's... good." He was more than good, but I didn't need to get into that. Not now.

Alicai smirked cruelly. "Oh, he's good, is he? Does that mean you finally gave in? I've heard he's *extremely* good in bed from several firsthand accounts. Apparently, he does this thing with his—"

"Seriously, Alicai?" Zavier groaned, a disgusted grimace on his face. "I don't want to know these things!"

Alicai's gaze was focused on me. "But Wren does. Or do you already know from personal experience?"

My cheeks burned, but not from embarrassment. The thought of Ryder in bed with someone...

I was already feeling murderous and didn't want to start dissecting the wrongness of jealousy where the prince was concerned.

"Shut up, Alicai," Zavier said dismissively. He moved toward the edge of his bed, leaning muscular forearms on his knees. "You have a point, Wren. *Why* target Ryder? Why not Lucio or the king himself? Why the brother who will never wear the crown?"

"Maybe it's personal," Alicai added. "Maybe our prince got himself mixed up with the wrong crowd. Maybe he said or did or—" he shot me a quick glance and winked, "*—bedded,* the wrong person." I fisted the sheets beside me. "Maybe our seemingly innocent Ryder isn't so innocent after all."

Ryder definitely wasn't innocent, but not in a way that made him a bad person. He was infectious in all the good ways. His charming personality, his humor and humility, how he cared deeply for people he didn't even know. He brightened up the darkest days. As if the sun forced its way through the clouds just to catch a glimpse of him. He once called me a breath of fresh air, but he was wrong. That was him.

But if I could lie to him so easily, who's to say he hasn't lied to me? I tried pushing that feeling of doubt away, but it lingered.

"I'm going to sleep," I mumbled, turning on my side. A few moments later, the candles were blown out, and the room fell to darkness.

And I dreamed.

I dreamed of bright blue eyes and a tangle of ebony hair. Asher. Beautiful like the midnight sky.

Then a second set of eyes appeared, in-between gray and blue. There was a head full of chestnut hair loosely curling around the nape of his neck. Ryder. Beautiful like a storm cloud over a quiet forest.

While both stood watching me, their feet planted on a blanket of soft grass, there was a space between them. In that space, a snake as black as night slithered through, hissing as it stopped beside them. It watched me through golden eyes. Then it began convulsing back and forth, shedding its top layer of skin.

When it finished, its new layer glowed a shimmering red.

Blood-red.

CHAPTER 33

The following morning I was up before the sun and out of the room before Zavier and Alicai even stirred in their sleep. There was plenty to do today, and at the top of my list was seeing Ryder.

I walked through the quiet halls so hurriedly, I almost took out a scullery maid mopping the floors as I turned a corner. With a quick and sincere apology, I continued moving.

I was outside Ryder's door a few moments later. Sanyulin and Easton stood on either side, their brows raised in confusion as I skidded to a halt. "I need to talk to the prince," I panted.

"Is something wrong?" Easton asked, confusion turning to worry. I didn't care at the moment if they wanted to make up rumors regarding my position here or complain that Ryder showed favoritism. I dealt with Flint and Micah yesterday, and I'd deal with these two if they had something to say.

I shook my head. "I just need to speak to him about his plans to go for a ride this morning. It's supposed to rain."

They cast each other a puzzled look before moving to allow me in. I pushed open the door to find Ryder seated on his chaise near the fire. His head quickly turned as the door slammed closed.

He stilled when he saw me, his hair tousled from another sleepless night. Although the circles under his eyes were deep and dark, his eyes themselves were bright. He was shirtless as he sat comfortably in a pair of gray sleep pants.

He must have just been finishing up breakfast, a tray of pastry crumbs in front of him. I pulled my headpiece off, clutching it between my fingers. "You didn't call on me."

He didn't say anything as he placed a teacup on the tray. Standing up, he stretched his arms back. "I'm not sure I know what you mean."

I wanted to touch him. Badly. I wanted to drag my fingers down his toned stomach and—

"Last night," I said tightly, clearing my throat and my traitorous thoughts. "You didn't call on me."

I was a fool. I came here to tell him what I overheard the captain and his father speaking about, but as soon as I saw him sitting there, all my logical thoughts went out the window. This was getting worse.

He took a hesitant step toward me. "I didn't think you wanted me to. I was giving you space after... everything." Or in other words, *After I tried to kiss you, and you pulled away like you were under attack.*

My mouth went dry as he continued moving closer. "I'm sorry," I whispered. It was the best I could do.

He stopped. "What could you possibly be sorry for? I crossed a line. I must've misread..." He let out a short laugh, shaking his head. "I should be the one apologizing to you."

You didn't misread anything, I wanted to say. I was confused. So confused about so many things, and as he reached out, running his thumb over my lower lip, I suppressed a shudder.

Ryder's eyes were focused on my lips as he said, "I won't kiss you, and I won't try again. Not until you want me to. *If* you ever want me to."

I shouldn't want this.

I told myself I'd be more restrained. Restrained for the both of us. I was failing miserably.

He dropped his hand, moving to sidestep me when I grabbed it, brushing my fingers against his. We stood side by side, neither one facing the other. The sound of our mingled breaths filled the quiet. It felt so intimate.

He spun me around and cupped my cheeks, lowering his lips to my forehead. They lingered for a moment on the space between my brows. On my scar. I closed my eyes, exhaling softly. Every inch of my body seemed to relax, my mind completely free of all the worries and challenges that lied ahead.

"I thought you said you wouldn't kiss me unless I asked."

Although my eyes were closed, I felt his smile. "Starting now."

I laughed. There was just this. Just us and this moment. Ryder and Wren. Not a prince and his guard, just two lonely people burdened with a life they didn't ask for. Two souls treading across a thin line of what could be and what could never happen.

Because as he walked into his dressing room, reality came crashing back down. Because he was a prince, and I was a guard.

Perhaps in another life, this unspoken desire and need we danced across like fire under foot could've been. In a life without crowns, lies, and covenants.

But this wasn't another life.

I pulled on my headpiece and walked out the door.

There weren't many people I disliked more than Ambrose Davincourt. It took maximum restraint that afternoon not to hit him with the dull end of my sword as he trained with Ryder.

The sun was shining bright, illuminating the stone walls of the prince's personal training room. I was stationed at the door with Silla, a strong man from Desmound, the town at the western border of the kingdom.

Both Ambrose and Ryder were shirtless, their sweat-coated skin glistening in the light. Ambrose was decently built. Thin but defined. Especially his shoulders as he raised his sword, lunging for Ryder who parried the blow, ducking and dodging around him.

Ryder was all lean muscle and shadows, moving with such fluid grace, it was like watching smoke dance through air. Besides his distracting body and beautiful face, I was mesmerized by his movements. He was definitely a worthy opponent, and maybe one day we could train together.

But right now, all I wanted was to speak to him. I wanted to see if he knew about this agreement his father and Blanning were speaking of. And then I wanted to find a way to ask for his help with Morters' End without revealing I was from there. Easy.

I tensed as Ambrose drove his elbow into Ryder's chest, causing him to stagger back. But Ryder only laughed as he repositioned.

"You should've blocked that," Ambrose huffed. "You would have if your head wasn't up your ass." He lunged again, and this time, Ryder was prepared. After the whirling clashes of swords and bodies, the next thing I saw was Ryder pinning Ambrose to the floor. It satisfied me to no end.

Ambrose grinned, holding his hands up in surrender. Ryder sheathed his sword and extended a hand, pulling Ambrose off the ground.

"Alright," Ambrose sighed, running his tunic over his sweaty face. "I take it back."

"Smart choice," Ryder said with a wink.

"Are you coming with us tonight?" Ambrose asked as he sat on the floor, resting against a stone pillar.

Ryder shook his head. "I don't know if it's a good idea."

"Oh, come on. Garrick's leaving tomorrow. You're really not going to join us for one last hoorah?" I remembered overhearing some of the courtiers talking about how Garrick was going to Tryfel with his father for the next month to work on a trade deal.

"And where exactly is this last hoorah taking place?" Ryder asked.

"Where do you think?"

"Do you have to answer every question with a question? Just tell me."

"Are you commanding me?"

"If I have to," Ryder teased. "I might even have the guards hang you by your ankles in the dungeon if you refuse."

Ambrose pressed a hand to his chest. "Is that how you treat your oldest and greatest friend?" I almost snorted at that.

Ryder kept a steady smile. A smile I'd come to think could make foreign kings drop to their knees before him.

"Fine," Ambrose said. "It's at the Iron Oak. We're all going, and don't use the excuse that your father forbade you from leaving the castle." He rested his arms on his knees. "You've never been one to listen to him anyway."

Ryder thought about it for a moment as he chewed his lower lip. "I'll see."

Ambrose glanced at me and Silla. "Why don't you bring some of your guards if you're going to be a baby about it? Just not in those uniforms."

Ryder looked at me, the gears in his brain churning. "Fine. One last hoorah."

Ambrose grinned, raising a glass of water up in salute. "The last hoorah."

CHAPTER 34

Yellow, orange, and blue tents were dispersed around the front lawn, while swinging acrobats dangled from hanging ropes above. Large beasts I'd never seen before were pulled on leashes, winding in and out of where women cloaked in glitter sold promising fortunes to the people of the city. *Circus de Torlei* was a traveling group from a small town called Brolare, and the castle was their final stop before venturing home.

I struggled to remain a step behind Ryder as he moved around the crowd, giggles and batting eyes blooming in his wake. I even heard one girl very descriptively announce what she'd like to do if she got him alone. I decided that *I'd* like to show her several tricks of my own, each one involving a different type of blade.

I noticed the smirk on Ryder's face as he overheard her. Was he considering it? *Even if he is, it's not your business,* I reminded myself as I dodged around a man with a mouthful of peanuts and a top hat.

Ryder had managed to shake the three guards who were with him. Fortunately, I'd spotted him walking solo from across the lawn and quickly caught up. I knew most of the others were here somewhere, so I needed to have this conversation quickly. I didn't want anyone else seeing us together and spreading more rumors about favoritism.

"I have to talk to you," I whispered as we strolled past Lord Plaztin and his soon-to-be bride gawking as a man shoved a sword on fire down his throat.

"If you're wondering what to wear tonight," Ryder said over his shoulder, "please make sure it's nothing scandalous. There's only so much self-control I can practice when it comes to you."

I stopped, my heels digging into the damp grass beneath me. "Don't say things like that."

He turned. "Why? I mean it." He raised a brow in question. "Unless you want me to lose control?"

I swallowed at the images whirling through my mind. "I need to talk to you," I repeated.

His head darted around, making sure no one was looking. I didn't think anyone was, considering we were on the outskirts of the main lawn, a distance away from the circus. But that didn't stop him from grabbing my arm and pulling me *through* the hedges beside us.

Before I could slap him, he let go. I looked around, taking in the small stone gazebo with two white benches in the center. Vines wrapped around the rails and wove through the rafters above. Various flowerpots shaped like angels and creatures I wasn't familiar with flooded the area, overflowing with different flowers. The circular space was surrounded by hedges and thick trees, concealing this little hideaway from wandering eyes. "What is this?"

Ryder dropped onto a bench, crossing his legs at the ankles. "The Hidden Garden of Dalia." I blinked, and he added, "The goddess of secrets and truth."

The irony of that didn't go unnoticed as I joined him, sitting on the adjacent bench. I wondered if he saw through my lies but was too respectful to pry the truth. He knew I was keeping secrets, that much was obvious by how he watched me. But where secrets made most people tread with caution, they made Ryder... intrigued.

"This place was built by my grandfather, King Abram, for my grandmother, Freya. The gardeners are the only ones outside my family that know about it."

"And me."

"And you," he repeated. We sat in silence before he cleared his throat. "So, what did you want to talk about?"

Rather than beat around the bush, I decided to just say it. "I overheard your father and the captain speaking about a group of Kindrahs that were spotted in Evamort. Blanning mentioned something about an agreement, and I don't know if you know anything about it, but I thought I'd ask since it seemed... strange."

Ryder angled his head, his features revealing nothing. "You're sure the word *agreement* was used in relation to the Kindrahs?"

"Considering I possess comprehension skills, yes, I know for a fact it was."

His lips quivered like he was fighting a smile. "No need to get defensive."

"Do you know anything about it?" I really didn't have time for teasing and games.

He cracked his neck, and I noticed the slight clench of his jaw before he said, "No, I don't."

That was all he had to say? Annoyance rushed through me as I swung my arms out to the side. "Do you really not care? They're hunting *you*, and I tell you that your father and captain were having a secret little meeting about the very people that want you dead, and you barely have anything to say?"

He stared at me, but I couldn't read the look in his eyes. "I don't know anything about it," he said gently. As if the slight change of phrase made his answer any better.

I let out a dry laugh as I paced, interlocking my fingers against the back of my headpiece. "You know they're heading for Morters' End? The Kindrahs. Your father told Blanning to let them enter the village and burn it to the ground."

I waited for a look of surprise, a show of emotion that resembled the kind prince I'd grown to know, but his face was as blank as a new canvas. He chewed his inner cheek, and after a moment said, "Good."

I blinked. "*Good?*"

It was one thing to lie straight to my face, which I had a strong feeling he was doing about the agreement, but *this?*

"Wren, the necromancers are responsible for my sister's death as well as Salma's and countless others throughout the years," he said. "They deserve to die alongside whatever other Kindrahs get trapped with them." His eyes hardened. "They killed my guards."

"I know," I said, my anger retreating slightly. "I know they did. But they won't be killed by fire, only the ordinary people will. There are innocent people there that will die. The necromancers and other Kindrahs will survive just to be trapped behind the shield. The fire will do nothing to *them*."

"People who sit back and watch while terrible acts are committed are *not* innocent," he said angrily. "You think those people haven't been brought back to life by the necromancers? *They're* the reason for all the death we see here. Actual innocent lives. Children who drop dead because someone in that gods forsaken village was resurrected. The fire might not kill the necromancers, but it will take away their call to power. They only do it because it makes them feel like gods. Taking and giving life. It's a *curse*. They all deserve what's coming for them."

Standing up, he exhaled a deep breath. I couldn't look at him. Couldn't meet the eyes of the man who'd just crushed my hope in the palm of his hand. While I understood his hatred for the necromancers and Kindrahs, I couldn't get behind the rest of his statement. He acted as if he knew the people in Morters' End. Like he knew what went on behind that shield when in reality, he knew nothing.

"What's wrong?" he asked.

I blinked back the tears forming in my eyes. I choked on the words I wanted to say but knew I never could because regardless of our comfortability, he was still a prince, and there were limits to what I could get away with saying. Even to him.

Shaking my head, I forced myself to smile. "Nothing," I said. "Nothing at all."

As we returned to the festivities, I knew what I had to do.

My last resort.

I just hoped he was in the mood to strike a deal.

~

My legs bounced in anticipation as I waited for Asher to show. Alicai was in the bathing room getting ready for the Iron Oak, while Zavier was with Tavrina.

Ryder, after much back and forth in the common room, agreed to four guards accompanying him tonight as long as they didn't *look* like guards. It would be me, Alicai, Easton, and Sanyulin.

I *dared* Flint and Micah to make a comment, but all they did was snort and roll their eyes. Really, I would have preferred if they went in my place. I wasn't crazy about this idea, especially with Bekencourt breathing down my neck. But he was away with Blanning, and Ryder saw that as an open opportunity.

I wasn't going to let my personal feelings get in the way of my job, as tempting as it might be. And while a part of me resented what Ryder said earlier, I tried my hardest to understand his perspective. If Angel could see me now, he'd say something about personal growth. But that didn't matter as I had more pressing things to worry about than the prince's feelings toward Morters' End. Like *saving* it.

We were leaving shortly, and I was running out of time. I needed to see Asher. I sat on my bed in black breeches and a bronze-colored tunic, Angel's hat gripped between my hands. I still had Ryder's cape which I planned to wear with the hood up for extra concealment. In the meantime, I was watching the clock.

This was one of the many things I hated about Asher. I could never summon him myself. He showed up when it pleased him, and nine times out of ten, his visits were unwanted.

I didn't know where he went when he wasn't with me, and he never told me. He didn't tell me a lot of things. I didn't know how he ended up dead at nineteen or when it happened. And I didn't know *why* he wouldn't tell me.

As much as I hated that secretive part of him, I couldn't deny it initially lured me in. The mystery that was Asher.

"I wish I could read your thoughts," he hummed as he appeared behind me. "Especially when I have a feeling they're about me."

"I need you to do something for me," I said, stiffening as his fingers grazed down my collarbone. He tucked my hair behind my ear, kissing the spot of my pulse.

It was so easy to forget everything as we danced across the blurred line of our feelings. Claiming, kissing, and marking with our lips and bodies.

"Asher," I bit out as he tilted my head back, fully exposing my neck. My eyes fluttered closed as he fumbled with the strings of my tunic, his lips a burning brand on my skin.

Warning bells rang in my head, forcing me to snap out of it. I jumped from his grasp, hands going to my half-open tunic. I scowled at him as I tied it back up.

A single black curl fell over his forehead as he braced his arms behind him. "Did you not ask me to do something for you?"

I grunted. "Not *that* kind of something."

His fingers brushed over my blanket. "From your reaction, I'd say that's *exactly* what you wanted."

"Can you be serious for a moment? I need your help."

"And what is it that I can do for you, my beautiful Wren?"

"I need you to find a way to keep the Kindrahs out of Morters' End."

He sighed. "And here I was thinking you wanted something simple."

I ignored him. "If they never pass the shield, Blanning will have no reason to torch the village."

"Let me ask you something. Do you *really* think the Kindrahs are stupid enough to get themselves trapped?"

I shrugged. "I'm in no position to play around with chances. The king and captain seem confident, and that's enough for me."

Asher's eyes shimmered with the knowledge I needed him. "What about your prince? You two seem so close, certainly he can help you."

My nails dug into my palms. "This isn't funny," I said through my teeth.

"Actually, it is. Coming to me for another favor when you haven't even held up your end of the last deal I struck with you."

I was waiting for that blow. Expecting it. So I said the one thing I knew would rattle him. "I'm begging you."

His expression hardened. "*Stop it*," he hissed. I didn't know why the concept of begging triggered him the way it did. One moment he was on my bed, the next he was in front of me. "What makes you think I can do anything to stop them?"

"I need you to try. Do something, anything. *Please*." I fought against my better judgement, raising a hand to cup his cheek. He seemed surprised by the gentle motion. My eyes searched his, those endless pools of blue placed perfectly on his face. "Where do you go when you leave me?" I whispered.

I hadn't meant to ask, it just slipped out. Another one of my intrusive thoughts.

"Is that important?"

"If it will enable you to help me, then yes," I said.

"I'll help you," he answered, and I sighed in relief. He cocked his head, and within seconds he was on me, his body pinning mine to the wall. His hands gripped my hips, fingers digging into my skin. He brushed his lips against my ear and said, "But just remember *who* it is that's helping you."

I pushed him off. "Thank you," I said, then paused. "What's in it for you?"

His smirk spread into a wide grin. "Who's to say I want anything?"

"There's always a price with you."

"All I ask is this. When you're in bed at night thinking about your *prince*, just remember it wasn't him who helped save your whole village. It was me. It's always me."

I opened my mouth, but the sound of a door creaking had me turning. Alicai stepped out of the bathing room, dressed in gray breeches and a navy-blue tunic. He raised a brow. "Were you talking to yourself?"

I glanced at where Asher stood, only to find the space empty. "It would seem so."

CHAPTER 35

The Iron Oak was a few streets off of the main road, and as we approached, I couldn't comprehend why they wanted to come here. Compared to the beautifully crafted buildings I'd seen in the city, the Iron Oak stood out. And *not* in a good way.

It was made entirely of aged dark wood and was slanting toward the right. Two rusted metal poles extended from the cobblestone street to the crumbling roof, keeping it from collapsing. I gave it a slight push, and the metal wobbled. *Wonderful*. The door creaked as a group of barely clothed women stumbled out, releasing a musty smelling odor mixed with cheap liquor and urine.

There were two windows. One near the front door, another on the side, and neither of them were clean enough to see through. Dust covered the fogged-up glass, allowing only the shapes of bodies to be seen inside. A wrought iron pole jutted out from above the door, dangling a sign that said, *The Iron Oak* in smudged black letters.

I looked at Ryder, brows rising in unison as if to say, *This is where you were dying to bring me?*

He shot me a look back as he wiggled his fingers. *Do you need me to hold your hand?*

I scoffed, turning just as Ambrose staggered out the door, leaning on Lorzo who seemed inclined to drop him, while Garrick filed out behind them.

"You made it!" Ambrose slurred, pressing his mug into Garrick's chest. I rolled my eyes. To my right, I noticed a stream flowing behind the buildings. What a shame it would be if Ambrose *accidentally* went for a little swim.

Ryder looked him up and down, shaking his head. Ambrose was filthy drunk already. "Are you going to block the door all night, or can we go inside?"

Ambrose cast a lazy smile, eyes glossy. "Your wish is my command, Your Magical Height-nass."

Alicai's eyes were tearing from containing his laughter, and Ryder seemed equally amused, mouthing that interesting title Ambrose gave him over again.

"Please take him," Lorzo groaned, pushing Ambrose into Garrick. "I don't know how he's this drunk already. We got here twenty minutes ago."

"Because, you idiot," Ambrose said, ruffling Lorzo's shaggy blonde hair. "I started drinking this morning at the circus."

I moved to say something to Alicai, but his eyes were trained on Ambrose. I'd have to talk to him later about why *that* would be a gods awful idea.

Garrick handed Ryder the mug and began walking to the door. "Oh!" Ambrose called over his shoulder. "Make sure your guards don't linger too close." His drunk eyes scanned the four of us. "You lot are off duty tonight! Have a drink!"

Being the last of us to enter, I pulled the door closed behind me and instantly regretted it. The Iron Oak was just as disgusting on the inside as it was on the outside. My boots stuck to the sticky floor, and as I looked down, I prayed it was spilt alcohol and not the alternative. Live music came from the far corner beside the bar top that ran the length of the left wall, while a hustling barmaid ran back and forth, fixing up drinks for the drunkards falling off stools.

Tables were scattered with mismatched seats, and only a few candles were lit, cloaking the room in shadows and voices. Alcoves were carved into the far wall with red silk curtains for privacy. Some were thrown open while others were closed, and it didn't take a genius to guess what was happening behind the thick sheet.

There was a mixture of people dancing, lounging, playing cards, and throwing darts at a board on one of the walls. I barely heard Ryder telling us to enjoy ourselves over the laughs and shouts. The other guards didn't need to be told twice. Alicai went to get a drink, while Easton hurried to an empty chair at a card table, and Sanyulin went—

Well, I didn't know where Sanyulin went. My hand itched for the dagger in my boot while my eyes wandered over every face in the crowd, marking each one to memory. Should anyone try anything stupid, I'd have this dagger embedded in their skull before they could draw another breath.

I already located each exit. The front door, a side door behind the bar, and the steps behind the musicians that led upstairs to a hallway connecting to the adjacent building. Oh, and the two dust covered windows. I'd break them if needed.

I was in the process of counting how many visible weapons I could see, when Ryder pulled the hood of my cape, knocking it over my eyes. I pushed it back up to find him smiling. "What?" I asked. I felt like I was constantly juggling my emotions when it came to him. A part of me wanted to scream while the other part...

"What are you doing?"

"My *job*," I said. I motioned to the other three guards. "Something they seem to have forgotten about."

"Do you think you can relax for one night?" He moved his coat to the side, revealing a shimmering rapier sheathed at his waist. "I can take care of myself."

"You came armed."

"I'm always armed. You're just too distracted around me to notice."

I clenched my jaw as he laughed. "You know what would be really distracting? If I gave the prince a black eye."

"You wouldn't."

"I would."

He inched closer, testing me. "Try it."

I angled my head, gazing up at him. "One day, I'll wipe that self-assured look off your face when I have you pinned below me with a dagger to your throat."

"That sounds extremely tempting. Is it a promise?"

"If you want it to be."

His eyes darkened. "Usually when I imagine us that close, it's *you* that's pinned below me. But I think I'd enjoy watching you on top."

Mine widened at what he was insinuating. "You promised you wouldn't say things like that."

He brought his mouth to my ear. "I said I wouldn't kiss

you unless you asked. I never said I wouldn't tell you *exactly* what I want to do to you. Just say the word, and I'm yours."

Before I could respond, he turned and headed toward the table where his friends were waiting. Thankfully, no one seemed to notice the encounter we just had.

No one but Alicai who was shaking his head at the corner of the bar. I prepared myself for whatever hurtful words he was about to throw my way as I sat down beside him. Without having to ask, the barmaid placed a mug of watered-down beer in front of me.

Raising it to my lips, I looked at Alicai. "Spit it out."

He sat with his back to the bar, eyes scanning the crowd in a seemingly innocent way, but I knew he was really searching for any potential threat against Ryder. So was Easton from the card table, and Sanyulin, who went to an alcove in the back for a clear view of this entire dump. Perhaps I misjudged them since they were all doing their jobs *while* enjoying themselves.

Alicai's dark gaze landed on me. "Does everything I say to you go in one ear and out the other?"

"What?"

He took a sip from his mug. "You're lucky no one else was watching you two. Your body language is ridiculously obvious."

I was about to argue and deny his allegations, but what was the point? I knew what I was doing was wrong and would undoubtedly end tragically, but it was like I couldn't stop myself. I was pulled to Ryder in ways I didn't understand.

Alicai's gaze continued drifting around the room. "In Telamar, on the fourth day of each month, everyone in the village is expected to bring gifts to the altar of Alteria. It's this giant white stone structure with four black pillars. Each pillar is said to symbolize the days it took for him to create the night sky. It's believed that if we bring gifts of our livelihood and wealth, Alteria will keep our nights safe and protected. He'll guard us while we sleep from any horrors that lurk in the dark."

I knew what Alteria was meant to protect people from, but that didn't mean anything. He was as much a false god to me as the rest. But I kept my mouth shut. Alicai hardly ever spoke about his home and life before this, and I was afraid if I breathed or moved the wrong way, he'd stop. I might not believe in the gods, but I did enjoy stories about them.

"Most people bring whatever they're willing to part with," he continued. "Whether it's fresh fruit, steaming bread from the oven, or even bags of gold coins. The children bring anything they can get their hands on. A ribbon for the hair, a fallen button from a coat, or even a secret." I waved the barmaid over for more drinks, careful not to interrupt him. "I was running late that day a few months ago. The streets were empty because after you bring your gift, you pass through the altar to the fields where a celebration is held. I remember running down the paved walkway. I saw the altar, it was just a few streets away, but the sound of crying made me stop. There was a young man crouched down in an alley with his head buried in his lap."

The barmaid brought over fresh mugs, and I silently thanked her. "When I got closer, I realized it was Lord Saymor's son, Randal." Leaning in, Alicai whispered, "Lord Saymor is a nasty old man who pretty much controls Telamar, in case you didn't know."

I nodded, my eyes locking on Ryder. I stilled as a redheaded woman approached his table. She ran her hands down her sides, highlighting her curves and breasts as they spilled from her bodice. Ambrose was drooling as he patted his lap, but she sauntered over to Ryder who was trying not to look. I watched as she bent down and whispered in his ear. He smiled, and that was about all I could take. I turned in my seat and asked the barmaid for something stronger.

"Well?" I asked Alicai. "Are you going to finish?"

He glanced at Ryder's table before turning back to me. Thankfully he didn't make any comments for once. "Anyway, Lord Saymor's son was crying in this dirty alley, and I wanted to know why. I'd never met him personally, but I knew he frequented the all-male brothels in the more discredited parts of the village."

The barmaid placed a glass of clear liquid before me. I didn't care to know what it was as I downed it entirely. I ignored my burning throat, urging Alicai to keep going.

He looked at my empty glass and shook his head. "Long story short, Lord Saymor learned about his son's... *preferences,* from someone who saw Randal kissing a man the night before. Saymor disowned him. His only son. His wife died four years prior from an illness, so he never had any other children."

Alicai ran a hand down his face. "Sometimes I wonder where Randal is now and what he's doing. I told him to join the guard, but he said a guy like him wouldn't last a week here." I dragged my finger over the chipped wood on the bar top. "I guess what I'm trying to say is, sometimes it's smarter to deny ourselves what we want most when the risks are too great." He motioned to the crowded room. "People are always watching and listening, whether you see them or not. And those people will talk."

I looked at where Ambrose was now dancing like an idiot on his chair. I really hoped the leg would snap so he'd fall. Lorzo was leaning back, laughing at something Garrick said, and Ryder...

He was watching me, but Alicai's words kept replaying in my mind. I was paranoid that someone would catch the hidden glances. I had no business looking at the prince in any way other than to protect him.

It was that foolish moment of distraction that cost us as the windows exploded.

CHAPTER 36

Screams and cries echoed through the room as shards of broken glass littered the floor. A few unlucky people seated beside the windows were bleeding, pieces of glass sticking out from their necks, chests, and eyes. The chaos that followed was overwhelming as tables were flipped, and people jumped behind the bar for cover. Others ran up the stairs, while a few stayed crouched over the injured and dead, trying to stop the bleeding.

My eyes darted around the room in search of Ryder. Alicai was already up and moving toward the table when I spotted Garrick and Lorzo huddled on the floor, backs pressed against the wall. Ambrose was crying on his side as he grasped his ankle. I spotted the chair he'd been standing on, and what do you know, one of the legs snapped. In any other circumstance, I would've been grinning. But I still didn't see Ryder. Easton and Sanyulin were charging toward us and—

There he was. Ryder. Kneeling over a woman in a puddle of her own blood. A second later, Alicai had him. I choked on my relief at seeing him unharmed. His eyes were wide as they scanned the crowd but relaxed slightly when they landed on me.

Safe.

We were both safe for the moment.

I pulled the sword from my belt and stepped over the body of a middle-aged man face down in spilt liquor and blood. I shoved that image to the place where I kept all the awful memories reserved for my nightmares.

We had to get Ryder out of here because if there was anything I knew, it was that windows didn't just explode on their own.

Alicai and Easton were helping Ryder up, while Lorzo pulled Garrick off the floor. Sanyulin groaned as he lifted Ambrose over his shoulder, the latter blubbering like a baby about his ankle.

I was a few steps away, carefully weaving through the crowd when the front door was ripped off its rusted hinges. Several screams followed as two towering men stomped inside, cloaked in black from head to toe. Their faces were concealed with a black cloth, the only visible aspect of their features being their eyes.

And those eyes… those cold, vacant eyes were all trained on one person. *My* person.

My breath caught as I moved quicker through the crowd, glass crunching under my boots as I shouted at Alicai to use the stairs. To bring them through that walkway to the neighboring building.

The next several moments seemed to happen in slow motion as Alicai gripped Ryder by the collar of his jacket, urging him to move his feet. But Ryder wouldn't budge. He was focused on the men moving toward him, all color drained from his face.

I'd never seen such horror and rage in his eyes. It was because of that look, I realized who these men were. The captain must have been fed the wrong information. The Kindrahs were never going to Morters' End. They were coming here.

They moved like solid night through the tavern, brushing tables and bodies aside as they went. Easton drew his sword first, pushing Ryder behind him. Sanyulin flew down the stairs after carrying Ambrose to safety. Garrick and Lorzo also fled, but Ryder was so damn stubborn. I watched him try shoving past the guards, drawing his rapier from its scabbard.

Sanyulin took a step forward, sword raised and ready to strike, when one of the Kindrahs lifted a gloved hand. A cloud of black smoke formed in his palm, and all I could do was watch in horror as he fired it at Sanyulin.

The smoke went up his nostrils, and a moment later, his body went limp. He dropped the sword as blood began pouring from his eyes and ears, his body convulsing.

I think Easton screamed, but I couldn't hear it. I couldn't hear anything as Sanyulin's mouth opened, blood dripping down his lips. His body began shaking faster than humanly possible, and then he just... stopped.

A second later, his back arched at an unnatural angle. I flinched at the sound of his spine cracking. Black smoke seeped from his eyes, ears, nose, and mouth. When it finally stopped, Sanyulin dropped to the ground. Dead.

Terrified screams erupted around the room as people dragged their bodies toward the hole in the wall where the door stood moments before. I'd never seen this type of dark magic. This was... *The kind that would make even the devil scurry back to Hell in hiding.*

Slowly, I turned to Alicai. His eyes were wide, hands trembling. Easton was breathing heavily as he gaped down at Sanyulin. And Ryder... Ryder fell to his knees as he watched another one of his guards die for him at the hands of the same wicked beings that slaughtered his others.

The two Kindrahs didn't say a word as they stared at the prince. Their stillness reminded me of the Faceling. Alicai, Easton, and I shared an understanding nod before moving.

Alicai lunged for Ryder, tackling him to the ground, ignoring his protests and screams. I met his gaze momentarily, and those storm cloud eyes pleaded with me not to do this.

I looked away, gripped my sword, and got to work. Easton lunged for the Kindrah who killed Sanyulin, while I went for the other. If I was going down, I'd go down fighting until the very end.

I slammed my body into the Kindrah, spinning as I slashed my sword across the back of his knees. He let out a muffled cry under his face covering, black blood spilling down his uniform. I smirked. I was going to enjoy this.

I blocked every swing of his fists and brought my sword down hard when he motioned to call on his magic. Their mistake was relying fully on their powers. I moved around him, ducking, rolling, striking, and driving my sword at every opening. I looked away for a second to see how Easton was holding up, and luckily, he was still fighting. Limping, but fighting.

"Alicai!" I screamed while dodging the Kindrah's massive fist. "Now would be a great time to get Ryder the hell out of here!"

"Don't you think I'm trying!" Alicai yelled back. I heard Ryder fighting him behind me, but I didn't dare break my focus again.

I was panting, but the masked figure didn't falter. No matter how much blood I drew or how many blows I dealt him, he kept moving as if nothing happened. As if he was indestructible.

The hilt of my sword slipped between my blood-coated fingers. In the two seconds it took to readjust, the Kindrah shot his hand out, a wave of black smoke blasting me off my feet. I was thrown across the room into the wall of bottles behind the bar. I heard and felt them shatter around me as I made contact.

Ryder screamed my name, but I couldn't move my mouth to form any words. I couldn't yell that I was okay, that I wasn't dead.

Shattered glass and alcohol rained down on me. Two dead bodies laid at my feet, one of them being the barmaid. A warm liquid dripped down the back of my neck, its coppery tang filling my senses. I was bleeding. I tried to lift my hand, but my arms were slack at my sides. I could barely breathe from the impact. I heard glass crunching, and a moment later, the Kindrah crouched down in front of me.

Alicai cursed as his grip on Ryder slipped, but I couldn't focus on anything aside from the blood-red shedding serpent embroidered on the right breast of the Kindrah's uniform.

He looked me over once, then raised his hand, a cloud of smoke forming in his palm. It was beautiful, in a dreadful sort of way. He was going to kill me. *Good,* a part of me thought.

I closed my eyes and prepared for the end. I just hoped Alicai and Easton would get out and bring Ryder to safety. I thought of Angel's sketches and his bright hazel eyes, so full of creativity and life. Of Mama laughing while Papa kissed her cheek. Of a time when my family was unbroken. Wherever death took me, I hoped I would see them again someday.

I exhaled a steady breath, clenched my hands at my sides, and waited.

And waited.

And waited.

The Kindrah gasped, causing me to open my eyes. Through sticky lashes, I witnessed him in a state of distress. His own eyes were wide, but he wasn't looking at me. He seemed to be looking *through* me.

"Are you going to kill me or not?" I coughed.

He blinked, refocusing on my face. "It would seem we have use for you."

The words were muffled, but I heard him. He glanced at whatever it was he saw once more, then his body folded in on itself and disappeared.

"What the hell?" Easton yelled from across the room. The other Kindrah must have vanished too.

I could barely keep my eyes open as blood continued dripping down my neck. I tried standing up, hissing as pain from the glass shards in my side sent me crumbling back down.

A second later, Ryder was there, dropping to his knees before me. I tried asking if he was okay as he grabbed my face, but I was too weak to talk. He rubbed tender fingers down my cheeks, worried eyes assessing my body.

I wanted to reach up. To smooth the harsh lines where his brows knitted tightly together. I didn't care who saw or what they might think. Not when I was certain I was going to bleed out.

I wanted to wipe the stray tear sliding down his cheek as he held my face, somehow gentle and firm at the same time. It was like he *needed* to feel me. To know I was there, even if I was slipping away.

He was saying something, but I couldn't hear. I could only see his mouth moving as he formed words I'd never know. I wished I'd let him kiss me.

His pink lips and panicked eyes were the last things I saw before everything went dark.

CHAPTER 37

I woke to Alicai staring at the hideous painting above his bed. He was gripping his chin, brows pulled together in concentration like he was trying to dissect the meaning behind it.

"You know, if you keep staring I might start to think you actually like that thing," I teased. He turned to me, eyes widening momentarily before relaxing.

"You're awake!" The bathing room door opened, heavy footsteps following. Zavier dropped to his knees beside my bed, the sleeves of his caramel tunic rolled up. His eyes scanned me from head to toe, dark lashes flickering as he assessed the damage.

"What happened?" I groaned. My head was pounding. They glanced at each other, expressions grave. Alicai opened his mouth but was interrupted by the creaking of the door.

I couldn't hide my surprise as Tavrina stumbled through, arms full of bandages and containers, her white healer's gown dragging across the floor. It was puzzling how she didn't trip.

Long brown curls spilled over her tan face as she glanced at the contents in her grasp.

"I've brought fresh bandages," she said softly. It was said that even the healers' voices carried medicinal qualities, and I saw why. Her words drifted through the air as gently as a summer breeze. "I also snuck into Clarabel's office and found the special salve she keeps hidden. Apparently, it works wonders for injuries to the—"

Brown eyes met mine, widening as she fumbled with the bandages. I realized I wasn't wearing a hat or my headpiece. I glanced at the small table beside the bed where my dagger rested. Alicai took a step, registering what I was about to do, but he was too late.

I shoved the blankets off my waist and grabbed the dagger, stars clouding my vision from the pain in my head. The quick movement also made the injured side of my stomach throb, but I fought through it, angling myself behind Tavrina, dagger to her throat. She dropped everything she was holding.

The smell of copper filled my nose as she swallowed, the movement causing her throat to jut out, pressing into my blade. She whimpered slightly. I *almost* felt bad.

Zavier stepped closer, his eyes darting between me and the girl whose life I now held in my hands. Literally. "Wren," he said calmly, but I heard the panic in his voice. "Put the dagger down. She just wants to help you."

Tavrina cried in agreement, shaking in my grip. From the look of her flawless skin, it was clear she lived a fairly safe life.

"You idiots," I hissed. "You let her in, and now she *knows*. I don't see any other option."

Alicai grunted. "Don't be so dramatic."

"Dramatic?" I echoed. I kept an eye on Zavier, pressing

the blade further into Tavrina's neck in warning. He halted, lifting his hands in surrender. "What's to stop her from running right to the captain and commander? Or even the king?" I pointed to Alicai. "You said you'd look out for me." He flinched at my words. *Good.*

"You have some nerve, really." Alicai was seething. "Preaching about maintaining your secret when you're always parading around with Ryder, not even trying to pretend something isn't going on. This is *your* fault."

I dug the dagger in further, and Tavrina winced.

"Wren," Zavier begged.

"I'm not going to tell anyone," Tavrina whispered, trying to keep still.

"We had to tell her," Alicai added. "Blood was pouring from the back of your head after you hit the wall." Memories began trickling in. Men cloaked in black, dark smoke, black blood, shattered glass...

"You should be thanking us, really. We managed to get you back here before all the chaos. Zavier snuck Tavrina in, and she stitched you back together." Alicai motioned to my side. "Even that one. She's been changing your bandages and making sure your wounds aren't infected for the past three days."

Three days.

My arms dropped to my side. Tavrina tripped over her dress, but Zavier caught her, pulling her against him. He smoothed her hair, kissing her forehead.

"I've been out for three days?" My voice sounded far away. Muffled, as my head continued pounding. I raised a hand, hissing as I pressed lightly on the bandages.

"Yes," Alicai said. " And luckily for you we've managed to

keep the extent of your injury under wraps. I was worried some of the guards would be asking about you, but you'll be glad to know no one seemed to really give a—"

"Way to be considerate," Zavier said with a shake of his head.

I blinked, then looked at Tavrina who watched me not with fear but... concern. "I'm sorry," I said on an exhale.

"You should get back into bed." She removed herself from Zavier's grasp and began scooping up everything she dropped. "I need to change the bandages and reapply the salve."

"We have a mandatory meeting with Blanning in an hour. All the remaining guards are to meet in the dining hall," Zavier said.

"We survived a Kindrah attack just for Blanning to kill us," Alicai mumbled as he fell back on his bed. "And before you start freaking out, he's only just gotten back today with Bekencourt. They've been gone for days. Not sure where they were, but you should really count yourself lucky. More people besides Tavrina would know your secret if they'd been here the whole time."

Tavrina's hand was on my back, ushering me to lay down, when I froze. "What do you mean remaining guards?" Those were the only words I could focus on.

Zavier clenched his jaw, then shot Alicai a look that seemed to say, *Do you want to take this one?*

Alicai sat up. "After the attack," he said slowly, as if his words were the match to an explosive. "The king thought it best if Ryder went to Cresta to join his mother until things relax here. Twelve guards were sent with him."

The words felt like tiny daggers through my chest as Tavrina helped me onto the bed. She lifted my tunic, cleaning the wound and changing the bandage. "Who's to say the Kindrahs won't find him there?" I asked, wincing as she removed the bandage from my head.

"They won't even know he's gone. Not yet, at least. He was sent off in the middle of the night in an unmarked carriage for the ports of Skantra," Zavier said.

"When?"

"The night of the attack. The city guards heard the commotion, and when they saw the crowd spilling from the Iron Oak, they rang the Red Bell," Alicai answered. "I carried you up the stairs into the neighboring building while Easton dragged Ryder into the street to meet the guards." He paused, then added, "He didn't want to leave you. He fought against Easton the entire time."

I twisted my hands deeper into the blankets. I still had so many questions, but it took all my energy to focus.

"She needs to rest," Tavrina said, running a hand in soothing circles along my back.

Zavier moved to the door. "We'll wake you before the meeting."

Alicai followed, looking back at me. "By the way, Easton knows. Your hat fell off when you hit the wall. But I wouldn't worry about him telling anyone." He smirked slightly. "Ryder was *very* descriptive about the punishment he'd face if he did."

I couldn't think about that right now, so instead I watched Tavrina pick up her things. "I'm sorry again," I said. She glanced up, dried blood smeared on her throat. A twinge of guilt coursed through me.

"Don't worry about it." She smiled and left the room. I had a feeling she'd never turn down helping someone, even if they held a knife to her throat. I understood why Zavier was so drawn to her. To her light.

A wave of exhaustion hit me hard, sending me back to sleep.

Our meeting with Blanning went just as expected.

I tried sitting still while he screamed, preaching his disappointment and outright shock at our disregard for orders, but the medicine Tavrina gave me was wearing off. My head throbbed with every word spoken, and the tight fit of my headpiece was not helping. When I breathed, the stitches on my side stretched, sending another wave of pain through my body.

Sweat dripped down my forehead as Zavier gripped my hand under the table, squeezing occasionally for comfort.

But there was nothing that could comfort the strained, broken feeling.

Sanyulin was dead. Alicai told me his body was sent to his family home in Val Mar where they performed a ritual water burial for him.

Easton was one of the twelve guards sent to Cresta with the prince. I wondered what Ryder had said to make him keep his mouth shut about me. Whatever it was, I hoped Easton kept his word.

Fortunately, there hadn't been any more attacks from the Kindrahs since then. I was still having trouble processing what I witnessed them do. I didn't even think Estelers could vanish into thin air the way they did. And aside from that, we weren't any closer to knowing *why* they wanted to kill Ryder, and I wasn't any closer to learning about this agreement.

For more than half the hour long meeting, I sat there, organizing my thoughts. I didn't tell anyone what the Kindrah said to me. *It would seem we have use for you.* I didn't understand what that meant or why he spared my life, but I had a feeling I was going to find out.

And that symbol. The blood-red shedding serpent. The Faceling knew and tried warning me. If it saw things before they happened, maybe it knew the reason behind these attacks. *Guard your prince, and guard him well. His enemies stretch far and wide, and even some reside at home.*

It had to know the truth. I just hoped it would come to me again and give answers. Preferably not in the form of riddles.

I was pulled from my thoughts as Blanning stiffly walked out the door. From the bits of the meeting I paid attention to, it seemed the remaining guards were being reassigned to castle patrol until Ryder returned. It was a slap in the face, but it could've been worse. He could have sent us all packing. He could have arrested us. He could have found out about *me*.

I fought against the growing panic attack in my chest. More and more people were learning the truth, and I hadn't even been here a year. This was all going downhill, and Alicai was right. It *was* my fault.

"That went well," Alicai sarcastically uttered from across the table.

I rested my elbows on the cold wood, rubbing the sides of my head. "Are you doing alright?" Zavier asked.

I nodded slightly. "I just need to lie down."

"Let's get you back to the room." He hauled himself up, and I followed, leaving the rowdy dining hall behind.

CHAPTER 38

I moaned as my body hit the soft mattress. After a quick bath, another dose of that wonderful pain medicine from Tavrina, and the bowl of lamb stew Alicai brought me, I could *finally* rest.

I was alone now, the silence weighing in heavy. I closed my eyes, sucking in a sharp breath as my head hit the pillow. I willed my mind to go anywhere else. To focus on anything besides the pain that lingered, even with the medicine.

My first thought went to Ryder. I knew he must be struggling with Sanyulin's death. *I can't have anyone else die for me,* he said that day on the balcony. I could still see the torment and guilt in his eyes. His dark circles a reminder of everything he lost. Everything he blamed himself for.

I knew that feeling. I knew the helplessness of standing by, being unable to do anything as the people I cared about were taken away. My fingers curled into the sheets. I would never be that useless again.

I remembered looking at Angel the day Papa died. His eyes

were closed, mouth moving. Praying. Mama's head rested on his shoulder, body shaking, while terrible noises escaped her lips. Noises I'd remember on my own death bed.

My eyes opened abruptly as I sat up, cursing at the pain from moving too quickly. Mama and Angel. Morters' End. Burning.

Guilt rushed through me for only thinking of it now. I needed to see Asher and know if I was right. That Blanning was misinformed about the Kindrahs going to Morters' End. Sweat soaked the strands of hair framing my face as my breathing grew labored. Then, as if he knew what I was thinking about, Asher appeared.

He leaned casually against one of the armoires, arms folded, feet crossed at the ankles. A slow, lazy grin was in the process of forming when he stopped. He looked me over, eyes lingering on my bandaged head. I sat up straighter, hissing as the stitches in my side stretched. My hand instantly went there, and so did Asher's eyes. Eyes that were now as dark as a storm struck sea.

He clenched his jaw. "What happened," he said quietly. Too quiet, considering how rigid his body was.

I shook my head. "Did the Kindrahs go to Morters' End? Did Blanning set it on fire?"

Asher stepped slowly toward me. "What. Happened," he repeated.

I huffed. "Like you don't know. I'm fine. Now tell me—"

He was at the edge of my bed before I could finish the sentence, pulling up my tunic to reveal the bandage on the right side of my ribcage. Gently, he peeled it back, eyes narrowing as they ran over the stitches. Over the dried blood from when I pulled at them earlier.

I allowed it for a moment, then as he growled, I swatted his hand away. "That's enough," I said dryly. "I'm *fine.*" I tugged my tunic down, ignoring the fuming look in his eyes. "Tell me what happened."

He unclenched his jaw. "You were misinformed. There weren't any Kindrahs invading Morters' End. The guards retreated shortly after they arrived. They didn't burn anything."

"How do I know you're not lying to me?"

"Unlike you, Wren," he said bitterly, "I'm good on my word." Without a look back, he vanished. I watched the space he occupied a moment longer before lying back down.

My chest felt somewhat lighter with the knowledge that my family was unharmed. It was because of that sudden, alleviating feeling I was able to close my eyes and fall into a much needed dreamless sleep.

~

The following weeks were strange. I hated my position at the castle gates while Ryder remained in Cresta, and I was growing so tired of people asking questions about what happened that night at the Iron Oak. I might have answered a few had I respected the guards I was stationed with. But it seemed they cared more for gossip than their jobs considering they could barely even hold a sword properly, let alone wield one. They were lazy, untrained, and useless. If someone tried to breach the gates, we'd be utterly and completely screwed.

With that being said, I did make one friend. One of the less aggravating guards named Axel. He was a middle-aged man who had a thing going with a kitchen maid named Grace.

We somehow got talking about chocolate, and I confessed I'd never had it. In his surprise, he told me Grace sneaks him chocolate truffles at the end of each day.

It was one of the only perks of this station.

As we munched on the delectable truffles, Axel told me his entire life story while all I could give him were fragments of mine.

He grew up in Skantra where he spent his younger years on large boats in the Aldric Sea, catching fish that was transported throughout the kingdom. He would have stayed and continued in the family business, but he had a falling out with his brother.

Axel was strongly built and handy with a blade, unlike the other guards here, so when he showed up at the castle twenty years ago, begging for a position in the guard, he earned his spot. He met Grace shortly after while patrolling the lower levels near the kitchen. They bumped into each other, spilling a tray of juice all over her apron and his uniform. They've been in love ever since. I found it hard to believe it was that easy.

Axel could talk, and I liked to listen. I was always listening. Listening for word of Ryder's return, updates on the Kindrahs, and whatever other information was whispered around the grounds.

My wounds healed nicely, the stitches dissolving on their own. I owed Tavrina a great deal as she spent countless hours tending, cleaning, and changing bandages. Zavier watched her every movement, his breath catching when she smiled. Every. Single. Time.

We fell into new routines as the days and weeks passed, but my mind always drifted back to Ryder. Through all the gossip I overheard, no one really spoke about him. No updates on how he was or when he was returning home. It was bizarre, considering how well loved and admired he was at court.

I missed him more than I cared to admit. I missed his contagious smile, his jokes, his company. I missed the unspoken words when we both knew what the other was thinking. I missed the late-night conversations and the way his face lit up when I laughed. As if it was the most breathtaking sound he ever heard.

Yet every time thoughts of missing him surfaced, I pushed them away. I still didn't believe he was being fully honest with me, but I'd gotten over the anger I felt before he left. I needed to let it all go. Nothing good could come from these deadly attachments. Especially with Asher chirping in my ear about fulfilling the covenant. It was safer if I didn't let myself feel anything.

Tonight made exactly five weeks since the attack at the Iron Oak. As I strolled down the streets of Caelestis alone, I shoved my hands in the pockets of my ankle length navy skirt. It had a slit up the right thigh, revealing brown, knee-high boots that kept my daggers hidden but still accessible should I need them. The lacy, cream-colored tunic I wore was undone at the top, revealing the swell of my breasts.

I avoided people as I headed downtown, the music from the city center growing dimmer with each step I took. It wasn't wise for young ladies to enter this part of the city alone. Or so I'd been told. But then again, most young ladies didn't know how to kill a man sixty-five different ways with a dagger.

After discovering another tunnel that led outside the castle, I started leaving on my own accord. I left my uniform beneath the bushes and ventured into the slums of the city. I'd been doing this a little over two weeks now, so I knew what to expect.

I learned that if I walked down the main road long enough, the perfectly paved cobblestones began to crack. The beautiful ivory-colored buildings with terracotta rooves were replaced with crumbling brown-brick structures, each one leaning onto the next like a drunk friend.

This was the Pit.

The section of Caelestis no one talked about. The place where pickpockets would rob you blind before you could breathe in the polluted air. Where people long forgotten hid in the shadows, waiting for the next foolish high-born idiot to make a wrong turn. It was a place where the dangerous and low-born members of the city resided. Where they thrived in the gambling halls and brothels, each one filthier than the last.

It was also the place, according to Axel, where there were whispers about Kindrahs passing through. That's why I trekked down here, playing the role of an innocent, helpless, young lady night after night for the past two weeks. Drunken fools and rowdy men didn't care to keep their mouths shut around a girl like me.

Alicai and Zavier were unaware of my late-night activities. They believed me when I said I was attending the music hall to hear the opera singers night after night. As if I'd be caught dead in a place like that.

So here I was, sipping on cheap beer in a collapsing tavern at the far end of the Pit. If I thought the Iron Oak was bad, it was nothing compared to the Rusty Nail. The name was fitting, considering the hundreds of nails jutting out of wooden beams along the walls. One scrape against the rusted tips and I'd probably be dead come morning from some strange disease.

Everyone knew about what happened at the Iron Oak by now. It seemed even the king couldn't falsely imprison every individual in the city that was beginning to realize the truth behind the last few attacks on the crown. The Kindrahs were here, and they were out for blood.

I didn't pay much mind to conversations about the past though. I was more focused on keeping my ears clear for whispers about current movements. I stayed at the bar where men spoke about things they had no business knowing. Every night I sat there, staring straight ahead, pretending not to hear the words exchanged a few feet away from me.

Most nights they rambled on about complete nonsense. But other nights, when their hushed voices dropped even lower, they drunkenly spilled information that could be useful. From bits and pieces of conversations I heard, the Kindrahs were drifting around parts of the city the guards didn't bother patrolling.

I was trying to hear a man three seats down, when a warm hand landed on my thigh. I looked at the wrinkled skin and bitten fingernails before raising my head. I wanted to see the face of the man who just made a very big mistake. He was older, specks of white in his ebony hair, pine green eyes, and a tanned, freckled face.

His grip on my thigh tightened as his gaze drifted down the opening of my tunic. From his height, I knew he could see everything. A darkness coated the greens of his eyes until they matched his pupils. Lust and desire. I knew the look well. "Get your hand off of me," I said.

He chuckled. A deep, raspy sound that had me fighting a

wave of nausea. Instead of removing his hand, he slowly dragged it higher, tracing circles over my inner thigh.

Subtly, I withdrew one of the daggers from my boot. Keeping it hidden, I repeated, "Get. Your. Hand. Off. Me." This time, more sternly.

He laughed again, bringing his mouth to my ear. "I enjoy a lady with a bit of attitude. Makes it more fun. And you and me? We're going to have quite a bit of fun tonight."

I remained still as his hand continued inching up further and further.

The barmaid was about to ask if we wanted a refill when her eyes locked on me. Whatever she saw on my face had her turning to the man beside me. "Why don't you leave the girl alone, alright?" Her tone held none of the warmth it had moments before when I ordered my drink.

He cocked his head. "How about you mind your own business. The lady belongs to me tonight."

She looked at me once more, and I gave her a tight nod. *I can handle this.* She hesitated for a moment, then went to the other side of the bar.

The man moved his hand again, bringing it further up my leg. Quickly, I shifted in the seat, pressing my dagger into his groin. "Please," he whimpered.

"Please? What's the matter? Not so sure of yourself anymore?"

He removed his hand from my leg, gasping as I gripped his sensitive area. I squeezed so hard tears ran down his cheeks. Keeping my hand there, I hopped off the stool and whispered, "I belong to no one." I squeezed one more time, hard enough that he expelled a cry, then walked away.

CHAPTER 39

"You're not from around here, are you?"

I paused near the door, turning to find the source of the voice. It belonged to a dark-skinned man lounging on a rickety old chair. The sound of his finger tapping against the wooden table drew my eyes downward. Four fingers on his right hand, the one beside his pinky cut off at the knuckle. He watched me curiously, his gaze drifting from the dagger in my hand, back up to my eyes.

"Actually I am," I said innocently, shoving the dagger into my boot.

A half smile crossed his face, a dimple pressing into his left cheek. "Most girls here don't put up any form of resistance, let alone have a man three times their size whimpering like a child."

I snorted, my carefully planned façade slipping. "Please. I could take anyone in this cesspit with my eyes closed."

He didn't seem surprised as he motioned to the chair across from him. With some reluctance, I sat. "Tell me, why has a young lady like yourself been parading through the Pit the past two weeks, drawing weapons in my tavern?" he asked.

I blinked. Crossing my legs, I casually lowered my hand, the hilt of my dagger in close range should I need it twice tonight. He smirked as if he knew exactly what I was doing.

"Are you following me?" *And did he say this was his tavern*? If anyone knew something of value, surely it would be the man who ran the place.

He sipped from his mug. "I don't need to follow you. You're walking through a place like *this,* dressed like *that*. People are going to talk." He leaned forward, bringing his face close to mine. I fought the urge to sit back. "And I want to know why a high-end girl like yourself is frequenting *my* establishment, armed to the teeth."

I shifted in my seat, keeping my expression blank. "I'm hardly high-end."

He shrugged. "Anyone from uptown is high-end to us down here."

I thought for a moment. I needed to play my words carefully to get the most out of him without raising suspicion. I folded my hands together on the table and smiled. "Have I been the only outsider around here lately?"

His eyes narrowed. "Who wants to know?"

I traced my finger across the chipped wood. "No one. I'm merely curious." He fidgeted in his seat, brows knitted together. Oh yes, he knew something.

I reached into my other boot and pulled out a small pouch. I dropped it on the table, the coins inside clinking together. Leaning forward on my elbows, I smiled again. "So here's how this is going to go. Tell me everything you know about the Kindrahs who've been sneaking around here, and the pouch is yours."

I didn't even know his name. Didn't care to ask, and definitely didn't plan on telling him mine. The less we knew about each other, the better.

I watched his eyes linger on the pouch. If there was anything I was sure of, it was that most men would do and say anything for money. Greed was an inescapable flaw of men like the ones in the Pit.

After a moment of rubbing his stubble-coated chin, his eyes met mine, and he nodded. "About a week and a half ago," he began, "four men in all black were spotted wandering around here. I didn't see them until they came in one night for a drink. I knew they weren't locals, but I'm not one to pass up on business. So, they sat at the bar and we served them."

He looked at the barmaid polishing glasses. "It wasn't until they got up to leave that I realized who... *what*, they were. They were going without paying, so Esme called them back. I watched from this seat right here." He tapped his chair for emphasis. "They all looked at her, and within seconds, the tallest one had some kind of black smoke shooting out of his hand. It wrapped around Esme's throat, pinning her to the wall. Place went silent after that, and no one dared to stop them as they headed out. They weren't spotted again. At least not in here."

"Why didn't you alert the guards?" *And why were the Kindrahs still in Caelestis? Didn't they know Ryder was gone?*

He scoffed. "They don't care to patrol this area, and they sure as hell don't come running when they're needed. Why would I help by giving them information?"

Fair point. "What else do you know of them?"

"Of the Kindrahs?" He snorted. "Nothing, and I don't really care what problems they've set out to stir. Only thing I care about is that they got free beer out of me." I fought an eye roll. This was hardly beer, and he knew it.

I reached for the pouch. "Well, since you insist on lying to me, I think I'll take this back."

He threw a hand on top of mine, stopping my movement. "Fine." He rubbed the back of his neck, debating how much information he wanted to throw out. "I don't know the specifics of what business they have here, but I do know quite a lot about their history. And from how much you're willing to part with..." He nodded to the pouch of money. "I'll bet you don't."

Good. We were getting somewhere now. I leaned back, crossing my arms. "Tell me whatever you know."

"They're dangerous, those with the dark magic," he said quietly. *No shit.* "But they weren't always like that. Just as the Estelers were given Purity from Tella, the powers of dark magic were also gifted from a god."

Now *that* I didn't know. "Which god?"

"His name was Aros, god of wind and storm. He's mostly forgotten now-a-days, lost to history. He was a minor god, not as powerful as Alteria or Tella, but powerful enough. He turned on the rest of them when they left for the skies. He wanted to rule on land, to be more powerful. So, he gifted many men and women in Enderya a fraction of his power. He willed it to manifest in different forms, to bend and change, to fulfill all impossible and terrifying feats. He wanted an army of loyal followers so strong, their power so unmatched, that even Alteria wouldn't be able to stop him."

"And what happened?"

"He showed his hand too quickly, and Alteria destroyed him. Brought him over to this continent, away from the abominations he created and rendered him to a pile of ash."

He paused as a crowd of drunken men and women stumbled out the door into the humid night. "They claim his remains were taken in the very wind he once controlled and landed in the village all the way east of Caelestis," he continued. "Morters' End, I think it's called."

I stilled, listening very carefully to his next words.

"Some believe that's how the necromancers came to be. That the ash of Aros formed his final group of loyal followers. I've heard that's why those in Enderya hate us so strongly. Because we have some of their people shielded away in a cage. Years ago, they bargained to have those necromancers freed and brought across the sea so they could be with their own, but the king wouldn't allow it." He leaned forward again, warm whiskey filled breath caressing my face. "I may also know why they have it out for the prince."

I clenched my teeth. "Do you now?"

His gaze drifted to the pouch. He tapped a finger against it. "Going to cost you a bit more for that information, sweetheart."

I laughed, pulling my dagger from my boot. I held it between my hands, pressing the tip gently into my finger. "You're going to tell me what I want to know, or this pretty dagger here will find itself embedded in your throat. Okay?"

His bitter expression was nothing short of murderous. "The pouch will do just fine then," he said harshly. "King Caldaris of Enderya lost his second born last year during an altercation with our soldiers. So if you ask me, this seems like retribution."

What? I'd never heard of any of this. While the reasoning would make sense, I knew better than to take the word of this swindler as stone-cold truth without confirmation. Surely if this happened Blanning would've informed us.

Wouldn't he?

"A second born for a second born," I said dryly. I needed to get out of here. Pushing the chair back, I paused. "If this was all kept under wraps, how is it you know?"

He grabbed the pouch, tucking it into his pocket. "People talk. Just have to be willing to listen."

I rolled my sleeves as I trekked up the streets of the Pit. It was hot. Unbearably hot for this time of night. The moonlight lit a path along the cracked and crumbling cobblestones, illuminating the rats scurrying down alleys. Half-naked women paraded the corners, calling over drunk men stumbling out of brothels. Some accepted, eager for a second round. I grinded my teeth together. This place was disgusting. A breeding ground for disease and illness.

I passed an alley, unable to discern the entanglement of limbs and bodies pressed against the side of a building. I might've thought they were dead, had moans and other sensual sounds not followed.

I was three steps away from crossing into uptown, when something caused me to stop. I was a trained guard, and even before then, my papa taught me well. I knew when someone was following me.

I pulled my dagger out slowly, gripped it at my side, then continued walking. Rather than going straight to the city center, I turned down a quiet street. It was empty, not even the sound of scurrying feet disrupting the eerie silence. I cut between two abandoned buildings and hid in the shadows, waiting.

Footsteps slowly followed, boots splashing through puddles. Whoever this was, wasn't as inconspicuous as they thought. As they crossed into a dim patch of moonlight, I jumped out and struck.

I slammed the pommel of my dagger into their back. From the deep grunt, I knew it was a man. He dropped to his knees, spitting out such vulgar words that I paused. I shoved him to the side, revealing his face.

Sighing, I put the blade away. "Don't expect me to apologize," I said, crossing my arms. "That's what you get for following me."

Alicai stood up, rubbing his upper back. He'd have a nice bruise there in the morning. His eyes burned into me as he said, "What the hell is wrong with you?"

"Do you really want me to answer that?" He rolled his shoulders a few times while wincing. "Why were you following me?" I demanded.

"Following you?" He looked up at the sky and snorted. "I was here for personal reasons when I saw *you* leaving the Rusty Nail. Are you out of your mind?"

"I can handle myself, in case you've forgotten."

"I haven't—" He sighed, eyes softening. Pinching the bridge of his nose, he asked, "What are you doing down here, Wren?"

"Doing what the rest of you *should* be doing," I said. "Getting information on what we're going up against."

He ran a hand down his face. "I know you miss Ryder, but—"

"This has nothing to do with that," I snapped. "And I don't miss him. I'm just curious."

"Yeah, okay. And I'm straight."

I looked him up and down, taking in his burgundy breeches and ivory fitted coat. Golden details were embroidered at the cuffs and in-between the buttons. "Where were you off to dressed like that? You look like you just stumbled off the stage of some ridiculous re-enactment play."

His amber eyes narrowed. "You're really funny." Grabbing my arm, he interlocked it through his. "Let's get back, nothing good happens here late at night."

"You realize we're two trained guards, right?"

He frowned. "I'd rather not press our luck again. Come on."

Just a few steps out of the Pit, and everything went back to perfection. Dying lights in windows flickered, and the cobblestones were polished and whole. The distant sound of music from the city center filled the air, mixing with the delicious scent of roasted, caramelized peanuts being prepared for the next day.

All the while back to the castle, I couldn't stop thinking about what that man had said. If it was true, then the Kindrahs wouldn't stop coming. They wouldn't quit until they killed Ryder. Hell, they killed all his guards in attempts to get to him. Who's to say they wouldn't do it again? I needed to learn the truth, and if Blanning wouldn't tell us, I'd need to take matters into my own hands.

CHAPTER 40

I wrapped myself in a towel as I stepped out of the bathtub that night. I would've waited until morning, but the lingering grime from the Pit resided on my skin. That was enough to have me running straight for the bathing room when me and Alicai returned.

Brushing through the knots in my hair, I felt like I was being watched. I looked at my reflection in the fogged mirror as Asher appeared behind me.

"And why is it," I asked casually, "that you insist on showing up when I'm usually naked?"

A smirk curled his lips as cold hands pressed into my sides. I felt every inch of him against my back. "You haven't seen me in over two weeks, and that's the first thing you ask?" He nibbled at my ear.

I twisted out of his grip. "And whose fault is that?"

"Sounds like someone missed me."

"Where do you go?" I asked quietly. I'd asked him this before. Plenty of times, but he never answered.

His smile faded. "A place you're lucky you'll never see."

I didn't know why, but I traced my fingers down the smooth skin of his neck. He stilled, completely motionless.

Asher was lonely. And a part of me knew that deep down, I was lonely too. But after everything I'd gone through, it wasn't the intimacy of *him* I craved anymore. Realizing that felt like the first breath of air after being submerged under water.

He lowered my hand, interlocking our fingers. His other hand brushed the damp hair off my shoulder, exposing my neck as he brought his lips to the space below my ear. Every kiss and touch from Asher felt like heavenly fire burning me alive, but I couldn't do it anymore. Even the strongest flames had to be put out eventually.

I pulled back, placing a hand to his chest. "No more."

He leaned in again. "If you're worried about anyone hearing—"

I pushed him harder. "*No. More.*"

We watched each other, and I knew he was reading in my eyes everything I couldn't voice out loud. I knew the moment he understood I didn't want him anymore.

He stumbled back like I just delivered a death blow. Those bright blue eyes shifted to a shade so dark, I felt afraid of him for the first time in my life.

He clenched and unclenched his hands several times. "So devoted to your prince. I must say, your loyalty is astounding." He clutched his hands behind his back, strolling around the tub. He chuckled to himself. A menacing sound that had me grabbing the hairbrush. It would do nothing to him, I knew that, but its firm weight in my hand was a comfort.

I watched him cautiously as he paced around the small

room. "I wonder," he added, perching on the lip of the tub. "Where is *my* loyalty, Wren? Where is my unyielding devotion and affection?" His pale fingers gripped the rim, bloodless veins surfacing under the skin.

When I didn't respond, he shrugged. "And where is your prince now? Ah, right," he hummed, a twisted smile forming. "He's not here." Asher stood up and moved toward me. I backed up until I hit the wall. Trapped.

He placed his hands on the smooth surface, locking me between his arms. "You were *mine* first. Did you forget every touch?" I shivered as he trailed his fingers down my bare skin. "Every kiss?" Dropping his head, he placed his lips on my temple. "Every memory?"

I looked at him. At the broken sound of his voice with those two final words. At the sullen expression coating his features.

Releasing a deep breath, I put my hand on his chest. "I didn't forget every touch." I pushed him, stepping away from the wall. "Every kiss." Another step. "And I certainly did not forget a single memory. Not one." I dropped my hand. "But no more, Asher. No more of those things."

The words felt like dragging a blade across my own throat. It killed me to say them, but it was killing him just the same. If not more.

"You were enough for me." My voice was so quiet. "Our little life together would have been enough. But it wasn't enough for *you*. You just couldn't let go of this need to come back from death, and in your efforts, failed to realize you were alive to me. You and me, Asher. The situation wasn't perfect, but it would have been enough." I shook my head, fighting back the tears I'd kept in for far too long now. "*You* wanted this. You ruined everything we were for this, so if you're suddenly okay with me not fulfilling—"

"You will fulfill this covenant whether you want to or not," he growled. He vanished and reappeared behind me, lips brushing my ear. "And one day, when your prince is dead, because he will die, Wren." He tucked the hair behind my ear. "Because although you might not love him yet, you will. And he... well, his feelings where you're concerned are unquestionable. No matter what you desire, you will kill him, I'll be free, and you'll see how easy it will be to pick up where we left off." He tugged the edges of my hair, snapping my head up. "You will always be *mine.*"

"I won't do it," I snapped as anger replaced the pain. "I'll never give you what you want. And you will never have me again. Not in any way your twisted mind can think of." He was no longer the boy who held my hand and kissed my lips on my bedroom floor in Morters' End. Now he was someone unrecognizable, the face of my most haunted nightmares.

He smiled, crossing the room. "Oh, Wren, you'll find both those things are one and the same. And no matter how you fight it or what you may think, I will have both."

My grip on the hairbrush tightened, and before I could stop myself, I chucked it at his head. He vanished just in time, the brush crashing against the wall.

I stood there shaking as Zavier and Alicai pushed open the door. Both sets of eyes were coated with sleep as they assessed the situation.

Zavier looked at me, the hairbrush, and then the wall. "I'll take it you won that fight."

Perhaps it was how small Alicai appeared beside Zavier, or maybe it was the joke he made. Or maybe... just maybe, it was the absolute disaster my life had become that caused me to drop to the floor in a fit of tears and laughter.

The following week, a few of us guards were reassigned to patrol the wall, a forty-foot stone enclosure around the perimeter of the castle grounds. We were stationed on a narrow walkway at the top, working six-hour rotations.

I had the sunrise shift. I didn't mind it, especially from this high up. I enjoyed watching as the red and gold hues lined the horizon, and although I stood with many other guards, there was something personal about it. The silence of Caelestis as the city still slumbered.

I held my breath as the sun rose. I was convinced that if I breathed even a slight breath as the first light began to show, it would vanish. As if I imagined the entire thing. Spending so many years in the dark did that to a person.

I'd always appreciate the light.

Standing here reminded me of the balcony at Ryder's townhouse. My chest tightened when I thought of him. I wondered if the shadows under his eyes had darkened in the weeks since I'd seen him. I wondered if he still thought of me.

I released the breath I was holding as the sun passed the horizon. The weight of the bow strapped to my back felt heavier than usual today. Rolling my shoulders, I did my best to shift the weight.

"Want one?" Axel asked, offering me a half-melted chocolate truffle. My new friend had been restationed with me.

I shook my head as I grabbed it. "I don't want to know where you're keeping these, but in this heat, you'd better finish them quickly." Plopping it into my mouth, I nearly moaned at the mixture of raspberry paste, dark chocolate, and sea salt.

"Would you believe me if I told you Grace restructured a part of my uniform to store them?"

I laughed, wiping my hands on my thighs. A tap on my shoulder had me spinning to find Rafael, one of the king's guards, standing behind me. Well, towering over me was more like it. I angled my head to see his face.

"You're wanted in the throne room," he said.

"Why?"

"Are you really in a position to be asking questions?" he shot back.

I cast a sideways glance at Axel who only shrugged as he chewed on a truffle. Turning back to Rafael, I sighed. "I still have three hours left of my rotation. I can't just abandon post."

A cocky grin took over his lips as he tapped a finger on the hilt of his sword, eyes drifting over my sagging shoulders. "That bow too heavy for you?"

I straightened, ignoring the pain of the strap digging into my shoulder. "Not at all," I lied.

He extended a hand. "Give it here." I fought the urge to drive my knee into his stomach as he reached out and pulled it over my head. I grinded my teeth as he smirked. The bow looked like a small toy against his large frame. "Get going, Hibreaker. The king said it was urgent."

I stiffened. What did the king want with me? Did he somehow figure out who I was? What if something happened to Ryder?

As if noticing my distress, Rafael added, "Not just you.

All Ryder's guards were summoned to the throne room. That's all I know."

With a quick goodbye to Axel and a grin promising violence to Rafael, I ran down the walkway. When I reached the corner, I pulled the metal hatch and descended the ladder.

I sprinted down the winding halls, my mind racing with possibilities of why the king wanted to see us. Finally, I arrived at the gilded doors of the throne room. Slightly out of breath, I hurried inside. The sun was shining through the windows, brightening the marble floors.

I found Alicai and Zavier almost instantly and hurried over to them. The nine others who remained at the castle were also present, lining the walls of the room. Captain Blanning was nowhere to be seen.

The king sat on his throne, chin resting on his hand. I couldn't read his expression as his eyes focused on the open doors. He'd done a good job the past month at reassuring the citizens that they had nothing to be worried about. That these attacks were being handled and treated with the utmost care. His calculated lies were like sweet poison to the people and watching him spin them so easily was sickening.

I was about to ask Zavier what the point of this meeting was, when movement from beside the king drew my attention. When did the queen return? And if she was here, then was Ryder back too?

Heavy footsteps sounded as Commander Bekencourt strolled in. Each step he took exerted a wave of confidence and cockiness. His smug expression didn't help either.

My stomach churned at the sight of him. I started retreating further into my skin, hoping he wouldn't notice me. During the past few weeks, he cornered me whenever I was alone, saying the same vague things. He tried prying information from me as well as scaring me into thinking he knew things he shouldn't. I never faltered though. And luckily, those uncomfortable interactions never lasted long as someone always walked by at the right moment.

His obsidian eyes drifted to me, lips twitching slightly in the corners. It would have affected me more, had I not been distracted by the chain he gripped. Attached to it was a man in all black except for a small red serpent woven into his uniform. A sack was thrown over his head as he stumbled behind the commander. A wave of tension spread through the room, and I reminded myself to breathe. Alicai stiffened beside me, memories from the Iron Oak resurfacing.

The chain branched off in two sections, each one attached to a hefty manacle that was snapped tightly around the Kindrah's wrists. I'd never seen metal with an iridescent shine before.

A moment later, ten of the twelve guards that went with Ryder to Cresta filed into the room. If they were here, that meant Ryder was definitely back.

My heart pounded in my ears as Alicai's warm hand gripped my wrist. His eyes seemed to say, *Not yet.* I nodded. I couldn't run out of here, especially when Bekencourt was undoubtedly about to explain—and *brag*—about how he caught one of the Kindrahs.

As the newly entered guards dispersed around the room, the commander dragged the prisoner to the dais. He pulled off the sack, revealing the Kindrah's face to the king only. I couldn't think of anything aside from Ryder. He was somewhere in this castle, and every atom in my body screamed to go find him.

I might've done just that had the Kindrah not turned his head to the side. I didn't see their faces that night at the Iron Oak, but I saw their eyes. And the coal black ones I saw now, sparkling with the promise of death should he get free of those chains, were the same eyes of the Kindrah who spared my life.

CHAPTER 41

As soon as the Kindrah was brought to the dungeons, I made a break for it. I couldn't believe Bekencourt managed to catch one of them. He said they'd found the Kindrah at the outskirts of the city in one of the wooded areas. His capture, according to Bekencourt, was largely due to the element of surprise and a type of metal that nullified magic known as talverite. It was extremely rare and found only in Tryfel which I guess explained the trade deal Garrick and his father negotiated.

I didn't understand how no one else was questioning this. I'd seen what that Kindrah could do with my own two eyes. I'd *felt* the extent of his power. I watched as that very power tore Sanyulin apart from the inside out.

Because of that, I couldn't wrap my brain around how Bekencourt, a few guards, and some metal managed to trap him. Especially without the help of Drestel and Pryler who I hadn't seen for weeks now.

The Kindrah didn't look at me again as he was pulled

from the throne room, talverite chains dragging across the black marble floor.

Once the commander had left, Blanning informed us that we were relieved from castle patrol now that Ryder had returned. Then he went on about the new safety precautions he wanted us to follow, which were pointless seeing as Ryder would sweet talk his way out of being trailed by a unit of guards no matter what Blanning instructed.

I moved steadily down the wide hallway, each step bringing me closer to him. After all these weeks, he was finally back. My heart raced in my chest as anticipation gnawed at me. Easton and Flint looked up as I approached Ryder's ivory door. They'd both gone with him to Cresta, and Flint's skin was now deeply tanned.

"Long time no see," Easton said.

I nodded. "Glad you're back. Mind if I have a word with the prince?"

Flint took a slight step, blocking the door. His narrowed eyes made it clear we still weren't on friendly terms. "No can do, Hibreaker. Said he didn't want any visitors."

I looked at Easton. He knew who I was now. Any fear of him exposing me faded as his eyes seemed to say, *Your secret is safe with me.* "Let him in," he said to Flint.

"But he specifically said—"

Easton shoved Flint to the side, allowing me to pass through. "Go ahead."

I mouthed *thank you* before walking into the room, the sound of them arguing muffled as the door closed behind me.

It looked exactly as I remembered it. Books covering the tables, the various assortment of detailed rugs spread over the floor, the cherry wood bed, black silk sheets...

And standing at the window, was Ryder. The curtains were pulled wide, allowing the morning light to penetrate the dark room. He stood with his back to me, arms folded across his chest as he gazed out. His hair was lighter now, a golden-brown that curled along the nape of his neck. From where I stood, I saw the strong muscles of his back flex as he lowered his arms.

I removed my headpiece, shaking out my hair as he stilled. He knew I was here. He always knew when I was in a room. It was as if the air shifted slightly, pulling him in my direction.

After a very long moment, he turned. His skin was a shade darker from his time on the island, eyes bright as they locked on mine. Those same eyes I dreamt of constantly over the last month. We stood that way for a while, relief and something else crossing over his features.

"Hi," I finally said.

He angled his head. "Your hair got longer."

I laughed, and that was all it took for him to cross the room and pull me into him. I breathed in his scent. The burnt sugar and... something else? Something new. I think it was lemon. It was an oddly intoxicating combination, and as I buried my head against his chest, I inhaled deeply.

"I missed that sound," he said softly.

"What sound?" I pulled back, straightening my uniform.

"Your laugh." He seemed mesmerized as he ran a gentle finger down my cheek. "I thought of that laugh every single day."

I scanned his face. That beautiful face. Although he didn't hold any physical scars, I knew the damage ran deep. His dark circles were drastically darker, his eyes red-rimmed. "How are you?" Possibly a stupid question, but we had to start somewhere.

A boyish grin crossed his lips. "Would you believe me if I said much better now that you're here?"

"Possibly." So many things... so many things I'd wanted to say. Had rehearsed in my head the countless nights I couldn't sleep. And now he was here, standing right in front of me, and I couldn't remember a single thing. "I'm glad you're home."

"I hope you missed me," he said. His eyes took on a devilish gleam that told me his thoughts were anything but innocent. "Because I missed... everything. I missed your fire and snarky remarks. I missed how you bite your cheek when you fight a laugh. I missed having you beside me. Having someone to talk to."

And while that was all wonderfully sincere, the next bit had me blushing. "I thought of you as I laid awake at night. It helped with the restlessness. I'd think about having you in that bed right there." He motioned behind him. "And I'd take you like—"

I smacked his arm, my cheeks burning. "You're so shameless."

He grinned lazily. "You love that about me."

"I'm sure there were plenty of beautiful women to entertain your fantasies while you were away."

He took an insulted step back. "There was no one. And there won't be anyone, unless you—"

"Things have been so interesting here," I cut him off. I didn't want to know what he was going to say. Not at all. I moved toward the chaise, dropping down comfortably. "The castle guards have it good, you know. I'm thinking about formally switching over." An absolute lie, but I *would* miss Axel's truffles.

Ryder sat beside me, draping his arms across the back. "Over my dead body would I let you do that. You belong right here. With me."

"Well, I'm glad your time at sea didn't put a damper on your charming personality."

He grabbed my legs, tossing them over his own. I tried thinking of anything besides his warm hands on my knees, his thumbs tracing idle circles above the fabric. I should have pulled away. I should have left. I should have done so many things.

"How was Cresta?" I asked, my brain suddenly foggy. My legs remained in place. "What did you do?"

"It was either train until I felt sick or join my mother and her court while they lounged around all day, sipping wine in the hot sun and rambling about nonsense."

"I'll take it you stuck with the former," I said, noting his muscles under his tunic. He'd definitely gotten stronger.

He flexed his fingers. "Speaking of training, I was planning on heading over to the sparring room. Care to join me? I'm in need of a partner."

My grip tightened on the hilt of the practice sword. It felt like an extension of my body. A part of me. I raised it, the dull blade glistening from the light in Ryder's sparring room. Sweat dripped under my headpiece, coating my lashes.

He panted across from me, and just the sight of him sweaty and bare chested was enough to bring out this unusually sharp desire. He managed to drive me out of my mind while simultaneously making me feel like the sanest person in the world.

Stepping back, I raised my sword and positioned my feet for the next round. He was a fair opponent, his skills greatly improved from his time away. "You must have really exhausted the guards who trained with you if this is all you did," I said.

The sound of metal scraping metal blended with our breathing. "I told you. It was either train or socialize with my mother's ladies. And trust me, I want nothing to do with them."

I parried his blow, driving to the right where he left himself open. "Why not?"

"They care for nothing but rank and status." We moved in a circle, swords raised in defensive positions. "I've lived my entire life surrounded by girls who want nothing but a title. They'll do and give just about anything to become princess."

"And you know that from experience?" What was wrong with me? Jealousy was a foul, disgusting beast.

His eyes hardened. "They mean nothing to me."

"Was Gisella—"

"No." He cut me off as he wiped his arm across his forehead, his curls slick with sweat. "Although she definitely tried."

"Well, you'll have to pick someone. Your father will want you to marry for advantageous purposes."

Something shifted in his expression but was gone before I could decipher it. "I don't have the luxury of choice in that matter. Ironic, isn't it? The prince who can have just about anything he asks for cannot marry for love."

"Is that what you want?"

He looked at me like I was the sun, moon, and all the stars in the sky. Before I realized what he was doing, he lunged, and I tripped, falling onto my back. He knocked the sword from my hand and gripped my wrists, pinning me to the ground.

I was completely at his mercy. And as he sat above me, knees on either side of my hips, something twisted in my gut.

His breathing was steady as he lowered his body over mine. "I've made it perfectly clear what I want, Wren. I want you. I want whatever we can give each other in positions as unfortunate as our own. Even if it's only stolen kisses and illicit meetings. I'll gladly accept whatever you give me because the truth is, there's no one like you, Wren Hibreaker."

"Maybe..." I tried moving, but his grip on me was firm. Clearly I wasn't going anywhere until we had this conversation. "Maybe in time you'll love whoever your father chooses for you to marry."

He frowned. "Do you really believe that?"

"I don't know much about love," I admitted. "But I know that sometimes it's not enough. I can't do this with you. It doesn't matter what you think you feel for me, we can't do this. And if you think stolen kisses and secret rendezvous will be enough, then you're crazier than you look. And what if someone found out? The list of people who know my secret is growing, and I'm more at risk every day. Maybe it would be better if I left."

He was a prince, and I was a guard. And like he said, he didn't have the privilege of marrying for love, and I wouldn't have crumbs of him while he belonged to another.

As much as I wanted to stay and finish my service to free Angel and Mama, I didn't know how much longer I could maintain this façade. Perhaps I would remain until this

Kindrah situation was resolved, and I knew Ryder was safe. Because I *did* care for him. But I couldn't imagine staying past that point. Things had grown too complicated. I failed.

"I can't lose you, Wren," he said, voice like gravel. He hovered over me, fear coating his blue eyes.

"Ryder, I—"

"I didn't know what happened to you."

"What?" I stilled as he pushed himself off me, leaning his back against a pillar, resting his arms on his bent knees.

"That night, I didn't know what happened to you. They wouldn't... everything happened so quickly after you passed out, I didn't know what happened to you. I didn't know if you were dead or alive. I didn't know for a week until Easton knocked on my door one night with a letter from your friend Alicai."

I didn't know Alicai had been writing to Easton. "He let me read it," Ryder went on. "And I knew you were okay when I read that you ignored the healer's orders to remain on bed rest and snuck out to train."

I smiled at the memory. Of Tavrina chasing me down the hall, waving bandages and salve in the air. *That* was something the courtiers would be unlikely to forget anytime soon.

Ryder, however, was unamused.

"Well, you know sitting still isn't exactly my strong suit," I teased.

When he didn't smile, I sat up. "I'm *okay.* See?" I patted my body, but his eyes remained on mine. I sighed. "I promise I'm okay, Ryder. I didn't—" I paused, huffing out a strained breath. "I didn't know if you were coming back."

"I didn't know either until a week ago when I was shoved onto a boat." He looked down at his open hands. "Sanyulin's family will be receiving monthly sums indefinitely for his bravery and selflessness. Money to care for their other three children. To make sure they live lives Sanyulin would be proud of."

My throat went dry. "I think... I think he would be very happy to know that."

He watched me again, shaking his head. "I thought you were *dead,* Wren." His voice cracked.

I crawled to him, positioning myself between his legs. Grabbing his face, I forced him to look at me. "I need you to hear me. *I'm okay.* My wounds have healed, and I'm okay." I brushed my thumb across his cheek, my gaze lowering to his lips. I swallowed. "It's going to take more than some silly magic trick to kill me."

Finally, he smiled. Even laughed a little bit. It was a sound that rang straight through my heart, encouraging beat after beat. He licked his lips, and I realized how close we were. How I was positioned. But I didn't pull away, not this time.

Grabbing his hand, I squeezed. "You're going to get through this, okay?" I didn't have to say it, he knew what I meant.

He squeezed my hand back in response. Finally, I pulled myself up. "What do we do now?"

A playfulness took over his features as he stood, and my chest eased at the familiarity of it. "I think I want to hear all about your adventures. Especially the ones that brought you down to the Rusty Nail."

How he knew about that, I didn't know. But his mention of the Rusty Nail brought me back to that conversation I'd had with the owner. "I may have an idea on why you're being targeted."

His smile vanished along with the color from his face. "What?"

"I talked to someone in the Pit. He told me something that helped this entire mess make sense." Ryder was uncomfortably tense as he watched me. "Did you know the King of Enderya lost his son during an altercation with our soldiers? I didn't know anything about it, but I did some research. I went to a library in the city, and after much convincing—and threatening—the librarian showed me the forbidden section. Last year, Tresdilian Eliadis, second born of Caldaris Eliadis, King of Enderya, was struck down and killed in the eastern grasslands near the Raptyrs, and it was kept quiet."

If this surprised Ryder, he didn't show it. If anything, he looked... guilty? "What is it?" I asked.

"I know," he said quietly. "I know about Tresdilian. I remember the day it happened."

"You *know*?" I echoed, shaking my head in disbelief. "You've known this entire time? When your own guards were being slaughtered in front of you?" He flinched at my words, but I didn't care. I was fuming. "You knew and didn't say anything? What else do you know? That's why they're targeting you, isn't it? Does this have anything to do with the agreement I overheard your father speaking about? You know, the one you *lied* about not knowing?"

I wasn't completely certain he *had* lied about that. It was only a hunch, but by the way he recoiled at the words like I'd just slapped him, I knew it was the truth. I stepped back, off balanced by my anger.

He looked at the floor. When he didn't respond, I spun on my heels and stormed from the room.

CHAPTER 42

Ryder lied to me.

I grinded my teeth as I headed down the hall of windows. The glass was covered by a sheet of pelting rain as dark clouds drifted above the castle.

He knew this entire time why the Kindrahs were after him, and he lied about it. His former unit of guards was slaughtered. Sanyulin died. *I* almost died.

And Ryder was keeping secrets.

I pushed open the door to the gardens, and thanks to the rain, no one was outside.

I stomped across the wet gravel to a stone alcove, pushed aside the hanging vines, and sat on a damp bench. My leg was shaking as I ran my hands down my face. The gods only knew what I looked like right now.

I just needed space. I needed to be alone to think, and the dark sky made me feel like I was back in Morters' End. Maybe it would've been better if I'd stayed. If I'd never agreed to Angel's ridiculous plan.

The crunch of gravel and rustling branches had me putting a hand on my restless leg, stopping its movement. As the sound drew closer, I grabbed my dagger, the hilt thrumming in my grip. If it was Asher, I'd find a way to stab him.

I jumped as a hazel eye peeked between the vines. Lowering the blade, I pushed them aside. "I was wondering when I'd see you again," I said.

The Faceling stared at me. "And what is it you wish to know?" Its melodious tune drifted through the air.

"No riddles today?" I asked, rising slowly from the bench. Although it wore my brother's face, the Faceling was still a predator. From its unnatural stillness to the way its eyes tracked my every movement, assessing if I was a threat. *Or food*.

It blinked. "What is it you wish to know?"

"You tried to warn me," I said, stepping away from the vines. Rain pinged off my headpiece. "About the Kindrahs. You told me of their symbol, the shedding serpent red as blood."

The Faceling said nothing.

"Why?" I added. "Why are you trying to help me?"

It shook its bony finger with a claw-like nail back and forth. That was something I hadn't noticed before. "You haven't heeded my warning to guard your prince from his enemies that reside at home."

"What enemies could he possibly have at home?" I wiped the water from my face. It was coming down harder now, the Faceling blurry behind a wall of rain. "Aside from the Kindrahs, who else is there?"

"You ask the wrong questions."

"Then what should I be asking? What role do I have to play in this?"

Its eyes widened momentarily, the first flicker of emotion I'd seen. "Do you truly know who it is you take to bed?"

I shook my head. "*What?*"

It repeated its words, this time like a song. "Do you know who it is you take to bed?"

"I don't understand."

Ignoring me, the Faceling changed its tune. "Your prince knows more than he is letting on, yet you do not know enough."

"Why can't you just tell me what you know?" I was at the point of begging.

It moved back. "The answers you seek are yours to find, right in your grasp, yet you remain blind."

Approaching steps had my head whipping to the right. I squinted, but the rain made it nearly impossible to see. I looked back at the Faceling, only to find it was gone.

I kicked the gravel, sending pieces flying across the garden. Crouching down, I brought my hands to my face, stifling the urge to scream.

"Wren?" I looked up to find Zavier towering above me. The water dripped from his headpiece onto his concerned face.

"What are you doing here?" I asked.

He squatted down beside me. "I passed Alicai in the hall. He said something happened that made you storm out of the sparring room in a huff."

I remained silent.

"What happened, Wren?"

"Have you heard anything about the prisoner?" I asked. I

debated telling him that our prince was a liar but opted against it for now.

"No. Is that why you're sulking out here alone? Don't tell me *you* want to oversee his torture and questioning."

I smiled slightly. Several minutes passed by, the heavy silence filled up by the raging storm brewing in the sky.

"Back in the Raptyrs, the rain is viewed as a gift from Exintrya, goddess of fertility," Zavier said. "It's believed to be a gift to help our crops and gardens grow. To encourage the next harvest to be abundant. So whenever it rains, we all gather outside and pray."

I turned to him. "Are you going to start praying right now?"

He chuckled. "No, I'm not. But when I told Alicai, he said I was a gullible idiot, and the next time I decide to pray outside during a storm, I should kneel beside a tree. See if getting struck by lightning is also one of Exintrya's gifts."

My shoulders shook as I laughed.

Zavier stood, extending a hand. I took it, and he pulled me up as easily as plucking a flower. "Thank you," I said. "For being my friend."

He tugged me closer, draping his arm across my shoulder. "Always, Wren. Always."

~

The damp grass glistened in the moonlight, soaking my bare feet as I trekked up the mountainside. Trees and wildflowers flanked me, the uncharted path I followed clearing with each step I took.

Closer and closer.

I was almost at the peak. I wasn't sure what I'd find when I got there, but I couldn't stop. Each step was against my own will. It felt like my legs were being pulled by strings, higher and higher…

The full moon shined directly above the mountain like it appeared for this moment only. I couldn't turn my head. Couldn't turn back or glance beside me. Only forward. There were none of the usual sounds of night either. The chirping of crickets, the distant howl of wolves, or even crumbling of dead leaves as small critters scurried across.

Nothing except a preternatural silence that caused my bones to tingle.

I was completely and utterly alone.

A few more steps, I told myself. I was almost there, even though I wasn't sure where *there* was.

Ten more steps.

The air was thinning, my lungs shaking as I struggled to breathe.

Five more steps.

I squinted through the gray mist that wrapped around me, tugging me forward.

Two more steps.

I stumbled over a rock, falling to my hands and knees. I couldn't get up. I dragged myself. Crawled, as my lungs burned and eyes watered.

One more step.

I made it. The peak.

And at the peak was a lake. I continued to crawl, my hands covered in mud as I neared the shoreline. I'd seen this lake before… the crystal-clear water, colorful stones, red flowers, and wild berries growing along the edges.

The path of moonlight shimmered across the surface, ending where I kneeled. It welcomed me. Coaxed me to come forward.

So, I did.

While something inside warned me not to look at my reflection, opposing voices whispered in my ears. Soothing and enchanting voices that caressed me. I leaned into those voices, completely mesmerized by the otherworldly sound.

I pushed on, my hands brushing through the lukewarm waters.

Slowly, I brought my head forward. I held my breath while my reflection came into view as clear as looking in a mirror.

Everything seemed normal. I looked like myself. Wavy brown hair falling against my chest, a freckled nose, emerald-green eyes, and a jagged scar between thick brows.

I was myself. Wren Hibreaker. Whatever that meant now.

As I focused on my reflection, I found the longer I stared, the harder it was to recognize the person looking back at me.

So much had happened. So much had changed.

I was no longer the same girl who'd left Morters' End.

I was about to get up, to start my descent down the mountain, when I noticed something.

A light. A light both bright and dark simultaneously forming behind me. Illuminating me. Outlining my figure.

It was cold yet warm, welcoming yet sinister.

It expanded, and the darkness took over. Hands as black as night pushed through, reaching for me. One wrapped around my throat, the other covered my mouth.

I couldn't feel it, the pressure as I watched one hand tighten around my neck. The other pressed further into my mouth, suffocating and choking me at the same time.

I couldn't feel it, but I could see it.

My eyes widened in horror as my reflection began to *move.*

I watched as my body convulsed, my face turning a deadly shade of blue as my eyes rolled back. I watched as my limp body collapsed into the water, face down. Those hands of night drifted over my soaking head, brushing my hair back.

I tried to scream, but nothing came out. I was trapped. My breathing grew rapid as I strained to move my body.

My eyes shot open, and I bolted upright, my hands going to my neck. I panted as I adjusted to the dark. As I gasped for breath, trying to decipher where I was.

My bed.

I was in my bed. Alicai and Zavier were in theirs, asleep.

It was a nightmare. Only a nightmare. I was okay, I was here.

I looked at the painting above Alicai's bed and shivered. It felt so *real.*

I brought my knees to my chest, rubbing the sleep from my eyes. There was something I needed to do. As quietly as I could, I changed into a clean uniform and wrapped my hair into the headpiece. Zavier was snoring on his back, Alicai face down in his pillow.

Moving like a wraith, I tugged on my boots. I was in the process of tying the laces when—

"What exactly are you doing?" I jumped at the hoarseness of his voice. Peering over my shoulder, I saw Alicai leaning on his forearms, eyes coated with sleep.

"Nothing," I whispered. "You're dreaming."

He snorted, sitting up. "Well now I know I'm definitely awake. Either that or having a nightmare if you're here."

I cast him a flat look. "You're an ass, you know that?"

Standing up, he stretched his arms to the side. "Yep, definitely awake." Ignoring him, I continued tying my laces. A minute later, he asked, "So where are we going?" I looked up to find him fully dressed, leaning against the armoire.

"What—" I blinked. "How did you—"

He tightened his sword belt. "In Telamar we have evacuation training once a week. Have to be out as quickly as possible. I guess the whole *getting dressed as fast as you can* bit came in handy."

"Evacuation for what?"

"Maybe I'll answer your questions when you start answering mine," he said. "So where are we going?"

I groaned as I pushed past him. "Is there an off switch for your annoying tendencies? Or am I stuck with this version of you."

He patted my shoulder and swung the door open. The candles in the wall sconces flickered from the movement. "You're sneaking out in the middle of the night. So, unless you're headed to Ryder's room..."

My face heated. "*No.*" I said sternly. "Absolutely not."

"Well then, looks like this is an adventure for two."

I rolled my eyes as I moved into the hall. "Fine," I sighed. "You can come. But no questions."

He swiped his fingers across his lips, eyes gleaming with delight. "I promise to be on my best behavior."

I hesitated, then turned on my heels, the outsoles of my boots dragging across the worn, red carpet.

Alicai trailed close behind, and I wondered if he'd keep his promise when he realized we were going to the dungeons.

CHAPTER 43

"Have you absolutely lost your mind?"

I ignored Alicai as I continued down the steep, winding steps. The moisture in the air made my uniform cling to me in the most uncomfortable way.

He grabbed my arm, stopping me. "What exactly is the plan here, Wren?"

"Alicai," I said calmly. "Let go of me right now, or I swear I'll have my dagger through your hand faster than you can say stop."

Slowly, he let go. "Okay, there is seriously something wrong with you," he mumbled as we continued. "Always threatening to put a blade through my hand."

"Oh, I'm sorry," I replied. "Are there any other body parts you'd prefer I puncture? Perhaps a lung?"

"You are so *violent*," he hissed. "I just want to know what genius plan you've concocted that has us sneaking into the dungeons in the middle of the night."

"One, you said you wouldn't ask questions." I hopped off the final step and grabbed a torch from the wall. The narrow pathway ahead of us was pitch black. "Two, we're not *sneaking* in. Just follow my lead."

"Oh, so now we're actors." His voice dripped sarcasm. "You should have told me we'd be performing, I would've warmed up."

I whirled on him, the light from the torch casting shadows over his face. "Would you be quiet? If you're going to ramble on, then go back to the room. I can do this by myself."

"Do *what*?" he demanded. "Tell me what you're doing down here, Wren."

If he was anyone else, I would've knocked him unconscious by this point. "I need to speak with the prisoner," I admitted. "He spared my life that night at the Iron Oak. I want to know why."

He glanced at me skeptically. "He spared your life..." he repeated slowly, breaking down each word. "...and you want to ask him *why*."

I nodded, tapping my foot on the stone floor.

He blinked. "I think Tavrina needs to do a full examination of your head."

"Are you coming or not?" I didn't wait for his reply as I walked into the darkness ahead.

The dungeons were a maze of winding passageways that flowed for a couple miles beneath the castle. Each individual cell was a small stone room with nothing more than a pile of hay, a torn piece of fabric for a blanket, and a bucket. The bars were all made of rusted iron, and as we passed an empty cell, I wondered how many diseases someone would contract if they cut themselves on it.

Most of the cells were full, at least where we currently were. I didn't know what these prisoners were in for, and I didn't care. We nodded to the guards unfortunate enough to have this rotation, and not one of them stopped us once they saw our uniforms.

In between the cells were iron holders containing torches that casted a dim light down the seemingly never-ending hallway. We'd been walking for at least fifteen minutes now with no success.

"Maybe he's not down here," Alicai whispered. "Maybe they're keeping him somewhere else. Somewhere isolated where he's less of a threat."

He was probably right.

We came to the end of the hall where a door of talverite stood between two stones. I recognized the iridescent shine from the manacles that had bound the Kindrah's wrists. I turned the knob, and to my surprise, it opened. We entered an even narrower hallway. The cells here were spaced further apart, the bars thicker. There were no guards, and as we walked, it didn't seem like there were any prisoners either.

I was about to accept defeat and turn around when I looked into the last cell. "Well then," I said as Alicai came up beside me. "Seems you were right."

Sitting on the damp floor, ankles and hands bound with talverite chains, was the Kindrah who spared my life. He raised his head slowly, hair white as moonflower framing his face. As his onyx eyes found mine, he stilled.

I held his stare as I said to Alicai, "Wait by the door."

Alicai hesitated but didn't object. I waited until he was gone before I said, "You might not remember me but—"

"I remember you," the Kindrah insisted. I looked at his

uniform soaked with black blood. I fought a wave of nausea as the bitter tang wafted through the air. But his face... whatever methods of torture they'd used on him, his face showed no signs of pain.

He leaned his head against the wall, the intensity of his gaze heavy. He didn't so much as blink. I gripped the bars, the strange metal sending tiny shocks through me. I quickly pulled back, flipping my hands over, examining them.

"Strange, isn't it," he said. "How it affects even those without magic."

I swallowed as I looked at his bound wrists resting on his knees. "What does it feel like to you?"

"Like my magic is suffocating me from the inside out while a thousand blades repeatedly slice open every inch of my body."

"Oh."

He smirked. Although his white hair was a marker of age, he looked no older than twenty-five. "I was wondering when you'd find me," he said.

I straightened, dropping my arms to my sides. "That night... you said you needed me. Why?"

"I said we have use for you."

I narrowed my eyes. "Who is *we*?"

"You're a smart girl, I'm sure you can figure it out."

Of course he knew I was a girl. My hat had fallen off once I hit the bottles. Frustration was growing inside of me. That, and the fear of being caught down here, conversing with the enemy. I needed to be quick. "What use could you possibly have with me?"

He extended a leg, the metal chain dragging across the floor. "Let's just say something's attached itself to you. Something dark. It's protecting you. I saw it when I moved to end your life, and I see it now. And this attachment just might be the key to what we've been looking for this whole time. I believe it'll make our goals more achievable in a way, through you."

He looked *through* me that night. And now he was saying something was attached to me, *protecting* me. I could only think of one person.

But what could Asher have to do with anything? I knew they wanted Ryder dead, but they knew nothing about the covenant.

"You see him," I said quietly.

"I see an aura. It's hard to explain. Think of it like a dark cloud surrounding you."

"How come no one else can see it? How are you the only one?" I shook my head. That wasn't the priority right now. "Who specifically sent you to kill the prince?"

He smiled, but there was nothing warm in the gesture. "So many questions. Most of which you could answer yourself if you only opened your mind, yet here we are..." He clicked his tongue. "And as for your prince, he knows more than he's telling you. Why don't you ask him for the truth? You two seem to have some sort of bond."

"We do not have a bond," I shot out quickly, causing him to pause. "We have nothing."

He raised a brow, the corners of his mouth tugging up. "No? Well, unless my eyes deceive me, that's not what I saw... what I see now." He chuckled. "You humans amaze me. Putting your emotions on display for all to see. And I saw *everything* that night."

I clenched my jaw. "You're human too."

"Am I?" he questioned.

"Where are the rest of you?" I pressed, not wanting to dissect that thought any further at the moment.

"Now why would I tell you that?" His voice was teasing, mocking. He wasn't going to tell me anything. "It's a shame you came all the way here for answers when your prince-lover and his father know everything."

"*He is not my lover.*" I was shaking.

"My mistake." His look was menacing, causing a chill to seep down to my bones. "We'll be seeing each other again, Wren Hibreaker."

I tried not to seem surprised that he knew my name. "Did the king of Enderya send you? Is this about Tresdilian?"

"You're on the right track but think bigger." He stood up, dragging his chains to his make-shift bed. Dropping onto his back, he crossed his ankles. "Now if you don't mind, I'd like to get some sleep. Big day tomorrow."

I opened my mouth, prepared to demand more answers, when Alicai ran over and grabbed me. "We have to go. *Now,* Wren."

I looked at the Kindrah once more. His eyes were closed, a smile staining his lips. I engraved it to memory. His bone-white hair, ink-like eyes... I memorized it all.

Alicai and I didn't say a word as we hurried through the heavy door, closing it carefully behind us. We were just in time as three guards walked by, not even glancing in our direction.

Honestly, they needed tighter security down here.

"Did your new buddy fill you in on why he saved your life? Maybe you two can be friends now. Go back to the Iron Oak and share a drink," Alicai whispered as we half-ran down the hallway.

I wasn't in the mood to argue. "Yes," I replied. "I got what I needed." *Somewhat.*

"Good." Turning the corner, we stood at the bottom of the staircase. Alicai whistled as he put the torch back in the holder. "Long way up. Lots of time for you to tell me all about it."

I shoved past him, taking two steps at a time. "My offer to stab you in the lung still stands."

"I know the concept of friendship is still a bit new to you, but typically, *sane* people don't threaten to stab their friends." He paused, then added, "*Repeatedly.*"

I smiled. "Well, I do."

Alicai gasped. "Wren Hibreaker, are you openly *admitting* that we're friends?"

I kicked my foot back and felt it connect with his stomach. He cursed, and if his foul mouth wasn't his most distinguishable quality... "Does that answer your question?"

"Yes," he croaked out, wheezing for breath. "Perfectly."

I smiled again as we continued up the stairs. In the silence that followed, mostly because Alicai was still gripping his stomach in pain, I allowed my mind to wander.

It seemed my instincts were correct. Ryder *did* know more. I didn't know what hurt worse, the fact he openly lied to me, or that he didn't trust me enough to tell the truth. There had to be a reason, something keeping him from speaking openly. *But what?*

My mind continued wandering through the Kindrah's words. How could he have possibly seen Asher's aura? And why was it enough to keep him from killing me?

One thing at a time, I told myself.

Tomorrow there would be no more lying. Ryder was

going to tell me everything he knew. Whether he wanted to or not.

CHAPTER 44

The week-long celebration of the Scorching began today. The castle was overflowing with white lilies as servants shuffled around, hanging banners and streamers from every pillar, window, and wall.

For the first day, the king would host a party for everyone to celebrate the magic gifted to the Estelers from Tella herself. A goddess who gave up her powers, the very essence of her being, for freedom.

For a chance to live. To love. To explore.

It was a nice story, but that's all it was to me. Nonetheless, I helped wherever I could. Especially at the entrance to the ballroom where Salle, one of the scullery maids, almost slipped off a ladder while stringing lily garland across the doorframe.

Not a single room in the castle was bare of decorations thanks to Queen Rosamund ordering servants around since sunrise.

It was mid-morning now as I stood in one of the less

extravagant hallways watching carts of lilies get wheeled toward the ballroom. I wasn't scheduled for rotation today, so after waking up, I headed to the healers' sanctuary to ask Tavrina for a favor. I wanted to borrow a dress. I'd only worn one other dress in my life, and that was the night of the ball. I would've gone for my usual breeches, tunic, and hat, but tonight was special for more reasons than just the Scorching.

Tavrina went all the way home to get the dress. She claimed it would fit me perfectly, but I wasn't sure about that since she was more filled out than me. She possessed all the womanly curves that my small frame never developed. Although I put on a healthy amount of weight since being here, the lack of proper nutrition I suffered from most of my life made the task strenuous.

The dress was made from wine-red silk with lace detail along the hem. I didn't try it on, just thanked her and left it in the sanctuary which she assured me would be empty for an hour before the Scorching began. The perfect window to sneak in and get dressed without being seen. *Or need any bees.*

Standing in the hall now, I backed up toward the wall as a group of gardeners lugged in a statue of Tella with lilies woven into her hair.

Before I could react, the door behind me clicked open, a hand wrapped around my waist, and I was tugged backward into the dark.

The door slammed shut, and in my disoriented state, I reached for the hilt of my sword, preparing for the worst. A gentle hand landed on my own, halting my movements.

"It's me."

"Ryder?" I hissed. "What are you doing?" After a

moment, my eyes adjusted to the dimness of the storage closet. It was so narrow, I felt the heat radiating off his body.

"I wanted to talk to you," he replied.

Funnily enough, I also wanted to speak to him. I tore the headpiece off, running a hand through the knots in my hair. "And you thought a storage closet was the best place? Where are your guards?"

"I lost them near the southern tower. They were distracted by a brawl between the musicians hired for the party tonight. Something about one of them stealing from their communal funds, I don't know." He brushed a stray curl from his forehead. "I wanted to talk to you alone. Without prying eyes or listening ears."

Gods. Blanning either needed to increase our training or get better guards because Ryder managed to avoid being trailed as easily as breathing.

"You could've called me to your room," I said.

"Would you have come?"

"Maybe." After everything I learned yesterday... probably not. But I *did* need to speak to him. I needed answers.

He smirked, and I hated how that simple expression still made my insides twist. That he still had such power over me.

"As much as I love having you in my room, I thought I'd surprise you." He leaned forward, lips brushing my ear. "To show you just how fun those secret meetings we discussed could be."

I shivered, and his smirk widened. "No." I pushed him away. "You don't get to do that. You don't get to pretend yesterday didn't happen. You don't get to pretend that you didn't lie to me."

He sighed. "That's why I wanted to speak to you. I want to tell you the truth."

I raised a brow. "Why the sudden change of heart?"

His eyes, grayer in the feeble lighting, focused on me. "When you stormed out yesterday, I wanted to run after you. I don't know when it changed or even *what* changed exactly, but something did. I realized I wanted to tell you the truth. I've told you things I've never told another soul, and I want to tell you this. Now. If you'll let me."

Well. I wasn't expecting it to be this... easy. I leaned against the wall, nodding for him to go on.

"You already know Tresdilian was killed in the eastern grasslands, but there was more to it. My father..." He hesitated, raking his fingers through his hair. "My father orchestrated the attack that killed him. He received word about their camp and that the prince was there. Instead of finding out what they were doing, he had them all killed in an ambush. Drestel and Pryler aided the small legion that was sent out during the night to slaughter Tresdilian and his men. The surprise gave Drestel and Pryler the upper hand, and they killed everyone except one. They left one alive to return to Enderya to tell King Caldaris. To warn him what would happen if any more of the Kindrahs were found on our lands."

"Your father ordered an attack knowing a prince of Enderya was there?"

Ryder nodded in disgust. "So as you see, the target on my head is much more personal than you thought."

"What do you think they were doing there?"

He shrugged. "Who knows? Maybe they were coming to attack us, and we got them first. Or maybe they were heading to Morters' End for the necromancers. Maybe they wanted to try brokering a deal to secure the necromancers' freedom again. We'll never know because my father acted in anger before asking questions."

I sank further into the wall. "And King Caldaris, he didn't do anything about it?" Even isolated in Morters' End, I was sure we'd have heard about a war between the kingdoms.

Something flickered over Ryder's features, but it was too dark for me to identify. "He just wanted the body returned. That was all."

"Was it returned?" I asked, and he nodded. "Do you think he's the one ordering these attacks on you now?"

I asked the Kindrah in the dungeons and he said I was one the right track. That I just needed to think bigger. Whatever that meant.

"No, I don't think so," Ryder admitted. "I think it's his people. The Kindrahs are a proud group. They believe justice is only served when the guilty party pays in equal. They'll go against their own king and risk the consequences for it. And in this case, justice ends with my head on a pike."

A second born for a second born.

"They can't..." I shook my head. "They can't do that." The words sounded foolish, but I didn't know what else to say. "Your father and Blanning. They know?"

"Yes. They're... handling it."

Handling it? "How is sitting back and doing nothing handling it? How many have to die before they act?"

The color drained from his face, and while a part of me felt awful for saying it, it had to be addressed. "No more," Ryder said flatly. "No more will die. I'd sooner die myself than watch another guard lose their life for me."

This was... I didn't know what this was. The more I learned, the more confused I felt. The motive for attacking Ryder made sense, but both kings' reactions had me puzzled. What kind of man—let alone king—would let the murder of his son go unchecked? And why was King Reid allowing them to consistently attack Ryder now without acting?

Ryder's smirk caught my eye. "Is something funny?" I demanded.

"I just like watching you. The way you scrunch your brows when you're deep in thought." He pushed off the wall, his muscles firm against me. I tilted my head back to find him gazing at my mouth. He looked like a man who was starved for far too long. "Are you satisfied with the truth?"

Before I could reply, he raised a hand, brushing his thumb over my bottom lip. My breath hitched as my body tensed. "You're so responsive to my touch." His voice was rough as he gripped my chin, our lips inches apart. "Tell me you don't want this. Tell me to let you go because so help me, Wren, if you don't in the next ten seconds, I won't be able to control myself. I'm a strong man, but I'll go to my knees and beg for just a taste of you."

I couldn't find my voice or the will to move.

"You've held my interest and possessed my thoughts from the moment I saw you hiding on that couch in the library." His eyes scanned mine, hungry and vulnerable. "I want no one else."

I looked at his lips. I wanted to kiss them. To feel them on every inch of my body.

So close. We were so close.

His hand drifted to the nape of my neck, and he tugged me closer. The air was thick, clouded with desire and boundaries yet to be crossed. His lips hovered above my own. "Five seconds, Hibreaker."

A stray tear dripped down my cheek as a memory flashed in my mind. A memory from years ago. Of a graveyard with a blue-eyed boy. Of blood and promises.

I couldn't do this. I pulled back, wiping the tear before Ryder saw it.

"I'm sorry." My voice shook as I tugged on my headpiece and pushed open the door without another glance at him.

Because if I looked at him, I wouldn't be able to leave.

He called my name as I closed it behind me, leaving him alone in the storage closet. I didn't know if he came out behind me. If he was following me or not. But I didn't dare turn back. As I crossed the open walkway to the guards' corridors, I felt something strain in my chest.

A feeling I hadn't felt in a long time. Hatred.

But not toward the prince or Asher or anyone else. It was hatred toward myself. Hatred for the feelings I could no longer deny. Feelings that would lead to inevitable death.

It was hatred that made me decide to leave. Tonight would be it. One last night of masquerading. And when the night ended, I was leaving. Leaving this castle. Leaving this city.

Leaving this damned kingdom.

CHAPTER 45

"You look nice," Alicai said as I closed the wooden door to the healers' sanctuary behind me. I left a sealed note in Tavrina's cubby thanking her for everything she had done for me.

I was struggling to keep the dress up. Of course it fit me everywhere except my chest, the sweetheart neckline drooping down my body whenever I breathed. "I can't go like this," I sighed.

Zavier was leaning against the wall, adjusting his cuffs when he looked up. He tore a bronze cufflink from his right wrist as he moved behind me. "Sure you can." He pinched the fabric along my upper back. It tightened the front, causing the loose material to cling to my chest. "We just need to secure it right here." Without another word, he shoved the cufflink through the dress and secured it on the inside.

Alicai snorted. "Hope Tavrina doesn't bite your head off for ruining her dress."

"How did you know to do that?" I asked, running my hands down my sides.

"Younger sister," Zavier answered with a shrug. He glanced at Alicai's untied shoes. "How many times do I need to remind you to double knot?"

He crouched down and mumbled something about dealing with children as he tied Alicai's laces. Alicai said something back, pretending to kick him. I turned away as a twinge of sadness coursed through me. We were such an unlikely trio, but we worked. My friends. Angel would've been so happy to know I'd found them. To know I had people who would look out for me no matter what. And I'd do the same. All joking, teasing, and fighting aside, I would kill for either of them.

It made the thought of leaving that much harder. I'd written two notes and slipped them under their pillows earlier explaining everything. I couldn't bring myself to tell them I was leaving because I knew they would never let me go alone. I didn't want to be a burden on their lives any more than I already was.

I stashed a few spare sets of clothes into my rucksack and hid it beneath a bush at the end of one of the tunnels. All day I'd been sneaking into the kitchen while the cooks were busy and managed to secure two blocks of cheese, a loaf of bread, and six apples. I had a decent amount of money saved and planned to use some of it to buy a horse. I wasn't a great rider, having only been horseback once, but I'd learn.

I planned to send word to Callin first. While I couldn't step beyond the shield of Morters' End without being trapped again, Callin could go freely, and I needed him to relay a message. Angel would need to be prepared incase Bekencourt decided to go after him and Mama. The commander threatened me numerous times, and I'd be a fool not to think he'd act on his word.

After that, I would go to Kalarois, the closest town to the Forgotten Mountains. According to some of the drunken travelers I'd spoken to during my time at the Rusty Nail, the people of Kalarois were the ones who would know how to potentially find the Estelers. *If* there were any others left. It was a giant leap, I knew that, but I had to take the chance. If I could get just one Esteler to help me free my family, we could leave this continent. We could go anywhere. I wouldn't need to finish my seven years of service. I knew it sounded ridiculous, but I had to try something.

I had to have some sort of plan because if I didn't, I would feel guilty for abandoning Ryder. I wanted to keep him safe, and the best way to do that was to leave. No matter how much it hurt.

The Faceling's riddle finally made sense. *His enemies stretch far and wide, and even some reside at home.*

It was me. I was the enemy. I was the threat to Ryder's life because of Asher.

Because of my foolish heart.

"You ready to go?" Alicai asked, pulling me from my thoughts.

I nodded, shrugging off all my worries. I wanted to enjoy this last time the three of us would be together.

Alicai extended an arm. I took it just as Zavier drifted to my other side and did the same. "Well," I said, "aren't we a dysfunctional sight."

Trouble flickered in Alicai's eyes as his lips curled. "Let's go watch the sky burn."

The halls grew busier and rowdier as we approached the

ballroom. We decided to enter separately to minimize the risk of anyone asking questions seeing as the ornately decorated space was already overflowing with people, young and old. The servants and gardeners had outdone themselves, transforming the spectacular room into something else entirely. Something otherworldly.

Red rose petals mixed with lilies covered the floor to represent the raining fire of Durling. Each marble pillar was wrapped in streams of white garland while matching ones hung from the ceiling and chandeliers. The doors leading out to the garden were thrown open, allowing a gentle breeze to flow into the room. Trays of that delightful golden liquid drifted through the crowd, and as I reached for one, Alicai yanked my arm back.

"Oh no you don't." He let go of me once we stood several feet away from the very confused server. "You might not remember the last time, but I do."

Ignoring him, I glanced around the room. "Where did Zavier go?"

Alicai motioned to the far wall, and I spotted them instantly. Tavrina's face crinkled with laughter, and Zavier... Zavier was watching her like he'd just caught a falling star.

"Alicai."

My head snapped back as Micah approached. I instantly looked down, afraid he'd recognize me.

"Micah," Alicai replied curtly.

"And who's this new friend of yours?" I could feel him gazing at me, but I refused to meet his eye.

"Resilia Frintwove," Alicai said a little too quickly. *Who the hell was Resilia Frintwove?* "You know, the daughter of King Reid's financial advisor."

"Ah, yes," Micah replied, although I highly doubted he knew what Alicai was talking about. "Pleasure to meet you, Miss Frintwove."

I nodded, keeping my head down. Micah mumbled something under his breath about rudeness before tugging Alicai away.

"Have you seen Hibreaker?" he asked. He wasn't as quiet as he thought he was, and I felt my body tense at the mention of my name.

"No, why?"

"You share a room with him, have you noticed anything strange?"

Alicai straightened. "What are you talking about, Micah." There was coldness to his tone.

"Do you not think it's weird that he's here when men much more talented than him were sent packing? And then there's his closeness to the prince. I don't know, I just don't trust him." He scratched his head. "I'm asking if you've seen anything or even thought the same because Flint, Dranic, and I are going to speak to Blanning about it tonight, and it would look better if there were more of us."

I saw Alicai's hand curl into a fist. "Really, Micah. We're meant to be a unit. A team. And here you are acting like a jealous asshole because the prince favors one of his guards. Get over yourself and get away from me."

I didn't see Micah's face as he stormed off, but I knew it wasn't good.

"I heard," I said before Alicai repeated the conversation.

"Shit, Wren," he rubbed a hand across his face.

"It'll be fine. We'll figure it out," Truthfully, I aimed to be long gone before their little meeting with Blanning took place.

"I'm going to go find Dranic and try to convince him he's being ridiculous. I think it's best if we stay away from each other tonight. There's too many guards here, both on and off duty, and if someone sees us talking, they might start looking a little too hard."

I swallowed and nodded. I so badly wanted the three of us to spend tonight together, but Alicai was right. "Go," I said. "I'll be fine."

With a clipped nod, he took off into the crowd.

I headed in the opposite direction, taking up space near the garden doors. There was still a half hour before the fire would start raining from the sky. The tears of a lover left alone.

I watched as a young man and woman ran down the steps, hand in hand, looking for a private place. I was envious as they laughed. How nice it must be to have it so easy. I snatched a flute off a tray and downed the contents in two sips.

"Woah, there," someone behind me said. The voice was uncannily familiar. "If you keep up that pace, you'll black out before the main event begins."

I internally groaned as Ambrose stepped in front of me. The last time I saw him was the night at the Iron Oak. His leg seemed to have healed as he stood with his weight evenly distributed. Shame. He wasted no time as his wandering eyes raked down my body. If he tried anything, the dagger at my thigh would finally see some action tonight.

I set the flute down on the table. "I can handle myself. Your concern is unneeded and unwanted."

He raised a brow. I forgot how much he loved the chase. "I apologize for overstepping," he said, a wry smile playing at his lips. I wanted nothing more than to smack it right off his face. "Is there anything I can do to make it up to you?"

"You can leave me alone," I said cheerily. I even added a smile.

"Have I done something to offend you?" He stepped closer. "If so, I apologize. I'm not used to being in the presence of such a beautiful girl. You have my mind spinning."

I almost threw up in my mouth. "You already apologized, and I don't particularly care to continue this conversation further."

As I turned to leave, he grabbed my wrist. I tried pulling away, but he tightened his grip to the point of pain. "Now you listen to me, you little—"

"Ambrose, I really hope you're not harassing the guests again."

Instantly, he dropped his hand and stepped back. Then he plastered the fakest smile I'd ever seen on his lips. "Well, the wayward prince returns." He patted Ryder on the back.

Ryder's expression was blank as he shoved his hands in his pockets. "I have." His voice was calm. Too calm. Like a clear sky before a storm. "I see you have as well."

"There isn't much to do in Reysitte," Ambrose replied. "And besides—" His eyes flashed to me. "I missed all the joys of residing at court."

Ryder shifted toward me, and normally, I'd roll my eyes at his possessive behavior, but right now, I wanted Ambrose gone. Ryder could act, say, and do whatever he wanted to make it happen. "Garrick and Lorzo are looking for you," he said.

Ambrose's gaze shifted to the other side of the room. He let out a laugh. "What do you know, your brother's back too."

I looked at the dais where Lucio was standing at the base, intimately close to a beautiful red-headed girl. Ambrose whistled. "Looks like he finally found someone new after that Tryfel princess left him. Maybe he'll get this one to stay."

My eyes shot to Ryder, but he was still watching Ambrose. He hadn't looked at me once. "Perhaps you should go and say hello," Ryder said.

Ambrose paused, eyes scanning us both. After a moment, he nodded in some sort of understanding. "I'll leave you to it then." He patted Ryder on the back again, winked, then strolled away.

I let out a breath I didn't know I was holding as Ryder finally turned to me. "Are you alright?" he asked.

I nodded, rubbing my hand over my wrist. His eyes didn't miss the movement. His face was flushed, a tiny vein pulsing in his neck. My heart pounded as his gaze drifted down my body before returning to my face. My lips. He shook his head. "What are you doing to me, Wren Hibreaker?"

"I don't know what you mean."

I hated how he was looking at me. As if I was... everything. I should have been angry at him for lying to me for so long, but I wasn't. When I looked at him now, all I saw was an illusion of happiness. Something I would never have.

"Yes, you do," he replied roughly, eyes trailing down me again. "Gods, you'd think after being rejected several times I'd get the hint, but I just can't seem to leave you alone or let you go." I swallowed, tilting my head back as he came closer. "Just seeing you in that dress is tearing me apart." He tucked a strand of hair behind my ear and whispered, "I think it would look better on my bedroom floor."

I knocked over the flute behind me. The glass shattered,

drawing several pairs of eyes directly toward us. Ryder tried hiding his satisfied smirk as a server ran over to clean up the mess. I was positive my cheeks matched the rose petals on the floor.

"It's starting!" someone screamed. I thanked the gods for the sudden lack of attentive eyes as everyone hurried through the garden doors to watch the fire fall from the sky.

I moved to follow the crowd when Ryder grabbed my arm. "Come with me." He wrapped his other hand around my waist, ushering me away from the doors.

"Where?"

I felt his smile as we exited the ballroom, venturing further into the castle. "A secret place."

"I think I've had enough of your secret places for today." And really, *where* were the guards meant to be watching him? If Micah wanted to get someone in trouble, it should be whoever was on duty right now because they were doing a terrible job.

Ryder laughed. "I promise this one's significantly better than a storage closet." Sliding his hand into mine, he broke into a run, pulling me behind. I allowed it. Just this once. Hiking up the dress, I matched his pace, my brown boots smacking against the marble floors.

There was something so childish and ridiculous about it. Running through the empty corridors. But also something... freeing, invigorating.

As we ran into the hall of mirrors, I couldn't stop the burst of laughter that escaped me. He watched me through the glass and smiled. That smile... I would never forget it. Just as I would never forget the sight of my reflection, hand in hand with the prince, as we sprinted through the castle.

I would never forget him.

CHAPTER 46

For as long as I could remember, fire was the closest thing I'd known to light. The flickering gold and orange hues dancing through pits of wood and ash, lighting up the perpetual darkness of Morters' End. That was it.

When I'd finally witnessed sunrises and sunsets for the first time, I realized how unique they were. While fire burned, the setting and rising sun was... different. It was warm, welcoming, and refreshing. It emitted the feeling of rebirth. A fresh start. A reset.

As Ryder and I sat on the hilltop overlooking the Tyro Forest, I held my breath. I held it as the sun drifted toward the horizon. As great spheres of fire fell from the sky in the distance, turning into embers and ash before hitting the ground.

The tears of Durling.

A god left to suffer alone as the love of his immortal life chose adventures and freedom before choosing him. If I believed in the gods and their stories, I'd find something quite tragic about it.

After a while, I said, "Blanning isn't going to be happy when he hears how easily you escaped your guards."

Resting an arm on his knee, Ryder snorted. "I'm with you, aren't I?" His gaze drifted to my extended leg. "I would bet the crown that you're armed underneath that dress."

My lips curled upward. "Perhaps."

For the next several moments, we sat in silence. Just the two of us, side by side on this tall, grassy hill. I realized why he took me to this spot. It was away from the crowd and confines of the castle. Open space and fresh air. It felt intimate.

I studied him. The prince who crushed and changed every initial thought I had of him. Who'd seen and gone through more in his short life than most people do in a lifetime. A prince who carried the weight of the lives lost on his account. Who blamed himself for everything, even though he shouldn't. I tried engraving each detail of his features to memory. I wished I possessed Angel's artistic abilities so I could paint him. So I'd have a piece of him forever.

I turned my attention back to the forest. The fire drops were beginning to slow. "I didn't see your parents back there," I said. "And when did Lucio return?"

"They like to watch from the balcony in their room alone. And as for Lucio, I had no idea he was returning until this morning."

"Why did he come back?"

"Does one need a reason to return home?"

"No, I guess not," I answered.

It was hard. Sitting here after everything with him. I was never short on words, but for some reason, right now I didn't know what to say. I was leaving. If I wanted to confess anything, now would have to be the time. But I was clearly a coward as my lips remained sealed.

I had to keep quiet because if I knew Asher, he'd find a way to exploit those feelings . He'd use them to his advantage, twisting them into something broken and destructive. Something deadly.

"The fire stopped," I said. As I looked at the horizon, all that remained was smoke and dark skies.

Ryder stood, extending a hand to pull me up. "There's something else I need to tell you." His voice was hoarse as he let me go, my fingers twitching from the loss of contact.

"Well, after the conversations we've had so far today, I'm not sure anything else you say will surprise me." I was joking, but the pain in his eyes made me start to worry. "What is it?"

He didn't get a chance to respond as the deafening sound of a bell echoed from the clock tower. If I remembered correctly, three consecutive rings meant—

My eyes widened. "A prisoner escaped."

And as the bell continued, I knew exactly which prisoner it rang for.

~

I knew the guards were trained for this type of breach, but training for and actually tracking down an escaped prisoner were two *very* different things. They were wasting their time as the Kindrah was probably long gone by now.

I heard people running through the corridors above. The heavy impact of boots on stone blending with the sounds of shouting. Lockdown protocol would undoubtedly begin any moment now.

And while all of this was happening, I was in the stone passageways beneath the southern tower. With Ryder. We hurried back to the castle as soon as we heard the bell, sneaking through a hidden door behind a rose bush.

I was seated on a ragged stone jutting out from a wall, legs dangling over the side. Ryder was still pacing back and forth like he had been for the past five minutes.

"We need to make our way back upstairs," I said eventually. "The guards are probably turning the place upside down looking for you." And I needed to go. *Now.* A distraction like this was the perfect time for me to slip away. But Ryder would never just let me leave, so I needed him to be taken care of first.

He continued pacing, his hair curling around his ears. "Ryder." I leaned forward, hands digging into the edges of the rock. "Did you hear me?"

He stopped moving. "Why?"

I tilted my head. "Why what?"

"Why do we need to go back?"

I pushed off the seat. "You can't be serious. That Kindrah wants you *dead*," I said tightly. "And you want to take your chances hiding in some musty, abandoned tunnel?"

"With you, yes." I didn't miss the admiration in his voice.

Sighing heavily, I walked along the wall, running my hands over the stones for any sign of a hidden doorway or hatch. "We need to get back upstairs." My voice held no room for negotiation. "How do we get out of here?" It was easy to get lost in the tunnels, and I didn't want to chance that by moving without a plan.

"Have you ever wondered about the other kingdoms?" I

turned to find him leaning against the wall, arms folded across his chest.

"What?"

Although his posture was nothing but trained princely calmness, his eyes were panicked. It was enough to have the hairs on the back of my neck stand up straight.

"I've always wanted to cross the Black Sea," he said. "Explore those distant lands we know nothing of. Meet foreign people and learn their cultures."

That was all well and good, but I didn't know how it was relevant to our current situation. "Okay," I replied. "When we get out of here, you should talk to your father about your sudden spark of wanderlust."

I knew he was stalling. I just didn't know why yet.

He frowned. "Do you not want to travel? To see the places of stories and books?"

I fought the urge to grab him by the collar and drag him until he revealed how to get upstairs. But regardless of our comfortability with each other, he was still a prince, and I doubted he would take kindly to being pulled like an animal.

I pinched the bridge of my nose. "With all due respect, *Your Highness*, do you really think now is the best time to talk about this?"

He angled his head, and I saw a shadow of a grin forming on his face. "Is it the fact that you're completely alone with me in a dark, confined location that's making you so desperate to run?"

"No," I lied. Being alone with Ryder was growing increasingly difficult as he made his feelings clear. He knew I was fighting it, my own feelings that I tried hiding even from myself. Because admitting them meant accepting what would surely follow.

And I refused to accept the fate Asher created for me.

"Then tell me what your plan is exactly, because currently, you don't look like one of my guards." His gaze ran down me like delicate fingers. "And I don't see how you'd have time to change into uniform and join the search. Not with every room and hall currently being checked."

I bit my lip. I hadn't thought of that. I *would* have if I wasn't so distracted lately. It would be easier to blame him, but really, I was the one at fault. I allowed this. The closeness between us.

"Alright, well what exactly is *your* plan then?" I dug my hands into the bottom of the dress, pulling it up. I kept my eyes on him as he watched my every move. As he stilled at the sight of my exposed leg. I lifted the dress up to my mid-thigh where my dagger was sheathed. In a quick motion, I grabbed it, allowing the dress to fall back down like spilled wine.

Slowly, Ryder's eyes lifted to meet mine. "Come with me."

"What?"

"You asked what my plan was." His voice was low and strangled, as if each word was being dragged across hot stones. I remained motionless as he came closer, the scent of burnt sugar and lemon closing around me. "Come with me."

"Where?"

"To those distant kingdoms. To lands far away from here where no one will know our names. Where we won't be a prince and a guard... just Ryder and Wren. Just us."

I lost all ability to speak. Did he know what he was asking? The depth of those very words?

"You can't possibly mean it." I stumbled, taking a step back. "Do you hear yourself? You can't just run away." *Even though that was exactly what I planned to do.* "Let alone to a place you know nothing of." I paused, waiting for him to laugh or admit it was only a joke, but he did neither. He was deadly serious.

I shook my head. "*Ryder.*"

His brows furrowed together as he reached for me, hands latching onto my waist. "Why not? Really, Wren, what's holding you back? You know how I feel about you. I'm willing to face anything as long as I have you with me."

I pushed his arms away. This was insanity. And yet, I couldn't deny the excitement I felt at what he was offering. "I know things are bad right now, but—"

His short laugh silenced me. I watched as he ran both hands through his hair, resuming his pacing. "You know nothing of it," he said under his breath.

"What is that supposed to mean?"

He kept moving, long legs striding back and forth across the floor. That sixth sense of mine kicked in. I couldn't shake the feeling there was still something he wasn't saying.

He stopped with his back to me. "I was going to tell you," he said. "But then the bell began ringing and..." His voice drifted out.

My heart hammered in my chest as he clenched his hands into fists. "You were going to tell me what?" I asked.

He spun around, his eyes the color of rough seas. "Do you remember when I told you King Caldaris only wanted the body of his son returned?"

I nodded slowly, not liking where this was going.

"That wasn't all he wanted. My father didn't tell me until

after Tresdilian's body was returned, but he erected an agreement with Caldaris." He slumped against the wall. "King Caldaris has a daughter. His firstborn named Saniya." The way he said her name made the blood in my veins turn to ice. "When Saniya turns twenty-one, we're to be married."

"And when will that be?" My voice was a shell of its normal sound.

"In three months."

I couldn't breathe as the sturdy walls I'd constructed around my heart began to fall. *He lied to me. He lied to me again.* "You've been engaged to someone this entire time?"

"Yes," he admitted.

I blew out a shaky breath. "Why? Wouldn't it make more sense to wed her to Lucio? What benefit could marrying you possibly have?"

"My father is not one to share his motives. Not even when they concern me."

I couldn't believe this. "The king has forged an engagement for you without any explanation? Have you not questioned the absurdity of it?"

Ryder looked like he was in physical pain. "Of course I have. Do you really think I wouldn't? He won't tell me anything. Whatever he's getting from this must be something worthwhile."

It would have to be to unite enemy kingdoms. But *what* could it be? And more importantly, what was Caldaris's angle?

I didn't have the ability to think about it right now.

Ryder is engaged.

The realization hurt. Badly.

"Who else knows?" I asked on a slow exhale.

"Bekencourt and Blanning." He hesitated, then added, "And now you."

"Not even your own mother?"

Ryder shook his head. "She'd never allow my father to agree to such a thing. He made me swear not to tell her. She'll find out when he announces it publicly."

I leaned against the wall. Real. The cold stone against my body was real. I needed to latch onto something existent as all the lies, dreams, and words blended together. "And the Kindrahs?" I asked.

"They know. Caldaris informed his people recently that a union would be formed between our kingdoms instead of retribution. A union to prevent future bloodshed. But it seems there's a rogue group still hellbent on getting their revenge, even if it means disobeying their king."

"Is that not worrying to you? What makes you think they'll stop once you're wed?" Why was he doing this? He was like a willing lamb going to the slaughter.

Ryder's smile was defeated. "My father seems to be under the impression he'll be able to dissolve the marriage as soon as he gets what he wants. That he'll be able to prevent my death. He'll probably want to ship me off somewhere far away afterwards. That's why I want to leave. Today, Wren. With you."

I rubbed my forehead, a nervous tic I'd seemingly adopted over the last few minutes. "Has your father alerted Caldaris that these rogue Kindrahs have been actively trying to kill you?"

"He's sent several missives regarding the attacks. Caldaris insisted he had no part in it."

How strong could Enderya be if the king couldn't even

control his own subjects? Perhaps they were struggling, falling apart and divided from the inside.

Regardless, I didn't understand why Ryder's own father would agree to such a thing. How could he believe after murdering Tresdilian in cold blood that Caldaris would just consent to a union? That they could just have peace? There had to be more going on here, surely King Reid wasn't that stupid. Besides, he hated dark magic, had scorned my entire village because of it. And now he was going to marry off his son to one of those people? *Could I even call them people?* What could possibly be worth this?

My head was starting to hurt. This was too much. "Everything you told me..."

Ryder was off the wall and in front of me in seconds, gripping my face with gentle hands. His eyes met mine. "Everything I told you was real. It still is real, Wren. What I feel for you, what I *want*... it's all real. I don't want this marriage, and I cannot imagine the princess does either." His thumb brushed across my lower lip. "I want *you.*"

I chewed my inner cheek, the pain keeping the tears away. I wouldn't cry. I wouldn't be so *weak.* After everything I'd gone through in my life, I refused to let him break me. "What about your family? Your mother and Lucio, you'd so easily run away and never see them again? What about your title?"

"The title is nothing to me," he said firmly. "You know how I feel about it. How I've always felt about it."

And I did. A life where everything was given, a life that left him with many companions but very few friends. A position where his entire existence was mapped out for him before he was even born. Where he had no choices of his own.

"There are things you don't know about me. To throw

away everything on—" I motioned to the space between us. "—whatever *this* is, is insane. You have to see that."

He shook his head. "I don't care. I know you have secrets, and I don't care. When you're ready to tell me, I'll be ready to listen. I know you're strong, brilliant, beautiful, and perhaps a little crazy, but so am I. What I said all those months ago still stands. You're a breath of fresh air, Wren Hibreaker, and I'm not ready to stop breathing you in."

"I'm from Morters' End," I said before I could stop myself. I needed him to drop this absurd idea, and if the only way was by admitting I was from the place he hated, then so be it. He could hate *me* if it meant he remained safe.

I watched as his brows scrunched together. Not in fear or anger, but in... confusion. He opened his mouth to speak, when another voice filled the silence.

"Well, isn't this just adorable," Asher purred. I dropped my dagger, the sound of it hitting the ground ringing through my ears.

My eyes instantly found him, as they always did.

His hair shimmered like obsidian stone, his mouth curved in a delighted, wicked grin. My body went rigid as he narrowed his eyes at Ryder's hands still cupping my cheeks. Something flashed across Asher's features as he took in our closeness, but it was gone a moment later.

From the corner of my eye, I noticed Ryder's head turn toward him. As if he could *see* Asher.

"What are you doing here?" I asked.

Asher cocked his head like a predator eyeing its prey. He crossed his arms, smile widening. "My beautiful Wren, I've come to collect."

CHAPTER 47

No. *No.*

All I could hear was the pounding of my heart echoing through my ears. Slowly, I let the words register. Let the weight of the situation I was now standing in register. Did I really think I could avoid this? That Asher would easily let me go? Gently, I shoved Ryder away. I couldn't bear to look at him.

Pushing off the wall, I walked toward the ghost of the boy I once loved. "There's nothing to collect," I said, keeping my voice as steady as I could. "You know as well as I do the terms of our covenant."

Asher uncrossed his arms. "Oh, Wren, you fool no one. Your love for him is as clear as the stars in the night sky." Perhaps I imagined it, but it seemed there was a hint of bitterness in his voice as he spoke.

I clenched my hands into fists. I knew Ryder was behind me, I knew I probably looked crazy, but I didn't care. I was ending this once and for all. "I don't love him," I spat. "I never did, and I never will." Taking a step closer, I felt my confidence rising. I had nothing to be scared of. Asher would never hurt me, he couldn't if he wanted to obtain what he desired most. His freedom. "I will never love *anyone*. I swear it."

Asher ran a hand through his hair, a short laugh escaping his parted lips. "Oh how you lie as easily as breathing. You forget, you love me." He was off the wall and behind me in an instant, his cold hands wrapping around my waist like chains pulling me into the depths of the ocean. "And as much as you deny it," he whispered against my ear. "You will always love me." He tapped my collarbone. "*However,* I know you also love him."

He spun us around, and my eyes landed on Ryder. His were wide and confused. It was then that I realized it. He could see Asher too. I tried to move away, but Asher's grip tightened around me.

"Wren," Ryder bit out, his voice strained. "Who is this?"

"It's fine," I said as calmly as possible. "He can't touch you. Just go. *Please.*"

Asher dropped his arms, striding toward Ryder. The sinister grin on his face had a certain panic shooting through my bones. With one quick glance at me, he slammed his hand into Ryder's chest with inhuman speed, sending him into the stone wall and crumbling to the ground. Ryder groaned in pain as he rolled onto his side, gripping his right arm against his chest.

Asher flexed his fingers. "It's a terrible thing to love something that death can touch."

My eyes widened in horror. "How did you do that?" I stepped forward, but my body suddenly felt unattached. "*You* can't touch anyone."

Asher sighed. "Really? Have you forgotten all the times I touched you?" He pointed to Ryder, but his eyes remained on me, burning with fury. "Does your little prince know all the things we did in the dark?"

One look at Ryder and I instantly regretted it. My heart ached at the clear pain on his face. Pain that had nothing to do with being slammed into a wall. I turned back to Asher. "You and I are bonded, you shouldn't be able to touch anyone but *me*."

Asher didn't say a word as he came closer again. I could smell the midnight breeze that reminded me of home. Except Asher wasn't my home. Not anymore.

"While I can't kill him," he finally said, "I *can* make sure he suffers. Do you want him to suffer, Wren?"

I wasn't surprised by his lack of answers. Asher was a moving shadow of mystery, only giving enough to keep me wanting more. I wondered if he could sense the fear coursing through me. Fear of what else he was capable of doing.

I wanted so badly to be numb to his betrayal and lies, but there was only so much I could take.

"Don't listen to him," Ryder begged. I winced as he spat out a mouthful of blood. I wanted to run to him, but the gods only knew how that would trigger Asher. "Don't do what he says, Wren, do you hear me?"

I shivered as Asher moved next to me, raking his fingers up my side. "Did you forget the way my hands felt on you? Is your mind so clouded with him that you've forgotten?"

"Touch her again, and I'll rip your throat out," Ryder snarled as he struggled to pull himself up.

Asher chuckled. "Such brave words for someone bleeding out on the floor."

"Please," I begged. "Just let him go. I'll go anywhere with you if you let him go."

Asher's hand stilled against my hip. "The only place he's going is to the crematorium after you kill him," he whispered.

I twisted out of his grasp, prepared to make a run for Ryder, when the sounds of hurried footsteps filled the space. I must have spun around several times, disoriented in the dark expanse of the tunnel. I couldn't locate the direction of the steps, couldn't brace myself for whatever might appear out of the darkness. It was then that I noticed Asher was gone. Without hesitating, I ran for Ryder, scraping my knees on the stones as I dropped down beside him.

"You're going to be okay," I said gently as I pulled his head into my lap, brushing his curls off his forehead. He was still spitting up blood, and it was too dark for me to make out where his wounds were. The footsteps were increasing, but I didn't care. "Come on, we have to get you up." He groaned as I shoved my arms underneath his, locking my hands across his chest.

"Wren?"

Turning, I squinted in the direction I thought the voice came from. A second later, I spotted cropped black hair and amber eyes. "*Alicai?*"

A few more steps and he was beside me, panting. "We have to go. Bekencourt—" He paused as he noticed Ryder's limp body in my arms. "What the hell happened?"

"Just help me get him up. He's going in and out of consciousness. We need to get him to the healers."

Alicai shook his head, snapping himself out of shock. "No, we can't. You and I have to go. *Now.*" He reached for my arm, but I pulled back.

"Are you out of your mind? I'm not leaving him down here! He'll *die*."

Alicai shook his head. "He'll be fine. Zavier and Easton weren't far behind me. They'll get him to the healers." He crouched down beside me, eyes wide with trepidation.

My brows scrunched together. "What is it?"

"You have to get out of here, Wren. I couldn't stop Micah from going to Blanning." Running a hand through his hair, he stood up, pacing. "He raised his concerns, and Bekencourt... he told Blanning and the king some made up bullshit."

"What is that supposed to mean?"

"He said that you were a spy for the Kindrahs. A female disguised as a male guard to seduce the prince and gain his trust. Bekencourt said he's had his suspicions for a while now but needed evidence, which he claims he has. He said that you helped orchestrate the attack at the Iron Oak and also released the prisoner. Everyone's looking for you, Wren." He dropped to a knee beside me. "We have to get the hell out of here."

I started shaking my head. "I can't leave him." I could tell Alicai was holding in a string of curse words he undoubtedly wanted to throw at me right now, but my focus shifted at the sound of more footsteps.

Alicai's head shot up. "Do you hear that? I told you. Zavier and Easton are coming. They'll get the prince." I watched as he carefully moved Ryder off my lap. As he slowly lowered his head down to the floor before yanking me up to my feet. Alicai gripped my wrist firmly. "Let's go."

I didn't know where he was pulling me or even how he knew his way down here, but just before we turned a corner, abandoning the narrow tunnel, I whirled around. With one final glance at Ryder's now unconscious body, I let a tear fall down my cheek. "I'm sorry," I mouthed.

And then I turned, allowing Alicai to drag me into the dark. I let him pull me for a good few minutes before asking, "Where exactly are we going? And how did you even know I was down here? How did you know where to go?"

He paused momentarily as we came up to a fork in the tunnels, then continued pulling me to the left. "Now is really not the best time for questions. And trust me, I've got plenty for you when we get out of here. Starting with what the hell happened to Ryder."

I bit my tongue so hard I tasted the metallic tang of blood. I tried to shove the images out of my head, but it wouldn't work. As if on a loop, my brain continued to replay the moment Asher slammed Ryder into the wall. As his body fell into a heap of broken bones onto the cold, stone floor. If Asher wasn't already dead, I would have killed him.

"Alicai." No answer. "Alicai," I repeated. "Where are we going?"

"We're getting out of here," he said as he finally dropped my arm. He ran his hands up and down one of the stones.

I laughed. "Let me guess, we're lost."

He continued to run his fingers across the edges. "Not lost." A second later, something clicked, and the stone moved open like a door. I was greeted by the Tyro Forest and the night sky. Standing up, he grinned. "Told you."

"Now what?" I asked, rubbing my arms as the night chill wrapped around me.

"Now we run."

By the time we were deep in the forest, my lungs were burning, and my legs were ready to collapse under me. Tavrina's dress was completely ruined, and I cursed myself for not grabbing the rucksack.

Dresses. Completely impractical.

The sounds of crickets chirping and the breeze blowing mixed with my heavy breaths. "Alicai, wait," I huffed out, resting my hands against my aching thighs.

"We don't have time to wait. We have to keep moving. Once they realize you're not in the castle, they're going to start searching the grounds. We have to be long gone by then."

"We?" I brushed a sweaty lock of hair off my forehead.

"Yes, *we*." He rolled up the sleeves of his shirt. "You didn't think I would let you go all on your own, did you?"

"Just give me five minutes to try and process everything," I pleaded. My mind was still whirling from the encounter with Asher and the secrets Ryder shared. I hadn't even begun to dissect the fact that Bekencourt pinned everything on me. I should've known he knew I was a girl. All those comments and threats and the way he watched me. For crying out loud, he *saw* me and Ryder in Caelestis together. He said nothing all this time because he was waiting for the perfect moment. This moment. But why? He had to know the accusations he made were lies, so what was *his* angle?

"Hello? Did you hear me?"

I looked up at Alicai's hand waving in front of my face. "What?"

"We don't have five minutes," he said through his teeth. "I'm doing this for *you*. Risking myself for *you*."

"I didn't ask you to do any of that! I had a plan!" I threw a hand back in the direction we just came from. "We don't even know if they got to Ryder. I should have stayed. He could be *dead* right now, and—"

"Why did you leave Morters' End?"

I blinked, losing my train of thought. "What?"

He stepped closer. "Why did you leave Morters' End, Wren? *Why*?"

I tilted my head. What did this have to do with anything? I was about to argue about how pointless this conversation was, but by the look on his face, I sensed there was no avoiding it. Letting out a deep breath, I said, "To be free."

He expelled a short laugh. "To be free," he repeated, pacing back and forth. "All you've done was trade one set of shackles for another. You've lived your life bound to places, people, and oaths. When have you ever lived for yourself?"

He was right. He was right, and I hated him for it. I lost myself in the lives, dreams, and desires of others. Somehow, while discovering everyone else, I lost track of myself. Who was I? Without the headpiece, without the shields of Morters' End, without a sword and dagger, and without Asher? Who was Wren Hibreaker? I realized I didn't know the answer.

A rustle in the bushes had me reaching for my dagger, only to find I'd left it in the tunnel. *Papa's dagger.*

Noticing the change in my composure, Alicai paused, raising a brow. I held out a hand, urging him to be quiet.

A second later, I heard it again. Someone was here. I kept my eyes trained on the thick bushes to my right. Even in the dark I could see the way the branches moved. As if whatever was hiding was preparing to jump out and strike.

Taking a silent step forward, I raised a finger to my lips. Alicai nodded, reaching for the hilt of his sword. The bush began moving faster, the entire thing shaking. Alicai drew his sword and turned, his arm pressing into mine.

I stumbled, leaning back into him as a mass of brown and black fur jumped out of the bush and scurried further into the forest on tiny paws.

I raised a hand to my chest as I tried easing my racing heart. Alicai burst out in a fit of laughter as he re-sheathed his sword. "Good eye, Wren. That was a close call. We were almost attacked by a bunny."

"You know what? Next time I sense a threat, I won't do anything. I'll just sit back and let—"

"Wren!" Alicai screamed, but his warning was too late. I was on the ground a moment later, my vision blurry. All I could focus on was the pulsating pain in the back of my head and the smell of fresh blood.

To my right, I distinctly made out Alicai cursing as he swung his sword at one of my attackers. There were eight of them. Or maybe it was five, I couldn't tell. I was incapacitated as the back of my neck turned damp, a steady stream of blood pouring from my head.

I was thinking about the irony of injuring myself in the same spot twice, when someone crouched down in front of me. They gripped my chin, tilting it slightly to the left. In any other circumstance, I may have found humor in this situation. As I locked eyes with the Kindrah who spared my life that night at the Iron Oak. *Definitely ironic.*

His black uniform was still stained with blood, and while the rest of the Kindrahs had their masks on, revealing nothing but their eyes, his face was completely exposed. His hair as white as the moon draped over his shoulders as onyx eyes searched mine.

I tried to laugh but it came out more like a cough. "I knew it was you that escaped the dungeons."

He smiled slightly. "I told you we'd be seeing each other again, Wren Hibreaker." He opened his palm, revealing a mass of black smoke. As if listening to silent instructions, it drifted up my nose. I didn't know if I expected it to have a scent, but there was nothing. Nothing but a tingling sensation.

My eyes grew so heavy, I couldn't keep them open any longer. I barely felt his hands as they slipped under my body, lifting me from the ground.

I knew we were moving by the shift in his weight and the crunch of the dirt beneath his boots. I couldn't hear Alicai's screams anymore. I hoped he was alive. There was nothing I could do but surrender as my limp body was carried into the unknown.

ACKNOWLEDGMENTS

A Covenant Forged in Blood marks my first published book. The fact that this all began as a short story I wrote during lockdown and is now a fully published novel is so surreal. It's been a long journey, and one I couldn't have done without the help and support of so many.

First and foremost, my most important thank you is to Jesus, my faithful savior. The strength and courage I find in You alone is immeasurable. Thank You for giving me a mind crafted for telling stories. Through You, all things are possible.

To Mom and Dad, thank you doesn't even begin to cover it. You both have supported me through every season and career path I thought I wanted to journey on. No matter what it was, you were always in my corner, encouraging me every step of the way. I finally think I found my calling, and I couldn't have done it without you. I am so lucky to be so loved.

To Chris, you might not dive headfirst into fantasy like me, but I've always felt your support and love throughout this journey. Love you, brother.

To Connolly, my wonderful editor. You helped me take this story and shape it into something better. Thank you so much for the time you put into working on this and for your absolute love of Ryder. Your comments on him were some of my favorite to read.

To Ben, who read this book twice before I put it out into the world. Thank you for the hours and hours we've spent discussing these characters and for all your suggestions to make it even better. Thank you for pulling me up from my moments of self-doubt and urging me to keep going. You're the absolute best. And on a side note, thank you for getting me into Star Wars. I don't know who I was before Anakin Skywalker.

To my friends and family that have been asking me for years when this book was going to be published, I'm glad to say we've finally made it! Thank you for the excitement and support you've shown me throughout this experience, even when I'm too shy to talk about it. I love you all.

Finally, to my readers. Thank you, thank you, thank you. Thank you for giving this book a chance. I've always dreamed of someone loving this story the way I've loved countless others, and I really hope you did. I can't wait to share the rest of Wren's journey with you all.

ABOUT THE AUTHOR

Josephine was born and raised in New York but can now be found living in Edinburgh, Scotland, the birthplace and home of some of the most famous writers in the world. Josephine has been an avid fantasy lover from a young age and would often make her entire personality based on her favorite book or movie. Having a flare for the dramatics and a love for writing most of her life, she knew being an author was her calling. Josephine then moved to Scotland in 2021, where she received her MA in Creative Writing from Edinburgh Napier University. Josephine's dream is to continue writing about made-up worlds with characters that tug at your heartstrings for many years to come.

Printed in Great Britain
by Amazon

55572295R00243